JUSTIN GRAVES
TERRY WRIGHT

2020, TWB Press
www.twbpress.com

Justin Graves
Copyright © 2020 by Terry Wright

This is a work of fiction. Names, characters, places and incidences are either a product of the author's imagination or are used fictitiously. Any resemblance to any actual person, living or dead, events, or locales is entirely coincidental.

Published by TWB Press, Centennial, Colorado

Cover Art by SaberCore23art.com

ISBN: 978-1-944045-72-2

The Gates of Hell

J ustin Graves recoiled against the smell of alcohol and disinfected air, but his guilt-ridden soul compelled him to visit his daughter at Deckers City Hospital where the thump and hiss of machines kept her on the precarious edge of life. Midnight had long passed as he stood at the door to her room and watched her lying there, the rise and fall of her chest, all the tubes and wires...

He shuddered.

The sight of her helpless condition threatened to rip his rotting heart from his bullet-riddled chest. If tears could have flowed from hollow eye sockets, he'd have been bawling.

A step into the room felt like stepping off a tall building. Dirt drizzled from his long coat but disappeared before reaching the floor. Standing at her bedside, he leaned over and examined her bruised face, one black eye and lips that were gray, cracked, and swollen. Her black hair was cropped short and mussed. She didn't even look like the same beautiful sixteen-year-old girl.

He removed his dusty cowboy hat and sat in a chair close to her bedside. "Christy," he muttered. "I'm sorry." He touched her doughy hand and choked on guilt. "If only there was another way to save you."

However, it was too late now. The mistakes had all been made. He looked down at the gleaming circle-star badge pinned to his dusty coat. His job had kept him on the move, chasing bad guys for the Texas Rangers. He didn't have time to stay home and raise a child. So this was the price she had to pay for him being a lousy father.

Christy never knew her mother. Eleanor died during the delivery. Nanny Jean had taken care of Christy until a truck driver out of Irvine drove away with the only mother she'd ever known. After that, Aunt Clara took her in.

Justin had sent her to boarding schools and summer camps, but he managed to make it home for holidays and birthdays...well, most of them. He hadn't even tried to give her a normal family life, but sitting in this hard chair, the bitter truth churned in his guts like maggots on rotting meat. Even as a part-time father, he'd failed miserably.

However, their life hadn't been all bad. He could remember her laughter, her songbird voice, and the way candlelight sparkled in her hair. She wore a blue flower-print dress, bobby socks, and shiny black shoes with big buckles. "I love you, Daddy." She blew out five candles on her birthday cake.

Justin kissed her glowing cheek and handed her a present wrapped with a red bow. "This is for my best girl."

"Oh, Daddy." She ripped off the wrapping. "Barbie." She hugged the doll close to her heart. "Was my mommy this beautiful?"

"Yes."

Justin's bones creaked as he leaned back in the hospital room chair. Carrousel music drifted in his skull. Deckers County Fair. He could still smell the stockyards and cotton candy. Christy wore cowboy boots, blue jeans, and a flannel shirt. "I want to ride a pony. Please, Dad."

The sign on the corral gate read: *You must be 9 years old to ride. $2.*

"Looks like you're in luck." Fishing two bucks from his wallet, he thought he would've paid ten times as much if a pony ride made her happy. "Be careful."

One day he came home from work and found Aunt

Clara in a tizzy. "I told her to clean her room." Clara jammed her hands on her hips. "She snuck out her window instead."

"That's not like her," Justin said in his daughter's defense.

"What do you know about her?" Clara stood in the dining room with a spiteful scowl on her brow. "You don't know about those boys she's mixin' with. You're never around."

"I'm still her father."

"Any sperm donor can be a father. It takes a real man to be a dad." Aunt Clara stormed out.

It was going on two a.m. when Christy returned, stinking of whiskey. Justin figured it was time for some tough love. "Where did you go, young lady?"

Christy glared at him. "None of your business."

Her face was all painted up with lipstick and rouge and eyeliner. He pointed to the bathroom. "Get in there and wash that junk off your face."

"My mother would've let me wear makeup."

"Don't argue with me."

"I'm thirteen, Dad. Almost a grown woman."

"That's no excuse to go around looking like a tramp."

"I hate you." She ran out.

So much for tough love. His daughter was slipping away, and he felt powerless to help her, to reel her back in, to keep her safe from the evils of the world; evils he knew so well. Crime and punishment ruled his life, but grounding her would make her rebel even further...

A noise down the hall interrupted his thoughts. He sat upright in the hospital chair, senses on alert for danger. A nurse walked in, strode right past him without so much as a nod, checked a monitor, and left. He felt invisible—because he was.

Settling back, he remembered the last time he'd seen Christy...before this tragedy struck. Wearing a plaid skirt, white blouse, and saddle shoes, she threw her books down on the breakfast table. "I'm not going to school." She stomped out of the kitchen.

Justin tried to be calm but firm. "Get back in here, young lady."

"You're not my boss."

"No, I'm not." He got up and moved to intercept her in the living room. "I'm your father."

"I wouldn't be braggin' about that, Dad." She plopped on the couch.

He sat next to her. "What's the problem?"

"What do you care? Go chase some bad guys."

"It's my job. You'll understand one day."

"You're never home. That's all I understand."

"You have to go to school, Christy."

"I can't wait 'til I'm old enough to get out of this stupid house." She retrieved her books and stormed out.

Then the stealing began. His wallet was emptied sometime during the night.

"I didn't take your money, Dad. You must've lost it."

He noticed a rose tattoo over her left breast, and her ears were pierced from top to bottom. "What have you done to yourself?"

She stuck out her tongue, revealing a silver stud.

If he'd had a pair of pliers, that thing would have been history. "What would your mother think if she saw you now?"

"She's dead. I killed her. Remember?"

"It wasn't your fault."

"She died giving birth to me, how can it not be my fault?"

"Christy..."

Billy appeared in the doorway. Her boyfriend. Billy Denton. Scraggly red hair flourished on his chin and he wore silver rings all down his earlobes. His neck was tattooed in barbed wire. "Crystal, let's go."

Justin flinched. "Crystal? Where did that come from?"

"It's my new name, Dad."

Billy strutted across the living room like a rooster in a barnyard. "You don't approve?" He jutted out his hairy chin like he was daring Justin to do something about Christy's name change.

Justin seethed inside. Billy Denton, punk of all punks with a rap sheet as long as his arm. "Get out of my house."

"Let's go, Billy." Christy took his hand in hers.

Justin couldn't believe this travesty was being perpetrated in his own home. "Christy, you're not going anywhere with him. I forbid it."

"He loves me, Dad." She kissed Billy on the cheek. "And I love him too."

Billy grinned wickedly.

Hot adrenaline surged through Justin. "You're only sixteen. You don't know anything about love."

"Looks like we're even. Until you become an expert, Dad, you can't tell me who I can love."

She left with Billy.

Tears stung Justin's eyes.

That was the last time he saw her... Until one night at headquarters, Justin was on duty with his boss, Captain Holland, a chubby, round-faced detective who wore a ten-gallon Stetson, turquoise bolo tie, and alligator boots.

"There's been a shooting on Deckers Boulevard." Holland handed Justin the call sheet. "Better get down there right away."

He threw on his long brown coat, cowboy hat, and grabbed his Winchester rifle from the gun rack. "What's the M.O.?"

"A drive by." Holland grunted. "Somebody fingered Billy Denton and his gang. He shot a kid."

Heat bloomed in Justin's chest. "I knew that punk would go too far one day."

"Justice." Everybody called him Justice. Holland put a hand on Justin's shoulder. "Reports have it your daughter was with Billy."

His stomach freefell. "There's got to be some kind of mistake...mistaken identity—"

"She's been hanging with that thug, selling his drugs, bangin' his homeboys and anyone else for a dollar. She was there."

Just thinking of her doing those things made Justin sick. Drugs: smoking pot, snorting cocaine, selling on street corners... *No. Not my daughter.* Prostitution: taking cash, seedy motel rooms, innocent young flesh writhing under fat, sweaty men, legs spread... *No. Not my daughter.*

"She's up to her nipple rings in trouble now," Holland said. "If patrol finds her, I'm counting on you to talk her down...give herself up, along with Billy."

"I did everything I could to stop her from running with that punk."

"You didn't do enough." Holland held open the door. "Now you're going to have to fight to get her back."

"Goddamned Billy Denton."

Racing to the scene in his squad car, Justin's heart filled with dread. If witnesses saw Christy with Billy during the drive by, she'd be guilty of the killing as well. Justin never thought his own daughter would become the focus of one of his murder investigations. If only she'd listened to him, about Billy, about makeup, about stealing money...

Justin swallowed. If only he'd been tougher on her, used a firmer hand, enforced his rules instead of feeling sorry for her because she'd lost her mother. Maybe if he'd spent more time with her and less time chasing bad guys none of this would have happened.

Gripping the steering wheel as if it were Billy Denton's throat, he swerved through traffic toward the scene of the crime, siren wailing.

Police cruisers blocked traffic on Deckers' main drag. Seemed like a million overheads flashed in a macabre disco of crime and misery. A uniformed officer led Justin to a bloody corpse on the sidewalk.

"Who is he?" Justin asked the lieutenant in charge.

"A hoodlum from the 12th Street Gang."

"And you're sure Billy shot him?"

"Yup. SWAT has him cornered in the abandoned warehouse on South Street. It's a gun battle down there, Justice. His whole gang is with him."

"Jesus. And my daughter?"

The lieutenant nodded. "Her too."

Alarm pumping through his veins, Justin dashed for his squad car and sped toward the warehouse, tires squealing and Holland's words rattling around in his brain. The time had come to fight to get his daughter back.

The scene at the warehouse looked like a war zone. Firearm reports banged through the night air. Spotlights lit up the old wooden building, peeling paint, dilapidated roof, and busted glass windows where muzzle flashes blazed from the gang's guns. Cordite and fear hung in the air so thick Justin could smell both.

Manning a bullhorn, Captain Holland ordered, "Cease fire."

Bullets ricocheted off police cars.

"Hold your fire, men. Billy. Billy Denton. Let's talk."

Billy's face appeared in a jagged window pane. "Go to hell, pigs."

Justin rushed to Captain Holland's side. "I've gotta get Christy out of there."

Through the bullhorn, "Billy," Holland shouted. "Send Christy out."

"Crystal stays." Billy pulled her to the window, revealing wide-open eyes ringed in white, her mouth gagged with duct tape, his gun pointed at her head. "Back off, you bozos, or she dies."

"Billy..." Justin stepped into the light so he could be seen clearly. "Take me instead." He dropped his rifle in the dirt and raised his hands. "I'm unarmed."

"I'm not letting her go," Billy yelled.

"Let me come in and talk to her."

"Talk from there." Billy ripped the tape from her mouth.

"No, Dad. Go home. He'll kill you."

"Christy, I won't leave without you."

"I'm sorry, Daddy. I should've listened to you."

Billy backhanded her and she fell out of view.

Justin's insides lit on fire. "I'll kill you for that, Billy."

"You wanna try? Come and get her, Justice."

"Don't do it," Holland shouted. "We can't cover you in there."

Justin spat. "I don't need any help with that punk."

"No. Stand down. That's an order."

In an all-out sprint, Justin ran toward the warehouse. The cops laid down a barrage of cover fire. Denton's gang fired back. Bullets were flying everywhere. He made it to the busted-open doorway and dove inside.

Firearms clicked. "Hold it right there, maggot." Several gang members surrounded him.

"Where is she?" Justin asked, hands raised.

"All in good time." Billy stepped out from behind a

stack of wooden pallets, gun in hand, the glow of police spotlights shining off his earrings.

"Come on, Billy, let me take her out of here before she gets hurt."

"Do I look like a fool?"

"If you love her then let her go."

Billy laughed. "Love her? She's a whore."

Justin's guts tightened. "Don't you ever talk about her like that—"

"Dad." Christy stumbled out of the shadows.

Billy grabbed her arm, pulled her to him and licked her ear with his thick, slimy tongue. "Tell him, Crystal," he hissed. "Tell him you're my whore."

"My dad was right about you."

"Your daddy is dead, just like your mommy."

"Leave him alone." She jerked free from Billy's grasp and staggered toward Justin.

He lurched forward and caught her in his arms.

Gunfire banged from Billy's gun.

Burning pain sliced through Justin's chest. The three bullets Billy had fired into Christy's back tore through her heart, exited her chest, and penetrated Justin's heart. Father and daughter's blood mixed in a hot boil. He felt suddenly lightheaded; his legs failed him, and he hit the floor. Still holding her tight, his next breath wouldn't come. Her body jerked and fell still as the warehouse around him faded to nothing.

Justin tumbled through darkness, a hollow place in time and space that reached into forever. Rolling and spinning, he squeezed Christy close, fighting an unknown force that was trying to rip her from his arms.

"W-what's happening?" Christy stammered.

"I think we're dead. We died at the same time. In each other's arms."

Terry Wright

"Are we going to see my mom now?"

"I don't know where we're going."

Christy stiffened and tried to push herself free of his embrace. "Oh no, Dad. Let go of me."

"Never...never again."

"You can't go with me. I'm going to hell." She screeched and struggled harder. "Let go. Save yourself."

"I go where you go." Easier said than done, Justin feared. He could barely withstand the force prying them apart. It was getting stronger and stronger every second.

Two lights appeared, one on the right bright as sunshine, and one on the left glowing red like furnace coals. Their gravitational forces were tearing at his arms, his muscles, his bones, and his soul.

The bright light called to him, *"Justice, let go, surrender to everlasting peace and happiness."*

"I can't."

"Eleanor awaits you with open arms."

"It's my fault Christy is in this mess. I should have been a better father. I'm not letting go."

"Wrong answer, Justice."

The bright light faded, and the red glow blossomed brighter. Heat radiated from its core and burned Justin's skin. He didn't feel any pain nor did he feel the pulse of life inside him. Death felt oddly natural.

"I'm afraid, Daddy," Christy cried in a childish voice that came to him without her speaking.

"Hang on," he said without a voice.

"I love you."

With all his strength Justin clung to her as they spiraled into the red glow. His hands became lucid, his arms, his coat, and his entire body felt weightless, without form or substance.

Christy's features, now aglow in a red hue, wavered in

the heat. Her hair grew long and flowed like lava. He feared she'd get so hot they'd both burn up like a meteor entering the atmosphere of hell.

The red glow pulled them into a fiery pit where flames leaped and flared all around them. Whooshing gases spewed from rock wall crevices and ignited into geysers of yellow and orange fire. Smoke billowed up from the abyss. Nauseous fumes gripped Justin's soul in black despair.

Bellowing laughter thundered in his head. Guttural words came to him from out of nowhere. "Justice, you don't belong here."

Justin felt a tremble deep in his ethereal soul, but he had to fight the fear. Christy needed him now more than ever. "My daughter doesn't belong here either."

"She's mine. Forever." More haunting laughter.

"But she wants to see her mother in heaven."

"I don't care about her mother."

Walls of fire erupted around Justin. Hissing and spitting gasses fed the angry inferno.

"Let her go and be gone," the devil demanded.

Floating in the flames, Justin held his daughter's soul tighter. "It's not her fault she had a rough life."

"She should have listened to her father."

"I'm to blame for not spending enough time with her. Take me. Let her live. She deserves a second chance."

"She deserves nothing. Her soul is mine."

Desperation formed his next words. "Her soul is worth a hundred souls."

"Only a father would say that."

"There are criminals running loose on the earth more worthy of hell than Christy. Let her go and I'll round up one hundred of them for you, starting with Billy Denton."

A gust of hot wind parted the fire, revealing an angry red face the shape of a ram's head suspended in smoke. The devil tilted his bald cranium. Razor-sharp horns shined like crimson agate. Glaring down on Justin with canted eyes the depth and color of crude oil, Satan furrowed his fiery brows. "You dare to make a deal with me?"

If he was alive, Justin would have peed in his pants. "A hundred bad guys for one mixed up girl. What do you say?"

"Criminals end up here sooner or later. Your offer is useless. I will wait patiently for them to die."

"Commendable," Justin said. "But isn't patience a virtue?"

"I have no virtues." Roaring flames seared the air. Granite walls quaked and rockslides rumbled into the depths.

"So my offer is valuable," Justin pressed and added a sly smile for effect.

The devil jutted out his pointy red chin as if he were the incarnation of Billy Denton himself. "You dare to mock me, Justice. We shall see who has no virtues. You're no saint either, no better than any killer down here." Fire leaped from his horns. "One hundred souls for one. So be it."

"How? I'm dead."

Satan drilled his evil glare into Justin's soul. "You shall walk the line between life and death until you have fulfilled your part of the deal."

Justin thought of his trusty Winchester. Gang-bangers would be easy pickin's. "She'll be out of here in a week."

"Not so fast." Flames churned and hurled black smoke into the upper caverns of hell. "You cannot kill anyone yourself. That would make you no better than Billy and equally worthy of eternal damnation. Your Winchester is useless in this deal."

Justin swallowed a fiery lump in his throat. "I can't

shoot the bad guys?"

"You must trick them into their own demise."

"How am I going to do that?"

"That is your problem to solve. If you fail, your daughter belongs to me." He snatched her soul from Justin's embrace. "Quit anytime you like, crossover to everlasting peace and happiness, but be forwarded. If you lose or if you quit, she will bear a million demons from my seed."

Laughter echoed off the rock walls of hell.

"Now go, Justice, before I change my mind."

"Daddy. You're making a big mistake. I belong here."

"I won't fail you this time, Christy."

The caustic abyss disappeared in an explosion of white light.

Sirens and flashing lights surrounded the warehouse in Deckers, Texas, where Captain Holland watched paramedics huddle around a lifeless sixteen-year-old girl. Anxiety grasped his stomach like a python coiled around a pig.

"Clear."

The defibrillator discharged as loud as a shotgun blast. Her body arched up and slammed back to the ground.

"I've got a pulse," a medic said. "But it's weak."

"Transport her right away." Holland hoped she'd make it to the hospital alive.

Cops carried Justin Graves' limp body out of the warehouse and laid him in the dirt next to his Winchester. They brought out Billy Denton, too. In handcuffs.

With tears stinging his eyes, Captain Holland stood over Justin. "He was the best damn homicide detective the Texas Rangers ever had."

"He was a piss-poor excuse for a father," Billy shouted as he struggled with the arresting officers.

Terry Wright

"You weren't much of a boyfriend, either," Holland shot back.

"She deserved what she got."

For a nickel he'd put a bullet in that punk and be done with him. "Justin gave his life for his daughter, thanks to you and your gang."

"Did you have to kill them all?"

"I spared your ass, didn't I?"

"You'll live to regret it."

"I'll be there when they put a needle in your arm. Be sure to remember this conversation as the lights go out."

Billy spat on the ground next to Justin. "Your jail won't hold me for long."

"Get him out of my sight."

The cops dragged Billy off and stuffed him in the backseat of a squad car.

Siren blaring, the ambulance sped away with Christy on board.

Holland tipped his hat. "Hang in there, girl."

The receding siren morphed into the thump and hiss of machines that kept Christy alive. Justin flinched and dropped his cowboy hat on the floor. As he stooped to pick it up, he heard voices and froze.

"How are you this evening, doctor?" A nurse's voice.

"Busy."

She handed him a clipboard. "How long do you think her coma's going to last?"

"Who knows? She's young. She has a chance."

Christy had no chance in hell if Justin didn't complete his deal with the devil. He retrieved his hat from the floor, batted dust from the brim and set it on his skull. A worm wriggled out a bullet hole in his chest. Thanks to the devil's sick sense fair play, he'd been reduced to a ghoul that had to animate his corpse and rise from his grave in order to walk in the land of the living. How many other rotten tricks did the devil have up his fiery sleeve? After all, the devil was the devil and couldn't be trusted.

Stepping between the doctor and the nurse, Justin stroked Christy's hair. "I love you, but I have to go now."

The doctor made a note on the clipboard. "No change."

He was right. Nothing had changed. Even in death, Justin was still chasing bad guys and leaving his daughter to fend for herself.

With a gust of wind the ghoul was gone.

The Wedding Ring

F red Regar pushed through the swinging door of Deckers Saloon and bulled his way toward the bar. His long coat smelled like the stockyards, and his rubber butcher's boots squeaked across the hardwood floor. Country music blared from the jukebox and emitted an irritating twang.

"Give me a beer, ya old cow," he shouted to the bartender.

Rita, a busty broad with two missing front teeth, looked up from the tap she was working for another patron. "God damn it, Fred, no trouble tonight, you hear me?"

"Screw you, bitch." He claimed his regular barstool off by himself near the back wall.

Nobody liked Fred. A ruffian and a troublemaker, they all figured he was just born mean. Another grueling day at the slaughterhouse had done nothing to soften his reputation. And like every night after work, an awful thirst burned in his throat.

"Hurry up with that beer, Rita."

Scowling, she slid him a full mug. "You behave yourself or I'll call the cops."

"Crawford had it coming," Fred spat and took a swig of beer. "He started the brawl last night. Bastard shouldn't be stickin' his nose in my business."

"And you shouldn't be beating your wife."

"You never mind about my wife."

Rita leaned on the bar and put her butt-ugly face in front of his nose. She smelled like dirty dishwater. "So tell me, Fred, why haven't we seen Sarah about lately? You beat her up so black and blue she can't be out in public?"

Fred showed Rita a fist. "Keep talking. You'll get some of this yourself."

"You don't scare me, Fred Regar."

"You should've been born a man." He cackled at his insult and went back to drinking his beer.

Rita waddled off to wait on somebody else.

Fred put down his mug and caught a whiff of rotting meat. He figured it was his coat, at first, but the odor quickly fumed up so badly his eyes watered. Pressure ballooned in his chest. In all his years of gutting animals, he'd never smelled anything so rank. His stomach threatened to heave.

Swallowing hard, he noticed the odor wafted in from his left. An old man had just sat in the adjacent barstool. He not only looked old, he looked ancient. The stranger wore a dusty cowboy hat and a long coat caked with dirt. His bony face bore prickly stubble, and his dark eyes sat in deep sockets. A gold ring on the little finger of his right hand looked out of place against his flaking skin.

Fred fanned the air with a hand. "You need a bath, mister."

The cowboy started flicking the ring in circles around his bony finger. "My name is Justin Graves," he said in a raspy voice. "But you can call me Justice."

Fred almost barfed up his beer. The man's bad breath was worse than his body odor. "Ever hear of breath mints?"

Turning slightly on his barstool, Justin lifted the lapel of his grimy brown coat to display the gleam of a circle-star badge. "I'm a Texas Ranger."

"You should see a doctor." Fred wheezed. "You don't look so good."

"I never felt better."

Fred chugged beer, hoping the cop wasn't here about

Terry Wright

Laura. Getting arrested wasn't in his plans for the night. Setting his mug on the bar, he figured he'd better be nice to the old fart. "So what brings you to Deckers?"

Leaning forward, the gnarly man whispered, "Laura Baker."

Fred's chest tightened, but he forced calm. "She died five years ago."

"And her husband was executed for killing her," Justin stated matter-of-factly.

"She shouldn't have married the bastard."

"He didn't kill her."

"Of course he did." Lucky for Fred, the cops botched the investigation. "You guys fried him in the chair. Good old Texas justice, if ya ask me."

"We made a mistake, but now I know the truth."

"You don't know nothin', old man."

Justin examined the ring on his finger. "I talked to her, you know?"

Yeah, right. He talked to a dead woman. "How much have you been drinkin'?"

"She came to me in the afterlife, told me what you did, told me what you said."

"She told you nothin'."

Justin glared at Fred with eyes that glowed with an eerie reddish hue. "*This one's for pinky.* That's what you said, wasn't it?"

Fred felt as if he were shocked with a cattle prod. Laura was the only one who knew about *pinky*, how it'd get all excited, and how she'd make him wait. *"After we're married,"* she'd said. But pinky didn't want to wait. Neither did Fred. She'd earned a black eye for that rejection.

How could Justin have known about pinky..? Unless he really had talked to Laura. Hell no. Fred wasn't drunk

~18~

enough to believe it. "Nobody can talk to dead people."

"I got myself killed a while back." Justin opened the flap of his grungy coat. "Took three bullets in the heart."

Holding his breath, Fred braved a look. Three holes, dead center in a soiled gray shirt, just like he'd said, but he'd failed to mention the exposed rib bones and rotting flesh. A worm wriggled out a bullet hole. Fred drew back aghast. "You've gotta be shittin' me."

"Dead people *can* talk to dead people."

Fred threw down a slug of beer. Common sense told him the old man was crazy, but still, he looked dead enough. And he certainly smelled dead enough.

Justin twirled the ring. "Laura didn't like you much."

Did he have to rub it in? "We were perfect for each other."

"But she married Charlie. Must've made you furious."

Fred blinked. Damn right it had pissed him off. How dare she dump him for Charlie? So what if he had six-pack abs? He worked as a hunting guide. The macho man had more guns than the army and never went anywhere without his Jim Bowie knife. That didn't make him a better man. "I got over it."

"You're still angry, Fred. That's why you berate women and beat your wife."

"That's none of your business." Talking to Justin was worse than talking to Crawford last night. Fred wanted to smash his fist into the ghoul's face and start another brawl, but decided against hitting a Texas Ranger...dead *or* alive. He'd end up in jail, for sure. Then who would keep Sarah in line? "What do you want from me?"

"Turn yourself in. Throw your sorry ass on the mercy of the court. Takes the death penalty off the table. You'll get life in prison without parole."

"You got no evidence against me." He drained his

beer.

"There are other ways to get justice for Laura, but let me assure you, those consequences are brutal."

"I'm not turning myself in, old man." Wishing the ghoulish ranger would disappear as fast as he appeared, Fred slid his beer mug down the bar toward Rita. "Fill it up, heifer."

Justin leaned in. "Laura's ethereal mental state won't allow her to cross over to everlasting peace and happiness. Her tormented soul can't be with Charlie until you are punished for what you did. They deserve justice."

"I didn't do nothin'." Fred held his breath, hoping the smelly ghoul would back off a few miles.

"You may think you got away with murder," Justin rasped. "But, I assure you, there's no such thing."

Fred exhaled. "They both got what they deserved."

"Have it your way." Justin removed the ring from his little finger and set it on the bar. "Charlie wants you to hang on to his wedding band."

"I don't want that damn thing."

"When it's back on his finger, you'll be headed for hell."

"Screw you, Justice."

A droning sound filled the saloon, getting louder and louder. The floor and the walls and the ceiling started shaking. Fred covered his ears, squeezed his eyes shut, and feared the ghoul had started an earthquake.

"What's the problem now, Fred?" Rita's voice asked.

"Huh?" He stopped shaking and looked up. She was standing in front of him with a frothy mug of beer.

"You're lookin' awful pale."

Embarrassment heated his cheeks. He'd been caught hunched over with his hands cupped on his ears. He glanced at the next barstool. The old man was gone.

~20~

Justin Graves

Stunned, Fred jerked upright and shook his head to clear the fuzz. "Where'd he go?"

"Who?"

"The old man."

"What old man?"

"He was sitting right next to me. Look." Fred pointed to the bar top where Justin had put the ring. "He left this ring." Fred felt belly-gutted. "What? It's gone."

Rita set the beer mug in front of Fred. "Crawford must've slugged you harder than you thought. You should go home. Get some rest."

Of course, he'd suffered a concussion and imagined seeing the old man...but he seemed so real. And he knew things...

With his mind swimming in confusion, Fred chugged the beer mug dry. Several rounds later, he staggered out of Deckers Saloon. A cold wind blew down from the mountains and knifed through his long coat. No matter how much he'd drunk, he couldn't get the gnarly image of Justin Graves out of his mind. How dare that son-of-a-bitch suggest Fred turn himself in? That made him mad enough to go home and beat the crap out of Sarah...twice.

As he did most every night, he staggered down Mason Street and weaved past the redbrick rectory of Saint Mothers. His tall shadow, cast from a streetlight, slanted across the side of the church like an apparition stalking the night.

He came upon a house with a single window aglow. Not just any house, but the old O'Shaughnessy place, which had been boarded up for years. Incredibly, someone had bought the dump and fixed it up...in only a day? New roof, new paint, and blooming flowerbeds.

Drunk as he was, he figured he was seeing things and shook his head. When he looked again, the silhouette of a woman appeared on the backlit window shade. Slim. Curvaceous. She was brushing her hair, an unexpected but intriguing sight.

As he stopped to watch her, déjà vu hit him like a board. The scene looked as familiar as the night he stood outside Laura's window and watched her brush her hair. After the wedding. After he'd stalked her to their honeymoon hideaway. Before he'd gotten his revenge.

The wind changed directions and turned from chilly cold to blistering hot, now blowing straight in off the Texas desert. He shrugged out of his heavy coat, then kicked off his boots and stripped down to his boxers. Why was it so damn hot? Why was he standing on the sidewalk in his underwear?

Strains of piano music tinkled in the air. A crowd gathered around a lighted Farris wheel rotating brilliantly down the block. People poured out of Saint Mothers, cheering and throwing rice at a couple who scrambled for a limo parked out front.

His heart climbed up his esophagus. All these people out so late at night, someone was bound to see him, report a pervert stalking the night. He gathered his clothes, and staying low, he followed the shadows, which oddly led him to the front of the O'Shaughnessy house. This close, his curiosity for the shapely figure inside drove him toward the window for a better view.

A dog barked from somewhere down the street.

He felt dizzy and chalked it up to too much beer. The sudden tingling in his fingers, though, he couldn't understand. And he was breathing as hard as a treed coon.

Reaching the lighted window, he ducked under the sill. The woman's silhouette played on the shade above his head. His heart beat frantically. The saliva in his mouth turned to sand.

He peeped over the windowsill and peered through a chink in the shade. The bedroom light revealed a wedding gown hanging on the closet door. A veil lay on bed sheets turned down. Over a chair, a tuxedo was draped, and on the dresser lay keys, change, and Charlie's Jim Bowie knife. Seemed the macho man couldn't even get married without it.

Laura sat at an elegant vanity. Her long golden hair swayed to the caressing of her brush. He could see her blue eyes in the mirror, sparkling with glee, and every soft curve of her face, magnificently beautiful. Under a petite white negligee, her plump breasts looked more inviting than ever.

He felt a warm swelling in his boxer shorts, but that feeling was quickly erased as the anger of five years ago surged through him again. The bitterness of rejection, humiliation, and downright betrayal was always in the back of his mind, ever present; and Justice was probably right about that being the reason he treated women like dirt, beat and badmouthed them—

His fingers tingled with more intensity. He glanced at his hands and got the shock of his life. The gold wedding band that Justin had set on the bar was now on his left ring finger.

Fred dropped down below the window, his heart racing. How did the ring get on his finger? How long had it been there? He tried to pull it off. The harder he pulled the more his fingers tingled. The ring wouldn't budge.

"Justice," he snarled under his breath.

A scraping noise above his head distracted him. Laura had parted the shade and opened the window, probably to let in fresh air for the fornicating to come. The sound of running water and the rattle of a pipe reverberated from the open window. Charlie was in the shower, getting ready for his wedding night with Fred's girl.

Terry Wright

His stomach roiled in anger. He'd failed to stop the wedding, but he would not fail to stop the honeymoon.

***

Laura stood at the open window and inhaled the scent of desert sage on the incoming breeze. She glanced out at the town of Deckers, Texas, savored the whirling Ferris wheel lights, the sounds of laughter and children at play on this festive night. Everyone in town knew her. Everyone approved of her wedding to Charlie. Everyone was glad she'd given Fred Regar the boot.

Again seated at the vanity, she resumed brushing her hair, entranced by the cheery glow of her blue eyes in the mirror. How different they looked now that she was married, shining with anticipation yet apprehensive at the same time. Getting naked with a man would be a new experience for her. She was a virgin on the verge of losing her virginity. This would be the most wonderful night of her life.

Her skin smelled of lilac from the bubble bath she'd taken earlier. Charlie was in the shower. The rattling water pipe grated on her nerves, but the thought of her nude husband set loose a swarm of butterflies in her stomach.

Finished with brushing her hair, she flipped off the light switch on the wall and lay down on the bed sheets. Shadows closed in around her and swirled on the walls to the rhythm of the Ferris wheel lights gleaming in through the open window. She arranged her nightie to show a lot of thigh then waited for her husband and the gifts of love they would give to each other tonight.

A tree branch swaying in the wind scratched against the house and made her feel uneasy, along with that irritatingly noisy water pipe. She wished Charlie would hurry.

A creak resounded through the bedroom doorway, striking a nerve of dread. Sounded like someone walking on the hardwood floor in the hall. But who?

The hair on the back of her neck prickled.

A man charged out of the darkness and reached her so quickly she had no time to scream. He covered her mouth with one hand and ripped off her dainty nightgown with the other.

Clutching his wrist, she tried to wrench his hand from her mouth so she could scream for Charlie, but the hand was too big, and strong, and stunk of cow dung and beer.

Charlie.

Her mind cramped in terror. She couldn't believe this was happening.

Charlie. Help me.

The noise from the shower pipe overpowered her feeble pleas. She shook her head back and forth. If she could get his hand off her mouth, she could scream.

He crawled on top of her with the weight of a thousand pigs. Stinging pain clawed up her belly where, only moments before, butterflies flittered about, butterflies for Charlie...her husband...on their wedding night. Now she could hardly inhale. One at a time, he lodged her arms under his hairy thighs and stole any hope of prying his hand from her mouth.

Why isn't he wearing pants? Is he going to rape me? She squirmed and kicked. *Get off me.*

He laughed with deep-throated glee. His breath reeked of beer. With his free hand, he reached for the Bowie knife on the dresser and held the point to her face. "Remember pinky?"

A horrifying recognition flashbulbed in her brain. *Fred Regar.* "You bastard," she sputtered into the palm of his hand.

"You should-a married me, Laura." He showed her the knife up real close. "Least you can do is let me kiss the bride." Ferris wheel lights from the window glinted off the blade.

Please don't kill me.

He put the point to her throat. "I'll remove my hand, but if you scream, I'll cut your throat and kill Charlie the instant he steps from the bathroom. Got it?"

She nodded the best she could.

He removed his hand from her mouth.

She choked back a sob. "What do you want, Fred?"

"How about that kiss?" He leaned to her face, and as his lips touched hers, she turned away.

"No. It's over between us. Get used to it."

"Why you bitch." He reared back and slugged her in the face. Then again and again...

Each blow tore into the fabric of her consciousness until the shadows and whirling lights blurred into a caustic soup of terror. But Fred Regar was having the time of his life.

"Charlie." She screamed.

In one quick move, he rammed the blade into her windpipe. "This one's for pinky."

Charlie!

The joyous Ferris wheel lights faded to nothing.

***

The gush of blood from Laura's throat didn't surprise Fred. He'd seen plenty of bleed-outs at the slaughterhouse. The red pool on the bed sheets grew for a few seconds...until her heart stopped.

"What's that, honey?" Charlie sing-songed from the noisy shower.

As Fred rolled off Laura, déjà vu flooded his brain. It

seemed as if time had gone backward, to Deckers five years ago. Everything looked and felt eerily familiar, the shadowy bedroom, dead Laura on the bed, and the thrill of finally getting his revenge.

This had to be a memory. A drunken stupor. It couldn't be real, but from the look of his bloody hands and the blood spatter on his arms and chest, he knew this murder scene was no hallucination. What happened was real, and he knew what he had to do to get away with murdering her, again.

He set the knife in the pool of blood on the sheet where Charlie would easily find it when he discovered Laura's body. He'd pick it up like he'd done before and get his fingerprints on the murder weapon.

By then, Fred would be long gone.

Heading toward the open window, his nostrils flared from the familiar stench of rotting meat. Pressure in his chest stopped him mid-stride. He remembered the old man at the bar, the dead Texas Ranger. "Justice? Is that you I smell?"

"Hello, Fred," a voice rasped from the shadows. "Up to your old tricks again, I see."

The ghoul's stench made Fred's stomach convulse. He had to make his break before he vomited all over the murder scene.

The shower water stopped running. The pipe stopped rattling. Charlie would be out any second.

"I'd love to chat with you, Justice, but I gotta go." Fred made a beeline for the open window.

It slammed closed all by itself.

Panic gutted him. He grabbed the latch. It wouldn't budge. He jerked up on the sash. It wouldn't budge. He slammed his fist into the glass. It wouldn't break. His fingerprints were all over the place. In Laura's blood.

"Justice, let me out of here."

"I can't do that."

Joyous whistling echoed in the bathroom.

"You set me up, you bastard."

"What's that, dear?" Charlie sang the words. "Are you ready?"

Fred backed into a corner. "He'll see me."

"I know." Justin's voice sounded low and ominous.

Charlie seemed playful enough. "I'll be finished in a minute, dear." More whistling.

Fred lunged for the bedroom door. It slammed shut. He grabbed the doorknob and pulled, but his bloody hands kept slipping off. More fingerprints.

"Damn you, Justice."

Justin stepped from the shadows. "You're the one who's damned." His long coat shed dirt that never hit the floor. He carried a Winchester rifle in one hand. "You should have turned yourself in."

Outside, sirens wailed. Tires screeched out front. Emergency lights flashed across the bedroom walls. Fred dashed to the window again. It still wouldn't open. He was trapped.

Police busted in. "Get on the ground." Several officers jumped Fred, threw him to the floor. Someone turned on a light. The bathroom door swung open. Charlie stepped out, towel around his waist, hair shiny and slicked back.

Fred saw terror in Charlie's wide-open eyes. He was looking at his new bride lying askew on the bed in a bloody pool. "Laura. My God." Rushing to her side, his hand landed net to the bloody knife he hadn't seen lying next to her. "Not again. Laura." He shook her. She didn't respond. "Laura."

"Screw you, Charlie," Fred shouted. "Now you can't have her either."

"Cuff him," Captain Holland ordered his men.

"Let me go," Fred hollered.

The cops wrestled his arms behind his back.

Worse, the stench in the room became nauseous to the tenth degree.

Justin snapped his fingers. Charlie flinched as if awakened from a trance. His body became nearly transparent. Laura's ghostly form sat up on the bed. Eyes blinking, she looked as if she'd just been roused from a deep sleep. Their bodies regained form and substance. She turned, saw Charlie, rose up and floated to him, threw her arms around his neck. "Thank God you're here. I was so afraid."

"I've finally found you."

"Don't ever let me go, Charlie."

Fred couldn't believe it. "Look at that...look at that."

"He's drunk," a cop said as they pulled Fred to his feet.

Paramedics surrounded the vacant bed, performed CPR on the ratty mattress, and hooked up a portable machine to nothing; it sounded a steady tone.

"What kind of joke is this?" Fred shouted.

"Get him outta here," Holland snarled.

"Wait. You guys are makin' a mistake."

The paramedics stood, heads bowed. "She's dead."

"Are you all totally crazy?" Fred yelled. "She's not dead. She's standing right there, next to her husband. Are you blind? Don't you see them?"

"He's hallucinating," an officer said.

Pulling a sheet over the mattress, a medic asked, "Who was she?"

"Laura Singleton," a sergeant replied. "She just moved into town. Someone called us about seeing a prowler at her window. We got here as fast as we could."

A patrol officer rushed in with Fred's clothes. "Found

these under the bedroom window."

Holland grumped. "Shows intent. He was probably going to rape her too."

"It was hot outside," Fred insisted.

The patrol officer looked around. "Why was she living in this dump?"

"She was going to fix it up."

"What are you talkin' about?" Fred spat. "This place is fixed up...looks brand new."

"It's a disgusting mess in here," the sergeant shot back. "Been abandoned for years."

As if an ungodly transformation had taken place right before his eyes, Fred saw cracked and water-stained walls, a flickering ceiling light, and a vanity mirror covered with cobwebs and dust. The bed was nothing but an old and rotted mattress on the floor. Trash was strewn everywhere, along with needles and meth pipes and the stink of human waste. The window was boarded up, and a cold wind now whistled in through the slats. Hot panic surged in Fred's veins. "Justice? What the hell have you done?"

Justin shouldered the Winchester. "Looks like Charlie has found Laura. That means you're going to hell...very soon."

"Bullshit. There's no Laura Singleton. She's just an illusion you concocted to set me up."

"You catch on real quick," Justin said.

"You can't get away with this."

"Shut up," Captain Holland yelled at Fred.

"You guys got this all wrong." Fred pleaded his case to the Captain. "She's not real. You only think there's a dead body on the bed. It's the ghoul, I tell you. He's playing with your minds. She's a figment of your imagination."

"Get him out of here."

"Wait, don't you see—?"

The cops pushed him toward the door.

"Justin Graves wants you to think I killed this woman because he thinks I got away with killing Laura Baker five years ago. He's staged this whole crime scene."

"Hold up, men." Holland gave Fred a stony look. "Justin Graves, you say?"

"You've heard of him?"

"He was a Texas Ranger, but now he's dead."

"Like hell. He's standing right there...look...in the corner."

Holland glared at Fred. "You must be drunker than a Texas sailor. There's nobody else here."

"Are you blind? Can't you smell him? And Laura Baker is standing right in front of him with her arms around her husband. She's not dead, either, I tell ya. Let me go."

"He must be crazy," someone said.

"Look...I even have the wedding ring on my finger, the one she gave her husband. Justin Graves gave it to me."

The Captain inspected Fred's hands shackled behind him. "Get this lunatic outta here. Book him. Murder One."

"What?"

"There's no ring on your finger, and Justin Graves is not in this bedroom."

Fred looked at the ghoul. "Where's the ring?"

Justin shrugged.

As officers shoved Fred out the door, Holland added, "And reopen the case on Laura Baker. We might have a serial killer on our hands."

"Justice. You can't do this to me."

Justin sneered. "Save it for the devil."

"Bastard."

They tossed Fred into a waiting squad car.

**

A hot wind whipped down Mason Street as Justin stood under the streetlight and stared at the boarded-up and weed-infested O'Shaughnessy place. He rather liked the sage-brush smell of the night air. The execution was over. Fred Regar had been convicted on all counts. Texas justice was swift and final. Sarah never shed a tear.

Laura and Charlie appeared next to Justin, cuddling each other. "You finally got him," she said. "Justin Graves got his man."

"I'm sorry I had to put you through that horror again, but it was the only way."

"Why didn't you tell me you were going to bring us back to that terrible night?"

"Would you have agreed to this charade, knowing what Fred was going to do to you?"

Laura shuddered. "It was worth it, though."

"Justice doesn't come easily," Justin said. "But thanks to you, Fred Regar has paid for his crimes. Now, the truth about Laura Baker is known, and Charlie, your name has been cleared."

"Thanks." He examined the wedding ring on his finger, finally back where it belonged. "If not for you, Fred would have gotten away with murder."

Justin shook his head. "There's no such thing."

"Now we can cross over and rest in peace." Laura hugged her husband. "Forever."

"How about you?" Charlie asked the dead detective. "Come with us."

"I can't. My deal with the devil has only just begun." He tipped his hat. "There's much work I must do to save my daughter's life."

"Good luck, Justice."

With a gust of wind the ghoul was gone.

Black Widow

In the shadows she waited, her long legs tantalizingly spread across her silken bed. She couldn't see him in the darkness beyond her doorway, but she knew he was out there: watching her, calculating his next move, betting on his chances for love.

Her heart skipped at the thought of what he would do to her. Touch her. Caress her. Take her. If he was strong, he could. If he was daring, he would. If he knew how desperately she needed his affections, he wouldn't keep her waiting long.

Teasingly, she twitched her legs. The silken bed shimmied beneath her curvaceous body.

He didn't appear.

Again. A twitch, this time with more intensity. More desire. More need.

Last night, under a sliver of moonlight, she'd seen him. A brief glimpse. Mostly a blur. He'd surprised her and made her jump.

He bolted.

Oh, what a tease he was. Intriguing her. Testing her. Making her long for him so deeply.

Tonight, she hoped, he'd venture closer. Climb into her bed of lust. Partake of her sweetness. Her body. Her love. How she desired to meet him. To smell him. To taste him.

She'd been alone for so long, struggling with the hardships of life. Love was never far from her mind, that warm coil inside her ever tightening, begging to be released in the ecstasy of true love, passion, and satisfaction. Could he be the one, the only one, to take her that high and hold her up there for so long?

But why did he make her wait like this, in torment? Torturous torment. Alone—

A blur of motion stopped her musing. He was there. She sensed him in the shadows. His breath. His aura. Coming closer. Stealthily.

Her heart raced with anticipation. She twitched her legs, frantically this time. *Please, please, let this be the night.*

A vibration on the bed made her body tremble. He was behind her now but not close enough. She had to force herself to remain still in spite of her instinct to turn and face him. He'd surely run away. She didn't want that to happen again. *Not tonight. Not now.*

Another vibration on the bed excited her. Yes. He was creeping closer. Her body oozed endorphins of love, flowing hot and smooth through her limbs. She breathed deep and slow. If she could quell her impatience, this encounter could end so sweetly.

She closed her eyes and twitched her legs again, just once, tenderly this time, hoping that he would play her lover's game. He had to know that his presence excited her... that she was willing to see this mating through to the end, to the scrumptious, fulfilling end.

He was right behind her now, his body vibrations strumming a love song on her heavenly silken bed. His presence was driving her wild, making her crazy with desire and the hope of finally finding the one who would carry her to the edge of total bliss and fling her over the side.

Oh, please. Do it to me now.

His touch felt soft and sincere, stroking her back, paralyzing her in place. She didn't dare move, didn't dare turn, didn't dare look at him for fear he'd flee. She could only imagine his slim and toned body—

He mounted her from the rear. Blood coursed through her body in hot waves. He was the one. She just knew it.

Don't make me wait. Please take me. Take me. Take me.

No brutal a lover there ever was. So quickly he had penetrated her, so hard, so fast, but so quickly he had filled her and finished.

No. No. No, don't stop.

But he was done. And he was leaving. She felt suddenly cold and alone. Again. Was that all he had to give her?

What about me? What about my feelings, my desires, my satisfaction?

He didn't answer. He had nothing for her, not even a word. Not a, 'Thank you.' Not a, 'That was great.' He just turned his back on her as if she were nothing but a receptacle for his seed.

You prick.

She spun around. There he was, the little bastard, running off without as much as a look back. Anger tore through her body, a rage that had to be satisfied. Now. She pounced on him hard and fast and sunk poison-spewing fangs into his spineless back.

***

The foggy light of the afterlife glowed around Justin Graves. In this place between earth and heaven, he languished in guilt and hate. His tormented soul cried for his daughter's salvation and screamed for revenge against his murderer, Billy Denton.

Pacing in surreal luminosity, Justin felt as if he were walking on clouds. His cowboy boots were soft as slippers on his feet. The circle-star badge shined from the left lapel of his long brown coat, cleaned and pressed. His freshly shaved face smelled of Stetson cologne. In the afterlife, he was restored to perfection. If only his soul were in such pristine condition.

"Justice," the light called to him. *"Relax."*

The brim of his cowboy hat shaded his eyes from the glow. "Not while Billy Denton is still breathing."

"Let go of your hate."

"Christy wouldn't have been running with Billy if I had been a better father."

"Don't harbor the guilt for her bad choices."

"She's in a coma at Decker's City Hospital. The devil let her live while I fulfill my end of the deal. It's up to me to save her."

"Nothing earthly matters anymore. Let go, Justice. Cross over to everlasting peace and happiness. Go to your wife, Eleanor. She is waiting for you."

Tempting as it sounded, he couldn't bring himself to turn his back on Christy. "I'm not going to cross over until Billy Denton's soul is burning in hell."

"Stay away from him, Justice. He's in jail for your murder. Let Captain Holland handle it from there. Only bad things will happen if you interfere."

"How do you know?"

"I know everything."

Justin stopped pacing and looked into the foggy glow but saw no one. "Are you God?"

"I am Wach-el, the formless archangel sent down from the Almighty's court to earn my fiery sword in your service."

"So you're stuck here too."

"Since you made your deal with the devil, the Lord of Hosts thought you might need a little help defeating Satan. We're a team, and there are plenty of tormented souls

languishing in the afterlife to keep us busy."

"Yeah." Justin felt a twinge of pride. "I got Fred Regar, all right."

"Charlie and Laura crossed over together, hand in hand into the light. You did a good job."

He felt humbled. His situation wasn't just about him and Christy. It was about all those souls who had been wronged in life so badly they couldn't cross over. And now Wach-el was counting on him to earn his sword.

"Yes, we're all counting on you, Justice, but the legal system took a while to play out for Fred Regar. Justice must come swifter or the devil will tire of the deal. You need to be more creative."

"All right. Who's next?"

"A woman serial killer is on the loose in Deckers. She kills her lovers."

"A Black Widow?"

"The gentler sex has a dark side. Take the English woman who murdered four husbands and five children. She poisoned them, as did a Black Widow in Budapest when she sent thirty lovers to their graves. Right here in America, a 300-pound farmer's wife poisoned her husband and dozens of suitors."

"Black Widows have no boundaries," Justin said.

"From Russia to South Africa, Canada to Brazil, they had names like Grandma Venom and The Poison Queen."

Justin shuddered.

"But the Black Widow in Deckers makes all the others seem docile. She's driven by fantasies of sexual fulfillment unrealized. Her M.O. isn't the quiet kill by poison, but instead, it's a bloodbath of unbridled rage. Her dead lovers are stuck here in the afterlife until she is stopped."

"Who is this blackest of Black Widows?"

"Meet Dennis Blaire. He is here to explain."

A slender man stepped out of the light, not ten feet from Justin. "Her name is J-Janet," he said in a shaky voice. "Janet Blaire."

Justin scrutinized Dennis, as any good detective would. In his mid-twenties, he wore preppy college clothes, brown slacks and a tan V-neck sweater. His dark eyes were ringed with sorrow and looked out of place on his handsome, clean-shaven face.

"She's killed every man who ever loved her," Dennis added.

"Please..." Justin motioned to the light from which two high-back chairs appeared. "Have a seat. Tell me about her."

The two men sat facing each other. Dennis wrung his hands. "I can't believe it, Justice. I wasn't the only man, I mean, since she killed me eight years ago, she's had thirty-seven suitors." Dennis buried his face in his hands. "She killed us all."

"Why aren't they here with you?"

"Since I was the first, they asked me to be their spokesman."

"What happened?"

"I married Janet in church... Saint Mothers, you know the one?"

"On Mason Street, yes."

"I'd been drinking at the reception. We made off to a ritzy hotel for our honeymoon. How could I resist her? She was a goddess, her eyes like ebony pools, long black hair that flowed over her shoulders. And she put on a black teddy and a red ruby pendant on a string around her neck. It rested perfectly in the V of her cleavage. I thought I'd won the lottery of love."

"So why did she kill you?"

Dennis swallowed. "I was pretty drunk. She went

crazy...stripped out of her dress so fast, I couldn't believe it. No bra. No panties. And she started clawing at my shirt buttons, my pants zipper. I couldn't get undressed fast enough for her. She shoved me on the bed. I landed on my back. She pounced on me...started kissing me...licking me...petting me with those silk gloves. I mean, she even bit me, you know, down there."

"Every man's dream girl," Justin said. "What did you do to piss her off?"

"I..." He looked horrified, like he was about to confess to masturbating in public. "It's not what I did. It's what I didn't do. I mean... I couldn't do it. I couldn't get it up."

Justin understood how hard it must've been for him to admit to his sudden case of erectile dysfunction.

"I was too drunk. She was so aggressive. Demanding. Boiling with lust. Her foreplay was rough, you gotta understand, Justice. I've been to friendlier fistfights."

Justin felt sorry for the guy. "How did she kill you?"

"I-I remember a knife in my stomach." Panic flushed Dennis's face. "She claimed an intruder killed me. The cops couldn't prove otherwise."

"Where is Janet now?"

"At another wedding." With a trembling hand, Dennis pointed to the light, which parted to reveal a scene in the land of the living.

***

Organ music pumped through the church on Rattlesnake Road in Deckers, Texas. Janet Blaire sat in the front pew next to the bride's mother and leered at the groom. He was standing at the altar, a sharp-looking young man, blond hair combed straight back, and he stood with perfect posture in his light-blue tuxedo. His best man stood next to him, looking equally as statuesque.

Terry Wright

The organ music heightened.

Janet liked weddings. For this one, as she did every wedding she attended, she wore a low-cut black cocktail dress, black silk gloves, and black high-heel shoes. Her favorite red ruby pendant, the size of a silver dollar, hung around her neck on a single strand of silk thread. She never wore nylon stockings, a bra, or panties. With her dress hiked halfway up her thighs, there was always the possibility that some special part of her anatomy might be revealed to a possible suitor.

She knew what men liked.

Crossing her right leg over her left knee drew a glance from the best man. She twitched her leg. Her shoe slipped off her heel and dangled by her toes. She could feel the heat of his stare on her tantalizing legs.

Men. They were so easy to please, but they were clueless when it came to pleasing a woman. Her dead husband, Dennis, the only husband she ever had, was a prime example. On their wedding night, he'd quickly satisfied his sexual needs then rolled over and went to sleep, leaving her lying there alone and yearning for her own release.

A venomous taste oozed in her mouth.

She'd gutted that mouse-of-a-man eight years ago, but the damage was done. He'd changed her attitude toward men forever. *To hell with those self-gratifying pricks.* She felt no pity, no remorse, only loathing for the men she'd bedded and killed since Dennis. Not a one of those pricks took the time or effort to satisfy her sexual needs.

But those losers hadn't stopped her from playing her games. She was always on the hunt for that one special man who could make her see the fireworks and hear the symphony of climactic bliss.

Her lustful gaze settled on the best man. She sent him

a flirtatious smile. Could he be the one to satisfy her? Would he dare take the chance? Her gaze slowly slipped from his wanting eyes to her long, shapely legs. She gave the dangling shoe a twitch.

Foolish man.

***

The scene in the church faded from the light. Justin had heard Janet's thoughts as clearly as if she had spoken to him directly.

"She's going to kill the best man." Dennis leaned forward in the chair facing Justin. "You've got to stop her."

"Who knows..." Justin shrugged, "maybe he'll send her to Fourth of July heaven."

"There's no satisfying her. She's frigid as a Frigidaire, and we paid the price for her frigidity."

Justin blinked. Thirty-seven dead bodies and no arrest? "How has she gotten away with all these murders?"

Wach-el answered from the light. *"The police are baffled. She's left no credible evidence behind."*

"No fingerprints?" Justin found that hard to believe.

"Black gloves," Dennis threw in. "She always wears those damn silk gloves."

"No hair? No DNA?"

"Without someone to link the evidence to, it's all useless."

"Link," Dennis said. "I almost forgot." He dug into his pants pocket and came out with a cufflink. "Show this to her."

"What for?" Justin took the cufflink. A green emerald sat atop a gold hasp, a unique piece of men's jewelry.

"I was buried with it. She'll remember it, and she'll believe you talked to me." Dennis stood. "We can't cross over until she's punished."

Terry Wright

"It's not that easy." Justin examined the cufflink. *To Dennis with Love* had been engraved under the emerald mounting. "But I have an idea."

***

The church organist pounded out the *Wedding March*. Janet stiffened in her seat on the front pew. The tune brought back memories of her wedding to Dennis, her great expectations, and that ultimate disappointment on her honeymoon night. She'd never forgive him. She'd never forget.

However, this was someone else's wedding, and she planned to take full advantage of everyone's heightened emotions. With flitting eyelashes, she flirted with the nervous best man. He already seemed mesmerized by her bare legs. He wanted her, all right. She gave her foot a little twitch, hoping he'd realize she was interested in him too.

He diverted his eyes to the bride, whose entrance at the back of the church had just upstaged Janet's tantalizing game. This required drastic measures. As the bride began her walk down the aisle, Janet uncrossed her legs, leaving a momentary gap between her thighs. A rush of cool air whispered across her smoothly shaved place.

Her offering hadn't gone unnoticed. The best man's eyes brightened and a smile touched his lips.

Foolish man.

With a rush of silk and lace, the bride glided by, her arm hooked over her father's elbow, her face hidden behind the veil. Janet had read about this upcoming wedding in the Deckers Herald. It hadn't taken her long to befriend the bride's family. They owned a convenience store, which Janet began to shop frequently. A little coaxing during idle conversation convinced them to invite her to their daughter's wedding.

Justin Graves

There was something about weddings that made men horny. Maybe it was knowing what the bride and groom would be doing that night. Maybe it was seeing so many pretty women gathered together in one place, all dressed up and smelling so fine. Maybe it was drinking alcohol and doing the chicken dance that made them all touchy-feely. Whatever the reason, Janet found weddings to be fertile hunting grounds.

The organ music ended. The bride faced her idyllic groom and his fidgeting best man. His eyes darted to Janet's distracting legs with increased frequency.

The preacher said, "We are gathered here today..."

A nasty odor crinkled Janet's nose, like somebody had dragged a dead cow into the church. A rotting dead cow. Her chest compressed under an unknown weight, a pressure or a presence she couldn't explain.

Looking around for the source of her distress, she noticed an old man had slipped in and sat next to her in the pew. He wore a dusty long coat and held a dirty cowboy hat in his lap. Gray hair touched his shoulders and his sunken face looked tough as beef jerky. He smelled like he hadn't showered in months.

"...to join this man and this woman..."

"Do you mind?" Janet sneered at him. "Sit somewhere else."

The old man plied her with steely eyes set deep in dark sockets. "Don't mean to offend you, ma'am," he said in a raspy-dry voice. "My name is Justin Graves, but you can call me Justice."

"...in holy matrimony..."

"I'd rather call the police," she hissed, keeping her voice low.

"I *am* the police," he said and showed her a gleaming circle-star badge pinned to the lapel of his grimy coat.

"Texas Ranger, homicide."

"You're stinking up this wedding."

"Did I mention that I'm dead?"

"If you were dead, you'd be in the morgue."

The old man opened the slat of his coat, revealing a chest full of bullet holes. White, slimy maggots squirmed in the rotting wounds.

Reeling from the gush of stench, Janet scooted away from him and shifted her eyes side to side to see if anyone else was disturbed by the old bum.

"...if anyone knows of any reason these two should not be joined together..."

Everyone's attention was on the ceremony. Maybe if she concentrated on the wedding, Justice would go away.

"Your husband sent me," the ghoulish Texas Ranger said.

"He's dead," she said out the side of her mouth.

"I know."

Her stomach turned upside down. She'd been cleared of any wrongdoing. His death was a cold case by now.

"...speak now or forever hold your peace."

"I know what you're thinking." Justin pointed a bony finger at the best man.

"You don't know anything." How could he know she was going to lure him into her bed of lust? Tempt him with her favors, lavish him with kisses and nibbles, and make him take her to heights that she'd never been taken.

"Leave him alone," Justin grated out. "If you don't, I'll see that the devil makes you pay—"

"Get lost, mister. You're nothing but a wedding crasher."

"...do you take this man to be your lawful wedded husband...?"

"Then how did I get this?" He produced a gold

cufflink with a green emerald stone.

Dennis's cufflink. She'd given it to him as a wedding gift, before he left her naked, cold, and wanting. Last time she'd seen it...on his shirtsleeve cuff...when the coffin was closed. So how did the old man get it? "You some kind of grave robber?"

"...do you take this woman to be your lawful wedded wife...?"

"I talk to dead people, Janet Blaire."

Her heart rate doubled. "You know my name?"

"And I know what you've been doing."

"Get away from me, goddamn it."

"Look at how you dress. You enjoy playing the part of a Black Widow."

"So what if I do? I have my reasons." She clutched the red pendant in her fist and wished Justin would go away.

"...to love, honor, and cherish..."

"You need psychological help, Janet. Turn yourself in to Captain Holland at the Texas Rangers headquarters here in Deckers. Tell him you're the killer they've been looking for. He'll see that you get the mental treatment and therapy you need."

"Get out or I'll scream."

"...through sickness and in health..."

Justin tossed her the cufflink.

She reached out to catch it but missed. It clattered on the floor. As she bent over to pick it up, she shouted, "Talking to dead people, Justice, you're the one who's nuts, not me."

"Shhhhhh."

Janet's face heated with embarrassment. Everyone nearby was looking at her. By the time she sat upright, she noticed the smelly old man was gone. Was her mind playing tricks on her? Nobody really talks to dead people.

She stared at the cufflink pinched between black-gloved fingers. *To Dennis with Love.* No. She wasn't crazy. She hadn't imagined him.

"...'til death do you part..."

The leer in the best man's eyes overpowered her concerns. He was watching her, calculating his next move, betting on his chances for love.

She spread her knees and let him see the prize awaiting him. *Come hither, you foolish man.*

"...I do..."

***

The motel room key clicked in the lock. Excitement rushed through Janet's body, tightening a warm coil inside her stomach.

With a strong arm around her waist, the best man toed open the door. They stumbled into the dimly lit room and tumbled onto the bed, flat on their backs.

"Honey, were home," he sang out and laughed.

Janet snuggled into the crook of his arm. "Why do they call you the best man, anyway?"

"Be...cause I am," he stammered and laughed again.

She kicked off her shoes. "Want to bet?"

"What do we bet?"

Your life. She sat up, and in one smooth motion, slipped the black dress over her head. Black hair cascaded over her bare shoulders and down her back. The red ruby pendent nestled into the valley between her breasts. She felt sexy and hot exposed to this man.

"Now it's your turn." Grabbing his shirt panels, she ripped them apart, scattering the buttons.

"Hey."

"What's the matter, best man?"

"That's a fricken rental." He tried to sit up.

Justin Graves

"So am I." She pushed him back down on the bed and undid his belt.

"I'm not paying..."

In the next moment, she yanked off his shoes and pants and dropped them on the floor, followed by his boxers. Her heartbeat jumped and sputtered at the sight of his naked body. Her eyes traversed his muscular frame to the thing between his legs that would soon set her free.

"I love you...ah..." He sputtered. "Janice...ah...Janet."

A coil in her belly began to tighten. "Show me how good you are, best man." With tingling fingers and palms on fire, she ran her hand through the mat of hair on his chest then down his tight abdomen to the soft nest of hair above his manliness.

Her own body swelled and throbbed and moistened.

Don't make me wait. Please take me. Take me. Take me.

"The room is spinning," he slurred out. "I think I'm going to be sick."

"Not until I'm done with you."

But he wasn't ready yet. She grabbed his limp member, squeezed it and stroked it. It remained as flaccid as a wet noodle. Undaunted, she went to work on him, pulling and twisting.

He could get hard. He was young and virile. He wouldn't let her down. *Not tonight. Not now.*

Squeezing him harder and stroking him longer, he still didn't respond, not to her kneading, not to her pumping and pulling. A wave of panic rippled through her. She got nothing from him. Not a thrust from his hips, not a moan. "Come on, best man. Be a man."

He let out a snore.

She looked up. The son-of-a-bitch had fallen asleep.

"You prick."

Terry Wright

She sat on his abs and wrapped her legs around his torso then pressed her hot place against his useless flesh, pressing and pushing as hard as she could. Her parts throbbed frantically, but she couldn't find the right rhythm. She couldn't climb that cliff to heaven all by herself. The more she humped him, the more frustration rooted in her belly.

She was losing the desire, that hot, steamy craving that should have sent her soaring through the sky by now. Instead, she was hanging there, clinging to the crumbling cliff face. Letting go meant defeat. She couldn't let go. She wouldn't. If only he was the best man he'd professed to be.

"You liar."

Frustration turned to rage, boiling hot in her chest, threatening to tear her from the anticlimactic cliff she'd been climbing and send her spiraling to the ground. The cold, lonely ground.

"Wake up, you limp-dick bastard."

She hung on with all her strength, gasping for air and hoping for the miracle revival of his manhood. He couldn't fail the test. He couldn't lose the bet. He couldn't leave her hanging over this insatiable abyss.

A disgusting odor invaded the throes of her carnal rage. Rotting flesh. Roiling maggots. The familiar odor of Justin Graves meant he was somewhere nearby. *Not Now. Not tonight.*

"Go away, Justice."

"I'm sorry it had to come to this." His gravelly voice rattled from the shadows.

The cliff crumbled in her fingers and let her fall. Down, down, down. It was over. The end. All she could do was keel over on the best man's chest and gasp for air. The fire between her legs smoldered and died. Tears burned her eyes. "Goddamn you, Justice. You ruined everything."

"I'm just getting started."

Her guts clenched and her lungs heaved. She felt suddenly ill and feared she might vomit on the best man.

"What are you doing to me?"

"You are what you are," Justin proclaimed.

Gasping, she searched the shadows for the smelly son-of-a-bitch, but hard as she tried, she couldn't see him in the darkness, which took on a deeper black than before, like she was going blind.

Her guts churned and twisted like something inside was trying to get out. Heart beating faster, she thought her entire body had caught fire. And the pain in her stomach was like her intestines had turned into coils of barbed wire. Her stomach started swelling and stretching. She hugged her abdomen in a futile attempt to stop the expanding muscles. Her head ached as if her brain were being attacked by the biggest migraine in medical history.

Justin bent over her. "You should've left the best man alone."

There's no such thing as a best man.

She couldn't speak out loud. The saliva in her throat had dried up and turned to dirt. She tried to swallow but couldn't. Her breathing became rapid, shallow panting.

"I gave you a chance to ask for psychiatric help."

Justice. What's happening to me?

"But you turned down my offer, and for that you'll pay the consequences, Janet Blaire."

Her belly split open and gooey liquid oozed from the gaping wound. Pain shotgunned up her spine. Three pair of spindly black legs unfolded from her torso. She screamed but no sound came out.

Her arm and leg bones broke into seven sections each, each with six joints. The bones turned to mush and her feet and hands fused into slender gripping claws, which would allow her to walk up window glass. She fell on her side, jerked, and kicked her new limbs. Her skin blackened and dried to a hard body shell.

Once sensuous lips crumpled into hard mandibles, and her teeth melded into sharp curving fangs that dripped poison. Splitting down the middle, her tongue formed two six-jointed, hairy appendages, which she would use to taste her food and feed herself.

Her brain imploded, and as if wiped away with an eraser, everything she ever remembered was gone from her blackboard of human life. Her abdomen ballooned into a hard-shelled ball, black and shiny.

Numbness replaced any sensation of pain.

And in the last surge of this hellish metamorphosis, her face peeled off and her forehead exploded, releasing eight eyes that could make out eerie shapes in the darkness. Shifting her eyes to her transformed body, she saw the red hourglass mark on her belly.

Instinctively, she rose up on her spindly legs and scanned the cavernous room. A shape towered close by, a human, she knew from instinct, a dead human she knew from the odor combing through her tongue hairs.

The fear of being crushed caused her to skitter off across the bright expanse of a soft surface and drop to the ground on a single strand of silk thread. She took refuge in a corner and quickly constructed a web.

Feeling safe, she clung to the silk strands and waited.

A sudden vibration rippled through her silken bed. Her heart skipped. *What was that?*

"You have company," Justin said.

The vibration came again, stronger this time. He had to be near, somewhere behind her. She didn't dare turn to face him. He'd surely run away. She didn't want to be alone. *Not now. Not tonight.*

She twitched her legs. He had to know she wanted him as badly as he wanted her.

Don't make me wait. Please take me. Take me. Take me.

***

It was almost noon when a knock came on the motel room door. "Housekeeping."

Justin was sitting on the bed, watching the black widow labor in her web. She'd killed her lover last night and wrapped the small body of the male spider in silk. He too had failed to satisfy her and paid with his life. She would lay her eggs on him, and when her babies hatched, they'd feed on their father.

"Housekeeping."

The best man awoke. He sat up and tried to shake off a hangover that would kill a horse. Sunlight glowed beyond the window shades. On the bed beside him lay a black cocktail dress, a red ruby pendant, and a pair of black gloves. His pants and her high-heel shoes were lying on the floor.

Slipping into his boxers, he vaguely remembered the beautiful woman he'd brought here last night. Damn. He was so drunk he'd passed out.

"Where did she go?"

The door to the bathroom angled open. She wasn't in there. Did she leave naked?

Another knock.

"Yeah, yeah."

"It's after check out time, mister."

"I'm coming." He finished dressing as best he could. His shirt buttons were missing. He found his shoes under the bed. Dizzy but in one piece, he opened the door. "Sorry I slept in so late."

Terry Wright

"You better go or they will charge you more for the room."

Justin watched the best man leave. He was a lucky bastard and didn't even know it.

The maid came in with her broom and started sweeping the floor. She moved to the far corner and stopped abruptly. Horror dug lines in her face. She screamed, "Spider..." then beat Janet to death with her broom.

Justin felt a pang of remorse for the babies she would never rear.

Dennis appeared in his ethereal form, glimmering like a mirage. "She won't be killing any more men."

The maid swept Janet's crushed remains into a dustpan.

"The devil has her soul now," Justin said. "It's over." He rose from the bed. "She was crazy, you know. You guys should feel sorry for her."

"We do."

"Then I'd say you're ready to cross over."

"What about you, Justice? Are you going with us?"

Justin blew dust off his hat. "I'm going after Billy Denton."

With a gust of wind the ghoul was gone.

The Bible Motion

R elaxing in the afterlife, Justin leaned back in a plush recliner the light had supplied. Polished boots stood neatly beside his chair. Thick socks pampered his feet. Clean-shaven and smelling of Stetson cologne, he anticipated a nice nap while waiting for word to come about Billy Denton's whereabouts, but Justin's name reverberated from the light in a low and deep and clear-as-crystal voice.

"Justice..."

He lowered the brim of his cowboy hat to shade his face from the light. "What is it this time?"

The light pulsed. *"There's a disturbance on the other side."*

"Nothing matters on the other side," Justin reminded Wach-el, hoping he would go away.

"I've summoned her to see you."

Removing his hat, Justin looked into the light, sat up and sighed. "Then I guess you'd better fill me in."

The light flickered, revealing a scene from the land of the living. Headlight beams illuminated a snow-slick highway as a curly-haired woman gripped the steering wheel with knit-gloved hands.

"The year is 1994, five-thirty in the morning on a cold February in Denver," the light explained. *"This is thirty-one-year-old Janice Cross. She's driving her Cadillac to her father's house. They're going to go fishing."*

Justin wondered why the light was showing him something that happened so long ago and seven hundred miles from Deckers.

As the Cadillac rounded a curve in the highway, two cars came into view, pulled far off the road. One was a blue Geo with emergency lights flashing. The other, a four-door sedan, was parked behind the Geo with headlights on and exhaust vapor puffing from its tailpipe. A dark figure stood by the sedan, facing a wiry-haired blond woman, who immediately bolted toward the approaching Cadillac. She had such a look of dread on her face that Justin knew she needed help.

"Her name is Rhonda Malloy," the light said.

The slowing Cadillac passed her, stopped, and backed up.

Already, the dark figure was running after Rhonda.

She flung open the Cadillac's passenger door. The dome light flashed on revealing her tear-streaked face, swollen eye, and a bleeding lip. "Thank you, oh God, thank you."

Just as she closed the door, the dark figure slammed into the window. "I'll kill you, bitch." He pounded on the glass. "You hear me?"

"Go. Go." Rhonda cried, sliding away from the window.

As Janice accelerated the car, the assailant ran alongside and banged on the roof. "Bitch."

Rhonda cowered low in the seat as the car quickly left the attacker behind.

Relief spread through Justin. She got away, saved by a Good Samaritan. He wondered why the light showed him this until Rhonda looked back through the rear window and saw the dark figure running up to his idling car.

"He's coming after us."

"W-what happened?" Janice shouted, obviously shaken by the sudden turn of events.

"He raped me," Rhonda cried. "For two hours."

"It's all right. You're safe now."

"But he's got a gun."

Bright lights suddenly drenched the Cadillac's interior. The sedan was right behind them.

Rhonda screamed. "Go faster."

The assailant's car sped up on the left, but Janice cut him off. Fishtailing, the sedan veered right, and as Janice swerved into its path again, gunshots shattered her back window, pelting them with flying shards of glass.

Janice ducked, suddenly losing control on the slick highway. The Cadillac careened onto the shoulder and scraped along the crash barrier, throwing sparks.

"The police station," she shouted. "Second exit. We can make it—"

Bang!

Justin heard the meaty thwap of a bullet striking flesh, saw Janice flinch, but she managed to cling to the steering wheel and steer the car back on the road. As Justin tried to assess the severity of her wound, the sedan sped up on the passenger side. Now he got a clear view of the gunman, a round-faced black man with dark eyebrows and bared white teeth. Hanging out his window, he rapid-fired a semi-automatic pistol.

Bullets ripped into the Cadillac. One tore through Rhonda's mouth, blowing blood and teeth all over dash. Janice managed to drive up the off ramp. She saw the police station straight ahead but couldn't make the turn around the median. With a tremendous jolt, the car went airborne across the divider and crashed on the cops' front lawn. Surely they'd heard the noise and would come running.

Seconds ticked by.

A rising cloud of steam sizzled from the Cadillac's broken radiator. Inside, wounded Janice lay slumped against the door, moaning. Rhonda was screaming. She must've been in horrible pain.

The sedan rounded the median, came back, and skidded to a stop behind the wreck.

Watching the assailant bolt from the car, Justin couldn't believe the man's fearless approach with gun drawn. He jerked open the passenger door and grabbed screaming Rhonda.

"You're not getting away from me again." He raised the gun to Janice's head. "You're dead, too, bitch."

She closed her eyes, lips muttering a prayer.

He pulled the trigger, but all he got was the click of an empty chamber.

Kicking and screaming, Rhonda fought him as he pulled her from the Cadillac and shoved her into the sedan. As it sped off into the icy night, Janice lost consciousness.

Justin felt as if he'd just been pistol-whipped.

The light dimmed. *"A week later, Rhonda's naked body was found under a bridge east of Aurora. She'd been raped repeatedly and bludgeoned to death."*

"And Janice?"

"Paralyzed. The bullet lodged in her spine. A single mom with three daughters no longer able to support her family."

"Who's the killer?" Justin wished he could kill the bastard himself, but he knew he couldn't...the devil's rules and all.

"Roger Hanson, son of a detective who'd turned him in. A jury sentenced him to death."

"So? Problem solved."

"The story doesn't end there." The light parted, revealing a blue-carpeted walkway. *"Let her explain it to you."*

From the darkness beyond, a young woman appeared.

Wavy blond hair spilled over her shoulders. Fair skin. A narrow but attractive face lightly freckled. She wore a flowing lavender gown that swayed with each step.

Justin recognized her immediately. He stood. His boots were already on his feet, and the recliner faded away. "How can I help you, Rhonda?"

"He stole my life," she said, now standing before Justin with clenched fists jammed on her hips. "My husband and I wanted kids, a family. I worked my fingers to the bone waiting Blackjack tables. And for what? So some bastard could kidnap me? Rape me? Kill me? And get away with it?"

"What happened doesn't matter on the other side," Justin said, wondering why she hadn't figured that out by now.

"The only thing that gave me peace was knowing that Hanson would die for what he did, that he would go to hell where he belongs."

"He got the death penalty. What more do you want?"

"His sentence was commuted to life in prison."

Justin couldn't think of any way that would have happened. The heinousness of his crime, the brutality: if anyone deserved to die for this crime, it was Roger Hanson.

"A juror consulted the Bible during the sentencing phase of his trial." Rhonda paced in the light. "She brought it into the jury room, showed the others, *an eye for an eye, a tooth for a tooth.* Seems that referring to the Bible is not allowed in Colorado." She stopped in front of Justin. "Some lawyer figured out how to twist the law to get Hanson off death row."

"If a man kills a neighbor's animal," Justin said, "he will replace it. If a man kills his neighbor, he shall be put to death. This concept isn't new, has its origins clear back to the Code of Hammurabi some 2,000 years before the Bible was even written."

The light flickered. *"By Colorado law a juror cannot consider evidence not presented at trial to sway the jury to the detriment of the defendant."*

"They're taking God out of everything," Rhonda cried. "Prayer from our schools, The Ten Commandments from our courthouses, *under God* from the Pledge of Allegiance is next, and now this. They called it the Bible Motion."

Justin understood her frustration. "Many people believe in the separation of church and state, Rhonda. It's written in the Constitution, though I doubt our forefathers thought it would be taken to such extremes."

"It's tipping the scales of justice in favor of criminals."

"Okay. So Hanson spends his life in prison without parole. What's wrong with that?"

A scene from the land of the living unfolded in the light. High walls, guard towers, a stone-edged sign that read *Colorado State Penitentiary founded in 1871.* Inside, a labyrinth of lime green brick and steel came into view. Clanking sounds. Footsteps. Four men, three guards and a tall suited man, the warden, appeared.

The guards approached a solid steel door. One unlocked a panel that covered a cavity just big enough to slide a food tray through. "All right, Hanson, you know the drill."

"Come on," he said, his voice echoing from inside the small cell. "You don't think I'd cause trouble now. Not after all my lawyer done to get me off death row."

"You've got a nasty temper," the guard replied. "Bible or no Bible, we've got rules, so do it now."

The killer turned his back to the opening, crossed his wrists, allowing the guard to reach in and cuff him.

"The prisoner is secure," the guard reported into his collar-mounted microphone. "Open number four."

With a clank, the steel door unlocked and slid sideways, revealing a six-foot-plus black man, his head hair only stubble, his baby face shaved clean. He wore white tennis shoes, orange coveralls over a white t-shirt, and a crafty smile. Standing tall, he stepped from the cell.

The warden stopped him. "You got lucky, Hanson."

"I don't remember killing anyone. I was blacked out drunk and high."

"That's no excuse."

Hanson looked over the waiting guards. "What are ya gonna do with me now?"

"Prisoner transfer," the warden stated flatly. "Limon Correctional Facility."

Hanson frowned. "I hope it's better 'n this shit hole."

"You'll die in *that* shit hole," the warden assured him.

"Don't count on it. I've found God. He's forgiven me. Why can't you?"

"It's not my job."

Two guards grabbed his arms and muscled him toward the exit. "I'm not a bad person." The scene faded out.

Rhonda scowled. "God grants forgiveness to those who repent. He's not going to hell, after all."

The light dimmed. *"In twenty minutes he'll be on a bus to Limon."*

Justin thought about repentance. Only the sincere would be granted everlasting life. In the end, God couldn't be fooled, but for now, the true nature of Roger Hanson had to be put to the test. If he failed, there'd be one more soul for the devil, putting Justin one soul closer to freeing his daughter.

He put a firm hand on Rhonda's shoulder. "I've got an

idea...but I'll need your help."

"Help?"

"You'll have to face your killer again."

***

This was no luxury bus, Hanson grumped, more like a rolling cage, but it was a wonderful bus rolling him out of Canon City. One guard and the driver, both rode up front. They'd stuck him in the cage back by the rear doors. His hands were cuffed in front of him, his ankles shackled, and his waist chained to the seat's steel frame. Beyond screened and bulletproof windows, Highway 50 reached out across the vast openness of Colorado's eastern plains clear to the horizon. He hoped this wasn't the closest he'd ever get to freedom.

Mile after mile, the bus hammered along until it turned north on Highway 71, a remote stretch of two-lane heading toward Limon. By now, Hanson's bladder ached. "How much farther?" he shouted to the guard.

"Shut up."

"Hey. I gotta take a leak."

"If we pull over, it'll only be to put a bullet in your head for killing that woman, so shut up."

He again tried to remember killing Rhonda, but that night was still a blank. For all he knew, it never happened. Sure, he'd gone to a Central City casino that night. Played Blackjack. The waitress brought him free drinks. She was nice to him. He kept losing. She kept bringing him drinks. He lost some more. But that was okay. The more he drank, the better looking she got. The last thing he remembered was snorting a couple lines of cocaine in the men's room.

The next day, he awoke in his bed. His clothes were caked with mud and splattered with blood. Scratches on his face and arms. A woman was missing. She waitressed in

Central City. His father, the great detective, put two and two together, turned him in to the cops. Bastard. People said horrible things about him. None of it was true, of course. He wasn't a bad person.

A horrible stench blew into the bus, like the sewer in his cell had backed up, but this bus didn't have a sewer. The smell made his stomach seize. He feared he'd puke. Swallowing bile, he glanced at the guard and driver. They were talking as if nothing were wrong. He tried to call out but only gagged on the putrid air he inhaled.

"Roger Hanson," a gravelly voice said.

"What..?" He looked around but saw no one. The smell was getting worse. Maybe this was a trick, he thought, panic rising. The bus was rigged like a gas chamber. They were going to kill him anyway. He had to escape, started thrashing on his chains.

"Let me outta here."

The guards kept talking like they couldn't hear him.

An old cowboy appeared in the seat across the aisle, long brown coat shot full of holes, a gnarly face, exposed teeth and bone. His dirty cowboy hat sat cocked on his head of ratty gray hair. "What is this, some kind of bus ride to hell?"

"I've come with a proposition," the ghoul rasped.

Hanson figured the bus fumes had caused him to hallucinate. Even the guard and driver were oblivious as they jabbered on. "Guards."

No response.

The cowboy tipped his hat. "My name is Justin Graves, but you can call me Justice."

Hanson tugged on his chains, but he couldn't scoot away from the ghoul. "What do you want?"

"You say you're not a bad person, can't remember shooting Janice and killing Rhonda."

Fear sucked the spit from Hanson's tongue. "How did you get in here?"

"I talked to her, you know."

"She's dead, you crazy bastard."

"So am I." Justin opened his coat, revealing bullet-riddled meat, exposed bones, and a circle-star badge. "Texas Ranger. Shot and killed in the line of duty."

Hanson figured it was possible the ranger was dead, considering how bad he stunk. "Shouldn't you be in a morgue?"

"Don't change the subject." The stench of rot wafted on his foul breath. "I'm here to talk about Rhonda. You got off easy. The Bible Motion of all things."

"I've got a smart lawyer."

"There are those who believe the jury was right to consult the Bible, others think it was wrong. I, for one, don't think it matters. You took a life; you owe a life. And I'm here to collect."

Hanson felt his blood heat up. "You're going to kill me?"

"Unless, of course, you're sincerely repentant."

"I'm a changed man." He said it, but he didn't think Justin believed him. Who would?

"Then I'll make you a deal...give you a chance to prove it. From here on, no one will remember your name, and no one will come looking for you as long you never do anyone harm. But if you do, every cop in the state will hunt you down and shoot you like a mad dog."

"You can't be serious."

"I can make anything happen." With a wave of the ghoul's bony hand, the locks fell loose from Hanson's chains. "You're free to go."

He looked in awe at his freed hands and feet. It was a miracle. God worked in mysterious ways, all right, but to

Justin Graves

send this smelly Texas Ranger...who would have ever thought that was possible. Hanson's heart beat wildly with excitement. "You're an angel. Aren't you?"

"Good luck." Justin dissolved into thin air.

Hanson rubbed his eyes as if that would erase the terrible image lingering in his mind.

Just then, brakes squealed and tires screamed. The bus tipped. Hanson clung to the steel cage truly believing his good fortune was about to come to a crashing end. Justin was an angel, all right, the angel of death. "Damn it."

The bus careened off the road, slammed into the gully and flipped on its side, now bulldozing through tall grass and yellow flowers until the rear doors flung open, and Hanson spilled out.

Unscathed and a free man.

Standing, he slapped dust from his slacks and polo shirt, amazed that he was no longer wearing orange prison coveralls. God was working overtime on miracles today. He screamed up to the sky, "Thank you, Justice."

Not far away, the bus's wheels spun wildly. Smoke swirled from the wreck. He thought about the driver and guard, wondered if they were all right, but decided it was their own tough luck if they were hurt. Besides, in seconds they could be out with their guns drawn. They'd already threatened to put a bullet in his head, so screw 'em.

He ran up to the road, a desolate stretch of two-lane blacktop with no sign of civilization at either end. Just a mirage of heat waves rising, from which suddenly emerged a red Cadillac with yellow flames painted on the fenders. How lucky was that? Another miracle? He stuck out his thumb for a ride.

The Cadillac pulled up, rumbling like a truck with no muffler. Tinted windows hid the occupants from view, just reflected his face, the practiced look of innocence he

Terry Wright

portrayed.

"How 'bout a ride?"

The passenger window rolled down.

He stooped to look inside. A woman driver, blond hair flowing over bare shoulders, narrow face lightly freckled. Lots of cleavage, short skirt hiked up. His heart rate jumped as he recognized the waitress from the Central City casino. What the hell was she doing out here in the middle of nowhere? "I know you."

"Can you read?" she asked, pointing down the road.

A yellow sign had somehow appeared, black letters: *Correctional Facility. Do Not Pick Up Hitchhikers.* Something weird was going on.

"Are you an escaped con?" Rhonda asked.

"I don't think so." He wasn't about to ignore another miracle, especially not a hot cocktail waitress who had come to his rescue. An image of her naked and writhing under him set his pulse racing.

"Get in," she said.

He grabbed the door handle, and like an electric jolt, a memory stopped him.

On a freezing February night in Central City, he followed the cocktail waitress out to a dark casino parking lot, the image so vivid it could have happened last night. He saw her hot breath vapors, felt the heat of her body as he shoved her into her little blue car, held a gun to her head. "Give me your money."

"Please don't hurt me," she said and dipped into her bra to reveal a wad of bills. "My tips for the night. Take them."

He grabbed the money, looked her up and down. Oh those beautiful legs, bare knees, he could almost see up her skirt. The barrel of the gun drifted down her neck, over her right breast, down the flat of her stomach to the hem of her skirt. Steel lifted the soft material. He saw the faintest hint of panties and grinned. This was going to be great.

"No, please no," she begged.

The gun swung up to her temple.

"Take it off."

Trembling, she struggled within the small confines of the car and removed her skirt.

He set the gun on the dash and tore off her panties.

Now she put up a fight, kicked and scratched him. It wasn't until he slammed a fist into her face that she quieted. The rest was easy. Afterwards, he had to pee, took the gun and left her lying unconscious across the seat. As he took a whiz on the tire, the car suddenly started and sped off. The bitch. He dashed for his sedan halfway across the lot, jumped in and chased her down the mountain to Denver where he finally rammed her car off the road.

How dare she run away from him like that? He wasn't finished with her. That rage began to boil inside him again. And then he remembered the bitch in the Cadillac driving up. The cocktail waitress ran to the car. She wasn't going to get away a second time. He showed them, goddamnit, took her back right under the cops' noses.

And he beat her. And he raped her. And he killed her. And he dumped her body under a bridge like so much trash.

The truth hit him square between the eyes. He wasn't a good person after all.

"Are you getting in or not?" Rhonda asked.

"Oh, yeah." Hanson felt off balance, a bit confused as he jumped in, slammed the door, and looked her up and down. The cocktail waitress was really Rhonda Malloy. And she wasn't dead. That meant she could tell someone what he'd done to her that night. Justin had set him free, gave him a new life, another chance, but Rhonda could ruin it all. He couldn't let that happen.

"Where you headed?" she asked him as the flaming red Cadillac roared off down the highway.

"Denver." He knew she didn't realize how much danger she was in.

"You have family there?"

He leaned back in the seat, felt sweat bead up on his forehead. How was he going to do this and get away with it?

"Better put on your seat belt," she said. "It's the law."

"Yeah, sure," he muttered. As he stretched the belt across his lap, he noticed a bulge in his right pant pocket. A quick touch told him it was a gun. How did he get a gun? Something was screwy here. The old cowboy must've known about Rhonda, known she could blab about what happened, and gave him a gun to stop her. It's the only thing that made sense.

Rhonda smiled at him. "So how did you end up walking on this highway?"

"You wouldn't believe it if I told you."

She giggled.

About a mile down the road, the Cadillac approached a bridge, a good place to dump her body. He felt hot adrenaline spill into his bloodstream. It was time. He pulled the gun, amazed at how heavy it felt in his grasp, and pressed the barrel to Rhonda's temple. "Pull over."

Terror flashed in her eyes, nothing he hadn't seen before. Crunching gravel, the Cadillac stopped on the shoulder. Hanson yanked the keys from the ignition and tossed them out into the tall grass.

"You're not getting away from me this time."

"Please don't hurt me."

He thought to pull the trigger, get it over with quick, dump her body and get out of here. He was perfectly capable of doing it again. That he knew, but all those years behind bars had left him thirsting for what he saw, long legs, bare knees. He saw no sense in letting that go to waste. "Take off your skirt."

"No, please no."

"Do it, or I swear, I'll kill you now and do you anyway."

She wiggled out of her skirt, revealing thin pink panties.

"It's not too late, mister. Get out now. Walk away. I won't tell anyone."

Like hell she won't. He envisioned having his way with her again. The brutality. The violence. His arousal grew with the anticipation, hot and hard, feeding on her fear.

Gun pointed at her head, he reached down with his left hand, touched the soft skin of her thigh. She flinched. This was going to be great. He found the thin panty strap and tore it off.

Rhonda screamed and kicked and scratched, like last time.

So he punched her in the face.

From out of nowhere, a dozen police cars surrounded the Cadillac. Officers piled out, took defensive positions behind open doors, guns drawn. "Let me see your hands."

He grabbed Rhonda for a shield, gun to her head. "What have you done?"

"It's called justice, Roger Hanson."

"You know my name?" He couldn't breathe.

She dissolved into thin air...like that smelly cowboy had done. His day of miracles had turned to a nightmare.

"Throw out the gun."

Fighting panic, he wished he hadn't tossed the keys. That ungodly smell mushroomed inside the car. "Not again." He turned, saw the cowboy lounging in the back

Terry Wright

seat as if this was some kind of taxi ride. "You."

"The Bible isn't going to get you out of this one."

"You said they wouldn't come after me."

"I gave you every chance to do the right thing, but instead, you showed your true colors. All that BS about you not remembering your crimes. You are a bad person, after all."

Hot anger flared up inside. "You son of a bitch." He shot Justin point-blank in the chest.

"Shots fired." The police responded with a barrage of firepower, a dozen guns blazing, bullets shattering every window, tearing into Hanson's body like hot pokers. He slumped to the seat, blood pumping out every wound.

One last breath. One last word: "Justice."

With a gust of wind the ghoul was gone.

Justin Graves

Riches to Rags

Surrounded by the warm glow of the afterlife, Mrs. Templeton sat in her favorite rocker and stroked Ginger, the longhaired white cat curled in her lap. Though the light supplied everything she needed in this serene domain, her soul felt like a lump of burnt coal. She missed her husband, Wally, who'd died fifteen years ago. He'd left her a fortune, so much money she couldn't have spent it all in ten lifetimes, even if she'd tried. As it turned out, that money had become the root of her despair.

Ginger purred.

Mrs. Templeton understood the rules. As long as she harbored hatred in her heart and the burning desire for revenge, she would not be allowed to cross over to everlasting peace and happiness. She could not be reunited with Wally until she let go of her hate. Let go of everything earthly. Let go of the good that her favorite charity could have done with the money she'd bequeathed them.

The light began to shimmer, and she knew a visitor was approaching. Her ethereal heartbeat stuttered. She was about to meet with her last chance for redemption. One man possessed the power to set her soul to rest.

Justin Graves.

In a dazzling display of radiance, a man materialized from the white light. His cowboy hat shaded a clean-shaven face and his chiseled good looks. A circle-star badge glistened from the left lapel of his long brown coat, and she detected the fragrance of Stetson cologne. If a saddled horse had trotted up behind him, she would not have been surprised.

Smiling at the man, Mrs. Templeton offered him a chair, which appeared from the light with a sweep of her hand. "I'm so glad you could come, Justice."

"You're looking well." He tipped his hat and sat down facing her. A cup of steaming tea materialized, which she set in the palm of his hand. "Thank you, ma'am."

"No trouble at all."

Meow.

"Ginger says hello."

Justin tipped his cowboy hat to Ginger. "How can I help you, Mrs. Templeton?" He sipped his tea, even held his little pinky up properly.

Mrs. Templeton felt comfortable in the presence of this handsome man in spite of their age difference. She could have chosen to look twenty again, with flowing blond hair and the long legs of a goddess, the bronzed and blue-eyed beauty of her youth. However, remembering those days, her insecurities and flightiness, how naïve she'd been back then, she'd opted for glimmering silver hair and pure white skin still wrinkled with the wisdom of her years. Her short stature and upright posture made her feel like royalty sitting with Justin as he sipped his tea.

"Wally and I used to have tea every afternoon at four o'clock." She felt a twinge of déjà vu.

Justin set his cup on his knee. "I'm a little pressed for time, ma'am. I—"

"Now, Justin," she cut in, "I know all about you. The light has told me everything. You're in a rush to get Billy Denton's soul for the devil."

Justin's good looks took on a hard edge. "I don't want him breathing one more day than necessary."

"His time of reckoning will come."

"I'm afraid he's going to escape Deckers' rinky-dink jail—"

"Take the advice of a wise old lady." She stroked Ginger's fine white hair. "Let sleeping dogs lie, get a good cat, and cross over to your wife. She's waiting, you know."

"You should take your own advice."

"I know what you're going through, Justin. I can't cross over either. If it wasn't for Ginger..." Tears shined in her eyes. "I wouldn't know what to do with myself. That horrible, horrible man, what he did to me. I can't shake my contempt for him."

Justin nodded. "We all have our Billy Dentons."

"Mine is Dwaine DuBois. I trusted him with my financial affairs. He stole my inheritance and left me for dead in a state-run nursing home, buried me in a pine box, in a pauper's grave. I don't even have a headstone, Justin."

"I'm sorry," he said and sipped tea.

"What's worse than that..." A tissue materialized from the light. Mrs. Templeton dabbed her eyes. "He doesn't like cats."

"Cats mean a lot to you?"

"The money he stole was supposed to go to Kitty Rescue. Sarah Wells, she's my hero. Now her organization is suffering because of that conman." She waved her hand at the light. "See for yourself."

The glow parted and revealed a scene in the land of the living.

***

Sarah got down on her knees and scrubbed the concrete floor. Hungry cats *meowed* from their cages, which she'd stacked floor to ceiling along the walls of this dingy, converted garage. She dunked the brush in the bucket of soapy water and scrubbed some more. The cats kept begging to be fed, but there wasn't any food to be had.

Sweat trickled down her cheeks. She had a lot of work

to do, and the only help she counted on was late. Or maybe Linda wasn't coming in at all. Normally, she was very dependable, an unusual quality for a teenage girl with boys on her mind. However, volunteer or not, she should have called and told her she wasn't coming in.

A lock of hair fell across Sarah's left eye. She stopped scrubbing long enough to hook it behind her ear. Her twenty-five-year-old body felt achy and stiff, and her knees throbbed. She surveyed the dirty floor she hadn't yet tackled. It might as well have been the size of a football field.

Four years ago, this rundown old building was the best she could find for the money, which lately had become as scarce as a good man. Since Mrs. Templeton died, donations had dwindled. The rent was late. Food supplies were gone. Sarah's dream of saving the lost and abandoned cats of the world was crumbling around her.

Hot tears stung her eyes.

The phone rang.

Sarah gathered her composure. Maybe it was Linda calling. What excuse did she have for not showing up?

Sarah struggled to her feet and dropped the brush into the bucket. The loose lock of hair fell again. She answered the phone. "Kitty Rescue."

A man's voice came over the line. "My wife's cat is missing. Black and white with a diamond-studded collar. Name's Missy. Would you happen to have her there?"

Sarah's mind shuffled through her inventory of unfortunate felines. Nothing fit Missy's description, and she'd certainly have remembered a diamond collar. "When did she turn up missing?"

"Last night."

"She'll probably return on her own."

"My wife is worried. We were just hoping—"

Justin Graves

"Perhaps you should check the city pound."

"The pound? They euthanize... Oh, God. If I'm too late, my wife will never forgive me."

"You'd better call them right away."

"Thanks."

"Could you send us..." the line clicked dead, "a donation?"

The door buzzer sounded. Someone had entered the front room. Sarah set down the phone and hurried out to the counter, expecting Linda, but her heart fell into her stomach when she saw Lou Ralston, her landlord. He looked mad enough to spit kitty litter.

"Where's my rent money, Sarah? I can't wait any longer."

"I'm trying—"

"You're not trying hard enough."

"Public service is threatening to turn off my power. I have to pay them first."

"You have to pay *me* first or I'll throw you and all them damn cats out in the street. You got that?"

Tears started to flow again. "Please, Mr. Ralston—"

The buzzer went off. Sarah shifted her attention to the front door. Linda was dragging something in. A bag of dog food?

"Sorry I'm late," she said, wheezing. "I had to stop by the pet store. My mom talked them into donating some food."

Sarah wiped a tear from her cheek. "But it's dog chow."

"We can soak it. Mash it up. It'll be all right."

Sarah stood flabbergasted as Linda shuffled her booty into the backroom.

Mr. Ralston wagged a stiff finger at Sarah. "You can't even afford to feed them cats?"

~73~

"Things are really tight right now."

"I couldn't care less—"

The buzzer buzzed again. Both Ralston and Sarah turned to the door. Wearing summer dresses, a young woman and a little girl stood in the doorway, both red-eyed from crying. The child held a brown and white calico cat in her arms.

"Oh, dear," Sarah said. "What's the matter?"

"This is Sammy." The little girl whimpered. "He needs a new home."

"But, honey—"

"My baby sister gets sick."

The young woman stepped forward, eyes cast down as if she were ashamed to be standing there. "You see...my newborn is allergic to cats. She breaks out in hives and can't breathe. We need you to take him...find him a new home. He's really quite gentle and loves to play."

"But I can't take any more cats."

"Please find Sammy a new home," the little girl cried.

"Don't you see? We don't have room for any more cats." Sarah's tears rolled out again.

Mother knelt to her child, and with both hands on her little shoulders, she looked into her eyes. "I'm sorry, baby. Sammy will have to go to the city pound."

"No, Mommy, no. They'll put him to sleep." Now the child was bawling.

Sarah couldn't stand the heartbreak any longer. "Okay. I'll take him. I'll take Sammy."

Now everybody was bawling, except Mr. Ralston. He looked like he was going to pop. "You have to be kidding."

"We'll work something out." Sarah took Sammy from the little girl.

"Thank you for saving him," she said.

Mother and daughter left the building in tears.

"Linda," Sarah called out and wiped her eyes on her sleeve.

Linda appeared from the backroom. "You rang?"

Sarah handed her the cat. "Find a place for Sammy."

"But where?"

"Put him in with Slinky. They'll get along fine."

"If you say so." Linda took Sammy to join the ranks of the unwanted.

"You are nuts," Mr. Ralston bellowed.

Sarah held her chin up high. "If I were rich like you, I'd have Kitty Rescue shelters all across the country."

Mr. Ralston grumped and stormed out.

***

As Mrs. Templeton stroked Ginger, the vision faded from the light. "Sarah would have made good use of the money I had left Kitty Rescue in my will...if Dwaine hadn't stolen it all."

Justin's empty teacup drifted into the light. He leaned forward in his chair. "Let me get this straight. He embezzled your money, and you want me to deliver his soul to the devil. Do you realize that means he'll have to die?"

"Yes." She'd said it without flinching.

"Theft isn't a capital offense, Mrs. Templeton. We don't execute people for stealing."

She swallowed. "I was dying in that nursing home hospice center, Justin, but I wasn't dying fast enough for Dwaine." She pulled up her sleeve and showed him the puncture wound the needle had left in the crook of her arm. "He helped me depart with a little potassium chloride cocktail. No coroner is going to autopsy an old lady who died in hospice."

Justin sat back, jaw-dropped. "My god. He murdered

you."

"For the money that belongs to Sarah Wells."

Justin rubbed his handsome chin. His crafty smile matched the afterlife's brilliance. "Where is he now?"

She nodded to the light. An image of a yacht came into focus, cutting though candy-blue Caribbean waters. Loud music blared from the deck speakers, and boisterous voices filled with laughter echoed throughout the afterlife. As if viewed from a helicopter sweeping over the speeding craft, bikini-clad women and buff men wearing Speedos came into view. They were dancing on the deck and drinking from beer bottles.

"I see," Justin said. "He's living the good life on stolen money."

"And he got away with murder, Justin."

"There's no such thing," he said. "I need your original will that proves you left the money to Kitty Rescue."

A legal document appeared from the light. Mrs. Templeton handed it to Justin. He looked it over, read: *Sarah Wells. Kitty Rescue. Two hundred million dollars.* If Justin were alive, he would have fainted. "I know someone who can help us with this."

"Who?"

"Captain Holland."

Meow, Ginger responded.

***

With a boatload of partygoers, the *Mary D. Light* sliced through the water toward St. Thomas Island. Heavy metal music pounded from speakers on the 86-foot yacht. Dwaine DuBois, wearing Bermuda shorts and a wife-beater shirt, sat at the stern deck table, drinking beer and loading his spear-fishing gun. His woozy head made the procedure cumbersome, but he managed to cock the rubber launch band and fit a barbed spear into the slot. Satisfied he was ready for their next dive, he set the loaded spear-gun on the table.

Time for another beer.

He staggered to the aft cooler, a casket-sized Thermos filled with ice, beer, and wine. As he popped open the lid, excitement coursed through his body like liquid gold. This was his beer; this was his cooler; this was his yacht. He was rich beyond the riches of the rich and famous. His newfound wealth had bought him a lavish lifestyle of jet-setting world travel. Now, only the finest restaurants and five-star hotels were good enough for Dwaine DuBois.

His head buzzing from alcohol and considerable self worth, he grabbed an MGD, spun around, and thrust the bottle in the air. "Here's to Mrs. Templeton," he cheered to his band of drunken pals.

A dozen bankers and lawyers and loose women hailed, "Amen."

"May the dumb bitch rest in peace." Dwaine opened the bottle and chugged down half the beer. He staggered toward his girlfriend, Peachy, who wore nothing but her bikini bottom. Must've been the skimpiest thong ever made. It cost a fortune for something so small. Two of his buddies-in-crime were ogling her breasts.

Christopher, Dwaine's top financial advisor, sat on a barstool in the shade. He raised his glass of wine. "To the best damn conman in the business. Let's hear it for Dwaine."

Boisterous cheers and applause followed.

"I couldn't have done it without you guys," he shouted over the loud music.

Lei, a flat-chested blonde and an expert at altering legal documents, laughed. "Can you believe she was going to give all that money to a bunch of cats?"

Terry Wright

"What a dumb old broad," Ralph crooned. He was a damn good lawyer and a better liar. He tossed a dart. It stuck in a picture of Ginger that he'd pinned to the dartboard.

Dead center. Left eyeball.

"Nice shot." Dwaine had to laugh. "Mrs. Templeton loved that damn cat. I got piss-faced drunk the day that prissy thing croaked." He wrung his hands around the beer bottle as if it were the cat's neck.

Peachy leaned against the starboard rail, her round-cakes glistening in the sunshine, her perky nipples erect in the breeze. "What's with you guys and cats, anyway? They're so soft and cuddly."

Dwaine swigged beer and spit on the deck. "I hate cats. They're the epitome of laziness, prissiness, and boredom. I can't stand the way women get all mushy over them when they should get all mushy over this." He pointed to his crotch. "Cats are like little girls and crybabies. Thank God, in his infinite wisdom..." Dwaine hiccupped, "God made me allergic to cats. They make me break out in hives. When they rub against my leg, I can't breathe. All that meowing a purring makes me want to puke."

Ralph threw another dart. "Nothing like the sound of a hardy barkin' dog."

Dwaine drained his beer. "If every cat in the world were dead, I'd sing hallelujah." He pitched his empty beer bottle over the side and staggered back to the aft cooler to get a replacement.

As he leaned in to make his selection, a nauseous odor assailed his nostrils. Gagging, he looked up, thinking a rotted whale carcass had gotten caught in the yacht's backwash. Peering over the stern, he saw the wake churned white and frothy.

Frothy. Like his next beer. He laughed at his own joke, leaned in, and grabbed another MGD. His chest started to compress from an unknown pressure. He couldn't breathe. Someone must've snuck a damn cat onboard.

"Hello, Dwaine," came a hollow voice from behind him.

He damn near jumped out of his Bermudas. Wheeling around, he saw a dusty old cowboy wearing a long brown coat encrusted with grime. He'd planted his muddy boots squarely on the deck.

"Where in hell did you come from?"

"Deckers," the ghoulish cowboy rasped. His face was shrunken and leathery like he'd been out in the sun too long...way too long, and his eyes were set in deep sockets that glowed red.

Dwaine blinked. He had to be seeing things, the burning sun and all the booze, it was probably just Ralph or Christopher standing there. Dwaine blinked again thinking his vision would clear...but no such luck. The smelly old man was still standing there. He must've stowed away in the black water toilet tanks. "Who the hell are you?"

"My name is Justin Graves," he grated out. "But you can call me Justice."

"You're stinking up my boat," Dwaine shouted, attracting the attention of his friends.

"What's that, Dwaine?" Ralph asked.

"Hey, you guys. Help me throw this fool overboard."

They laughed, flipped him off, and went back to their frivolities.

"What's the matter with you guys?" Dwaine shouted at his friends.

"They can't see me," Justin said. "Only you."

Dwaine felt a chill in spite of the tropical heat. The smelly cowboy was beginning to raise the hairs on the back of his neck. "What do you want?"

"Justice for Mrs. Templeton."

"The old bag is dead."

"She told me how you killed her with a shot of lethal injection."

The chill became a deep freeze. "How did you know that?"

"I talk to dead people."

"Yeah. And I'm Miss America."

Justin peeled open his brown coat, revealing a rotted rib cage roiling with white, slimy maggots. "Believe me now?"

Dwaine stepped back, his throat choking from the stench. Justin was dead all right. Only a ghost could've gotten aboard this speeding yacht. If he was here to con the best conman in the business, he was on the wrong boat. Dwaine offered him the MGD. "You look like you could use one of these."

With a flick of his bony hand, Justin declined. "I have a proposition for you, Dwaine DuBois. Liquidate all your misbegotten assets, keep a million dollars for yourself, and give the rest to Sarah Wells and her Kitty Rescue Foundation. All will be forgiven."

"Are you crazy?"

He shrugged. "Not since the last time I was checked."

"You want me to give two hundred million bucks to a bunch of cats? You can't be serious."

"I'm dead serious."

"Go to hell, Justice, and take that cat-lovin' old woman with you."

"I take that as no."

"Take it anyway you like." Dwaine screwed the lid off the beer bottle and flicked it overboard. He wasn't going to entertain any of this bullshit. He was drunk. That's all there was to it. After slamming the cooler lid, he flipped his middle finger to his imaginary apparition.

Two steps back toward the party, he heard a creaking noise from deep within the yacht. Then a groan. He stopped mid-stride. His heart rate shot up a notch. "What was that?"

Justin showed him a gnarly grin. "Seems your boat just got a hole in the hull."

The yacht listed hard to port. Dwaine dropped his beer bottle. As it rolled under a chair, spewing foam, the chair started sliding toward the stern, which was going down fast. The liquid gold in his veins turned to hot adrenaline. He grabbed the railing and hung on for his life.

The engine sputtered and quit, slowing the boat until it stopped dead in the water.

Christopher fell off his barstool and slid to the aft railing. The dartboard flew off the wall and bashed Ralph in the forehead. Dazed and bleeding profusely, he tumbled over the railing and into the water.

Peachy screamed.

Dwaine clung to the rail and looked down to the water. A blue and yellow fuel slick oozed from the hull.

Screeching like fingernails scraping on a chalkboard, the table slid down the sloped deck and slammed into the aft railing, just missing Dwaine. The loaded spear-gun almost catapulted over the rail, but Dwaine grabbed the gun and turned it on the ghoul. "You'll pay for this, Justice." He pulled the trigger.

With a twang, the gun launched the spear, driving it into Justin's throat. He staggered back, his eyes pulsing red with anger, but he didn't go down.

"We're sinking," a naked man shouted as he charged up the steps from the below-deck cabins. He held his naked girlfriend's hand and pulled her along. "Abandon ship."

Sparks popped and arched across the tilted deck. The

boat's electrical system shorted out, killing the loud music. Crewmen were lowering the lifeboat. A cable snapped. The lifeboat plummeted into the water, capsized, and disappeared under the choppy surface.

"Now what are we going to do?" Peachy shrieked.

Dwaine threw the spear-gun overboard. "Justin Graves is sinking my boat." He turned an accusatory finger on the cowboy, but he must've already jumped ship.

The boat listed so badly, waves were already lapping over the stern and port transoms.

"Jump." Lei leaped overboard, feet first. Christopher struggled to his drunken feet, threw her a life preserver, and flung himself over the rail. The other shyster bankers, lawyers, and whores followed suit.

Clinging to the rail, Dwaine watched in horror as triangular fins broke the surface and raced toward his swimming cohorts at breakneck speed. His heart almost stopped. "Sharks."

There must've been a hundred of them, attracted by Ralph's blood in the water. Three slick gray bodies struck him from behind, jaws gnashing. The blood-red water became a boiling caldron of fish and flesh, a feeding frenzy of unspeakable horror.

Lei screamed. Her face twisted with terror. She went under, lifesaver and all. A red stain floated to the surface.

Dwaine clung to the rail, knowing that if he jumped, he would die. He could only hang on and watch as a speeding fin sliced up behind Peachy. "No."

In a rush of white water, savage jaws rose up around her body and clamped those beautiful round breasts in razor-sharp teeth, raking the flesh into long, bloody gashes before pulling her under.

Dwaine thought he was going to puke.

Deck chairs slid to the rails and piled up like pickup

sticks. An umbrella tumbled over the stern. Horrible sounds echoed up from below deck, a kind of mechanical wailing as hot steel met cold water. Even the yacht was crying out for mercy.

Fighting the burn of panic in his veins, Dwaine looked for something that would float, something he could hang on to, something big enough to keep him out of the water and away from those man-eating sharks.

The beer cooler, of course.

Hope drove him to action. He hooked a leg on the aft rail, and with all his strength, he flipped over the cooler, spilling its contents. He set it upright, climbed inside, and closed the lid just as a rush of waves set it afloat.

With a hissing gasp, the *Mary D. Light* went to the bottom.

Set adrift, Dwaine had no sense of time. An hour might have passed. Maybe two. As the sun beat down on the cooler, it became hot as an oven inside, but he didn't dare open the lid for fear of the marauding sharks.

Even under these terrifying conditions, with death swimming within mere feet of his arc, Dwaine started to laugh. That stupid old Justice Graves had failed to kill the best conman ever born. *Didn't he know crime pays?* He'd buy another yacht. Buy some new friends—

He felt a bump against the bottom of the cooler. His breath seized in his lungs. Shark? Another bump. Same shark? More sharks? Then a heave as the cooler shot upward, tipped, and started rolling over and over. The lid flew open. He was suddenly flung out into the water. Expecting to be greeted by sharp gnashing teeth, he screamed...and fell face-first in sand.

Sand?

Scrambling to his feet, he couldn't believe his eyes. He'd landed on a tropical island. The cooler had bumped the shallow bottom of the lagoon. Rolling waves had shoved it to shore. He'd fallen out before a rip current pulled the cooler back out to sea. So there he stood, on a beach edged by stands of fruit trees and groves of palms swaying in a gentle breeze.

Paradise had saved him.

He fell to his knees and grabbed two handfuls of sand. The grains sifted through his fingers. Mad with delight, he looked up to the sky. "Justice, you failed again, you smelly bastard."

A boat engine roared nearby. If Dwaine was going to spend any more of Mrs. Templeton's money, he'd have to get back to civilization as quickly as possible. He jumped to his feet and started waving his arms. "Over here." The boat wasn't far away; the passengers should have been able to see him, but the boat cruised away. "Hey."

A speedboat churned across the lagoon. He chased after it, down the beach, yelling so loud his throat hurt. Clambering over rocks and racing through dense vegetation, he waved and jumped up and down, but sill, he couldn't get their attention. Not even a slow moving double-decker tour boat, packed with people, stopped for him. He felt as if he were invisible.

In all his efforts to be rescued, his wife-beater shirt was ripped to rags. His Bermudas were tattered worse, exposing his Fruit-of-the-Looms, and his arms and legs were scratched all to hell. Not long ago he had riches beyond his wildest dreams. Now Justin had reduced him to wearing rags.

Exhausted, Dwaine fell to the sand, closed his eyes, and thought he'd take little nap to restore his energy.

Meow.

Dwaine froze.

Meow. Meow. Meow.

He opened his eyes to a terror that struck deep to the core of his soul. Cats. Two, three, ten, twenty, he couldn't count the number of them prancing toward him, tails in the air, meowing and purring, agate eyes glaring, little cats and big cats of every imaginable color. He tried to get up. He wanted to run, but he was too exhausted from chasing phantom boats.

The cats swarmed over him, licking his open wounds, meowing and purring, rubbing against him as if he were their greatest love. His throat seized.

"Justice."

***

On a hill overlooking Cat Island, Justin pulled the spear from his throat, leaving a half-inch hole through his neck. One thing good about being dead: the wound didn't hurt. One thing bad about being dead: the wound would never heal. He broke the spear in half, dropped it on the ground, and made a note to himself: *be careful*. His rotting body was the only transportation his soul would ever have when he came back to earth. If it was going to last long enough to finish his deal with the devil, he'd have to take damn good care of it.

Mrs. Templeton's ethereal form appeared next to him. "It's lovely here."

A salty sea breeze tugged at Justin's brown coat. He was a long way from Deckers, Texas, but he'd been farther. He'd been to hell and back. This was his first Caribbean vacation, and as it turned out, a working vacation at that.

Wally, a baldheaded man of short stature, appeared as a shimmer next to his deceased wife. He took her hand for the first time in fifteen years. "We can't thank you enough, Justice."

"I've got my Wally back," Mrs. Templeton chimed in.

Terry Wright

"For eternity."

"I'm happy for you," Justin said with a twinge of jealousy in his empty chest. His time for happiness was coming, but not for a while. Not until he'd satisfied his demons, the one in hell, and the one tearing his soul to shreds...his hatred for Billy Denton.

Watching the cats mill around Dwaine and rub their bodies against him, Mrs. Templeton sighed. "They're such loving creatures."

Justin kicked a rock with his boot. "Dwaine's attitude toward cats says a lot about his attitude toward people."

"I'm glad he's allergic to cats. Serves him right, but I feel sorry for all those young folks who had to die because of what he did."

"Things are not always what they seem," Justin said. "I wanted you to see them punished for what they did to you, but only Dwaine will pay the ultimate price for sticking that needle in your arm."

She held out her arm to show Justin the wound had healed.

"Truth is, the *Mary D. Light* sailed into Galveston Harbor. Captain Holland and a contingency of local cops were there to apprehend the gang of white-collar criminals as they got off the boat."

"I'm glad that boat didn't sink." She petted Ginger, who'd magically appeared in her arms. "It was a pretty boat."

"The story the gang told Captain Holland was much different from what you saw in the light. Dwaine got drunk, freaked out from too much sun, dumped the cooler, and jumped overboard with it. By the time the crew got the yacht slowed down and turned around, all they found was the empty cooler floating in the sea. They assumed the sharks had eaten him."

Down on the beach below, Dwaine wheezed in agony. Hives had already festered up on most of his exposed skin, but the loving cats wouldn't leave his side.

"He won't last much longer," Justin said. "The devil is waiting to greet his soul in hell."

"And the money?" Mrs. Templeton asked.

"A judge confiscated your stolen assets and reinstated your original will."

"The one I gave you?"

"Somehow it showed up on Captain Holland's desk, as if it had materialized out of thin air."

"You old prankster, you." She pinched his ear.

"Sarah will get a fortune to fund her Kitty Rescue."

"She hasn't received the money yet?"

"Soon, but not until she's stretched Mr. Ralston's patience to the limit. He needs to learn a little humility. I think he's going to become one of Sarah's most ardent supporters."

Wally spoke up. "Maybe she'll give you a proper burial, dear, and a headstone as grand as any in the cemetery."

"Oh. I hope she doesn't spend any money on me."

"There'll be no stopping her," Justin said. "She misses you very much."

"Tell her I'm fine now but what about you, Justice? Are you going to take an old woman's advice and cross over to be with your wife?"

"Someday." Justin said. "Not today and probably not tomorrow. But someday."

With a gust of wind the ghoul was gone.

The Beauty Queen

Twin spotlights swept the night sky above Deckers Town Theater on Main Stage Road. The final round of the beauty queen pageant was underway. On stage stood ten girls in the six-to-eight-year-old category. One girl would be chosen to wear the Little Miss Central Texas crown.

Mrs. Sandy Brandish stood behind the red curtains and watched the contestants pose in their evening gowns. Mothers had primped their girls to perfection: lipstick, mascara and rouge, hairstyles upswept, and high-heel shoes. The fragrance of expensive perfumes caressed the air, and she could feel the heat of the stage lamps on her face. As the finalists' names were announced and the girls strutted the runway, thunderous applause excited every nerve in her body.

She'd finally come home.

Five years had passed since she'd attended one of these gala affairs. Five years since—

"A fine group of girls we have this year," Mr. Shepler, the pageant's aging announcer said as he stepped back from the podium to speak with Sandy. "It's good to see you here."

"I must confess...I'm a little nervous."

Shepler sighed. "I remember when you were standing up there."

Cameras flashed.

"A lot has happened since then."

"It must've been horrible. I can't imagine losing a daughter like that. She was destined for stardom."

"As I was...once."

"Did the police ever find her killer?"

"No."

"I hear Victor took it pretty hard."

"Yes." Her husband had put on a good show for the cops and the media.

Another round of applause filled the theater.

She scanned the girls, their bright smiles and nervous twitching. Some beauty queen contestants were better poised than others, the result of constant coaching from their mothers, mothers insistent on winning, mothers who lived vicariously through their daughters. Mothers like Sandy.

"Where is Victor tonight?" Shepler looked around.

"He doesn't know I'm here." Sandy pushed back a lock of flowing black hair. "Beauty pageants have been my life. My mother entered me. Her mother entered her. Pageantry molds girls into fine, upstanding young women. Victor doesn't understand that I have to put Renee's death behind me and move forward."

"He'll come around, in time."

The last girl rejoined the line. As she turned around to face the audience, the photographers snapped some final shots of her. In the flashbulbs' glare, Sandy could see the girl clearly. Blond hair. Blue eyes. Same size. Same stature...a spitting image of...Renee?

Blood rushed to Sandy's head in a dizzying swirl. Memories spilled out like red wine on a white tablecloth, the stain of her past flooding into the present. Renee, the beauty queen, once a dead child cradled in her arms, now seemed alive on stage in all her radiant splendor.

Shepler stepped up to the podium microphone. "There you are, ladies and gentlemen, this year's Little Miss Central Texas finalists. Please wish them well by giving them a big hand."

The audience applauded.

Sandy's gaze met the blonde girl's eyes, and they locked on each other, staring as if they were the only ones in the theater. Weak knees threatened to send Sandy to the floor. "My baby."

As she came to that realization, a horrid stench ballooned in the air, the smell of rot as bad as any Texas highway road kill. Wrinkling her nose, she noticed a man standing next to her. She hadn't heard his approach, and his unexpected appearance gave her a fright. She stepped back, aghast.

Tipping his dirty cowboy hat to her, a flurry of dust swirled from his long brown coat. His face looked sickly thin, cheeks sunken and weathered as old rawhide, and a bit of bone showed on his jaw. Scraggly hair hung down to his shoulders. The hole in his throat must've been from a tracheotomy that had gone horribly wrong. The stinking bum looked out of place at this formal event.

Sandy gagged on his stench. "Go away, mister."

"I didn't mean to startle you, ma'am," the man said in a sandpaper-rough voice. "My name is Justin Graves, but you can call me Justice." He extended a bony hand to her.

She cringed at the thought of touching him. How dare he walk in here and stink up this beautiful pageant. He was beneath her high-society dignity and didn't even deserve another word from her. She refocused her attention on the child who resembled her dead daughter.

"Pretty girl, isn't she?" Justin said. "Her name is Suzie May."

How could this ugly vagrant know anything about Renee's look-alike? Sandy crossed her arms, irritated that this unsightly creature would even look at a child so beautiful.

"She's an orphan."

Sandy blinked. He must've been family to her, a long lost uncle twice removed. Make that ten times removed.

"She needs a nice home."

Putting her social status aside, she braved a conversation with the bum. "Why are you telling me this?"

"Just thought you might be able to help her out."

Sandy stuck her high-society nose in the air. "I suggest you leave before I call the authorities."

"I'm a homicide detective for the Texas Rangers." Justin pointed out the circle-star badge pinned to his coat lapel. "Is that enough authority for you?"

She'd had her share of pushy homicide detectives... Since Renee...

"That's why you won't call anyone," Justin said, as if he'd read her mind. Affording him a glance, she feared she'd vomit from the looks and smell of him. "What do you want?"

"Justice for Renee."

Her heart almost stopped. "How is it you know Renee?"

"Doesn't everyone?"

The entire world knew Renee, but for all the wrong reasons.

"I suggest you tell the police what happened to her."

"An intruder killed her."

"That's not what she told me."

Sandy turned her head away from Justin with as much snobbery as she could muster. "She's been dead for five years. You couldn't have talked to her."

"I talk to dead people," Justin said.

"Do I look stupid?"

"Do I look alive?" Justin opened the flap of his coat. "See for yourself."

She ventured a glance and saw rotted flesh hanging from bleached-white rib bones. Slimy maggots writhed in the goo. The sight drove her eyes shut like a slap to the face. "That's disgusting."

"The house of the dead is a mighty big place," Justin said. "Those who check in, never check out. Except me."

"What are you getting at?" She wished the old man would just go away.

From his dusty pocket, he removed a silver barrette studded with red jewels. He set it in the palm of his right hand and offered it to her. "Renee wants you to have this."

Sandy couldn't breathe. Her daughter had worn that barrette on the night she died. It was the only item of jewelry she was buried with. Sandy remembered clasping it to a lock of Renee's hair just before the coffin lid was closed and sealed. Now here it was again, in the hand of this filthy and definitely dead Texas Ranger. She snatched the precious barrette from his dirty palm. "What if I believe you?"

"You and Victor have the financial resources and the political clout to adopt Suzie May. It would please Renee if you'd let her wear that barrette."

Sandy clutched the barrette close to her heart and looked at the child standing on stage. Yes, there was a place in her heart for Suzie May, a place in her home, a room of her own; she'd never want for anything. Sandy could have her daughter back. Together they could compete in beauty queen pageants across the country. Suzie May could be the next Miss America, and Sandy's life would be complete again. All she had to do was convince Victor to adopt the little girl.

She looked at the barrette in her hand, and then she looked at Justin, seeing him in a totally different light, knowing that he had spoken with Renee. "How is she?"

Justin Graves

"She forgives you."

"And Victor?"

"Not so much. Because of him, she can't cross over to everlasting peace and—"

"Come up on stage, Sandy," Mr. Shepler unknowingly interrupted Justin. "The crowd wants you to say a word or two."

"Yes, of course." She looked back at Justin. He was gone.

***

The Brandish mansion stood on a five-acre plot in the Cactus Flats subdivision of Deckers, Texas. Sprawling green lawns and lush gardens stood in harsh contrast to the surrounding tarantula-tracked sands.

Victor was sitting in the breakfast-nook sunroom, reading the Deckers Harold financial section when Sandy stepped in, leading a child by the hand. "Victor, here she is. Suzie May."

Victor turned in the chair, looked the girl up and down, a cute little thing, and then returned to his newspaper without saying a word. His position as President and CEO of Brandish Microwave put him in contact with powerful people in his community. He hobnobbed with the rich and famous. The last thing he needed was another child in his life, especially someone else's reject.

"What do you think, Victor? Isn't she precious?"

"Take her back to the orphanage."

"But you said—"

"I said I'd meet her. So, I met her, and I don't want her here."

Suzie May climbed into the chair next to his, put her elbows on the table, and cradled her chin in her hands. "Why don't you like me?"

~93~

Victor looked up from the paper and got a close view of Suzie May. Sandy had dolled her up with lipstick and mascara, a lacy gown, as if she were Sandy's very own living dress-up doll. The girl could've passed for Renee's twin sister. "I don't like anybody."

"You liked Renee."

"I loved her..." He tossed an accusatory glare at Sandy. "What have you told her about Renee?"

"Not a word...I don't know how she knows—"

"How many times have I told you not to talk—?"

"Victor." Sandy thrust her shoulders back. "I want to adopt Suzie May."

"Are we going to take in every stray dog that comes along?"

"I'm not a dog," Suzie May said.

"I need her."

"You need what she can give you." Victor folded the paper. "The answer is no."

Sandy leaned on the table and put her face nose-to-nose with his. "I'll tell."

Victor's jaw muscles clenched. "You wouldn't dare."

"I'm bored, Victor."

"If you tell...you go to jail."

"And so will you."

The acid in Victor's stomach started to sizzle. "You'd throw all this away?" He swept his hand indicating the mansion and her high society life. "Because you're bored."

"I've endured this self-imposed isolation for five years. It's time to get on with my life. Suzie May will help me. And look at her. She's bright and cheery—"

"And smart," Suzie May added.

"And she needs me as much as I need her."

Victor felt ganged-up-on. "For what?"

"She's a beauty queen contestant."

Justin Graves

"I told you to stay away from those pageants."

"I should've never listened to you, Victor."

He slammed his fist on the table. "You'll do as you're told."

Suzie May reached over and put her small hands on his clenched fist. Her touch was electrifying. Calming. Welcoming. "Please adopt me."

She showed no fear of him, but his fear of her climbed his back with sharp claws that dug in deep.

***

Before long, Sandy's high-society lifestyle was back in full swing. Preliminary competition on the state level had brought Suzie May up on the registry as a serious contender for the beauty queen's crown.

And for the first time since Renee's death, the Brandish mansion was aglow with Christmas tree lights. Harry Tilden, a hoggish man with a long white beard and Santa Claus costume, passed out presents to children bused in from the orphanage on Deckers' lower east side.

Victor snapped photos of the festivities, many with Suzie May as the center of attention. Sandy had dressed her up special for this party, short red dress with white furry trim, and gold-buckle shoes. She'd applied Suzie May's red lipstick a bit heavily and overdid the eyeliner, as well. Suzie May looked as hot and seductive as any exotic dancer...

He downed another rum-laced eggnog.

"Go easy on that stuff." Sandy knelt beside Susie May for another picture.

Victor aimed the camera. "It's a party." He pushed the shutter button. "With lots of pretty girls."

"Ho. Ho. Ho," Harry chimed in.

The children squealed.

Terry Wright

Victor sat back in his easy chair and studied Suzie May, this unbelievable child with all Renee's wit and charm, vibrantly alive on this Christmas Eve, as happy as Renee had been...before...

Suzie May adjusted her sitting position on the floor and inadvertently exposed her pink panties to Victor. His eyes locked on her crotch. She must've seen him looking. Her eyes made contact with his. She smiled. That yearning in him began to rise, that terrible secret he had kept from everyone...including Sandy, until Renee...

He tossed back a shot of rum straight up and closed his eyes.

Sometime later, he awoke to a dark room. The Christmas tree lights were off, but multicolored outside decorations twinkled around the window frame. He looked at his watch. The blurry, glowing dial read 2:00 a.m.

"Damn." Sandy had left him alone to sleep in the chair. His wife thought more of her new daughter than him.

He got up and drunkenly walked down the hallway toward the bedroom. Noticing Suzie May's door slightly ajar, he stopped to close it, but as he reached for the doorknob, he saw her lying on the bed. She was on her back, legs spread, the sheet covering only one foot. Her nightgown was hiked up to her waist, and her panties glowed eerily in the dim light of a streetlamp outside her window...where it was snowing... A white Christmas in Deckers, Texas? Suzie May would catch a cold uncovered like that, so he stepped into her room and moved to the bed.

Before he pulled the sheet over her, he stood there a moment and watched her peaceful breathing. A silver barrette in her hair sparkled with red jewels. That wonderful feeling inside him welled up like warm spring-water. He quietly bent over and ever so gently placed his hand on her thigh.

Justin Graves

Her eyes popped open, fully alert. "Not tonight, Daddy. Please don't make me—"

"Hush," he whispered, wondering why she had called him daddy. "You'll wake your mother."

"But it hurts when you do that."

"I'll be gentle this time." Excitement tingled through his fingers as he reached to slip off her panties. His mouth began to water.

"Please don't, Daddy, don't—"

"You bastard." Sandy's voice shrieked through the room. The lights flared on. She stood in the doorway with a golf club clutched so tightly in her hands that her knuckles were white. "Get away from her."

She lunged forward, swinging the club. Victor ducked just in time. The club struck Suzie May. A bloody gash opened up on her forehead. Her body went into spasms; her arms and legs flailed.

Victor jumped back. Terror raked his chest. "God damn you, Sandy. Look what you've done."

"Oh...oh, my God. No. You made me do it." Sandy dropped the golf club and rushed to her adopted daughter. "My baby. Baby. I'm sorry."

Her body went limp on the bed. The spill of blood from the gash stopped leaking.

"No. No. No." Sandy clutched the dead child and scowled up at Victor. "You son of a bitch."

"I was just going to touch her," he said, backing away from the body. "But you killed her."

"It was an accident." Sandy wailed as she hugged Suzie May's corpse to her breast. "God knows I didn't mean to. It was you, Victor, you animal. Now it's happening all over again...but...but this time I'm telling the cops what happened. This time I'm telling them what you are...what you did."

Anger made a fist in his stomach. He wouldn't tolerate talk like that. If word got out that he was a pedophile, no one of any importance would ever associate with him again. He'd face jail time and humiliation as a registered sex offender. Victor wouldn't let that happen. He had to get Sandy to cooperate...like before.

Stepping forward, he put his hands on Sandy's trembling shoulders. She was hunkered over the dead child, weeping terribly.

"You're not going to tell them anything about me," he said with words as cold as the snow falling outside the window. "But if you want them to know you killed Suzie May, just like you'd killed Renee, good luck."

"I'll tell them I meant to kill you," she wheezed out. "Both times."

"I'll tell the cops Renee wet the bed. You went berserk and beat her with a golf club."

"I'll tell them how you defiled her. How you had sex with her. How I caught you—"

"You're the one who made Renee desirable. You dressed her up in sexy clothes. You made her wear makeup and grownup hairdos. And you did the same with Suzie May. What did you expect?"

"We were having fun, but you couldn't keep your filthy hands to yourself."

"Go ahead, shoot your mouth off. I'll deny touching either of them, but you'll have admitted to murdering them both."

"We have to tell them what happened this time." Sandy sobbed.

"Fine...but they'll execute you, not me."

Her sobbing stuttered. "Execute?"

That hit a nerve, so he hit it again. "Bye bye, Sandy, the killer of beauty queens. The press will eat it up."

She hugged the lifeless child. "I don't want to die."

"Then do what I tell you."

"Like last time?"

He picked up the golf club. "Leave it to me."

The murder weapon had blood on it, so he went through the house turning on the lights on his way to the kitchen. He washed off the blood in the sink and returned the golf club to the caddy in the hall closet. Rushing to the basement, he jimmied the latch on a window and toppled over some boxes to make it look as if an intruder had entered the house.

He found some rope, thinking he'd tie it around Suzie May's neck to make it look like the intruder had beaten and strangled her. Duct tape across her mouth would enhance the illusion of an attempted kidnapping gone bad. He could fix things...just like last time, five years ago, when Sandy killed Renee in a fit of rage. He'd make another false trail to send the police on a wild goose chase while he bided his time to inadvertently find Suzie May in the storage room. He could rip the tape off her mouth, untie the rope from around her neck, and perform CPR, contaminating the crime scene right under the cops' noses. Then with his power and influence in the Deckers community, he'd block any attempt the cops made to interview them.

They could get away with murder again.

Rushing upstairs to Suzie May's room, he discovered it empty and searched the house for Sandy. He found her in the master bathroom. Grief-stricken, she was bathing Suzie May in the tub, talking to her as if she were still alive.

"Get hold of yourself, Sandy."

"I can't go through it again," she cried as she shampooed the dead girl's hair. "The media attention...the accusations...people pointing fingers and you not letting me say a word in my defense...how I caught you—"

"How did you know I was in her bedroom?"

Sandy sniffed. "Something woke me. The golf club was in my hand. I heard voices in Suzie May's room."

"What woke you?"

Sandy rinsed Suzie May's hair, careful to keep her face out of the running water. "I don't know...but can't you see? There's something wrong. It's snowing outside, for Christ's sake. It never snows in Deckers. It's Christmas and there's another dead child in our house. It's happening all over again..." She gasped. "Oh, God." She looked at him with wide open eyes. "I wonder if that stinking bum had anything to do with this."

"What bum?"

"There was a man at the beauty pageant. He said he talked to Renee."

"Was he drunk?"

"His name was Justin Graves."

Justin Graves? "I've heard that name before."

"He smelled awful. I tried to get rid of him, but he gave me that." She pointed to the barrette sitting on the edge of the bathtub. "I'd put it in Renee's hair before we buried her."

"It can't be the same barrette."

"It is. I had it made especially for Renee. One of a kind. She gave it to Justin Graves."

Justin Graves. Now he remembered where he'd heard that name before. A Texas Ranger was shot and killed in the line of duty. It was in all the papers and on all the news channels. Fear fell across Victor like a cold, dark shadow. If Justin Graves had talked to Sandy, it meant he wasn't dead, after all, or he wasn't dead enough.

Victor rushed to the bedroom closet and pulled a box from the high shelf. In it, a 357 Magnum was loaded with hollow point bullets.

Sandy entered the bedroom carrying Suzie May's limp body wrapped in a towel. "What are you doing with that gun?"

He stuffed the gun behind his belt and covered the butt with his sweater. "If Justin Graves comes around here, he'll live to regret it."

"He's already dead."

"If you talked to him, he's not dead. Are you so stupid—?"

"You're stupid." She laid Suzie May on the bed. "You screwed up our lives. Now two little girls are dead, and we have to go into hiding again. I can't stand it."

"You'd better get used to it, Sandy. I'm not going down with you. You're the murderer. You'll do what I tell you, damn it."

"Damn you, Victor." She started brushing Suzie May's hair and talking to her again. "I love you so much." Sandy clipped the jeweled barrette to a lock of hair. "Renee wanted you to wear this, honey." She slipped a clean nightgown over the dead beauty queen's head, much like a child would dress a doll, and struggled to get her limp arms into the sleeves. After tying the neckline bow just right, she looked up at Victor. "We're ready."

He followed her downstairs to the storage room. Sandy put Suzie May on a stack of boxes. Victor tied the rope around her neck, tightened it enough to pinch the skin, then ripped off a length of duct tape and taped it over her mouth. Stepping back, he said, "Now you've got a note to write."

They locked Suzie May in darkness.

***

Captain Holland wasn't comfortable with these high profile cases, rich parents with a kidnapped child: a beauty queen, a celebrity at seven years old. He secured the Brandish Mansion crime scene and hoped they'd soon find the child unharmed.

The parents were in the kitchen, drinking coffee and nervously watching the phone, waiting for it to ring with demands from the kidnappers.

Holland sat on the ritzy front-room couch and reexamined the most bizarre ransom note he'd ever seen. The block letters looked distorted, as if drawn by a grief-stricken hand. The kidnapper claimed to be part of a militant group Holland had never heard of, The Deckers Militia, and they demanded an astronomically high amount in exchange for the safe return of the beauty queen.

And if that wasn't strange enough, last night's freak snowstorm had left Deckers covered with a couple inches of snow. That was enough to snarl traffic, but not enough to stop the media from getting through. Their vans were parked along the street, satellite dishes aimed skyward, and reporters pressing against the crime scene tape with microphones extended to anyone who would talk to them.

The Brandish couple was big news, again.

Lieutenant Simmons entered through the front door, kicking snow off his boots. He was a young detective with a pretty wife and a rambunctious six-year-old son at home. "I've walked the perimeter, Captain. No footprints anywhere in the snow."

"How did the kidnapper get to the jimmied window? Fly?"

"Maybe the storm covered up his tracks."

"It didn't snow long enough." Holland folded the ransom note. "I think the girl never left this house."

Victor stormed in. "You mean the kidnapper failed?"

"I'm not sold on a kidnapping. She's here—"

"We've got to find her," Victor shouted. "I'll check

the basement while you and your men check upstairs."

"Wait." Holland stood. "We'll stay together."

"It'll go faster if we split up," Victor insisted. Sweat beaded on his forehead.

"What's the rush?" Holland asked, noting Victor's nervousness and his fixation on the basement. "We'll start in the basement."

***

Downstairs, Victor escorted the officers through all three bedrooms, two baths, and the recreation room. The place was as tidy as a model show home. "Nothing," he said, knowing he had to be alone when he discovered Suzie May's body in the storage room. "Let's check upstairs."

Captain Holland nodded, and heading for the stairs, he stopped abruptly and looked down at his feet.

Following the cop's gaze, Victor saw a jeweled barrette lying on the floor in front of the locked storage room door. His heart skipped with dread. The barrette must've fallen out of Suzie May's hair when Sandy carried her into the room.

Holland picked up the barrette and examined it with suspicious eyes.

"That's Suzie May's," Victor said, making light of the find. "She plays down here sometimes."

"Plays?" Holland glanced around. "Really? Where are her toys? I'd expect to see a dollhouse or an Easy Bake oven, some stuffed animals or games..." His eyes landed on the locked door. "What's in there?"

"It's just a storage room," Victor said. "Besides, it's always locked. She couldn't be in there."

"Open it."

Victor swallowed hard. "But..." An ungodly stench filled the air, causing his throat to close up. "I mean..." His eyes started to water, the room smelled that bad. Rotting flesh, he was sure of it, but it couldn't be coming from Suzie May's body. She hadn't been in that room long enough to decay.

He coughed and covered his nose with his hand, hoping the cops didn't notice the odor.

Sandy bounded down the stairs and rushed to Victor. "He's here," she whispered. "Nothing stinks as bad as Justin Graves."

"Justin Graves?" Holland asked.

Victor gasped. "It's a god-awful smell."

A raspy voice echoed through the basement. "Open it, Victor."

Holland didn't seem to hear that. Who did Justin think he was coming into this house uninvited? "Get out of here."

Captain Holland and Lieutenant Simmons shared a confused look.

From the corner shadows, Justin appeared to Victor and Sandy, his grimy coat drizzling dirt. He tipped his dusty cowboy hat. "Tell them the truth, Victor." His eye sockets glowed crimson.

Victor was more pissed off than afraid. "You put that barrette on the floor."

"I did not," Holland said. "Open the door or I'll bust it down."

"You set us up," Victor yelled at Justin.

Captain Holland responded to the accusation by kicking in the door. He saw the dead child and staggered back. Shock distorted his pudgy face with hard lines of horror.

Victor had to act fast. "Suzie May." He ran to the door. He had to get in there, scoop her up, and pull the duct tape off her mouth. He had to touch her while the cops were watching. Contaminate the crime scene—

"Stay back," Simmons ordered, blocking the way.

Victor couldn't get to Suzie May, but he had a clear shot at Justin Graves standing in the corner. "You're not going to get away with this, you bastard." He pulled the 357 Magnum out from under his sweater and got off two shots.

One bullet hit the ghoul dead center in the cowboy hat. It went flying off his head in a puff of dust. The second bullet blew a hole in Justin's forehead.

Gunfire rattled through the basement as Simmons and Holland unloaded their guns on Victor. He felt the burn of bullets tearing into his chest. His legs gave out. He stagger-stepped back and collapsed on the floor.

Somewhere along the way, he'd dropped his gun. Simmons had it now, standing over him, shouting into his radio mike. "We need ETMs at the Brandish mansion right away."

Captain Holland, gun still drawn, appeared in the haze over Victor. "Who the hell were you shooting at?"

Sandy dropped to her knees beside him. "Victor. Victor. Can you hear me?"

The haze turned black.

***

Sandy slapped Victor's cheek as he lay on the floor in a growing pool of blood. "I told you...Justin's already dead."

Captain Holland yanked her up off the floor. "What are you talking about?"

"He was shooting at Justin Graves."

Holland looked gut-punched. "Justin? Where?"

"He's standing in the corner. Can't you see him?"

Holland looked toward the shadows where Sandy pointed. "I don't see him. Nothing."

Terry Wright

Sandy could see him just fine. "Why did you have to kill my husband?"

"He gave us no choice," Holland said. "Shooting up the place like that."

"Victor's soul belongs to the devil now," Justin grated out, "for what he did to Renee."

"But he didn't kill Renee," she shouted into the corner. "I did. I killed her. I didn't mean to."

Justin grinned. "You just confessed to murdering your daughter."

"Arrest her," Captain Holland ordered Simmons. "Murder One."

Justin stepped from the shadows. "I gave you a chance to come clean about Renee's murder. Now you're going to do it the hard way."

Simmons wrenched Sandy's arms behind her back and clamped on the handcuffs. "You have the right to remain silent."

"It was an accident," she cried.

"Anything you say can be held against you," Simmons went on.

Justin extended a bony hand toward Suzie May. Renee's translucent spirit rose from the dead body. "Renee wants to speak to you, Sandy."

"My baby." Tears flooded Sandy's eyes.

The ghost-girl wore a long flowing gown that sparkled with glitter and a diamond tiara. She glided to Justin's side. The red bejeweled barrette glistened in her hair. "Suzie May wasn't a real person," she said in an echoing voice.

"Not r-real?" Sandy stuttered.

"She's an apparition. Justin made her look like me so you'd love her and help us expose the truth about my death."

Only now did Sandy understand she'd been set up.

Victor got what he deserved. "I didn't know he was molesting you."

"You didn't want to know, Mom. You wanted me to be a beauty queen like you were. That's all you cared about. I just wanted to be a little girl and have fun."

"I'm so sorry."

Justin retrieved his hat from the floor. "Suzie May played her part to get Victor to show his true nature. Her body will disappear from the morgue." He examined the bullet hole in his hat. "No one will be able to explain it."

"I'll see her again, back in the afterlife," Renee said.

"Tell her I'm sorry."

Justin set his hat on his head. "This time, talk to the police, Sandy. Tell them what happened. You'll do some hard time in prison, but not as hard as Victor is doing in hell."

"I'll tell them everything."

Justin looped his arm around the ghostly beauty queen. "With Victor dead and the truth revealed, Renee can now cross over to everlasting peace and happiness."

A glowing orb of soft light appeared in the center of the room.

"Are you coming with me, Justin?"

"I still have work to do here. You go ahead."

Renee glided toward the light. "Goodbye, Mom." In shimmering luminescence, her ethereal form dissolved into the glow.

Tears streamed down Sandy's cheeks. "I love you."

"Shut up." Captain Holland grabbed Sandy's arm. "I'll take her out to the car," he told Simmons. "You stay with the girl until the coroner gets here."

Justin followed them outside.

Handcuffed and weeping, she walked in front of the TV cameras and reporters. Her high-society life was ruined.

Holland stuffed her into the back of a squad car.

She saw Justin watching from a distance. "I know you're not going to believe me, Captain, but Justin Graves is helping you solve crimes."

"Justin is dead." Holland slammed the car door and glanced around. "I think."

A reporter rushed forward, microphone leading the way. "Is it true? Is Justin Graves helping you?"

"Don't be ridiculous."

Now a herd of reporters ganged up on him.

"Did you see him?"

"Is he a ghost?"

"How did you solve the Renee Brandish murder?"

"Someone had to have tipped you off."

Holland's round face looked like it might explode. "No comment." He stormed back to the house; he had a crime scene to process.

With a gust of wind the ghoul was gone.

Judgment Day

At Texas Rangers Headquarters on Saddle Tramp Road, Captain Holland held the phone to his ear in disbelief. The State Police should have arrived yesterday. Though Deckers lay off the beaten path, they shouldn't be dragging their feet where Billy Denton was concerned.

"We're sorry about the delay, sir," the dispatcher said.

"Christ. It's been a week already."

"I'm sorry the judge denied him bail."

"Are you kidding? We're not letting that killer loose. It's your job to transport him to the county jail."

It was a two hundred mile trek across some of Texas' roughest terrain, but Justin Graves' killer required special handling. "If I had the manpower, I'd haul him over there myself."

"Just keep him locked up until we get there." The phone clicked dead.

Holland slammed down the receiver. "Lieutenant Simmons, get over to city jail. Backup Deputy Pender. Looks like we've got Denton for another night."

"Right away, sir." Simmons grabbed his suit coat off the back of his desk chair and rushed out.

The desk phone rang. Holland picked up. "Homicide."

"Is there any truth to the rumor about you and Justin Graves?"

"No." He hung up. Ever since he'd solved the beauty queen murders, the phone had been ringing off the hook, reporters asking questions that had no logical answers. Holland had to wonder, though, as cold cases had suddenly gotten new life, and how Mrs. Templeton's lost original will had showed up on his desk; nobody could explain that.

Holland shuddered. He had bigger problems right now. Each moment that passed gave Billy Denton another opportunity to make good on his threat to escape. He'd be getting more and more desperate with each passing hour, knowing it wouldn't be long before he was transported to county where security was much tighter. Even that weasel couldn't weasel his way out of a lockdown as secure as the county jail. He'd have to make his escape tonight, or never.

With that thought banging around in his brain, Holland threw on his ten-gallon hat and Texas Rangers jacket, and then checked the clip in his Glock.

Three men on guard duty tonight couldn't hurt. They could take turns sleeping and guarding Billy Denton.

***

Deckers City Jail wasn't much more than a cracker box, built sometime between the Alamo and the Civil War. Billy Denton watched Deputy Pender through the only door that led from the backroom cellblock to the front office. Pender was sitting at the squad desk, his feet propped up and his eyes shut like he was taking a nap. A ring of keys dangled from his leather belt, and his holstered Colt hung on a wall hook by the fire extinguisher. The things Billy needed most were way out of his reach from his position on the cot in cell number two.

Jo Joe Peters, the town drunk, was locked up in cell number one. Lying on the concrete floor, he hacked and snorted in a drunken stupor, his weathered face and bulbous nose flushed as Santa Claus. He hadn't combed his wiry hair and scruffy beard for months, and his BO smelled worse than cat piss.

Cell number three was empty.

Other than Jo Joe's belching, the jailhouse was quiet. Billy preferred it that way. Gave him time to think in peace. Like he'd told Captain Holland, this jail wouldn't hold him for long. Billy rubbed his goatee. One slipup...that was all it would take. The cops could kiss his ass goodbye.

Billy pushed his empty dinner tray aside and leaned back in his cot, watching Deputy Pender nap and thinking about the keys and the Colt.

Jo Joe stirred, grumped and cursed, then started puking out his guts on the floor.

As if the urping and splattering sounds weren't enough to make Billy sick, the disgusting odor of bile ballooned in the air. His guts constricted in an instinctive response to the stench. He was going to lose his supper. Jumping up to the bars, he had all he could do to inhale enough breath to shout, "Pender. You better get Jo Joe outta here before I blow a gasket."

The deputy just snorted.

"Pender."

Jo Joe coughed and spit. "Mind yer own beeswax, boy. I'm in my glory here, can't ya tell?"

"Puke in the damn toilet, ya pig."

"If I coulda made there, I woulda." Jo Joe let loose another gush of vomit. It splattered on the floor and added to the toxicity of the backroom air with a fresh tidal wave of nauseous stench.

"What the hell did you eat, old man, rotten mule dung?"

Arrauggggg. More puke spewed out of Jo Joe.

The smell was sucking the juices out of Billy's stomach. Already the back of his throat burned with churning stomach acid.

"Pender."

A gut-wrenching spasm took hold of Billy's innards

and shook him like a rabbit in a coyote's jaws. He made a mad dash for the commode but upchucked before he got there. Puke hit the wall, the floor, and drenched all down the front of his prison coveralls.

Jo Joe joined him in another chorus of barfing and gagging.

"You fools are making a mess," Pender shouted. He was standing at the cell door, keys in hand.

***

In the afterlife, Justin Graves watched the scene unfold at Deckers City Jail. He stood before the light, feet spread and his long brown coat hanging open as Pender unlocked Billy Denton's cell door.

"Oh, oh." Justin had just a second to pull his cowboy hat low over his eyes and tuck his elbows in tight to his sides in preparation for a quick transition back to the land of the living. Pender was going to need some help.

In a flash, he was speeding through a spinning black void of time and space, his insides seething at the thought of confronting Billy Denton. Finally. Justice for Christy.

The ethereal plane suddenly shifted. His speed increased. He should have been transported to his grave in Deckers Memorial Gardens by now.

In the distance, a red glow appeared, expanding like a tumor on a chunk of liver. He'd seen it before, not long ago, with Christy, right after they'd died in a shootout with Billy Denton. Now, for some ungodly reason, the devil had summoned him back to hell. He couldn't have picked a worse time.

Nearing the smoke and fire of hell's growing inferno, Justin's cowboy hat flew off. The brown coat stripped away, his shirt, his pants, his boots, and finally his flesh and his bones until all that remained was his soul, the very essence of his being now fully exposed to hell's impending fury.

Justin didn't have time for a social call. He'd seen Pender open the cell door. He'd seen Billy Denton's wicked, scheming gaze. Something terrible was about to happen, but down Justin spiraled into the fiery caverns of hell, unable to do anything about it. With flames licking hot tongues of damnation all around him, he couldn't help but wonder if the devil had deliberately intervened on Billy's behalf.

Fire seared the air, and the stench of burned flesh rose from the pit as he tumbled in. Hissing gasses belched plumes of flame from craggy rock walls that trembled and rumbled in an eternal earthquake of unnerving proportions. The bellowing sounds of laughter echoed inside his soul, a haunting cackle, both despondent and chilling.

"Justice," the devil shouted. "Now your soul is mine."

Floating in smoke and ash, Justin felt the essence of despair surround him, as if hearing the devil's decree had made the words true and unforgiving. He expected to see Christy materialize in front of him, her flesh and hair on fire, her mouth agape in an everlasting scream of anguish. Casting off the horror of his unearthly imagination, Justin shouted back, "Why have you brought me here? I haven't yet fulfilled my end of our bargain."

"Silence, fool." A red and yellow ball of fire billowed up from the depths of the pit. "You have broken the rules."

"What rules?"

"Janet Blaire is dead because of you."

"I didn't kill her," Justin said in his own defense. "The maid beat her to death with a broom."

"But you turned her into a spider, which directly led to her demise."

Justin couldn't believe how the devil had twisted the

rules to suit his own evil agenda, but then again, Justin should've expected it, after all, the devil was the devil and not to be trusted. His evilness probably cheated at solitaire. No pact was sacred, no handshake binding, no honor set in stone. Such was the character of the nemesis Justin had to appease or his daughter would be condemned to eternity in Satan's service. Justin had to fight to save her, but here in hell his only weapons were words and reason.

"She was a Black Widow at heart," Justin shouted into the hot air around him. "I only made her see what she really was. A poisonous spider. And spiders die just because they're spiders. Nearly everyone on the planet hates spiders or fears them or thinks nothing of the lives they possess. It's the evil in human nature that makes them stomp the life out of something so small and defenseless. And who is responsible for that evil? You are, Satan. Evil is yours, so the Black Widow's death is your fault. Not mine."

"Damn you, Justice." Fire roared and churned up from the abyss. "Your point is made."

"Then quit your bitching. She's serving you now. That's what this deal is all about, you getting the bad guys."

Rock walls spit gasses, parting the clouds of smoke and revealing the devil to Justin's soul. Razor-sharp horns glistened in the firelight. Satan's face glowed red with rage. "You think you are so damn righteous, but you are no saint, yourself."

"I give everyone a chance to redeem themselves."

The devil's evil eyes canted. "Does the same go for Billy Denton?"

Justin's soul trembled. "He's different."

"No different from you."

"I'm not a cold blooded killer."

"You would kill him if you had the chance. You want

to kill him."

"Of course I want to kill him, but he killed me first."

"An eye for an eye," the devil rasped. "It proves that the evil in Billy is the same as the evil in you trying to break free, Justice. It's only a matter of time before you show your true human nature. And when you do, Judgment Day is coming for you and your precious daughter."

"Leave Christy out of this."

"She is your weakness. Because of Christy, hatred and revenge will be your downfall, and I will get my satisfaction."

"Never."

Flames shot upward. "You may be powerful, Justice. You can bend time, change human flesh into an arachnid, make cats appear, and conjure up ghosts to play your little games, but I am more powerful than you can even imagine."

"You're just a bully."

"Silence." The devil pointed a talon-spiked finger at Justin. "Rounding up souls for me has been too easy for you. It's time I leveled the playing field."

"You can't change the rules in the middle of our deal."

Hell spit fire and belched putrid smoke. Laughter bellowed from the devil's evil throat. His hot breath blew Justin's soul out of hell and back into the spinning black void.

"It has already begun."

***

Deputy Pender bent over Billy Denton. He was convulsing on the cement floor of cell number two. His face was pale as a ghost as he hacked up vomit. The goop was getting all over Pender's boots. "Jesus Christ, Billy."

In the next cell, Jo Joe harmoniously heaved his guts, as well.

"God damn it, Jo Joe."

Pender could hardly breathe with the way his stomach was lurching in protest. "You guys are cleaning up this mess."

Jo Joe hiccupped. "Did you see that punk lose his supper? That was soooo gross."

"Shut your mouth, Jo Joe." Pender grabbed Billy's collar and dragged him to the toilet where he wretched violently. The smear of puke on the floor made Pender's stomach clench tighter. "I'm never going to get the smell out of this place." He left the cell door open and rushed the few steps to the maintenance closet. Keeping an eye on Billy, he started hosing water into a mop bucket.

Billy sat up beside the toilet and wiped puke from his lips with his shirtsleeve. "Jo Joe. I'm going to kill you for that."

Jo Joe laughed like a hyena with asthma. He stood and grabbed the bars. "I wouldn't wanta be in yer shoes where they're takin' ya for killin' Justin Graves." In his drunken state, he couldn't have realized the sting in his words. "Them fellas down there at county, they'll be real sweet on yer young ass."

Billy scowled at the drunk.

"Here comes the bride," Jo Joe sang like it was the *Wedding March*. "Sweet cheeks spread 'em wide."

Pender grabbed a mop. "Sit down and shut up, you old coot." He wheeled the bucket out of the closet and into Billy's cell. "On your feet," Pender ordered, almost puking from the stench. "Mop up this mess, right now."

"Mop, mop, mop yer puke," Jo Joe sang to the tune of *Row Your Boat*.

"Shut up, Jo Joe," Pender shouted. "You're getting the

bucket next."

Billy stood, and glaring at Jo Joe, spit and took the mop from Pender. "I'm going to kill that old man."

"Nobody's killing nobody," Pender said. "Now get to work."

Billy started mopping the floor.

Pender turned to walk out the cell door. He heard a sudden whoosh behind him, but never felt the mop handle crack against the back of his skull.

***

Billy hit the deputy again and again; the adrenaline-charge in his bloodstream brewed a storm of uncontrollable rage. He hit the cop so hard the mop handle broke, so he used the broken piece to beat him some more, beat him senseless, beat him to death.

Jo Joe tugged on the cell bars like a caged ape. "Yer killin' him, Billy. Killin' him."

Blood splattered on the wall and pooled on the floor. Red spatter splotched Billy's prison jumpsuit and peppered his face. He only stopped when he was satisfied Pender wouldn't be able to thwart the upcoming escape. Tossing down the broken mop handle, he wiped his bloody hands on his bloody clothes. A warm feeling of pride welled up inside him. He was making good on his threat to escape. Captain Holland was going to be pissed.

"Holy bejesus, Billy. You gone and done it now."

"Shut up, Jo Joe. I'm trying to think."

"It's a jailbreak, by God. Let me outta here too."

Billy spit. His mouth tasted like the bottom of a toilet. Fighting off another wave of nausea, he made a dash for Pender's Colt hanging by the door.

"Get the gun, get the gun," Jo Joe hollered through the cell bars.

Just as Billy made it to the holstered Colt, the front door swung open.

"Hey, Pender." It was Lieutenant Simmons.

Hiding behind the open door, Billy froze. He looked back to the doorway leading to the cells. Pender's body was clearly visible, sprawled on the floor.

"Pender?" Simmons rushed into the room.

Billy drew the Colt.

Must've been the sound of steel sliding on leather that stopped Simmons. He turned around, his shocked eyes locking on Billy then shifting to the gun barrel coming down. Instinctively, his hand went for his own gun, but Billy had the drop on him. And fired.

Simmons keeled over and hit the floor.

"Nice shootin'," Jo Joe shouted. "You got him, Billy Boy. You got him. I seen the whole thing."

Billy was about to split out the door when he realized Jo Joe had to die, not because he witnessed the killing, the cops would figure out who done it on their own, but on account of general principles alone. The old man was a whack job who needed whacking. Billy kicked the door shut and rushed back to the cellblock. Endorphins of murder filled his brain with ecstasy. He was walking through a dream, in slow motion, gun coming up and now aiming through the bars.

Jo Joe stumbled backward, his eyes wide with fear and puke still dripping off his beard. "You lily-livered coward." He fell back against the cot.

"Screw you, old man." Billy fired two rounds, one striking Jo Joe in the heart, the other spraying brain matter goo all over the back wall.

Captain Holland burst in through the front door, gun drawn, obviously alerted by the gunshots that killed Jo Joe.

Damn. Billy should've made his break when he had

the chance. Now all he could do was duck behind the maintenance closet door and hope he could blast his way out.

"Throw the gun down, Billy," Holland ordered. "Come out with your hands up."

"Go to hell." Billy leaped from behind the door and shot two rounds at Holland.

Holland returned fire, bullets now zinging through the air and pinging off cell bars. Empty shell casing tinkled on the cement floor like metal rain.

Crouching low, Billy fired again, but Holland had ducked behind the squad desk, firing back. Billy dove into the closet, gasping air that tasted like vomit. The gun battle reminded him of the standoff at the warehouse the night he'd killed Justin Graves and his whore daughter. They both got what they deserved. Holland was next.

Billy ejected the clip and counted the number of bullets he had left. It didn't take him long.

One.

"Shit." He slapped the clip back into the Colt, chambered the round, and wondered how one bullet could defeat an army of cops, which he was sure would be charging into this battle any minute.

"Give up, Billy."

He'd need another weapon. The broken mop handle lay on the other side of Pender's body. To get to it, he'd have to cross into Holland's line of fire. A quick scan of the closet revealed a screwdriver and a Crescent wrench on a shelf. A box of floor soap. A sponge. Totally useless.

"Throw out your weapon."

Billy got an idea. If he could make Holland *think* he was unarmed...

"Don't shoot," Billy shouted. "I'm out of bullets."

"Toss out the gun."

Billy grabbed the Crescent wrench from the shelf. "Here it comes." He slid the wrench across the floor in front of Pender's corpse, hard enough to send it skidding past the doorway and into a dark corner. Holland wouldn't have been able to see it, but the clatter it made on the concrete sure sounded like a gun, and from Holland's point of view, it could have looked like a gun in the split second it had been visible to him.

"I give up." Billy put his hands behind his head, the Colt firmly in his grasp, barrel pointed down the nape of his neck. "I'm unarmed." He stepped out of the closet and faced Holland in plain view. "Don't shoot."

Slowly, Holland stood, gun pointed at Billy. "Get on the floor."

Dropping to his knees, Billy felt his heart pounding as if it would burst from his ribcage. The stench of puke on his clothes made his eyes water. Holland looked like a big, blurry wraith stepping toward him. Billy held his breath. He had to be cool, if only for another moment, even though he wanted to crack up laughing at Holland for falling for his fake gun toss.

"Don't move a muscle." Holland reached back with his free hand for the cuffs hanging from his belt loop.

The gun felt slippery in Billy's sweaty hand. In less than a second, Holland would be close enough to see the gun. It was now or never. He brought the gun around and pulled the trigger. The shot reverberated through the jailhouse like the clap of a howitzer.

Holland dropped the handcuffs and clutched his chest. A bloodstain blossomed under his hand. Staggering backward, he raised the gun and fired a round that went wide and ricocheted off the doorjamb. His eyes glazed over. He fell.

Billy picked up Holland's dropped gun, and this time

he wasted no time making good his escape.

***

Amidst the bloody carnage, Justin materialized in Deckers City Jail, but he was quick to realize he'd arrived too late. It wasn't hard to figure out the devil had a hand in aiding and abetting Billy's escape.

Dust and dirt rained down from Justin's cowboy hat and long coat, as he'd just dug himself out of his grave, which had burned up more time in the devil's favor. He stepped over Simmons' body to Captain Holland sprawled on the floor by the squad desk. Seeing him lying there in a puddle of blood ignited in Justin the fires of hate and revenge that even the devil would envy.

He stepped to the door to the cellblock, spotted Pender's bludgeoned body in one cell and an old man shot to death in another, but no Billy Denton.

With Billy on the loose and the death penalty hanging over his head, now he had nothing to lose. Justin wondered how many more innocent people would be murdered before he could stop him? Billy wouldn't be taken alive. Justin would have to kill him, which would prove the devil was right. Christy's soul, and his own soul, would be condemned to hell forever. *So be it.* Resigned to his fate, Justin picked up the squad desk phone and punched out 911.

"What is your emergency?"

"There's been a shooting at city jail," he told the operator in a raspy voice. "Four dead."

"Is the gunman still there?"

"No." A moan came from behind him. Justin whirled around and immediately located the source. Captain Holland. His eyes were open and focused on him, wide with disbelief.

Terry Wright

"I've got a survivor. We need an ambulance." He hung up.

Holland wheezed. "Justice? Is it you? My God. It is you. I must be dead."

Kneeling beside his fallen boss, Justin lifted Holland's head up from the floor. "Hang in there, Captain. Help is on the way."

Coughing, Holland grabbed Justin's dusty coat sleeve. "We're in hell, aren't we. You can tell me. I can take..." he choked, "bad news."

"Don't talk," Justin rasped and checked Holland's wound. His shirt and jacket were soaked in blood. It looked bad. Real bad.

"Your eyes. Your face? What happened to you, Justice? You don't look so good...and what's that god-awful smell?"

"Try to relax."

"Is the devil here? Have you seen him?"

"You're not dead, Captain."

"I'm not?"

"You're wounded. An ambulance is on the way."

"Wounded? How?" Terror wrenched Holland's round features as if a recollection had claws and fangs. "Where's Billy?"

"He got away, but don't worry. I'll get him."

"Did he shoot you, too?"

"He was gone when I got here."

"There's a bullet hole...in your hat."

Justin removed his cowboy hat and poked a bony finger into the hole in his forehead. "It was a through-and-through shot." He felt like a soldier showing off his war wounds as he pointed out the hole in his throat. "Spear gun."

"My God. You're still...on the job. You're helping me

catch bad guys...like Sandy Brandish told me."

"I'm not doing it for you or the Texas Rangers, believe me."

"I didn't believe her."

Paramedics rushed in with a stretcher and all kinds of equipment, which they started hooking up to Captain Holland.

"Get Billy for me, Justice," Holland shouted. "Arrest him. Bring him back."

A paramedic held up a pair of scissors. "Easy, sir." He cut off the Captain's jacket sleeve.

"I may have to kill him," Justin said, knowing it was wrong to even say it, but he feared Billy wouldn't give him a choice.

"Don't do anything stupid, Justice. Like last time...at the warehouse."

The paramedic said, "He's hallucinating...thinks he sees Justin Graves."

"He's losing blood fast," another medic replied. "It's affecting his brain functions."

"Back then, I did what I had to do," Justin grated out. "And I'll do what I have to do now."

"No, wait. Justice...tell me...how did you come back from the dead?"

"Please, sir. Be still." The paramedic inserted an IV needle into Holland's arm.

"It's a long story," Justin said, wincing at the sight of the needle going into Holland's vein. "I have to go. I have to find Billy."

"Justice. Justice. When will I see you again?"

"Take it easy, sir." The paramedic grabbed the Captain's fist, the one he was holding in the air, the fist that held on to Justin's coat sleeve, the coat sleeve only Holland could see.

Terry Wright

"I'll be in touch." Justin broke free of the Captain's clenched fist. "After I get Billy."

"Don't take the law into...your own hands."

With a gust of wind the ghoul was gone.

***

Justin rematerialized in the light of the afterlife. The image of an ambulance appeared before him, racing toward Deckers City Hospital with Captain Holland on board. He was hanging on to a thin thread of life.

In front of City Jail, a coroner's van idled at the curb, awaiting its gruesome cargo: the bodies of Simmons, Pender and Jo Joe Peters. With the desire for vengeance sweeping through Justin's soul, hot as the fires of hell, he shouted into the light, "Where is he, Wach-el? Show me where Billy is hiding."

"Justin..." Wach-el's deep voice resonated from the intense glow. *"Beware."*

"That punk has no respect for human life, no remorse for his victims, no sorrow for shooting Christy in the back, and the devil has the nerve to say that I am no different than him. Billy's more like the devil than me. He's as evil as the devil ever was."

"The devil isn't evil. Man is evil. The devil simply feeds on the misery humans cause one another."

"And God lets him get away with it."

"Since Adam and Eve lived in a beautiful garden and begot two sons, one of whom killed the other in a fit of jealous rage, God has given mankind a choice between good and evil, peace or violence. It's called free will."

"But even God isn't immune to violence," Justin shouted, his ethereal mind racing back through history. "He demanded offerings of lamb's blood, drowned the Pharaoh's army in the Red Sea, swallowed up Hebrews in

~124~

an earthquake at Mount Sinai, he even sacrificed his own son on the cross—"

"Think about it, Justin. Man was made in God's image."

Justin's ethereal stomach dropped. "That means violence is rooted in our origins. We inherited violence from our maker."

"And the horrors began," Wach-el proclaimed. *"The Romans enslaved and slaughtered millions, killing man and beast for conquest and sport. Christian armies butchered their way to prominence in the name of their God. Islam even wrote jihad into their creed. Religious zealots branded innocent women as witches and burned them at the stake."*

The light revealed more images of man's barbarism, soldiers clashing on a field of battle, North against South, hundreds falling under a volley of musket and cannon fire.

Gas drifted over rows of barbed wire and miles of trenches filled with dead soldiers. Hitler's scowling face appeared, his right arm raised in a Nazi salute. Behind him, emaciated bodies were piled up like cordwood. Battleships exploded at Pearl Harbor. Soldiers keeled over on the beachheads of Normandy. A mushroom cloud billowed over Hiroshima.

Guilt clawed up Justin's backbone. He felt ashamed to be a member of the human race.

A naked Vietnamese girl ran along a dirt road leading away from her burning village, her skin charred and blistered, her face wrenched in agony. Helicopters landed, and wounded Marines were loaded aboard while B-52 bombers rained death on Hanoi.

Oil field fires blackened the skies over Kuwait, and on the *Highway of Death*, retreating Iraqi troops were mowed down by war planes from a nation professing peace. Bodies and equipment lay scattered for miles, broken and burning.

And as if the passage of time meant nothing, the light revealed a smoldering Federal building after a truck-bomb blast. A fireman stumbled from the rubble carrying a limp and lifeless child in his arms. The North Tower in New York City crashed to the ground in a cloud of dust and fluttering papers.

Justin's stomach sickened at the horrible loss of life displayed before him. Man's atrocities against his fellow man, there seemed to be no end to the carnage. He lowered his cowboy hat, shading his eyes from the light. "Stop. I've seen enough."

"Violence is ingrained in the human experience, Justin. You are no exception."

An angry heat wave coursed through Justin's soul. "Whose side are you on, anyway?"

"Look again, Justin, and learn."

Two preschool boys appeared in the light, playing in a sandbox. They were fighting over a toy shovel, screaming and kicking and punching each other until the weaker boy finally submitted and ran away crying. The victor remained alone in the sandbox, content to play with the spoils of his own little war. A mother's shouting voice echoed eerily from the light. "If you don't share with your friends, they won't play with you anymore, Justin."

"Mom?" Justin had no recollection of what he'd just seen, but he now understood that violence was inherent in all humans. Even within him.

"Children must be taught to be kind to each other. Those who don't learn this from their parents are destined to grow up to be like Billy Denton, Ted Bundy, Timothy McVeigh, or the suicide bomber sitting on a crowded commuter train."

As the image of the sandbox faded, an involuntary shudder seized Justin's chest. "Now I see what the devil meant."

"Be sympathetic, Justin, even unto the worst of these killers."

"You're right. I can't kill Billy, no matter what, or the devil will be proven right."

"Trouble is, he's going to test your resolve, Justin." The light parted. *"Look."*

It was the middle of the night in Deckers, Texas. The familiar hulk of a huge building came into view.

"City Hospital?" Justin wondered why Wach-el was showing him the place where Christy lay in a coma.

A motion revealed a dark figure emerging from the bushes. He lurked in through the back delivery door, ducked into a supply room, and quickly slipped into a gray smock he'd found hanging on a wall hook. The nameplate read: *Ruskin.*

But it wasn't Ruskin.

It was Billy Denton: red goatee, silver rings up and down his earlobes.

Dread filled Justin, sure as the dirt that filled his grave. "What's he doing?"

"Christy is not safe there anymore."

"She's in a coma. Helpless. He wouldn't dare—"

"The devil is forcing your hand, Justin. He's going to give you a reason to kill Billy. A reason you can't ignore."

"That's because he's a cheating bastard."

"It's Judgment Day, Justin. You'd better get down there."

His ethereal body began to tingle. In a brilliant flash of light, he was on his way to stop Billy, once and for all.

The Assassin

With anger gnawing at his insides, Billy Denton hunkered down in the supply room at Deckers City Hospital and took inventory of the rounds in the Colt he'd taken from Captain Holland just before he died in the world's greatest jailbreak. Six bullets in the clip, one in the chamber. He slipped the gun under his belt next to his sheathed hunting knife then closed the gray doctor's smock he wore over both weapons. He was on a mission, one final strike against Justin Graves.

The nameplate on the smock read: *Ruskin*. He hoped Ruskin wasn't a black man or a woman. One last detail: Billy removed his earrings and the ring in his eyebrow and stashed them in the pocket of the jeans he'd stolen from a homeless camp down by the river. There was nothing he could do about his scraggly goatee. Satisfied he'd blend in with the hospital personnel, he commandeered an empty cart, threw a towel over it as if covering something for the night's rounds, and pulled open the supply room door.

City Hospital wasn't a big facility: four floors and two wings. This time of night, after visiting hours, he encountered only a janitor while wheeling the noisy cart down the hallway. The reception lobby sat on the main floor between the wings. There he held back, made sure no one was around, then casually pushed the cart to the counter. Sneaking behind it, he flipped through the admissions log, scanned a list of patients, and found the name he was looking for: *Room W214, upstairs, west wing.*

Suppressing a grin, he headed for the elevator, the cart wheels rattling with speed.

Justin Graves

***

Slowly, Captain Holland became aware of his breathing and noises around him, the whir of a fan, tennis shoes squeaking on floor tiles, and the rhythmic beep of a heart monitor. His chest felt like it had been hit with a pickaxe. Opening his eyes to a dimly lit room, he fought off a wave of panic, knowing where he was but not sure how he'd gotten here.

"He's coming around, Dr. Payne," an angelic voice said.

Holland turned his head toward the voice, saw radiant red hair and a halo, all fuzzy around the edges. He blinked.

She stepped back.

A tall man in a white smock bent over him. "Can you tell me what day it is?"

What day? Tuesday...or maybe...Friday? He couldn't be sure.

"I don't know." The sound that came from his throat gave him a fright. "What happened?"

"Do you know your name?"

My name? Yes. "Justice. I mean...Justin Graves."

"He's doing it again," the angelic voice said. "He kept shouting that name, over and over, when they brought him in."

"He's still groggy," Dr. Payne said. "Captain Holland. Harold Holland. Does that name sound familiar?"

"But I saw him. I saw Justice."

"You were in shock, delirious."

"Justice," Holland shouted. He couldn't have been wrong about what he'd seen. "Where are you?"

Dr. Payne patted Holland's shoulder. "Calm down now."

"Justice."

"He's dead," Payne said.

Terry Wright

"No he's not. I saw him."

"The surgery went well," Payne slipped in, as if he could change the subject. "We removed the slug from your upper chest."

"Billy Denton shot me. It happened so fast."

"The bullet was lodged under your collarbone."

"Did they get him? Did they get Billy?"

"Don't worry about him. You'll be out of here in a few days."

Groaning, Holland thought the pickaxe had turned into a bulldozer parked on his chest.

"Get some rest," the angelic voice said.

The room went dark.

Pain rifled through Holland's body as if the anesthesia had suddenly worn off, the horror of the jailbreak and the gun battle now returning to his memory in all its bloody terror. He wished he'd never heard the name Billy Denton.

A single wedge of light from the hall angled through the doorway, across the floor, and up the wall. Holland struggled to get comfortable, to cope with the damage the bullet had done to his body. He wished he could sleep, but that vision in his mind wouldn't let him rest. With his own eyes he'd seen Justin Graves. The image couldn't have been born of shock or delirium. The wraith was as real as the bullet wound in his chest.

Justin didn't look like any wavy and transparent Hollywood ghost. He wore his long coat and cowboy hat, as always, but they were dirty and dusty, like he'd just crawled out of the ground. His voice was raspy, and his deep dark eye sockets were filled with death. However, most convincing, the ghoulish homicide detective smelled like rotting flesh, as if his body had been locked in a car trunk for three days under the blistering Texas sun. That was one smell a cop never forgot.

Justin Graves

Justin Graves was back from the dead.

A noise in the hallway caught Holland's attention. It sounded like one of those rattling hospital carts, probably a nurse coming to wake him up, to check his bandages, poke him and prod him, and otherwise keep him awake, as if he needed any help with that. Maybe now he could ask for a stronger dose of pain meds.

The cart stopped just outside his door. A shadow invaded the wedge of light on the floor. Holland blinked, craned his neck, and tried to focus on the silhouette of a man now standing in the doorway. He seemed uncertain about entering, looked back and forth.

The angelic voice spoke from the hallway. "May I help you?"

"I'm looking for W214." The shadow stepped back.

For a split second, before it moved from the light of the doorway, the shadow-maker's face appeared: a red goatee and a barbed wire tattoo on his neck. Holland's heart about stopped.

Billy Denton?

His shadow remained cast in the light on the floor.

The nurse's shadow approached his, their shadows now coming together. "I've not seen you around here before," she said.

"It's my first night." The shadow of his hand pointed to his chest. "Ruskin. See?"

Her shadow stepped back. A gasp. "Maria Ruskin is a woman. What are you trying to pull—?"

In a heartbeat, his shadow drew a big knife shadow and thrust it into the shadow of her belly. He plunged it deep and jerked it upward, burying the blade in her heart.

Her shadow went limp, buckled over, and his shadow caught hers in his arms.

Terror pumped through Holland's body, making the

pain in his chest do double-time. He wanted to call out but stopped short for fear of giving away the fact that he'd witnessed the killing.

Billy dragged the dead nurse into the darkness of Holland's room. Her body hit the floor with a dull thump.

Keeping one eye open just a crack, Holland feigned sleep, hoping the rapidly beeping heart monitor wouldn't alert Billy to the helpless man in the bed. Or perhaps that was the reason Billy was here, to finish him off after he'd survived the shootout at Deckers City Jail. If that was the case, Holland was a dead man. He didn't have the strength to fend off a knife-wielding assassin. All he could do was wait in silence and hope the monster in the room didn't see him.

Instead of approaching the bed, Billy left and wheeled the noisy cart away.

Relief flooded Holland, but his investigative instincts squashed the feeling. If Billy hadn't come to kill him, why was he here? Who had he come to kill? Christy? Her room was down the hall...at the end of the wing. Holland had to stop him. Somehow. He had to try.

He sat up. Pain slugged him in the chest. Hard. He thought he would faint.

Justice. Where are you...when I need you?

***

Billy moved down the hall, pushing the rattle-wheeled cart, the towel now covering his right hand, the one that held the knife, the one he'd bloodied killing the nurse. If anyone saw that blood, he'd be busted for sure. They'd sound the alarm. Security would come running. He couldn't afford to be recaptured. Not now. He was too close to his goal, his target, his final blow to Justin Graves.

To Billy's relief, the hallway was silent as a morgue.

He encountered no one. The path was clear to do this thing he'd come to do.

He left the cart in the hall and pushed open the door to W214, just a little at a time, cautiously, without the reckless abandon of his jailbreak. His mouth went dry as he stepped inside the room, the bloody knife clenched in his right fist. Using Holland's Colt would make too much noise. This would be a silent kill, like the nurse, and then he'd slip away into the night.

Too easy.

In the soft glow of streetlight that beamed in through the window, he could see his victim, comatose, unaware of the rasping ventilator and beeping heart monitor. Every nerve in his body tingled as he approached her bed, quiet like a cat stalking a bird. It would be a quick death.

He raised the knife above her chest, began the plunge, but hesitated to stab those beautiful breasts.

His mind recounted the times he'd violated Justin's little whore of a daughter. Christy didn't look so good right now, with all the wires and tubes sticking out of her. But she'd been a fine bitch before she chose her father over her boyfriend. He didn't know how she'd survived the hail of bullets at the old warehouse. Luck he supposed. He'd shot her in the back three times. Whatever the case, he was about to rectify the situation.

This time he placed the knife tip on her left breast, prepared to plunge it home, but a stirring in his loins stopped him. Maybe first he should cop a feel: one for the road, for old time's sake. She'd never know. She couldn't stop him. What the hell could it hurt?

Reaching for the bed sheet, Billy felt a rush in his jeans and a rise in his heartbeat. He threw back her covers and took hold of the hem of her hospital gown. Slowly he lifted it, revealing raven-black pubic hairs glistening in the glow of the street-lit window. He licked his lips and pulled her gown higher, exposing the white skin of her belly, then her rounded breasts, slack nipples, and more wires. His heart rate doubled. He began to salivate. This could be better than ever, the final disgrace. He'd violate her one more time before killing her. Justice's failure as a father would be complete.

Billy didn't waste any time, now that he'd made up his mind. A cackle rose in his throat as he tossed the knife on the bed-stand, and the Colt too. He ripped off Ruskin's gown and dropped his jeans to his ankles, his blood-gorged flesh now throbbing. This wouldn't take long. *Slam bam thank you, ma'am.* Or better yet: *Slam bam screw you, Justice.* He spread Crystal's legs and put a knee on the bed to climb aboard. A bit of rattling came suddenly, from behind him, the familiar sound of wheels on the cart he'd left in the hallway. As fast as the realization came to him, he spun around.

Captain Holland screamed like a Comanche, his face pale, grimacing in pain, and his bandaged chest hunched over the cart handle as he rammed the cart into Billy's groin, launching him backward into the window, which exploded with a glass-shattering bang. The wind came out of his lungs, and he felt the sensation of nothing around him: falling, falling, falling, and then crashing through spiny bushes that tore at his skin like a million razor blades. Striking the ground flat on his back, he fought for air, paralyzed almost. This sudden turn of events made him want to scream, but he couldn't get the air. Through clenched teeth, he forced a breath into his lungs and struggled to his feet. Gasping and staggering about, he pulled up his pants and swore he'd be back to kill Christy...and Captain Holland, as well.

***

Holland staggered and tripped and fell against the windowsill. Shards of glass cut into the palms of his hands. Something inside him felt like a hot poker, torn stitches perhaps, or the sudden hemorrhage of a bullet-weakened artery. Below the window, Billy stumbled off into the night. Holland gritted his teeth and collapsed into darkness.

Opening his eyes, Holland didn't know how long he'd been out. He was back in his room. The wedge of light on the floor looked familiar; the fan whirred. The heart monitor beeped. The murdered nurse's body was gone, but something was different: the smell, the god awful smell. Medical examiners must've left a dead body on an autopsy table downstairs in the morgue...for a month. The stench turned his stomach over. He swallowed bile and wished someone would put him out of his misery.

A raspy voice came from the shadows. "Captain." It was a familiar voice, the one he'd heard in Deckers City Jail. And a grated kind of breathing disturbed the air. Holland's throat clutched. Slowly, he shifted his eyes to the shadowy corner of his room where a ghostly cowboy began to take form.

Justice.

Though instinct told Holland to scream, to cry out for someone to witness this abomination, he held his breath and stifled his fear.

"I owe you one," Justin said in a raspy voice. He stepped from the shadows. Dirt and filth rained down from his long coat but dissolved before hitting the floor. His breath smelled of decay. The brim of his hat hid his eyes.

"Justice...is it really you?"

The ghoul's cowboy hat bobbed. "You saved Christy's life."

"How...I mean...why are you here?"

"I'm trying to save my daughter's soul."

"She...she's not safe," Holland managed to say. "As long as Billy Denton is alive, Christy is in danger. You've got to kill him before he kills her."

"I cannot kill him. It's against the rules."

Holland tried to ignore the ghoul's foul stench but couldn't. "She's in deep shit, Justice. What rules could possibly—"

"The devil's rules, Captain."

"Jesus." A jolt of adrenaline attacked Holland's chest like shark teeth. "You made a deal with the devil?"

"I must deliver him one hundred souls in exchange for Christy's life."

"Christ, Justice. What were you thinking?"

"She deserves a second chance."

"And if you fail?"

Justin lifted his hat brim, revealing lifeless eyes sunk in black pools. "Hell is a horrible place for a little girl."

"She's a teenager, Justice. She made her choices."

A huff of air came from Justin's hollow chest. "Because of me...it's my fault she took the wrong path. I didn't make her listen. I wasn't there for her. Parents like me raise children like her. I can't let her pay the price for my incompetence as a father."

Holland tried to sit up, failed. "I said you'd have to fight for her...but I didn't realize you'd be fighting the devil himself."

"I can't cross over to everlasting peace and happiness until she is safe, but I need your help."

"Help?" Holland had no idea how he could help a dead detective. The whole affair sat in his guts like a pile of rocks. "What can I do?"

"Put a twenty-four hour guard on Christy. Two men. Maybe four."

"That won't stop Billy." Holland coughed. "He'll find

a way to get to her. I'm sure he'll stop at nothing now."

"Then you'll have to kill him for me."

"Kill him yourself." Holland regretted saying the words as soon as they came out. He didn't agree with taking the law into one's own hands.

"If I kill him, it'll prove I'm no better than him. Christy and I will be condemned to an eternity in hell. So you have to do it for me."

"And condemn myself to hell? No thanks."

"In the line of duty, Captain. He's an escaped cop killer. He won't be taken alive anyway."

Justin was right. Billy would never surrender to the law. "I don't know where he is. We don't even know where to look."

"You've got to find him. Get Billy...or Christy and I are doomed."

With a gust of wind the ghoul was gone.

**

In the desert outside Deckers where rattlesnakes, scorpions, and tarantulas reigned supreme, Billy Denton inhaled the sweet smell of freedom. His back hurt some from the fall out of the second floor window of Deckers City Hospital. If it hadn't been for the bushes that broke his fall, he might have been killed. That damn Captain Holland hadn't seen the last of Billy Denton.

Sitting on a big rock, he peered across the ravine below. He'd grown up wandering the flats and craggy hills of this sun-baked hell on earth. By now he knew every inch of the place known as *Irongate.*

He'd named his hideout after the rusted wrought iron gate that lay askew alongside the trail that led up to the mouth of an abandoned mine. Old Penelope they'd called her back in the old days, and Billy knew her history well.

His great, great grandfather had stolen the mine from a geezer named Rascal. It wasn't hard for Billy to imagine how the theft played out some hundred and fifty plus years ago, right on this very spot. He could see them and hear them plain as day.

***

"Yah claim jumpin' varmints. Just wait 'n see what I has in store fer your hides." Cackling, Rascal worked under a scorching sun, talking to himself, as usual. "Confounded squatters."

With ropes, he'd already hoisted up the iron gate, the one that came from San Francisco, and now he went to work tightening hinge bolts to posts he'd sunk on either side of the trail. He scratched his gray beard. "Deckers...*hump*...what kind a name were that for a town."

The geezer spit chaw, some of which dribbled down the front of his dusty coveralls and splattered on his *church* boots. He called them church boots because they was *holey*. He latched the gate with a lock and stepped back to admire his handiwork. "That oughta keep them varmints out."

He scrambled down the dusty trail, now blocked by his gate, and made his way across the ravine. High up on the west bank, a wooden shack sat atop a pile of mine tailings, and from the rock face, shoring timbers poked out a square, black maw in the hillside. He'd named his claim Penelope.

For the longest time, his mine had been barren as a barroom whore. Near on ten years. But never mind that now. He'd already figured a way to drop her shaft another hundred feet, follow the bedrock seam, and whittle out another vein of gold. He was going to be rich, and he wasn't about to give it up to them thieving squatters they

Justin Graves

called townsfolk of Deckers. Puke.

Hoisting a shoulder-load of timber, he hunkered down and trudged into Penelope. The air took on a chill. Rusty lanterns lined the tunnel, not many, though just enough to break the darkness into flickering shadows. Dripping water echoed from the depths, and his church boots crunched dirt.

Several tunnels went off to the left and the right and crisscrossed this way and that. Some tunnels were dead ends, and some broke out into steep crevasses that'd leave a man without a foothold. Others had trip beams that would bring down the ceiling and false floors that could collapse underfoot, dumping a man into subterranean washes to drown. Rascal placed his feet carefully, counting each step, as he scrabbled deeper into Penelope's rocky bowels.

"Claim jumpin' varmints 'll get killed comin' in here."

***

Billy Denton had to chuckle. It had long been known that mine was no place for a stranger to wander around. The stories were legend in these parts. And so was his great, great grandfather, Roger, a legend in his own time. Billy came from a long line of tougher-than-granite men, and he was damned proud of it.

***

Roger Denton spurred his steed down Deckers' main street, his gang of thieves riding behind him, horse hooves clomping dirt. Women and children scurried in every direction. Wagons laded with wood planks and roofing tar rumbled through town, stirring up dust. Hammers struck nails, saws rasped wood, and men groaned and sweat under the Texas sun.

Signaling his gang, he dismounted in front of the Devil's Roost Saloon, hitched his horse, and took to the

Terry Wright

boardwalk where his boots clunked and his spurs jingled. From behind swinging doors, honky-tonk piano music spilled into the street. Voices yammered from within, some drunkenly. "I tell yah, boys," someone said. "Rascal hit it big. I say we bushwhack the old coot and do our own diggin'."

"Penelope is a worthless old hole in the ground," somebody else shouted.

"Not so," another voice said. "I seen Rascal at the assayer's office day before last. Weren't no fool's gold he was handin' over."

"I say we all go out and jump his claim...*hic*...find out fer ourselves."

Denton pushed his way through the door, and with his gang, sidled up to the bar. Talk of claim jumping came to a quick end. Cigar smoke clouded the air. "Sarsaparilla," he said to the bartender, a pudgy fellow with more hair under his nose than on his head.

"We don't want no trouble, Mister Denton."

Some fool at a card table laughed. "Sarsaparilla?" He chugged hooch straight from the bottle. "My pappy used to say, if you're gonna walk like a man, yah gotta drink like a man."

His card-playin' buddies howled.

Hands on their pistol grips, Denton's gang turned away from the bar and focused their murderous gazes on the loudmouths.

"Easy, men," Denton said. "I'll handle this." He eyed the drunken cowboys. They were probably in town just for the night. Tomorrow they'd be back to driving their stinking cattle east toward Fort Worth. A couple of them didn't look much older than snot-nosed kids just weaned from their mamma's teats.

At the next table, a dapper looking bunch of gamblers

leaned back in their chairs, their eyes shifting about nervously. One big fellow in a black bow tie and vest stroked a bar floozy's thigh while she sat in his lap. "Can a man play poker in peace around here?"

Now that Denton had everybody's attention, he twitched his mustache. "What's all this talk about jumpin' old man Rascal's claim?"

"What's it to yah, mister?" This smart remark came from a dusty cowpoke in need of a shave. He hadn't been playing cards with the cowboys, but stood at the end of the bar, sipping straight Kentucky bourbon.

"If anybody jumps that claim, it'll be me and my men. Rest of you stay away."

"And if-in we don't?"

"You die."

Piano music stopped.

The dapper gambler stood, dumping the floozy on the floor in a heap of petticoat lace. He wore a black glove on his right hand like some gunslingers did from Dodge City. His eyebrows canted menacingly. "Says who?"

"Now, gentlemen," the bartender said.

"Stay out of this, Shorty." Denton stepped forward, glaring at the fool who would stand up to him. "Time for you boys to move along." His hand hovered over his holstered Colt.

The gun-slinging gambler flexed gloved fingers and poised them above the ivory handle of his six-shooter. "I think you better—"

Denton drew and fired. Cowboys scattered. Chairs upended. Grimacing, the gambler stagger-stepped back then fell face first and hit the floor like a sack of horse oats. Blood pooled.

The floozy screamed.

In the next second, Denton spun around. Sure enough,

the dusty cowpoke at the end of the bar was going for his gun, but Denton had a bead on him and pulled the trigger. Blood and brain matter spattered the wall.

The Denton gang pulled their guns and covered all the wide-eyed saloon patrons. As the floozy whimpered over the dead gambler, Denton strode up to the cowboy who'd badmouthed sarsaparilla. "Didn't pappy ever tell you to hold your tongue?"

Cowering on the floor like a whipped dog, the drunk cowboy stuttered, "I-I didn't mean no harm."

"But I do." Denton fired a bullet into the cowboy's forehead and turned to his gang. "Come on, men. We got a claim to jump."

***

With a rope and a good horse, Denton's gang pulled down Rascal's new iron gate and left it bent and twisted on the side of the trail. Whooping and hollering, they rode into the ravine, a dozen or more thieving bastards firing their guns.

Rascal had hold of his shotgun and watched the whole thing from the window of his shack. Beard itching, he leveled the barrel on the nearest claim jumper and pulled the trigger. With a boom, the man came out of his saddle and landed in a cactus bed.

"Varmints." Rascal spat chew and reloaded.

Bullets started ricocheting off his shack, some zinging through the window and dislodging pots and pans from the wall. "Yer askin' fer it now." He unleashed another shotgun blast that tore the head off a man riding in at full gallop. "Yer not takin' my Penelope."

A rain of bullets pummeled the shack, forcing Rascal to retreat into his mineshaft. Extinguishing lanterns as he ran, he found it more difficult to place his feet safely. He

Justin Graves

lost count of his footsteps. His booby traps now became a harrowing problem. He started counting steps between beams, but he wasn't sure which beam was which. Was it four steps or five then sidestep left…or was it right? In all the mayhem, he'd become confused. He should've been at beam seven by now, but this beam had a wood knot half way up, like beam ten. Or was it beam eleven? "Tarnation."

Gunfire rang out from Penelope's entrance. Men's silhouettes now blocked out the glow of daylight. "Give up, old man," someone shouted. "We might let you live."

"Drats."

"Spread out, men. Take the tunnels on the right and left. Holler if you find him."

Moments later, a long scream echoed through Penelope, faded, and ended with a thump. A rumble belched from a tunnel on the left, followed by a quick scream and an *ugghh*. Rocks crashed down, and dust swirled in the air.

Now Rascal grinned. "Served them thievin' bastards right." He turned, took three steps forward and one step left. The floor gave way underneath him. He immediately realized he'd gone beyond beam twelve. "Curses." Crashing downward, falling rocks knocked him senseless. He never felt his body hit the roiling subterranean wash.

***

Denton peered into Penelope's black throat. "Anybody there?" His men had rushed in, but none had come out.

Eerily, only the sound of dripping water and an occasional rock fall echoed back.

"Rascal?"

Silence.

With lantern and shovel in hand, he entered Penelope.

Dirt crunched under his boots and echoed away. Shadows danced on rocky walls. Timbers sagged and creaked. About ten yards in, rocks cascaded from the ceiling, and dust choked the air. From somewhere in the dark abyss, he heard a moan.

"Who's there?" Denton shouted.

"Go back, boss. Save yourself."

A scream echoed away.

Rocks clattered.

A wave of panic swept over Denton like an icy waterfall in December, chilling him to the bone.

"Hello?"

Silence.

"Answer me, damn it."

The ceiling spit more stones. Penelope groaned.

Panic took over Denton. Acting on their own accord, his feet raced for the mine entrance and daylight. Once outside, he bent over, put his hands on his knees, and gasped fresh air. He'd lost his entire gang to Penelope. The old man had turned his mine into a death trap, a gauntlet of unspeakable horrors. It would take an army to dig through the cave-ins, shore up the walls, and patch the floors to recover the bodies. How many men would die in the process? It wouldn't take long for word to get around Deckers that the mine was cursed. Nobody would work a suicide pit. Gold or no gold, Penelope was too dangerous. She would take revenge on whomever entered her dark domain.

Roger Denton spent the rest of the day boarding up Penelope's entrance. He painted a skull-and-crossbones sign, big and black. After pounding the last nail in place, he rounded up the horses and galloped them off toward town, thinking how he'd explain the deaths of his men.

***

Billy Denton laughed and jumped down from the big rock. Pride welled up inside like a warm breeze. His family history was something to be proud of.

Those were the days.

At the entrance to Penelope, he gaped at the weather-worn skull and crossbones his great, great granddaddy had painted on the wooden barricade. Billy yanked on a couple of pre-loosened boards and crawled into his hideout.

***

Justin Graves, slick and trim in his pressed trousers and button-down shirt, sat in his favorite recliner in front of the light. Like the biggest big screen ever, the ethereal glow revealed Captain Holland with his left arm in a sling and a diagonal bandage across his chest. He'd insisted on leaving the hospital right away. Lives were at stake. Now he sat on the front porch of the old Denton Mansion, iced tea glass in hand and talking with Morton McAllister about Billy Denton.

"The war started about the time Roger Denton's gang disappeared," McAllister said. "Roger Denton told the townsfolk his gang had lit out to fight."

"And Rascal?"

"Just another miner swallowed up by his own greed. The mine's been closed ever since."

Holland adjusted his aching frame in the rocker. Bandages pressed on his chest wound just below his left clavicle. "How long have you been caretaker around here?"

"My great granddaddy helped Mr. Denton build this place. They made their fortune in cattle rustling back then. Grandpa stayed on after Denton died. My father and I followed in Grandpa's footsteps. This has always been our home."

"I hear Roger Denton's misses was a barroom floozy

before she took up with him."

"Frightful woman she was."

"Do you remember Billy's great grandfather?"

"Samuel Denton." Morton shook his head. "I was nine when they hung him. Don't remember much more than that, except his son was only four at the time."

"Billy's grandfather?"

Nodding, Morton examined his own glass of iced tea. "He grew up mean."

"I hear Billy's dad was brutal."

"Rattler got the bastard. Billy's ma died when he was sixteen. Courts couldn't handle him. Nobody wanted to foster him. Kept causing trouble and running away. He's been mostly on his own."

Looking around the neatly trimmed grounds, Holland inhaled the scent of freshly-mowed grass. "Why didn't he stay here with you?"

Morton sighed. "After my Margret died, it was like the devil moved into young Billy's soul. He ran off. Spent most of his time up in the hills. Got mixed up with them drug fellas after that. Killed Justin Graves and his daughter. Guess he was destined to be the devil's advocate."

Holland twitched. "The hills, you say. Could it be that he went back to the old mine?"

"Only a fool would go in there. The place is cursed, you know. Nobody who went in ever came out."

"I never said Billy had any brains."

"Be careful there, Captain. He can fool you."

***

The light dimmed. Holland's image faded. Justin had seen enough. He rubbed his smooth chin and leaned back in his recliner. Tipped forward a little, his cowboy hat sat on his head just right. His long brown coat smelled of fine

Justin Graves

leather, and his boots shined like he was going to a wedding.

"Shall I find that mine?" the archangel Wach-el asked in his hauntingly deep voice from the light.

"It's our only lead. Take a look. See what's there."

For a moment, which could have been a split second or a week in the afterlife, Justin wanted to end his torment over Billy Denton and the devil's deal. Rounding up souls had proven to be a difficult task that he wished he hadn't taken on. All he had to do was kill Billy Denton for revenge. The devil would win. Christy would die and go to hell. Justin would join her there for eternity, though he was sure he'd never see her.

A supernatural pain stabbed Justin's chest as if it were punishment for entertaining such thoughts. That fiery, smoky abyss was no place for Christy. He couldn't let his daughter down like that. Not ever.

As the light brightened, a twisted iron gate appeared alongside a dirt trail that led up a ravine. A breeze rustled sagebrush. Rotted wood planks, remnants of a decayed shack, lay strewn about the steep face of a tailings pile, and a trickle of water cascaded down from a crevice above the black mouth of a mineshaft. There, in the shadows behind an old skull and crossbones sign, his back propped against a shoring timber, his knees propped up, napped Billy Denton with his forehead resting on his arms. Earrings glinted, and his barbed wire tattoo was clearly visible.

Anger boiled inside Justin. As long as Billy was alive, his daughter was in danger of being murdered in her sleep, in her coma, murdered in her bed. He wanted to transform himself into his ghoulish state and appear to Billy, then choke him to death with bare bony hands.

With that thought, a vision of the devil appeared in his mind, laughing while flames lapped around him. *"Do it,*

Justice," the devil crowed. *"Your journey to hell will be complete."*

"You're not getting my daughter."

"Do me proud, Justice. Show the world the killer inside you."

"Never."

"Do it, do it, do it."

The hellish vision faded.

Justin's ghostly heart hammered.

Billy lifted his head and turned his evil eyes toward Justin. The punk's piercing glare seemed to penetrate the light and dare Justin to do the devil's bidding.

In all his years of investigating homicides, Justin never hated the murderers he tracked. Not until now. The face that glowered at him in the light was the face of his killer, the defiler of his daughter, the epitome of everything evil, an evil that Justin must snuff out once and for all.

A growl came from deep inside Justin's soul as he curled into his long coat and began the transposition back to his grave.

***

From his position at Penelope's entrance, Billy peered across the ravine, his eyes squinting against intense sunlight. An eerie feeling crept through his body. Though the temperature must've been a hundred and ten degrees, he felt a chill. It seemed as if someone out there was watching him.

A dust devil swirled down the trail below. Sagebrush rustled. A hawk soared on thermals above. But nothing else stirred. Satisfied he'd not been discovered, he leaned his head back against the shoring beam and groaned.

Justin Graves' daughter played in his mind. Christy, or Crystal as he preferred to call her, lay spread-eagle on a hospital bed. She looked helpless, the perfect lover. He had approached her. Wanted her. Brutally. Then that damn Captain Holland had ruined the upcoming quickie.

But that didn't stop his imagination from taking up where reality left off. He climbed on top of her anyway. Her skin smelled stale, her shallow breaths smelled like plastic, probably because of the ventilator. A charge of air entered her lungs and lifted her breasts to meet his bare chest. She gasped. Her eyes shot wide open.

The ground trembled, and from deep within the mine, Penelope belched dust. A ghastly odor wafted from the depths.

Billy's fantasy fled him. Gagging on putrid air, he struggled to his feet and looked down Penelope's dark throat, thinking a rockslide had unearthed the rotted remains of the bodies entombed there long ago. The air smelled like a thousand maggot-infested corpses. About to lose his lunch, he started crawling toward the loose boards and fresh air.

"Billy," a coarse and echoing voice rumbled from Penelope.

He froze.

Silence.

It must've been his imagination, the tone of creaking timbers having taken on the sound of his name. But the odor wasn't a figment of his imagination. It was getting worse. He scrambled for the entrance.

"Billy."

He stopped. Stomach reeling, he gritted his teeth. "Who's there?"

Heavy footsteps crunched dirt in the darkness.

Right about now he wished he hadn't set Pender's Colt on the bed-stand in Crystal's hospital room. He spun around to face the voice. "What do you want?"

From the depths of the mine, the form of a cowboy appeared. He looked as though he'd clawed his way up from the mine's muddy innards, his long coat caked with dried clumps of grime, his hat shedding dirt with each step. Tangled gray hair touched his shoulders, and worse, the skin of his lipless, toothy face dripped like thick goo.

Billy bent down and picked up a splinter-infested board that must've been a hundred and fifty years old. "I'm warning you." Cocking the board behind his shoulder, he took a step backward. "I'll waste your ass."

"You already did," the aberration said in a raspy voice, now standing an arm's length away. "Name's Justin Graves, but you can call me Justice."

Billy's stomach clutched. "No way."

The ghoul patted dust from his coat lapel, revealing the gleam of a Texas Ranger badge. Billy saw bullet holes in the coat and shirt, and exposed rib bones and rotting flesh. The awful stench sent salty bile surging up to the back of Billy's throat. He swallowed. "It *is* you." Without hesitation, Billy lunged at the ghoul and swung the board, smacking Justin upside the head. "I thought I was through with you. How dare you come back? Now I've got to kill your ass again." He beat Justin with the board.

The ghoulish detective raised his arms to ward off the onslaught. "I'm already dead, punk."

"You're not dead enough." Billy walloped him again. "And neither is your daughter. I'm going to kill her again too."

"That's why I'm here."

Again and again, Billy pummeled the ghoul. Dust flew from his coat. His cowboy hat fell off.

"You should've stayed buried where you belong."

"I had to come back. You gave me no choice."

The board splintered and broke. Billy threw it down

Justin Graves

and balled his fists. "Come on. It's just you and me." He threw a right jab.

Justin bobbed left. "You have no idea how much I want to kill you."

"Talk is cheap." Billy threw a roundhouse, almost hit Justin on the jaw.

"But I can't kill you. I made a deal with the devil."

"You came here to tell me that?" Billy jabbed with a left-right combination.

Justin landed a right punch that sent Billy reeling backward. "If I kill you, the devil wins. He takes my soul...and Christy's."

"She deserves to go to hell." Billy spit blood. "But what's the devil got against you?"

"I play by the rules."

"Bet he hates you for that." Seeing Justin drop his left fist a little, Billy took a quick swing and slammed his fist into the ghoul's left cheek. Rotting flesh splattered and exposed his jawbone.

"That's disgusting," Billy choked out while shaking the goo from his knuckles.

"So I've been told."

Billy kept his fists high and out in front of him while he stared at the horrific sight before him. Once Justin Graves was a picture of health: a clean-shaven, well-groomed officer of the law. Now, reduced to this smelly ghoul, his fate hinged on the only thing he had left, his principles. The only way Billy could hurt the dead detective was to convince him to abandon those principles. The devil would take care of the rest.

"You've got a lot to learn about bad guys, Justice."

"And you're going to teach me, I suppose."

"Don't you get it?" Billy sidled right, his eyes locked on Justin's sunken orbs. "The rules are different with us.

You good guys don't impress us. We only look up to other bad guys...in fact...the badder the better."

Justin raised his fists. "And you, you're the baddest?"

"I am." Billy's mouth hurt on account of the knuckle sandwich Justin had fed him. "I don't like good guys, wouldn't give them the time of day. But if you were a bad guy like me, there's nothin' I wouldn't do for you."

"I don't want anything from you."

"Ah...but if I were the devil, you would."

Justice stepped left. "Like what?"

Billy crouched, his guard up. "Your daughter, man. Wouldn't you try to impress me to save her?"

"I'd do anything to save her."

"Then impress the devil. Break the rules. Do what he least expects."

"He expects me to kill you."

"Okay, second least thing." Billy stepped in, jabbed and stepped back. "If he likes you, he'll be more inclined to do you a favor, like spare your daughter. If he hates you, he'll never give in, and you'll never win."

Putting his fists down, Justin snarled. "It's not worth taking the chance. If you're wrong, Christy will spend eternity in hell." He stooped to pick up his hat. "So I'm not going to kill you."

"Then why are you here?"

"I'm asking you, man to man, to leave my daughter alone."

"And if I don't, what are you going to do to stop me?"

"I don't know. But I have friends."

"Like Captain Holland?"

"Don't give him a reason to kill you. Stay away from Christy."

Glaring at the ghoul, Billy showed his teeth. "You were no help to her before she died, always out chasin' bad guys. Well, here you are, still chasin' bad guys, and you can't do anything to help her now."

"Billy," a loud voice blared over a bullhorn. "Billy Denton, we know you're in there. Come out with your hands up."

Panic shot like a bullet thought Billy's brain.

Justin sneered. "I can't stop you, but those cops can."

"How did they know I was here?"

"A little birdie told them."

"You. You ratted me out." Billy pressed his back against the rock wall and eased himself toward the mine entrance. On the trail below the tailings pile, Captain Holland stood, legs spread and a bullhorn at his lips. He'd brought a fricken posse with him. "Shit."

"Come out, Billy."

"You better give up," Justin said.

"Never."

Justin cupped his hands around his mouth and hollered in Billy's voice. "I'm unarmed."

Billy pushed him. "Damn you."

Now a dozen men scrambled up the tailings pile.

Heart hammering, Billy took off running down the dark tunnel and into Penelope's treacherous arms.

Justin's voice echoed behind him. "Don't go in there."

Groping in the dark, Billy made his way deeper into the mine, counting timbers as he went. He figured Penelope's reputation would dissuade the cops from following him, for a while anyway.

"Billy."

At beam seven, he stopped, and feeling along the crossbeam, found the flashlight he'd stashed for an emergency like this one. Justin and his police buddies would have to get up early to outsmart Billy Denton.

Up ahead, the tunnel forked. He stayed to the left. The

air felt colder now and tasted like dirt. Just past beam twelve, he had to place each step carefully as he worked his way around a hole in the floor. Loose rocks cascaded over the edge, shattered against bedrock, and splashed into an underground wash. Shoring timbers creaked and groaned.

"Give up, Billy."

Running footsteps echoed behind him. The fools. Didn't they know danger lurked at every turn?

A scream. A thump.

Rocks clattered.

"Officer down. Officer down."

Billy stepped over a trip-beam that held up the ceiling.

"Take the right fork," someone ordered.

Another scream.

"Take the left fork."

A scream and a splash came next.

"Hold up, men. It's too dangerous to go any farther."

"I'll get him," a raspy voice echoed.

Turning, Billy shined his flashlight back down the tunnel. Justin's ghostly shape flew toward him, his long coat flapping like Superman's cape, his eye sockets glowing crimson under his hat brim. "Shit." He had to think of something...the trip-beam. "Come and get me, Justice."

Justin landed just in front of the beam, an arm's length away from Billy. "Go back with me. There's no way out of here."

"You're wrong." He stepped backward.

Justin stepped forward. "Be reasonable."

Billy turned and took off running.

Justin leaped for him, tripping the beam in the process. A horrendous rumbling wracked the tunnel. The ceiling crashed down. Billy looked back. Huge rocks slammed into the ghoul, crushing his cowboy hat and smashing him to the floor, crushing his body under tons of rock.

Billy stopped to watch the pile grow and the dust swirl. As the maelstrom subsided, he brushed his hands together. That was the end of Justin Graves. Now Billy had to get out of this mine and finish off Christy.

Negotiating Penelope's hazardous tunnels, he looked for one that would circumvent the cave in. It had to be here somewhere. Rascal wouldn't have left himself without an escape route, but the more Billy searched, the more he began to worry. Water dripped from a brittle rock ceiling and trickled along the floor in muddy little streams. Goosebumps covered his arms. The air smelled stale and tasted bitter in his throat. He'd never ventured this deep before. Panic strangled his chest. He was lost.

Throwing caution aside, he frantically scrambled through tunnel after tunnel, finding only dead ends or deep fissures. He wandered this subterranean hell for hours. His pants were soaked, his shoes were muddy, and any minute now, he was sure he'd freeze to death. Finally, as the flashlight batteries died, Billy gave up hope. He slumped to the tunnel floor and cursed Justin Graves. This was his fault.

And Crystal's too. If she hadn't sided with her father during the siege at the old warehouse, none of this would have happened. One minute Billy was her hero—the next— a bum. Anger coiled in his guts like a pissed off snake. What gave her the right to do that? She had to pay, big time. He wasn't going to let this mine keep him from killing her for real.

Struggling to his feet, he threw the dead flashlight, and groped the darkness one step at a time. He banged into rock walls and tripped over fallen timbers, all the while swearing he'd not become another one of Penelope's victims. He twisted his ankle and wrenched a knee. But his resolve to escape grew with each setback.

Then, as if preordained by Penelope's revenge on all who entered, the floor gave way under him. Falling, he managed to grab hold of a jagged rock outcropping. His stomach felt like a ton of boulders. Hanging by his fingers, his feet dangled in thin air as he hung on for dear life.

Penelope made a belching sound.

Tiring quickly, his fingers ached and his wrists burned from the strain. Time was running out. Every effort to pull himself up failed. No foot holds. No stable ground for his fingers to grasp. One more breath, maybe two, and then his fingers would let go. He could only hope his death would be swift.

A whooshing sound echoed overhead, followed by a glow on the ceiling and the stink of a thousand corpses. The ghoulish detective took shape in the incandescent ghostly light.

Billy gasped. "You...you're alive?"

Justin looked confused. "I am?"

"Help me."

"The devil expects me to save you, don't you think?" Justin asked in a sandpaper voice.

"Yes. Save me."

"He'd least expect me to let you fall. You might be right. If I did, he may think kindly of me. Right? He might do me a favor. He might set my daughter free. All I've got to do is let you fall."

Billy clung to the rock, his feet flailing above the dark abyss. "It was a lie. I tried to trick you into giving up your principles."

"Yes. Good idea. I think I will let you fall. Now's the perfect time to impress the devil."

"No. Please." Billy gulped air, every precious lungful he could get. His fingers slipped a little. "Help me."

"Goodbye, Billy."

"No, wait. Wait. I'll make you a deal. Save me and I'll leave Crystal alone."

"Christy."

"Christy, all right. Christy. I promise. Just don't let me die."

"And I should trust you?"

Billy's fingers slipped again. "Screw you, Justice. If you let me die, your daughter goes to hell."

From out of the ghostly glow around Justin, a hand reached down. "Take my hand."

In an instant, Billy grabbed the ghoul's wrist, first with one hand and then the other, his body now dangling in midair, swinging back and forth. "Pull me up." He thought his heart would burst.

As Justin pulled him toward safety, the rotting flesh on his forearm started peeling away from his bones.

"Justice. Your arm—"

"Hang on."

Clutching soggy muscles and stringy tendons, Billy fought desperately for a firm grip, but his lifeline was turning to putrid mush: Justin's wrist, his hand, and now his fingers: the skin and meat stripped from his slimy, slippery bones.

"Justice."

In the next heartbeat, Justin's dead flesh gave way.

At first Billy felt weightless. A rush of air surged from his lungs, an involuntary scream. A thump came next, dull and painless, as if he'd entered a dark room and someone hit him with a pillow.

***

Falling, tumbling, spinning around and around, arms and legs splayed, the clothes ripped from his body, Billy no

Terry Wright

longer felt the pulse of life surging through his veins. Down, down, down, he spiraled into an ethereal void where sight and sound seemed only imagined, as in a dream, until that dream turned to a nightmare of guttural screams that rose from the fiery depths. Shrieking cries echoed all around him. Searing flames and the heat of a blast furnace engulfed his naked soul, a soul made of hell-flesh, an endless source of pain and suffering.

Only now did he realize the cries and screams were his own.

Hellish toil began with the sting of a lash, the curse of a demon. Billy felt the weight of heavy chains on his legs, a shovel in one hand and a fire in his throat from a thirst like none he'd ever known. A line of the doomed stretched out before him, a multitude of faceless souls chained together, trudging down a well-worn path that wormed its way through fire-lit cambers. Long shadows of the condemned paraded across granite walls as black ash swirled in the air. Red-hot pain jabbed his flesh with every step he took down, down, down into the depths of hell.

Sobs of misery came from all sides. Muscular men and women, their naked skin shining with sweat, swung picks. Rocks shattered. The damned made piles of coal stone into which he now thrust his shovel and lifted out a heavy load. Plodding down to the bottom of the pit where walls were made of flame, he pitched the stones into the fire, as did the others, as they had done for millenniums, as they all would do for eternity.

Screeching demons tossed condemned souls into the flames, their hell-flesh bodies igniting like gasoline-soaked rags, their screams echoing their torment for all to hear and be afraid. Again and again, they were pitched into the fire. Over and over, hell's torment would be their lot, forever, until the end of the universe. The awful, sickening stench of burned flesh filled the pit of horror. Then it started over again, back on the path, the condemned souls reappeared, moaned, and groaned in agony, and began another trek down, down, down into hell.

Billy Denton screamed, "God damn you, Justin Graves."

Laughter echoed through hell's chasm.

Billy found himself standing on a tower of rock with only enough room for his feet. Flames leaped up all around him. The chains and the shovel were gone, but the echoing laughter remained.

"What's so damn funny?" he shouted over the roaring inferno, not caring if he sounded offensive. After all, he was already dead. He was in hell. How much worse could things get?

"You fool," a throaty voice rumbled from the fire. "Your fate was not in the hands of Justin Graves."

"He let me fall. He let me die."

"It was not his fault that rotted flesh should fail to hold your whiney ass."

"He said he wanted to kill me. Now you can take Christy's soul."

The devil cackled. "You just want her here with you."

"Nothing would please me more."

Churning flames billowed up from the deep. "She's mine." Gasses hissed. "She will mother a million demons from my seed."

"Serves the whore right."

"But Justice is protecting her. I must defeat him first."

"He won't break the rules."

"So it seems." Black smoke curled through fire-laced air. "But he will when we get done with him."

"We?" Billy folded heat-blistered arms across his soul and spat hell dust.

"Yes. You will be my advocate in the land of the living."

"Say what?"

"You shall walk the line between life and death as Justin does. Seek out and destroy his daughter. He will certainly break the rules and kill you himself."

"Kill me? How can he kill me? I'm already dead."

The devil laughed. "It's called intent. I don't care how he does it. He can shoot you, stab you, or break your neck. He can set you on fire for all I care."

"Will it hurt?"

"No more than toiling in my kitchen."

If that was hell's kitchen, Billy didn't ever want to see the workshop. He had no desire to go back down there, but still, opportunity was knocking, and he was one to always take advantage. "What's in it for me?"

Fire roared. "You dare to make a deal with the devil?"

"Where I came from, I was the baddest of the bad. Give me command over your demons, and I will give you Christy."

"You fool. I'd rather cast you into a cauldron of burning oil."

"Justin won't give up his principles. He'll complete your stupid deal, and you'll lose Christy. I'm your only hope."

Hissing like a thousand demons, flames shot up a hundred feet. The curtain of fire parted revealing the crimson face of evil, white fangs and sharp horns glistening in hellfire. "How dare you taunt me."

"No deal? Okay then. Do with me as you please." This was called the bluff.

"I shall."

"And you'll lose to Justin Graves."

"I never lose."

Justin Graves

"Never say never," Billy said with as much sarcasm as he could muster.

The ground began to shake. Rockslides clattered. "Very well. But if you fail to make Justin succumb to his inherent human nature, the fate that awaited him will be yours."

Billy felt a twinge in his soul. "What fate would that be?"

"Maggots will feed on your hell flesh for eternity, a never-ending feast of pain and suffering."

Being dead and in hell *wasn't* the worst thing that could happen to him, after all. "Send me back. I got a date with Christy."

***

Billy found himself standing in the middle of Deckers on Mason Street, a car bearing down on him at high speed. "Shit." He dove for the curb but didn't make it. The car hit him square on. He rolled into the gutter, sprang to his feet, and quickly patted his chest and head in search of injuries, but he didn't find a single scratch. He didn't feel any pain. What a rush. He recognized the feel of his old blue jeans, t-shirt, and tennis shoes and rubbed his goatee.

Not bad for a dead guy.

People milling around the bus stop seemed oblivious to his presence, as if he were invisible. Could that be?

A creaking sound came from behind him. He spun around. A boy on an old bike rode right into him. He braced himself, and for an instant, the bike disappeared as it passed through him. By the time he turned around, the boy was peddling away as if nothing had happened.

Billy smiled. Being dead could have its advantages. He rushed to a department store window, and to his delight, didn't see his reflection. As he touched the glass, it became invisible. He leaned on the glass and fell forward into a display case with a half-naked mannequin. Whipping around, he expected to see shattered glass. The window was intact.

How cool was that?

He walked into a wall...and strolled right through it into a ladies' restroom. A young woman with long brown hair stood at the mirror, adjusting her bra.

This was better than anything he could have imagined.

Laughter echoed inside his head. *"I know what you're thinking,"* the devil said.

"Give me a break."

The woman didn't flinch. She couldn't see him, she couldn't hear him either.

"Don't get sidetracked. You're on a mission."

"But this could be so much fun." Billy slinked up behind the woman at the mirror and pinched her ass.

She let out a yelp, spun around, and froze, her eyes wide with disbelief. "W-who's there?"

Billy stood real close to her now, so close that if he were breathing, she'd feel the heat of his breath on her neck. Though he thought of lustful things he'd like to do to her, he got no response from his junior partner. He reached down and touched himself. There was nothing there. He was Ken Doll smooth.

"You bastard," he shouted to the devil in his brain.

"Last time you had the chance to kill Christy, you couldn't control your urges. Now you have no choice."

"This wasn't part of the deal."

"Perhaps you feel as though you are being treated unfairly?"

Hell's kitchen came to Billy's mind. Backing away from the trembling woman, he snorted. "It's your lucky day, bitch."

Justin Graves

"Use your powers wisely, Billy."

"Yeah, Yeah."

"Christy is heavily guarded now. There are cops on every floor of the hospital."

"Then I'll need a gun."

Laughter.

Rushing down Mason Street, Billy came to a pawnshop. *We Buy and Sell Guns*, the window sign read. He walked through the door, through a couple of customers, and through a display case of camping supplies before stopping in front of a counter at the rear of the store. A balding clerk paid him no mind...because he was invisible.

Yeah.

Rifles hung on the wall, some shotguns, a couple deer rifles, and a selection of AR-15s. He huffed. Too much hardware to carry around. In a glass case, he spotted an array of handguns, several old Army-issue Colts, a Remington or two, Lugers and Glocks. The latter caught his attention: A Glock .45 with a thirteen round clip. On a shelf below the rifles, boxes of ammunition had been neatly stacked in order of their caliber. Forty-fives came in standard and hollow point. Why not? He waded into the counter, helped himself to a few boxes of hollow points, the Glock, and a couple spare clips. The items became invisible when he touched them, so Billy knew the clerk wouldn't see them float away.

He had to laugh.

At the camping display, he noticed a nice hunting knife, a good six-inch blade complete with leather sheath. That went with him too. He walked through the back wall and into an alley where he hunkered down behind a dumpster and loaded the clips and the gun. Those cops at Deckers City Hospital would never know what hit them.

~163~

It had happened so fast. Billy was gone. Justin didn't want him to die. Sure, he'd taunted him, but in the end, he'd tried to save him. "It wasn't my fault," he shouted. His voice echoed through Penelope's innards. He looked at his rotted arm, the meat half torn away, his hand, stripped to the bone. Or would the devil think it was his fault...his dead body's fault?

He felt a jolt. Christy. If the devil blamed him for Billy's death, he'd take her soul. Justin's hollow chest panged. "You can't blame me for this."

In the back of his skull, he heard laughter.

Leaping into the air, Justin dematerialized and made the transposition to Penelope's entrance. There, he chose to stay transparent in the shadows as he assessed the situation. The cops had torn down the barricade boards.

"Get those ropes up here, men." Sweat shined on Captain Holland's round face. The armpits of his white shirt were soaked. His left arm was useless in the sling. "We need some more shoring timbers."

"This stuff is rotten, sir."

"Jensen and Niles," Holland shouted. "Get down to Deckers Lumber. We need some new four-by-fours."

Penelope groaned and creaked.

Fear creased his brow. "Make that eight-by-tens."

"More lanterns too," someone put in.

"Here's a first-aid kit," a lieutenant said. "In case you find any survivors."

"Hurry, men." Holland stepped back into the mine with a flashlight, swept the beam back and forth. "We have to find those guys."

Justin caused dusty air to swirl around Holland.

"What the hell?"

"It's me," Justin said in a raspy voice. "Your men are

dead. And Billy too."

"Justice? Where are you? Show yourself."

"What's that, Captain?" the lieutenant asked. "What did you say?"

Justin's voice reached Holland again. "Get everyone out of here. Tell them the mine is going to cave in, but you stay here. We need to talk."

"I don't think it's going to cave in."

"A cave-in, Captain." Justin kicked rocks. "You want more of your men to die?"

Turning to his officers, Holland flailed his arms. "Get back. Get out. The ceiling is going to fall."

The officers scrambled down the tailings pile.

Holland stayed behind. "Where are you, Justice?"

Justin materialized in the shadows and took a step forward.

Holland's face turned a putrid green color. "Christ, Justice. Don't you have any kind of deodorant for that smell?" He batted the air. "God—what happened to your arm?"

"Billy had hold of my wrist. I tried to save him, but he fell anyway."

"I'm gonna be sick."

"How do you think I feel?"

"You can't go around looking like that." Holland rummaged through the first-aid kit and pulled out a roll of gauze bandage. Stepping toward Justin, Holland screwed up his face. "Give me your hand."

Justin held out his bony arm, the meat hanging like moss on an old tree branch. "I need your help."

"What happened to your face?"

Justin knew half his jawbone was exposed. "Billy landed a lucky punch, but we have bigger problems."

"Worse than this?" Holland held his breath, gathered

together the stringy, rotten flesh around Justin's bones, and started wrapping his wrist and hand.

"You've got to understand," Justin said, his voice hollow as an empty drum. "Billy's dead. If the devil blames me for his death, he'll take Christy's soul."

Holland's cheeks bulged, and he made urping sounds, but he kept wrapping Justin's hand.

"Radio your men standing guard at the hospital. Find out if she's okay."

Holland didn't look up from his chore, but held his breath.

"Your turning blue, Captain."

Finally, as he tied a knot in the bandage, he exhaled, turned around, and gasped air nearest the entrance. "Second squad will notify me if they have a problem at the hospital. God, Justice, you're a mess."

"I got caught in a cave in. If I hadn't dematerialized, I'd be pancake-flat forever."

Holland coughed. "Your body is falling apart."

"It ain't what it used to be." Justin inspected his wrapped wrist and hand and wiggled the bony fingers that stuck out from the bandage. "Nice job." He looked at Captain Holland. "Now call the hospital."

Holland stepped to the mine entrance and pulled a two-way from his belt. "Second squad, report."

Static.

Justin frowned.

"Second squad, report."

Static.

Holland frowned.

***

In his transparent state, Justin dodged speeding gurneys and frantic staff as he rushed through the halls.

Deckers City Hospital looked like a war zone. He stepped over the limp bodies of Texas Rangers and Deckers police officers. Some had been shot, some stabbed; others' throats were slashed. Doctors bent over the wounded. A defibrillator discharged. Men moaned.

Justin's empty chest overflowed with panic and despair.

"Doctor Maples to ER, stat," the intercom echoed.

A nurse rushed by with a tray of bloody bandages.

Second squad had suffered a horrible defeat.

Justin flew up a bullet-riddled stairwell and headed for the west wing. A warning alarm wailed from the vacated nurses' station. Pools of blood on the floor marked spots where officers had fallen. The place looked as if it had been attacked by an army, the walls scarred with bullet holes, windows shot out, and ceiling panels scattered about. It looked as though the officers had fired their weapons wildly, in every direction, as if they'd been attacked from all sides, or worse, by an unseen attacker. For all Justin knew, the devil had sent a battalion of demons to take Christy's soul back to hell.

The door to room W214 hung on bent hinges as if it had been kicked in. Justin materialized and stood in the doorway, his empty chest throbbing with dread. One part of his soul ordered him to rush into the room. Another part told him Christy was already gone. A question suddenly haunted him. Where did he get off thinking he could beat the devil? His failures in life would be his failures in death. He had made mistakes, and now Christy was destined to suffer for them.

"Justice." Captain Holland had topped the stairs and was running toward him. "Don't go in there."

"I have to."

"You know what you're going to find."

Terry Wright

"My daughter."

"She's dead."

"No."

Holland approached as if Justin's smell didn't matter. "The alarms are coming from W214. She's gone."

"No."

"You have to let her go."

"I can't."

He grabbed Justin's bandaged wrist. "Go back to your afterlife, Justice. Cross over. Rest in peace."

"Not without Christy." Hardening himself against his fear of the unknown, Justin stepped into her room. The heart monitor wailed a steady tone; the respirator sputtered.

Justin felt a chill, colder than the depths of his grave.

On the bed, Christy's lifeless body lay in a shroud of blood-soaked sheets. Her chest had been splayed wide open and her heart cut from her body.

"Christy." Justin clutched his bullet-riddled chest and fell to his bony knees. "No, Christy. No."

Holland set his hand on Justin's shoulder. "There's nothing we can do here."

Justin raised his eyes to the Captain, saw a message cut into the wall with a bloody knife:

Screw You Justice!

A rage shook Justin's body. "It's Billy."

"You told me he was dead."

"He is." Justin stood and wobbled on grief stricken legs. "But he's come back, like me, only he's the embodiment of evil. He's the devil's assassin. Look what he did to her. He cut out her heart. Now she'll never get a second chance. I'll kill him for that."

"You can't."

Justin balled a bony fist. "I've had enough of that punk."

~168~

Justin Graves

"Now take it easy, Justice. Think about what you're saying."

"My daughter is dead because of him." Every bone in Justin's decayed body wailed for revenge. "And I'm dead because of him. Don't think I'm not going to do anything about it."

Holland grabbed Justin's coat sleeve. "Now wait, think like a cop for a minute. Look at motive. Why would the devil send Billy to kill Christy? He could have taken her soul himself, isn't that right?"

"He can do anything he wants."

"So you see? This isn't about Christy." Holland shook Justin's arm. "It's about you, Justice. That's why the assassin killed Christy in such a brutal way. He knew it would piss you off, make you do something stupid. The devil wants *your* soul."

Justin yanked his arm from Holland's grasp. "We'll see about that."

"Justice, no."

With a gust of wind the ghoul was gone.

Heaven's Door

T he afterlife. The light. Bathed in a warm glow, Justin felt only torment, for he could never cross over to eternal peace and happiness as long as this hatred boiled inside him. Billy Denton had to be destroyed, but Justin had to find him first.

"Wach-el. Why did you call me here?"

Mist poured from the light and began to swirl. *"Justice, beware,"* came the deep voice from the light.

"You always say that." He set his Winchester in the gun rack the light had supplied. "I've got to find Billy."

"You need to know your troubles have just begun."

The light parted, drowning the afterlife in a crimson glow. Now roiling, the mist became billows of black smoke. Flames licked the air. In the middle of it all, Christy appeared, dressed in a red bikini, her hair now red and long and flowing, and her skin coppery tan and shiny. She sat on a throne of fire. Chains made of human bones shackled her ankles to a lava-rock floor. Dead eyes stared blankly ahead.

Cynical laughter echoed through Justin's mind. The devil appeared next to Christy, sitting on his own fiery throne, the king and queen of hell together in total misery.

Justin's heart lurched. "Look what's become of her."

"She did this to herself, Justice."

"But it's my fault for being a lousy father."

"She is where she belongs. Do not blame yourself."

"I failed her."

"The past cannot be changed, only the future. Your future. Cross over now."

"I'll never give up." Justin wiped away a tear. "What

did she do that was so wrong, so unforgivable?"

"She embraced evil."

"That was Billy Denton's doing."

"Free will, Justice. Billy gave her the opportunity, and she took it. She shunned her father. Broke the law. The penalty for that is predictable."

"What about forgiveness?"

The vision of Christy shackled in hell faded from the light.

"She never asked."

"She's just a kid."

"You want to end up in hell with her? Don't let the devil take away your eternity. Let go of your hate and cross over."

Justin bowed his head. "Not until Billy is destroyed."

"You should reconsider. You have much to lose. "

"I do?"

The light brightened, and the mist receded. *"You have a visitor."*

"Who?"

"Justice, beware."

From out of the light, a woman appeared, her face a blur in the bright glow. She wore the white gown of an angel and floated in the air as she approached Justin. He removed his cowboy hat and stared.

"Justin." Her voice carried the harmony of a church choir. "Is it really you?"

Music drifted in, soft classical music that soothed the pounding in Justin's chest. He stepped forward, somehow drawn to this beautiful creature, as if by recognition or déjà vu. When her face came into focus, he felt an unexpected surge of bliss. "Eleanor?"

She stood in front of him and put the palm of her hand on his smooth cheek. "I've missed you so."

Terry Wright

"I've missed you too." Without hesitating, he dropped his cowboy hat and gathered her up in his arms. "How did you get here?" he whispered in her ear.

"I don't know." Her voice sounded soft as a summer breeze. "Just hold me."

Her body, so warm and familiar, made his head spin. The sweet smell of lilacs and roses tantalized his senses. And something stirred inside him, something that had been dead for so many years. The music got louder. A violin. A harp. Now flutes and a cello.

He closed his eyes. Every nerve in his body tingled. A voice from the past came to him. His voice.

"May I carry your books?"

He found himself standing next to her on a sidewalk shaded by oak trees, their leaves turning yellow and red and burnt orange. A bell rang from the halls of Deckers High, just across the park. Someone had told him her name was Eleanor. She'd just moved here from California. He didn't think she looked like a California girl: no blond hair or bronze tan. Black curls cascaded over her shoulders, soft as mink, and her deep brown eyes reflected a glint of sunshine, like the twinkle of a star. Her skin was ivory white.

"Thank you," she said shyly and handed him her books.

"My name is Justin."

She smiled. "I know."

Things became a blur after that, the light revealing memories to Justin at a breathtaking pace: high school football games, cheerleaders, sock hops and senior prom. That night, dressed in her dazzling silk gown, she looked like a princess, an angel...the way she looked right now.

He held her a little tighter.

"I love you," she said in his ear with a whisper-soft

breath.

Wedding bells chimed. Organ music filled the air.

"I do."

"I now pronounce you husband and wife. What God has joined together, let no man put asunder."

He remembered how the police academy had taken him away from her for a while. Then FBI training at Quantico. He recalled his rookie year with the Deckers Police Department, where he met Captain Holland during a murder investigation. The Texas Rangers occupied a lot of his time after that. One muggy night, between assignments, he'd gone home. His back hurt from the long drive up from Houston.

Eleanor met him at the door. "This is for you." She handed him a small box wrapped in pink paper with a little white bow.

"I didn't bring you a gift."

She smiled. "Your being here is enough."

"What's the occasion?"

"Open it and see."

Inside the box, he found a tiny pair of pink booties.

"You're going to be a father," she sang.

He'd never been happier. And on the day of delivery, the wailing cries of a newborn baby girl were suddenly overpowered by the steady wail of Eleanor's heart monitor, her life lost while giving life to another. He remembered the funeral, the preacher's mournful words: *"Ashes to ashes, dust to dust, I commend you to the house of the Lord."*

Sixteen years of heartache followed. Sixteen years of sorrow. Sixteen years of mistakes. And now eternity awaited him, wrapped in Eleanor's arms, her fragrance intoxicating, but guilt dampened his rising passion. He couldn't get Christy out of his mind. Her affliction in hell was his fault. Surely Eleanor knew.

"I'm sorry about our daughter," he said.

She placed a finger on his lips. "Shhhh."

"I let her down."

"Pray you don't do the same to me now." Her lips met his.

He pulled away. "I can't."

Her gentle gaze made Justin melt. "I grant you the serenity to accept the things you cannot change," she said and tore open the front of his shirt. "The courage to change the things you can," she added, stroking his muscular chest. "And the wisdom to know the difference."

Desire overwhelmed him, as if her heavenly words had taken away all his guilt.

"Justice, beware."

A symphony played on in the afterlife, drums beating feverishly now, tubas and trumpets blaring. The light began changing colors from yellow, to blue, to passionate red, a kaleidoscope of emotions twirling around in a sensual whirlwind.

He touched her angelic face, smooth and inviting. Her gown dropped to the floor next to his cowboy hat. Embracing her naked body, he drew her to his bare chest, felt her warmth against his skin.

"It's been so long," she said breathily. "I want you so bad."

A bed appeared in the light, its white satin sheets folded down and pillows piled high. The orchestra let out a crescendo as they tumbled onto the mattress, their bodies locked together in a passionate embrace. Her lips touched his, ever so slightly; her breaths came hot and fast. For the first time since his death, Justin felt warm inside.

The symphony played on.

Shivers of delight shot up his spine as her long hair

swept across his skin like a soft breeze. She raised her eyes and met his. "I can't wait any longer."

"Justice, beware."

That haunting voice from the light kept echoing in his brain. What was the danger? A while ago, he truly believed he had nothing to lose by destroying Billy. Was the light simply trying to prove him wrong? Could Eleanor be the one thing that would bring him peace? Eternity with her could be his reward for abandoning his deal with the devil and his vendetta against Billy Denton. Let them have Christy. They all deserved each other. Deserve each other. Deserved each other—

"No." His heart felt stabbed with a hot poker.

"It's all right, Justin. We don't worry about earthly matters on the other side."

"Our daughter is in trouble."

"You can't change that, Justin."

"I've got to try."

"Forget about her. Love me, Justin. Think about us together. Forever. In eternity." She began to tremble, to breathe harder and let out little moans of pleasure. "Make love to me."

The depths of hell were never hotter. The light was never brighter.

"I'm all yours, Justin. Just say the word."

He couldn't breathe. He didn't want to. Was this her promise to him, an eternity of bliss? He felt sure she meant it, meant it with every strand of her heavenly being.

"Come with me through heaven's door, Justin." She rose up and floated above him. "Cross over."

Moments stretched on and on, until finally, he decided. "I love you, Eleanor, but I'm not going anywhere without Christy."

"She doesn't matter anymore, Justin." With beckoning

Terry Wright

arms, she backed away and faded into the light. "Follow me."

"I can't."

He heard the devil's laughter echo from the light. Every muscle in Justin's body tensed.

The light turned gray and cloudy, a storm with bolts of lightning and claps of thunder. "You fool," the devil's voice cackled. "You should've gone with her."

The bed disappeared and Justin found himself holding his cowboy hat again. He felt as though he'd been mentally raped. "What have you done?"

"I gave you one chance. I tempted you to abandon your daughter, to let her spend eternity with Billy and I, in exchange for your wife, forever, but like the fool you are, you turned her down. Now you know what you will never have. You are mine, Justice."

"You've got nothing left to bargain with. Christy is dead."

"And you want revenge. Admit it, Justice. You want to kill Billy with your bare hands."

"It's crossed my mind more than once."

"You have lost your daughter. Your wife made you an offer you refused. Why is that, Justice? Because you haven't settled the score; you haven't finished your guilt trip. My will is inevitable. You will kill Billy, and your soul will be mine."

Justin growled. "All I have to do is walk away, forget about our stupid deal, cut my losses and cross over."

Laughter. "It won't be that easy now. Captain Holland is Billy's next victim. If you cross over, he will die, along with his entire family."

Terror seized Justin's soul. "You wouldn't."

"Holland's your only friend. Billy will kill him, just like he killed your daughter."

Justin recalled the carnage at City Hospital. "He doesn't stand a chance against Billy."

"Question is, what are you going to do about it?"

"You cheating bastard."

Laughter echoed. "You should have never made a deal with the devil."

Justin shook his head. "I see it's a no-win situation."

"For you, but for me, it's a win-win." The devil's laughter faded away.

Shaking his head, he now realized the futility of his plight. Christy was in the devil's clutches. Eleanor had showed him Heaven's door. Billy stood between him and his family, him and eternal peace. Now Captain Holland was marked for death, another victim of Justin's failures. The key to ending it all was Billy. He had to be destroyed.

"Justice, beware."

"I'm sorry, Eleanor," he said into the light. "I can't let this go. Billy has to be stopped before more good men die. Please grant me the courage to change the things I can."

She didn't answer.

He slumped into his recliner, which appeared from the light. Just then he heard the sonic crack of a high-powered rifle. He wondered where the shot came from.

The light parted and showed him a scene in the land of the living.

Terry Wright

Sniper

Crawling on his belly, Specialist Fourth Class Rodney Gantz was sure his camouflaged fatigues and blackened face would meld his features into the surrounding jungle. Sweat seeped from under his helmet as he made his way through dense underbrush, barely making a sound. A bayonet was clamped between the wiry Marine's teeth. Without mercy, he was ready to silently dispatch any perimeter guard he encountered.

Stealth was his greatest asset. Success or failure of his mission depended on his uncanny ability to get in undetected. And Gantz was a pro. His target would never know what hit him.

Commander O Ben Lai was due to arrive by bus. Back at HQ, Rodney's general had briefed him on the situation. The enemy was planning to overrun the base. Hundreds of GIs would be slaughtered if O Ben Lai wasn't stopped...here and now. The United States and the Marine Corps were counting on Rodney Gantz to fulfill his mission and get the kill, a responsibility and an honor that he embraced wholeheartedly. He had trained with tenacity and brilliance, achieving the highest marksman ratings with his Harris M-89 sniper rifle at 1000 yards, the same rifle he'd lived with, slept with, and now crawled with strapped to his back.

He knew the outpost in the clearing just beyond this thicket was heavily guarded. The general had warned him that soldiers would surround O Ben Lai when he disembarked from the bus. A clear shot would be difficult, and Gantz would have only seconds to escape afterwards.

His route was well planned, though. His confidence was high.

Reaching the edge of the clearing, and now shielded from view by leafy bushes, Rodney took in the scene before him through powerful binoculars. Heavily armed troops scurried in and out of their headquarters, a large building off to his left. It had a glass façade and automatic doors, which he thought strange for a military post. In loose formations, soldiers marched across the compound, a blacktopped area sectioned off in rows of parallel sections. Jeeps, tanks, and armored personnel carriers had been parked neatly inside each of these sections, a show of strength and strict organization. Rodney grinned. He was about to show them just how vulnerable they really were.

"General to Sniper One, come in," a nearly inaudible voice said.

Rodney set aside the binoculars, grabbed the bayonet from his mouth, and keyed the satellite radio mike clipped to his collar. "Sniper One is in position," he whispered.

"We're all counting on you," the general said.

A movement through the trees on the other side of the compound caught his attention. It was the bus. "Over and out."

With heart beating wildly, Spec 4 Rodney Gantz knew it was time. He sheathed the bayonet and retrieved the sniper rifle strapped to his back. Settling into a prone position, he firmly planted his elbows in the loose soil and focused the scope's crosshairs on the scene. His nose itched, but he ignored it. Nothing was going to distract him from this history-making shot.

And he waited.

The goddamned bus was delayed at a red light. For the briefest of moments, he wondered why the enemy had erected a stoplight this deep in the jungle. Undaunted, he concentrated on the view in his scope, the bus driver's head now framed dead-center from three hundred yards, well within the rifle's calibrated parameters. Because there was no wind to correct for, he knew he could place a bullet square between the driver's eyes.

However, a professional sniper would not take such a high-risk shot. At this range, center chest was not only a bigger target, but it had a higher kill rate by severing arteries, collapsing lungs, and with a perfectly placed shot, exploding heart ventricles. Rodney considered himself a chest man and waited with the patience of a vulture.

He didn't have to wait long. The light turned green, and the bus proceeded into the compound, stopping in front of the headquarters building. And just as the general had predicted, a throng of soldiers emerged from the bus. Rodney tightened his finger on the trigger, crosshairs aligned and steady. Seconds went by, maybe five, maybe ten, and then there he was, Commander O Ben Lai. Rodney could tell by the bonnet he wore, the blond hair flowing to his shoulders, and the small soldier hanging on to his hand.

Rodney held his breath and squeezed the trigger.

Bang.

A perfect chest shot. Now Rodney slipped silently away. He had to report back to the general.

***

Deckers Department Store parking lot turned to bedlam, women screaming, children crying, men cursing. In an instant, terror filled the air as everyone scrambled for cover behind cars and benches. Someone had even crawled under the bus.

Mr. Carlson, the veteran driver, crouched in the doorway and shouted out, "Somebody call 911." On the asphalt in front of him, Mrs. Henry, her long blond hair in a tangle, was sprawled out, motionless in a growing pool of blood. Her 5-year-old son, Danny, had fallen to his hands and knees and now shrieked in horror. His mother's blood was splattered all over his face and shirt.

"Good God." Carlson wished he were invisible as he scanned the thicket just west of him. The shot had come from that direction, with the crack of a bullet breaking the sound barrier, and as Carlson knew from his Gulf War experiences, it was fired from a high-powered rifle at long range. A sniper, he was sure of it. Fear pumped through his veins, fear that the killer had framed someone else in his scope, perhaps a shocked and helpless bus driver. One shot, one kill, the sniper had to be an expert. Carlson didn't want to become his next victim. In a leap of faith, he dove under the bus.

Sirens pierced the air. Deckers police were on their way, and hopefully an ambulance, though it wouldn't be of any benefit to Mrs. Henry who lay lifeless in the hot Texas sun not ten feet from where Carlson cowered.

***

The escape had gone exactly as Rodney had planned. He'd broken down the sniper rifle (something he could do blindfolded) and stashed it in a toolbox behind the front seat. Quickly, he changed into street clothes and wiped the black grease off his face. As he drove down Deckers' Boulevard in his Jeep, he had to chuckle at the incompetence of the reinforcements racing toward the compound where Commander O Ben Lai lay dead on the ground. He knew the general would be pleased. All his men had been saved by one well-placed shot.

Arriving at HQ, he burst through the door and across the front room. The place smelled like chicken soup, which he thought was strange for Marine Corps headquarters.

Terry Wright

"Mission accomplished, sir."

The general was sitting at his desk, his back to the door, hunched over some paperwork. His gray hair was tied up in a bun, and he was wearing a flower-print dress.

"The target was terminated."

The general spun around in his wheelchair. "What are you babbling about, boy?" For a general, his voice was squeaky as an old woman's.

"I got.him..." Rodney gulped. Something wasn't right about this. "I mean, I..." He suddenly realized he wasn't at HQ. And something was wrong with the general. He looked like...like... "Ma?"

"Don't stand there gawkin', boy. Eat your lunch." She indicated an empty seat at the table, a sandwich on a plate, a bowl of chicken soup, a glass of milk.

"I..." Rodney felt sick in his stomach. "Where's the general?"

She glared at him with bloodshot eyes. Some of her sandwich was stuck between her teeth, and soup dribbled down her prickly chin. "What general? They done kicked you out of the Marines, if you ain't forgot. You're nothing but a screw-up."

"I was a marksman, the best shooter on the firing range."

"Well you shouldn't 'a stole their rifle."

"They couldn't prove it."

"Got you a dishonorable discharge anyway."

"That was *my* rifle, damn it. I wanted to show it to my father."

"You're a damn fool for trying to please that man. He knew you were a screw-up too." With quick command of her wheelchair, she spun around to face the table again, leaving him staring at her hunched back. "Your father was right about you."

Rodney's insides started to squeeze the life out of him. The thought of his father festered hatred and spite. There was no pleasing that bastard. To him, his son was nothing but a bum, a failure, a screw-up, and not a day went by that he didn't pound that into him with words and fists, over and over:

You're a bum, a failure, a screw-up.

In everything Rodney did in his life, he strived to prove his father wrong. However, in everything he did, Rodney failed, just as his father had predicted: the Marines, college, marriage, everything. He was a bum, a failure, and a screw-up. But not anymore. Now he was the general's main man. "My father was wrong about me. Don't you see?"

She gave him a canted look. "I see just fine, boy. It was that darn floozy you took up with, what's her name, Sarah Shitforbrains?"

"I loved her, Ma."

"She showed you things that weren't no good for you, and you, the screw-up that you are, you lapped it all up like some kind of puppy dog. God knows what she saw in the likes of you. She made more money than you ever did, that's for sure. Hell, I don't blame her none for dumpin' your sorry ass. She didn't want you, your father didn't want you, the Marines didn't want you—"

"They made a mistake; they know that now. I saved them all, Ma."

"Who's gonna save me, I ask you? I'm stuck with your lousy good-for-nothin' ass." She chucked a mouthful of sandwich. "You gonna eat your lunch?"

Rage rolled in Rodney's guts. "I'll show you. I'll show my father. I'll show the Marines. I'm the best sniper in the world."

"You're a screw-up."

Terry Wright

Rodney stormed out. He was going to show them all.

***

Captain Holland sped to the shooting scene, siren wailing. Chatter over the radio was frantic. A sniper had taken a victim, by all accounts a random innocent victim, and all officers were on extreme alert, barricading roads and searching citizens' vehicles. Weapons drawn, they had no idea who they were looking for or what kind of person would do such a thing. Neither did Captain Holland.

By the time he arrived at the crime scene, Deckers officers had cordoned off the area with yellow police tape. The body of a young woman lay still on the pavement, covered with a white sheet, her blood already seeping into the fabric. In a nearby police car, a policewoman held a crying child. They were awaiting the arrival of a Social Services agent. Holland approached the lieutenant in charge. "What've you got?"

"A shot came from the woods over there," he said, pointing. "My men are combing the area now. We're hoping to find some trace of the shooter, a spent cartridge, anything."

Holland felt totally inept. "Has her husband been notified?" He indicated the victim with a tilt of his head.

The lieutenant nodded. "He's being questioned downtown. We're not leaving any stone unturned."

"This is going to be a tough one to solve. It's so random and senseless."

Now the lieutenant regarded Holland solemnly. "Word has it, you've got connections, sir."

"Connections?"

"You know, with Justin Graves."

"He's dead."

"Sir, rumor has it—"

Justin Graves

"That's all it is," Holland snapped. "A rumor."

"Maybe..." The lieutenant paused thoughtfully. "Maybe he can help us on this case."

"Not likely." Holland didn't want anyone thinking he was some kind of loon talking to a dead man. He headed for his squad car. "Call me if you find anything."

***

Again, Specialist Rodney Gantz found himself in the middle of a war zone, this time Sarajevo in the former republic of Yugoslavia, now under siege by Serb forces. He again wore his camouflaged fatigues and blackened face. The general had given him a covert assignment, one that only a professional sniper of Rodney's caliber could accomplish. Bring the citizens of Sarajevo and the U.N. troops to their knees.

"General to Sniper One, do you read?" The satellite radio crackled during the high-tech transmission. Spec 4 Rodney Gantz could be reached anywhere in the world, such was his high status with the Marines. Burrowing deep in the woods with a clear view of a white U.N. truck and the citizens gathered around it, he triggered his mike. "I'm in position, sir."

"Good work, Sniper One. Now do your duty."

Rodney didn't answer. He knew his call to duty was of the highest priority. Terrorize the community; paralyze the city. A sniper's mere presence instilled fear in the enemy and decayed their morale. The general would be proud, his father would be proud, for Rodney Gantz was as brave and loyal as they came. And he was about to prove it.

With the enemy all round him and stealth as his only shield, Rodney trained his M-89 sniper rifle on a small boy holding his mother's hand as they talked with a U.N. trooper sitting in the white truck. At one hundred yards, this would be a chip-shot. He found the boy in his scope sight, looked at his chest, and squeezed the trigger. With practiced speed, he chambered another round and shot the boy's mother in the stomach. She would die a much slower and painful death, but she would live long enough to see her son's life bleed out on the ground. Now, the community of Sarajevo knew even their children weren't safe and the U.N. couldn't protect them. With the skill of a surgeon, he'd accomplished his mission. Assured the general would be proud of him for the terror he'd inflicted on the populous, Spec 4 Rodney Gantz slipped through the underbrush and made his getaway.

***

From the seat of his white ice-cream truck, the ice-cream man heard the first gunshot, and then the second. He recoiled instinctively and dropped a Fudgesicle that he was holding out for a little girl's wanting hand. A crescendo of screaming and crying suddenly drowned out his dinging music box. Mayhem had erupted around his truck, and filled with dread, he searched for the cause. His worst nightmares could not have prepared him for what he saw. By the rear tire, 7-year-old Timmy Stewart lay face-down on the ground, blood spilling from a hole in his chest. His mother writhed in pain on the sidewalk, clutching her stomach, her hand and arm soaked with her own blood.

"Timmy. Timmy."

The boy didn't move.

A jolt of adrenaline shot through the ice-cream man. Children scattered in every direction, and he feared he'd see them cut down by a hail of bullets as they ran. A madman was on the loose in Deckers, but in spite of the danger, he rushed to the wounded woman's side.

"Timmy. Oh God. Why Timmy?" she wailed.

He was sure nobody could survive a shot like that, but he didn't want to be the one to tell her Timmy was dead. "I think he's out cold."

"Help him. Please help my Timmy."

"You're hurt, ma'am. Please be still. Help is on the way."

She moaned, fell unconscious in his arms, and died.

***

Captain Holland parked his squad car in the shade of an oak tree, just down the alley from Deckers Family Restaurant, where trashcans in the rear were piled high with garbage. His car radio was going crazy. He jotted down details in his notepad. Reports were coming in at an unbelievable rate. The sniper was killing people all over town. A child and his mother were shot while buying ice cream. A policeman directing traffic took a single bullet to the chest; he was dead before he hit the ground. Two supermarket employees were gunned down while gathering carts in the parking lot. A florist, a mailman, a paperboy, they were all dead, all killed by the same high-caliber rifle. It was an afternoon of hell on earth.

"Justice. For God's sake, help us."

***

In the light of the afterlife, Justin watched the horror that plagued Deckers. Thoughtfully, he rubbed his smooth chin. The aroma of Stetson cologne filled the air. He felt uncomfortable, conflicted about Eleanor, but the light was correct. He was needed in Deckers. His problems with the devil and Billy Denton would have to wait. Again he would have to return to his smelly, decaying body and dole out justice for those who could no longer speak for themselves. He grabbed his Winchester, cocked the lever, and chambered a round.

"Be careful, Justice. Don't turn Deckers into the gunfight at the OK Corral. If you shoot the sniper, the devil will have your soul."

"I need an advantage. What do you suggest?"

"One thing is in your favor. A sniper's rifle is not intended for multiple firings, one right after the other. Such overuse causes the heavy contoured barrel to heat up and distort enough to throw off the sights. After ten consecutive shots, Spec 4 Rodney Gantz won't be able to hit a barn door at fifty yards."

Justin strapped his Winchester behind his back. "I wonder if he knows that."

"He does, but he's a screw-up."

"So you suggest I set myself up has his target?"

"You may have to take more gunshots than your rotted body can withstand. Remember, it might not be much, but it's the only body you have."

"I'll take my chances." Justin rode a bolt of lightning down to his grave and dug himself out.

***

There wasn't anything Rodney wouldn't do to prove his father wrong. The general had faith in him. Why else would he have recruited him for this mother of all missions, the most clandestine, the most dangerous of all? After today, the name Rodney Gantz would be enshrined in the history books. *He wasn't a screw-up after all.*

"General to Sniper One," the satellite radio squawked. God how he loved his status with the Marines, the respect he commanded. Even the general's voice sounded full of pride, for this mission was the highest honor, the envy of all Marine snipers. They all knew Rodney Gantz was the only soldier capable of an assignment of this magnitude.

"I'm in position, sir."

In the oil fields of Iraq now, with his M-89 rifle cleaned and polished, he crouched behind a row of 55-gallon oil drums that smelled like restaurant trashcans full of garbage rotting in the sun. He thought that was a strange odor for crude oil. Flies buzzed all around him. Undeterred, he spotted his priority target sitting in an official car at the end of an alley of towering oil derricks. Shaded by an oak tree, which Rodney thought an odd sight out here in the desert, the man was talking into a radio mike and writing notes on a tablet pressed to the steering wheel. The target would never know where the bullet came from.

With practiced precision, Rodney framed the doomed man's head within the crosshairs of his sniper scope and put his finger on the trigger.

"I've acquired the target, sir."

"Presidential clearance has arrived," the general reported. "Take out the terrorist. You'll be a hero, Sniper One."

"Good as done, sir." He worked the rifle bolt, chambering a round from the M-14 magazine. Though a head shot was high risk, at this range, he couldn't miss.

Just then, the smell of oil drum garbage swelled in the air. The stench of maggots and rotting meat made his stomach clutch and his aim waver. It felt as if an Abrams tank had parked on his chest. His concentration began to falter, and bile rose up in his throat; he thought he would be physically ill. Holding his breath, he fought for control of his senses and his rifle. This would be the big kill. He dared not fail now or his father would be proven right. The general would discharge him from the Marines as a disgrace to the sniper corps. No. He had to finish his mission in spite of the horrid conditions under which he'd suddenly found himself working.

Terry Wright

"Specialist Fourth Class Rodney Gantz?" a grating voice demanded from behind him.

He whirled around in surprise. A stinking old man stood in the desert sand, a dusty cowboy hat shading his gnarly face, a Winchester rifle held at his side. Slimy worms wiggled out holes in his long coat, which was caked with mud and sticks and leaves as if he'd just crawled out of some ungodly foxhole. He was wounded, his left hand bandaged. "Who are you, soldier?"

"The name's Justin Graves," he said hoarsely. "But you can call me Justice."

"This is *my* kill," Rodney shouted. "Get out of here."

"Drop your rifle," Justin ordered. He opened the flap of his coat, revealing a bullet-riddled chest and protruding rib bones. "You can't win."

Reeling at the stench of this glory hound, Rodney showed him teeth. "The general gave *me* this mission."

"He thinks you're a screw-up."

"You're lying." Spec 4 Rodney Gantz had performed gallantly under fire. The ghoulish cowboy was just trying to steal his thunder and turn the general against him. He raised the M-89. At this range, he didn't need a scope. Point and shoot. It would be an easy kill.

He pulled the trigger. The bullet tore into the old cowboy with horrendous force, square in the chest, and knocked him backward, but to Rodney's amazement, the apparition just stood there and grinned. Now Rodney Gantz went to work, showing off his skill at operating the rifle bolt and firing rapidly: two rounds, four rounds, eight rounds, ten. Pieces of Justin Graves went flying: rib bones, an ear, and shreds of his long coat scattered in dusty clouds. Rifle reports echoed down the alley of oil derricks. The M-89's barrel was turning blue from the heat. And the whole time, not once did Justice raise the Winchester in his own defense, which Rodney thought strange. "Why don't you shoot back, old man?"

"It's against the rules."

Rodney thought the cowboy must've taken ten direct hits. "Why aren't you dead?"

"Oh, I'm dead all right."

"Then you're on your way to hell, soldier." Rodney chambered another round and fired.

"You missed," Justin said.

"I never miss. The bullet went right through you."

"Are you sure?" He pointed to an oil drum next to him, a fresh blast hole oozing garbage.

"Drop the rifle." a stern voice ordered from behind him. Rodney spun around in total disbelief. The terrorist had been alerted by all the gunfire. He was approaching from down the alley, a Winchester rifle propped in his right arm, and a silver badge glistening in the sunshine, a Texas Ranger badge. Now that was really bizarre. A Texas Ranger in Iraq?

"Drop your weapon."

With imminent failure staring Rodney in the face, he didn't have time to think twice about a last-ditch effort at redemption. He jerked the M-89's scope up to his eye, framed the terrorist's chest in the crosshairs, and pulled the trigger.

The target flinched but kept walking forward. "You missed."

Panic raced through Rodney's mind as he suddenly realized that his rifle barrel was overheated. His scope was useless. Now he'd have to adjust his aim, but how? A little higher and to the left, or perhaps lower and to the right, or left? In his confusion, one thing became perfectly clear. He'd screwed up.

"Drop it," the terrorist ordered.

Rodney chambered another round. "I'd rather die." He raised the M-89 again.

"Have it your way." The terrorist fired his rifle, the bullet tearing into Rodney's stomach and exiting out his back, painfully dispensing parts of his insides on the ground.

Staggering, Rodney turned around clutching his wound. "Justice."

"Your father was right," Justin said. "You *are* a screw-up."

"Sniper One to the general. May Day. May Day." Spec 4 Rodney Gantz choked on blood and fell into the garbage cans, scattering flies.

Holland ambled up to the dead body. "What the hell were you shooting at?"

"Me," a grating voice said.

Looking up with a start, Holland saw Justin Graves shot full of holes. "Christ, Justin. Look at you...you're a walking sieve."

"One good thing about being dead, it doesn't hurt."

"You've gotta stop showing up like this. People are starting to talk, like they think you and I got a thing going to get the bad guys."

"Let 'em say what they will. I'm just glad I got here before that sniper popped you."

Holland glanced down at the body. Already the flies were buzzing around the bloody bullet wound. He looked up at Justin. "Thanks, my friend. Seems you've saved my life."

"Now I've got to find Billy."

"Let me and my men worry about that punk."

"He's dead, remember? The devil gave him the same powers as mine. So watch your back. He's gunning for you next. I've got to stop him before he succeeds."

"What am I supposed to do in the meantime? Hide in a corner somewhere?"

"Dynamite the old mine. Destroy his hideout."

With a gust of wind the ghoul was gone.

Terry Wright

The Baddest Demon

Billy Denton took the high point of rock down in hell's Cavern of the Damned, which was lit by torches mounted to rock walls. The heat had become bearable for him, if not somewhat comfortable. Stroking his goatee, he looked over his new gang.

Flickering flames cast an eerie red glow on the legion of demons assembled before their new master. As the devil had agreed, Christy's delivery into hell was rewarded most adequately.

These demons were an unsightly bunch of squatty-looking gargoyles. Their blood red bodies were mostly smooth, completely unclothed, and smelled of vinegar. They had hairless heads, piercing black eyes, and pointy tails that bent at sharp angles. The horde standing shoulder-to-shoulder swayed back and forth and chanted *Cara, Tara, Shara. Cara, Tara, Shara.* A show of allegiance to their new leader.

This was going to be the best gang ever.

As Billy scanned the hellish members of his new gang, his eyes were drawn to a demon standing in front. He appeared to be older, his skin looking scaly, not smooth like the others, and one place on his chest appeared scarred. Billy pointed at him. "Come up here."

With the moves of a monkey, the demon clambered up the rock, slouched at Billy's feet, and twisted his neck around so his inky eyes looked up. "Master?" His voice came out like gravel on a washboard.

"I'm going to need a little help with these guys."

"Leon, at your service," the demon said, and with a

Justin Graves

twinkle in his eye added, "They call me the baby killer."

"Admirable." One thing Billy liked about demons, they enjoyed bragging about their evil exploits and the ghastly deeds they'd committed to gain rank and favor with the devil. "You'll be my right-hand man."

Leon hissed his approval and turned to the legion.

Cara, Tara, Shara. Cara, Tara, Shara. The cavern echoed their allegiance.

Billy extended his hands, palms down. "Listen up, boys."

The chanting subsided, leaving only the gaseous sound of fiery torches.

"You've been draggin' ass around here for too long. Things are gonna be different now."

The demons stopped swaying and began murmuring to each other.

"I expect twice as many souls fried in the fires of Hell's pit. You got that?"

Now the demons eyes narrowed, and they hissed loudly.

Leon looked up at his new master. "What's the rush? We got all eternity."

"Are you going to argue with me?"

"But we will need to increase fire rock production. Forge more chains, enslave more diggers. New gas lines will have to be run and more wells drilled. The logistics of such an operation is mind-boggling."

"I don't want to hear none of that crap," Billy shouted. "Tell my gang-bangers to get on it."

"But—"

"Do it."

"You don't understand."

Billy's eyes narrowed to threatening slits. "I'll tell the devil. He'll cast you back into the hell fires along with all

Terry Wright

the other losers in this frickin' place."

Leon flinched, paused in thought, then turned and crouched on all fours, his tail angling upward. "You heard the boss."

The demons began to sway. *Cara, Tara, Shara. Cara, Tara, Shara.*

Feeling the rapture of his power, Billy thrust a fist in the air. "Now get to work." As the demons filed out of the Cavern of the Damned, he turned to Leon. "You take care of things around here. I have another matter to attend."

"Justin Graves?"

"The devil is obsessed with him, which works in my favor."

"They are worthy opponents."

Billy huffed. "I'd like to see them choke each other to death."

"They're already dead, master."

"Dumb luck, I guess."

Leon sat on his tail. "Because of them, you get to go back up there and raise a little hell of your own. Some of us down here would call that lucky."

"It's boring," Billy said with a sigh. "I mean, being invisible and sneaking up on people to slash their throats and blow their brains out was okay at first, but what I really want to do is make them piss their pants."

Leon's brow arched. "Then you need to learn a few tricks."

Billy peered quizzically at the old demon Leon, the killer of babies. "Tricks?"

"Lighten up on my boys, I'll show you."

"If you make it worth my while, I might."

"Follow me."

In a whirl of smoke and ash, Billy found himself transported to another rock-walled chamber. Leon led him down a sloping tunnel that smelled of oily decay, swampy and tarry. Skeletal bats clung to ceiling rocks with sharp claws and protested the intrusion of their roost with high-pitched chirps. Billy felt a chill. This place was darker and colder compared to the rest of hell. "Where are we?"

"Down here," Leon said, loping along with a crab-like gait, "are many secrets of the dead, where horrors abound, and the tools of terror are at our disposal. One of my favorites is just ahead."

The tunnel's end opened into a steamy cavern where, in its center, a dark red pool oozed and bubbled. Billy expected to see a woolly mammoth flailing in its midst. "Tar?"

Leon squatted on a flat rock at the pool's edge. "Looks can be deceiving."

Billy knelt at the icky pool and scooped up a handful of the red goo. "What is it?"

"The stuff nightmares are made of."

***

Captain Holland set his binoculars aside, satisfied the ravine was clear of personnel. The punishing sun gleaned sweat on his brow, which he dabbed with a handkerchief. Justin had told him to destroy the mine, and that's what he was about to do. "Get ready, men."

A dozen holes had been drilled into Penelope's walls. Dynamite was planted and wired. In a few moments, Holland would blow Billy Denton's hideout to smithereens.

"Charging." Lieutenant Richter had been a demolition expert back in Afghanistan. Both his hands rested on the raised T-handle. Both his eyes glittered with anticipation. The light on the detonator glowed solid red. "On three, sir?"

"Just blow the damn thing," Holland spat.

In an instant, the ravine disgorged rocks into the air with a mighty boom. Penelope belched and fell in on herself. The tailings pile gave way and cascaded to the bottom of the ravine. Dust billowed up like an afternoon storm.

***

Back at Texas Rangers headquarters, Deputy Ryan held the phone. "I promise," he said to his wife. "As soon as they get back."

"I need that prescription right away," she said. "Lisa's skin is breaking out in hives."

"I'm on duty. I can't just leave."

"Don't give me that *line of duty* crap. Your daughter needs your help."

"I'll get it. I promise. Just need to find someone to tend the station."

"Then hurry—"

The line went dead. Deputy Ryan couldn't believe his wife would hang up on him. He clicked the cradle button several times without raising a dial tone. Just great. Something went wrong with the phone line. As he set down the receiver, a burst of wind threw open the front door and a red tempest swirled in.

He'd seen strange phenomenon before, this one reminding him of a rampant dust devil wreaking havoc through town, blowing open doors and knocking over potted plants, but this one was different. Its amoeba-like form defied physics as it moved about the room with deliberate intent. Papers on the desk began to fly around. Chairs toppled. He could hear faint laughter.

Then the anomaly took the form of a-a...it looked like an undulating glob of liver. Quickly, it moved toward him, loomed over him, made a rasping sound like heavy breathing. Ryan's hair whipped in the wind, and he felt heat radiating from the apparition. Knives the size of machetes sprang from the red glob. His chest seized with fright.

***

Captain Holland's men threw the last of their equipment into the back of a county maintenance pickup truck, which they had borrowed for the demolition chore. "Return the truck," Holland told the lieutenant. "I'll meet you back at the station."

Favoring his painful chest, he slid behind the wheel of his black Texas Rangers squad car. It had a silver circle-star emblazoned on the front door and a multi-colored light bar mounted on the roof. He clicked on the air conditioner and picked up his radio mike. "Two-Adam-Forty-four, Command."

Static.

Holland frowned. "Command, come in."

Silence.

"Deputy Ryan?"

No answer. A shot of adrenaline spiked Holland's heart rate and caused a sharp pain in his healing chest wound. The doctors had told him to take some time off, get some rest, but that hadn't been possible. Seemed every time he turned around, Billy Denton, Justin Graves, or some criminal or another interfered with the doctor's orders. Now Holland's radio calls were going unanswered, and considering the way things had been going lately, he instantly feared something was wrong at the station. He switched the radio frequency to mobile. There might be another patrol car in the vicinity of headquarters to check on Ryan. "Two-Adam-Forty-four. Captain Holland, here. Any unit respond."

Silence.

He switched to the Deckers Police frequency. "Two-Adam-Forty-four, dispatch."

"Go ahead, Forty-four," a female voice came back.

"Call the Ranger's headquarters on the phone. I can't raise my man by radio."

"Right away, sir."

Filled with dread, he dropped the transmission shifter into drive and tore off down the desert road toward Deckers.

"The line is dead, sir."

Holland's throat clutched. "Send one of your black-and-whites to investigate. I'm on my way." He flipped on the overheads and siren.

***

A Deckers black-and-white cruiser skidded to a stop in front of the Texas Rangers' headquarters. Sergeant Baxter looked at his partner, rookie Steve Mosier. "Watch my back."

Baxter piled out of the car and headed for the front door, gun drawn and Mosier on his heels. Strange, Baxter thought, how the door stood wide open, and papers littered the steps leading up to it. With a quick wave of his hand, he cautioned Mosier to stay back until he had a chance to scope out the situation.

At the doorway, he stopped, peered in, saw no one in the lobby. The place looked like it had been hit by a tornado. Creaking, a wall-mounted fire extinguisher swayed crookedly on its broken hanger. And the glass partition between the lobby and squad room had been shattered, indicating that someone had breached internal security. His heart started pounding.

Chairs and tables lay scattered and broken on the littered floor. Signaling Mosier to close the gap between them, Baxter entered the station, his gun held barrel-up in both sweaty hands.

Inside, past the counter, he carefully advanced toward the squad room, every nerve in his body on full alert. Years of training and experience kicked in: clear right, clear left, advance. Looking back occasionally to check his partner's progress, he hoped the rookie was keeping a keen lookout.

At the shattered doorway to the squad room, Baxter stopped and listened. Nothing stirred inside. He'd been in this room before, on several occasions, back when the Texas Rangers and the Deckers Department of Safety and Training met to discuss tactical maneuvers and what they called Critical Incident Procedures. He never thought he'd have to enter this room under these critical circumstances. He worried over what he would find inside. According to dispatch, Deputy Ryan was supposed to be on duty. He wasn't answering the radio, and his telephone was out of commission. Instinct and devotion to duty pressed Baxter to move onward.

However, no form of training could have prepared him for the carnage he found inside the squad room. The walls were awash with blood, some smears still dripping rivulets toward the floor. Bullet holes pocked the walls and ceiling. Furniture was upended, and he could smell gunpowder in the air. Wide-eyed and heart drumming, he worked his way around the room. Gun ready.

Mosier entered the room after him, pulled his gun but had difficulty holding it steady. Baxter hoped the rookie wasn't in over his head. They cased the room together.

Behind an upended desk, Baxter found a torso, no hands, no legs, no head, the severed neck bones clearly visible. A bloody nametag on the torso's shirt read: *Ryan*. Bile burned the back of Baxter's throat. Whoever had done this was the most gruesome, evil person on the planet.

Baxter's stomach lurched, but he refused to vomit.

Mosier, on the other hand, upchucked his guts. The stench of bile knifed through the air.

Baxter grimaced. "Stay alert."

White as a lily petal, Mosier wiped puke from his lips with his shirtsleeve.

Baxter, his gun hand trembling now, searched the room for Ryan's legs and arms...and his head. Under tossed tables, toppled chairs and piles of papers, he found nothing. He looked everywhere. The blood and gore scrambled his insides, but he was sure of one thing; the perpetrator had left the scene and taken body parts with him. He pressed the switch on the radio mike clipped to his collar. "One-Baker-Nine, dispatch, we need the coroner over here," he paused, "and CIT."

"The Crime Investigation Team?" the dispatcher asked. "What happened?"

"I've never seen anything—"

Suddenly, the air in the room turned sauna hot. An unexplainable wind stirred up litter. Baxter froze.

"One-Baker-Nine, say again."

A scream came from behind him. He whipped around, saw Mosier pressing his back into a corner. Baxter followed his partner's terror-stricken gaze to Deputy Ryan's missing parts, his head lolling atop a ten-foot undulating glob of...of what? Raw liver? Coagulated blood? The glob stood on Ryan's legs and flailed Ryan's arms like some morbid version of Mr. Potato Head.

"One-Baker-Nine, come in." The dispatcher sounded frantic.

Baxter tried to step back, but his feet wouldn't respond. He tried to raise his gun, but it weighed a million pounds. Some unexplainable force had hold of him, something evil, straight out of hell.

"Baxter, what's happening over there?"

He couldn't take his eyes off Ryan's hideous decapitation. The look on his face was that of a man who'd seen the devil first hand, his mouth wrenched in pain, his round eyeballs staring out blankly. Baxter saw the same look in Mosier's eyes.

"Hang on, officers," the dispatcher relayed. "SWAT is on the way, code three."

The grotesque being lurched forward stiffly, its arms outstretched. A scream emanated from its core, a scream that hurt Baxter's eardrums. Hot adrenaline spilled into his bloodstream, spurring him to action. He fired his revolver again and again, his mind blinking in and out of reality, at first expelling any notion that this was real, then recognizing the pure evil before him.

As the grisly anomaly approached, unyielding to the barrage of bullets, Deputy Ryan's head bobbed, his arms flailed, and with each step, his bloody boots clunked on the hardwood floor with the clumsiness of a marionette.

Baxter's gun ran empty.

The amoeba-shaped body pulsed and throbbed like a living glob of red goo, oozing fluid from multiple bullet holes. But it kept lumbering toward him. Unstoppable.

By now, Mosier had regained his composure and started firing his gun. The screaming beast, the firearm reports, and Mosier's cursing made for a macabre cacophony of sounds echoing around the room.

Fighting panic, Baxter started reloading his gun, but the glob was nearly on him, two feet away, when suddenly a third arm shot out, wielding a long knife. Baxter jumped back, but he was too slow. First, he felt a stream of urine run down his leg, then second, a sharp pain across his throat, followed by a bright light, and then nothing.

***

In front of the Texas Rangers headquarters building, Captain Holland careened up next to a black-and-white cruiser with its overheads still flashing. There was no one in it. Trepidation mounting, he got out of his car and headed toward the entrance.

A scream shrieked out the open front door, then: "No. Don't." It sounded like Deckers' newest rookie, Steve Mosier.

A guttural moan came next. Then silence.

Holland bolted inside, gun drawn, his chest-wound on fire. The place was in shambles. In the squad room, his stomach tightened. He found two officers down, probably the rookie and Sergeant Baxter whom he'd known a long time, though they were difficult to recognize in their beheaded conditions. Mouth agape, Baxter's head lay on its left cheek in a puddle of blood, his gray hair wadded up in gooey red tangles. From a nearby corner, Ryan's lifeless eyes stared out of his decapitated head. It looked as though it had rolled there, several yards from his torso, which Holland found behind an overturned desk. Mosier's head was nowhere around. There was no one else in the squad room, no one else alive. "Christ."

Pivoting, gun in both hands and elbows locked, he scanned the bloody room, thinking the masochistic killer had to be near, maybe hiding in the adjoining office, or perhaps the locker room down the hall. He couldn't have gotten far. Only moments ago, just seconds, Mosier's life had been snuffed out, his body brutally dismembered and left piled about, along with Ryan's and Baxter's body parts and pieces, like a grotesque game of pick-up sticks. The stench was awful: upchucked bile, congealing blood, excreted bowel matter. Flies were already buzzing around their newfound feasts.

Sirens wailed in the distance.

Justin Graves

About then, Holland heard a rustle of paper and felt a rush of hot air on his face, stiflingly hot air that sent a chill rippling down his backside. A gooey substance began to ooze from the walls and the seams of the hardwood floor, seemingly from everywhere all at once. It came together before him, a glob suspended in mid-air, undulating, stretching, and expanding. Within the glob's membrane-thin walls, Mosier's head bobbed in blood-red fluid, his face distorted: eyeballs nearly popped out of their sockets, mouth agape in an eternal scream, and his skin stretched so tight the form of his skull was clearly visible.

Holland's throat went dry. He stepped back in total disbelief, wanting to fire his gun but at the same time knowing instinctively how futile it would be. He'd never known fear like this before, and he had all he could do to keep from crapping in his pants.

The apparition grew larger and larger, maybe four-foot by five-foot or more. Mosier's head suddenly popped out on top of the glob and waggled like the head of a hand puppet.

Holland stepped back again, this time tripping over Baxter's decapitated body. Everywhere he stepped, he stepped in blood. With every breath he took, he inhaled stank that soured his insides. He thought he couldn't take anymore. "What are you?" he shouted, still clinging to his weapon, yet not firing and not knowing why. Was it the natural inquisitiveness of a homicide detective, or was it morbid curiosity? As a captain in the Texas Rangers, he'd seen a lot of disgusting things during his career. This beat them all with a stick, one hell of a big stick. "What do you want?"

The sirens were getting louder.

A new face appeared in the belly of this monstrosity, large and alarming, with pierced earlobes and a chin beard.

~205~

It was a face Holland thought he'd never see again.

Billy Denton.

The face glitched on and off in horizontal lines. Billy opened his mouth, and an eardrum-shattering scream filled the squad room, like feedback from a rock and roll band's speakers, drowning out the approaching sirens and snapping Holland's sanity. He began firing his weapon like mad. "You son of a bitch."

Now he heard crackling laughter.

The blob sprouted knives, a dozen or more, clinking and clanking as the blob undulated toward him. Holland kept firing. The sirens and the promise of approaching help seemed so far away.

Holland's back hit the blood-streaked wall; his gun clicked empty. The stench of death swelled in the room like a nuclear blast. He knew this was the last moment of his life.

"Billy," a familiar grating voice called out.

The glob stopped and turned to the voice.

Holland looked left, saw Justin standing next to him, his dusty cowboy hat canted on his head, his feet planted apart, and his long coat drizzling dirt and worms. Deep eye sockets dominated his shrunken face, now glowing crimson, but even through the ravages of decay, Holland could see determination in Justin's expression, feel the power in his clenched jaw, and hear his exposed molars grinding together. In one hand, he held the CO_2 fire extinguisher. In the other hand, he held his Winchester.

"Justin Graves to the rescue?" the ghostly Billy Denton asked, cackling from inside the glob. A malicious smile twitched the corners of his mouth.

"I know you're not in there, Billy," Justin said. "You're just a projection from hell."

"Mirror, *crackle,* mirror on the wall. *Crackle.* Who's

the baddest demon of them all?" Billy's laughter sputtered in and out.

"You're right, Justice," Holland muttered. "It's not him. His voice is hollow, like a bad speaker connection."

"You can't win," Billy's voice said.

"Watch me." Justin squeezed the fire extinguisher handle. A spray of carbon dioxide, colder than dry ice, shot from the nozzle.

Knives lashed out from the glob, some slicing into Justin's coat, some plunging into his bullet-riddled chest, some slashing him across the face, but he held his ground and kept the icy spray aimed on the glob.

Holland ducked behind Justin.

In seconds, the glob began to ice up. The freezing temperature caused the apparition to become sluggish. Mosier's head fell to the floor, made a cracking sound. The knives retracted.

"Damn you, Justice." Billy's voice sounded tinny from inside the icy core. "I'll get you for this."

"Chill, punk."

The glob lost buoyancy and sank to the floor, no longer able to levitate in mid-air. The absolute cold zapped Billy's satanic vehicle, and the colder it got, the less it moved, until finally, it became a totally immobilized gob of frozen goo. Justin poured on the freezing carbon dioxide until the extinguisher sputtered empty. Tossing it to the floor, he raised his Winchester. One shot, dead in the center of the frozen glob, shattered it. A million pieces flew through the air like shards of glass and landed on the floor, tinkling about like tossed marbles.

Holland thought that was the most amazing thing he'd ever seen. "You killed it," he cheered.

Justin shook his skull. "Don't be so sure."

Sirens wailed outside, and the sound of squealing tires

Terry Wright

in front of headquarters gave Holland a total sense of relief.
"Come out with your hands up," somebody shouted
into a bullhorn.

Justin turned to Holland. "I warned you the devil was
out to get you, through Billy, but I never thought he would
do something this horrific."

"Then give up, Justice," Holland demanded. "If he
wins he'll have no reason to kill me."

"I'm not giving up on Christy. I'll do my best to
protect you."

"Listen to me, damn it. Christy is not your fault. Cross
over. Be done with it."

"That may not be enough to stop Billy. I can't give
up. You're the only friend I've got."

Holland patted dust from Justin's shoulder. "Friends
like you will get me killed."

The bullhorn crackled. "Don't make me send in the
SWAT team. Come out. Now."

An eerie scraping sound came from the floor, over by
the bloody wall, in the far corner. Justin turned, and
Holland followed his eyes. Splinters of frozen goo melted
into droplets and moved toward each other, now racing
across the floor as if drawn together by some evil magnetic
force. Hundreds of globules skittered about in a frenzy.

Holland felt an ache in his throat. "It's not dead."

"We're coming in," bellowed from the bullhorn.

Justin cocked the Winchester. "You'd better get out of
here, Captain."

Just then, the globules seeped into the floor cracks as
if suddenly siphoned back to hell.

"Where'd they go?" The astonishment in Holland's
voice was laced with a sharp edge of fear.

"The devil's on Billy's side." Justin's hollow eyes
were a distant stare of impending disaster. "He'll be back.

Who knows what form of evil he'll take next time."

"Let it go, Justice. You can't win against the devil."

"This is *my* fight. It's not over until I say it's over."

An angry gust of wind nearly knocked Holland over. Justin was gone by the time the SWAT team busted in to secure the crime scene.

Holland figured he'd be up all night with this one.

***

Down in the cavern of terrors, the pool of red goo expelled a glob of itself into the fetid air, as if hell had burped a big bubble of snot and swallowed it again. Billy Denton stepped back as an arm and a leg sloshed up to the rocky shore. The gore didn't faze him but sent Leon into a fit of cackling laughter. The skeletal bats that clung upside-down to the rock ceiling joined in and gave new meaning to the term *bat-shit crazy*.

The devil was not amused. "Billy," echoed throughout the chamber. "You're wasting time with this nonsense." The rock walls trembled. "Go back up there and get Justin Graves to kill you."

That sent Leon rolling on the rocks.

"Are you kidding? And miss all this fun?"

A hand of goo rose up from the pool, grabbed laughing Leon, and pulled him under, silencing the laughter and the screaming bats. Some took flight, a seemingly impossible feat with wings of bone and no flesh, fur, or feathers. Billy ducked to dodge a swooper.

Fire spewed from crevices and hissed with fury. "Justin Graves is delivering souls to hell at an astounding rate. He could win this deal and make me out to be a fool."

Billy turned a full circle, arms spread, palms up. "He just might impress you when he kills me." Bat skeletons swirled around him.

"Your charade with the blob didn't fool him. He knew you weren't really in there. All you managed to do was kill some good guys."

"Oh, he's steamed about that, all right."

"I don't get those souls, you fool."

"Just you wait and see what I'm going to do to him next...at Christy's funeral. He'll kill me, and you'll have his soul before you know it."

Child's Play

A deathlike silence crept into the dining room. Edgar glanced up from his plate and noticed his wife, Delores, seated across the table from him, wasn't eating her meal. He grumped and returned his attention to his mashed potatoes. What did she have to complain about anyway? They lived in a nice house in the suburbs of Los Angeles. His job at the consulting firm afforded them a lavish lifestyle. He was doing well for a prematurely balding man of thirty-two.

Delores pushed her dinner plate away. "I can't take any more of this." She'd said it in a whisper-soft voice.

He pretended not to hear her.

"This marriage is a joke," she said, louder this time.

Edgar shrugged. He knew she wouldn't do anything about the marriage. Divorce wasn't allowed in her Church of the Holy Scriptures. She hadn't done anything to stop his 'entertainment' for the past ten years. Besides, wives never told on their husbands. The revelation would be too embarrassing for her. Those snooty friends of hers would say stuff like, "She's the one with that pervert for a husband."

Sticks and stones.

He stuck a fork in his meat loaf. What did they know? He wasn't doing anything wrong.

But Delores had to go and open her yap again. "You shouldn't be allowed to work around all those children."

"Why don't you just shut up?" He chucked meat loaf in his mouth and pointed his fork at her. "You want all your snobby friends at church to find out?"

She just glared at him.

"I thought not." His consulting firm was handling the new contract for the county's preschools. He was now working on site, elbow to elbow with the administrators and teachers, and blissfully in direct contact with children every day.

Rising from her chair, Delores took her plate to the sink. "You better not touch a one of those kids."

"Go to bed."

She was right about their marriage. It was a sham...a front. After all, he had to keep up his image. He was a devoted husband, a deacon of the church, and an upstanding citizen in the community. No one would ever suspect he had desires contrary to the norm.

After dinner, he went upstairs, showered and donned a robe, which he left hang open down the front. Delores closed her bedroom door without saying goodnight, as usual.

Relieved she was out of the way, he stepped into his study and shut the door behind him. This was his private room, decorated with reminders of his boyhood, his model airplanes, his old catcher's mitt, and his favorite comic books.

Sitting at his computer desk, he unlocked the bottom drawer and pulled it open. Inside lay his greatest treasure, the scrapbook, which he took in his hands as lovingly as Romeo had taken Juliet. His mouth began to water. He levered open the cover, his heart beating fast with anticipation.

On the first page, a little princess gazed out at him. This beauty queen's picture was said to be the most widely distributed photo among pedophiles. She posed in a white dress with ruffled trim, and her curly blond hair cascaded down to her shoulders. Mascara on her eyelashes and red

Justin Graves

painted lips gave her that certain look of maturity that masked her true five-year-old innocence. Her parents were foolish to present their daughter to the world this way.

On the next page, a montage of clippings from various Sears catalogues showed little girls modeling short dresses and smiling at him. His fingers tingled as he turned the pages with gentle strokes. In some poses he swore he could see the slightest glint of panties. His robe fell open, exposing himself to the air-conditioned room. He shivered with delight.

Now he was ready for more serious stimulation.

Turning to his computer, he logged online as *Lidlwacker* and opened his mailbox. There, he found an email from *The Club* with the daily password he needed to get on their website. With pulse racing, he worked the keyboard. The screen soon displayed a picture of his boldest fantasy, a naked man hunched over a small child.

Edgar's excitement became intense. Moments later and dreamily exhausted, he forwarded his latest find to one of his *buddies* online: *Pearlfancy*.

***

Howard sat in front of his computer and eyed the flashing icon indicating a new download had arrived in his private folder, *Pearlfancy*. A 30-year-old and handsome man, he fancied himself a pearl among pedophiles. And he was good at deception. Even his new wife didn't know his secret.

"I'm going to work now," Rachael called out from the hallway. She worked the night cashier position for Oklahoma City Market. He worked in the bakery department there. Everybody loved him, especially all the wonderful children who came in for the free cookies that he'd set on the counter.

Terry Wright

"The kids are in bed. Bye."

"I love you," he replied, though he really didn't love her. She was a necessary part of his secret life. He had to keep up the façade as loving husband and caring stepfather in order to get close to her angelic children.

The front door closed. His heart rate went up a notch. Now that she was gone, the fun could begin. He opened his *Pearlfancy* folder. The attachment was from *Lidlwacker*, some closet pedophile in Los Angeles. He'd forwarded a tantalizing picture that made Howard's imagination run wild. The line between fantasy and reality dissolved. With his palms sweating, he forwarded the download to *Crotchpotato,* and then stalked toward his stepchildren's bedroom.

***

Mrs. Drake shouted up the stairs to her 27-year-old son. "Your breakfast is on the table." The door to his room was closed, as usual. "When are you going to get a job?"

"Shut up, Mother. I don't need a job."

"You lay around all day watching TV with the neighbor kids. How do you expect to get anywhere in life?"

Darren drew the bedcovers over his head. "I work on the computer."

"That filthy smut box?"

He hated when she started nagging him. *"Find friends your own age. Wash the BMW. Get a job."* Darren liked things just fine the way they were. His room was his sanctuary. Here he could play with his erector set and his model cars. And some of the neighborhood kids would come over and play with him, too. What was wrong with that? "Leave me alone."

"I want the kitchen cleaned up by the time I get back from Deckers Golf Haven."

~214~

"Go to hell." Darren didn't give a damn what she wanted. After all, she was the one who married that prick. His father was the one who had taught him how to intimidate, humiliate, and control children. Kids were vulnerable. In their innocence, they truly wanted to please others. All his dad wanted to do was belittle and shame them. Even his own son, god damn it, so Darren had no use for adults or friends his own age.

The car cranked, and his mother drove off.

Darren's rage boiled inside. He remembered when he was a boy, how his father would call him a dickhead and make him do unmentionable things to him in the tool shed out back. Child's play, he had said it was. *"This is how we love each other."*

Afterwards, Dad would threaten to tell Darren's friends what a nasty little boy he was, what a filthy dickhead. He could never tell anyone what he'd done. How humiliating that would have been. Fear kept him from telling anyone what his father was doing to him, but he could not contain his anger. In school, he mistreated his friends, bullied them, and frightened them away so his father wouldn't have anyone to tell what went on in that shed.

When his father died, he'd left Darren a lot of money. Guilt money, he surmised, but he still didn't have any friends. Since then, he learned that many parents in the neighborhood didn't give a crap about their kids, where they spent their afternoons or whom they were with. That was the trick, spotting the kids who were bored, the lonely kids with idle time on their hands. They were perfect kids for child's play.

He got out of bed, sat naked at his computer, and signed online: *Crotchpotato*. There was an attachment from *Pearlfancy*, a picture that didn't particularly move him.

Terry Wright

He'd done all that before.

The doorbell rang. *Shit! They're here.* Not ready for visitors, he threw on his favorite pair of baggy shorts and bounded down the stairs. Quickly, he combed fingers through his curly brown hair and opened the door.

"Hi, Uncle Darren," Mikey said, a neighbor's six-year-old son. "I brought my sister. She's already seven."

"You're just in time for *The Power Rangers*." Darren poked his head out the door, looked up and down the street for any adults, and seeing none, ushered the children inside.

Now the seven-year-old girl had his full attention. She wore yellow shorts and a white top. Her skin looked creamy smooth. "What's your name?"

Her pigtails flailed back and forth as she refused to answer.

"It's Sadie." Mikey rushed to turn on the VCR.

Darren could already feel himself getting excited inside his baggy shorts. "Would you like a Coke, Sadie?"

"I do." Mikey plopped on the floor in front of the TV.

Sadie nodded and knelt next to him. She was nervously quiet, and Darren wondered if he could convince her to play with him. "Help yourself to the candy dish." He always kept candy on the coffee table. It helped loosen up the reluctant ones.

In the kitchen, he poured two glasses of Coke and spiked them with vodka. He remembered how his father drank vodka, how it made him friendly, touchy feely, and hoped Sadie would feel the same way. If not, he'd have to force her—

Unwelcomed anger invaded his thoughts. Now he wasn't in the mood for child's play. His father's memory ruined the fun again. Darren decided he'd rather just get on with the final act, do the deed and dump the body. Teach one more kid that adults couldn't be trusted, though it would be a lesson learned too late.

After inserting straws in the glasses, he returned to the front room. "Drink up."

Sadie sipped on her straw. "This tastes funny."

"Don't be a brat. Just drink it." When he sat on the couch, he made sure he exposed himself to her through the baggy legs of his shorts.

Sadie saw him. "You don't have any underwear on."

"You want to touch it?"

She gasped. "I'm telling my mom. Come on, Mikey." She grabbed her brother's arm. "We're going home."

Darren leaped from the couch. He'd had enough of this child's play crap, anyway. First his mother was on his ass, then his father's memory pissed him off, and now this little bitch was going to blab to her parents. They'd call the cops, for sure.

He blocked the door with his body. "You're not going anywhere."

***

Deckers Gulch was abuzz with police activity. A small and naked body floated face-down in stagnant green water. It was Sadie Cross. Her little brother, Mikey, was still missing. Texas Ranger Captain Holland and his team of homicide detectives were working the crime scene. This was the third dead child this year. The investigators found footprints in the mud. Forensics was making plaster casts of the impressions, but the consensus was these tracks would match those found around the other bodies. A madman was on the loose in Deckers, assaulting and killing children.

In the afterlife, the light revealed the hellish scene to Justin Graves. He was sitting in his favorite chair surrounded by a warm glow, clean-shaven, and he smelled of Stetson cologne. His clothes were neatly pressed, and his cowboy hat sat comfortably canted on his head. Normally this would lighten his battle-weary soul, but what he saw in the light darkened his mood. It seemed as if the devil himself had brought the worst imaginable suffering to Deckers, Texas: the slaughter of innocence.

"Did Billy have anything to do with this?" Justin asked the angel, Wach-el, in the light.

"Put aside your hate for Billy Denton, Justice." Wach-el's deep voice echoed through the ethereal firmament. *"Help Captain Holland save the children."*

"In the meantime, who's going to save my child?" Christy was dead, murdered by Billy Denton, and now sitting at the right hand of Satan on a throne of fire. If Justin didn't deliver a hundred souls to the devil soon, she'd be giving birth to a million demons from his wicked seed.

Rape was commonplace in hell.

"Patience, Justice. You'll soon have a visitor. She will help you."

"You know I work alone."

"She's the seven-year-old girl floating face-down in the water. She was abducted, sexually assaulted, murdered, and discarded like everyday garbage."

Justin's problems seemed suddenly small. "Who did it, some perverted pedophile?"

The light dimmed a little. *"Pedophiles have recurrent and intense sexual urges, which arouse fantasies involving adult sexual activities with children. It's a psychological disorder that usually does not involve a criminal act."*

"Sounds criminal to me."

"Pedophilia becomes a crime when the pedophile acts out those fantasies. The vast majority of pedophiles do not cross that line, but those who do are called 'child molesters.' They seduce children by offering gifts and

Justin Graves

appealing to their emotional weaknesses. These molesters can have hundreds of victims before they are discovered."

"And one of these whackos is terrorizing Deckers?"

"Worse. What you have in Deckers is a 'child abductor.' These are the most dangerous molesters of all. They snatch children off the streets, take them from their front yards, and even grab them out of their beds in the middle of the night."

Justin's mind couldn't fathom the depth of horror an abducted child faced. "All for their own twisted sense of sexual gratification?"

"Like rape, most sexual molestations are about power and control. Children are weak and easily coerced. When sex is not the main driving force, the pedophile is classified as a 'situational child molester.' His choice of victim is strictly based on availability and not physical attraction. His motivation is criminal in intent and often fueled by abuses he'd suffered during his youth. Abuse breeds abuse, Justice."

"That's no excuse. Free will, remember?"

"Your point is well taken." The light brightened. *"Sadie is here."*

From out of the glow stepped a young girl with tears streaming down her cheeks. She could have been anyone's little girl, so fragile and so broken. "There now," Justin said, sitting up straight in his chair. "Everything is going to be all right."

"I can't find Mikey," she sobbed out. "I was supposed to take care of my little brother."

"Where did you last see him?"

"At Darren's house."

Justin removed his cowboy hat. "Do your parents know Darren?"

"No, but all the kids hang out there. He has the Power

Terry Wright

Rangers on TV and gives candy to everyone."

"Where does he live?" Justin asked softly.

"By the silver car down the street from my house."
Her small shoulders lurched with giant sobs.

"Did your parents ever talk to him, to find out why
their kids were going to his house?"

"No."

"That kind of activity should have raised red flags to
parents in the neighborhood."

"My mom didn't care if Mikey went there. Darren
was like a free babysitter. I saw right away he wasn't a nice
man. He wanted me to touch him, you know, down there. I
wanted to go home and tell my mom, but he tied us up and
started hurting Mikey. And then—"

"*Justice,*" Wach-el interrupted. "*You'd better see
this.*"

The light flickered and parted, showing Justin a scene
in the land of the living. A small bed appeared on which a
young girl was napping. She wore a short pink dress, bobby
socks, and saddle shoes. Suddenly, she sat up and
screamed.

***

Sally's little heart was pounding like mad. She darted
her gaze around the bedroom, looking for the snake. Her
afternoon nap had run overtime. Now the dim light of dusk
seeped in around the curtains. Everything looked familiar
and safe to her, but she feared the snake wasn't really gone.
There was no sign of it on the floor between the bed and
the door. Her mother would be in the kitchen. She would
protect her from the bad snake.

Sally sprang from the bed and sprinted to the door, her
wide open eyes on full alert for the snake. She made it to
the hallway and ran for the kitchen. "Mommy, Mommy."

Justin Graves

Her mother was sitting at the table, a stinky cigarette clamped between two fingers and the phone pressed to her ear. Her words came out slurred. "What did she say, for Christsake?" Empty beer bottles lay all around like sleeping puppies.

"Mommy?" Sally tugged on her mother's shirtsleeve. "I had a bad dream."

"Shhh."

"I'm frightened."

Mom clutched the receiver to her chest and glared at Sally. "Can't you see I'm talkin' on the phone? Go watch TV or somethin'."

"It's broken."

"Then fix it."

"Gee, Mom, I'm only six."

"Then go outside and play."

"But it's getting dark."

"Go."

"I'm hungry."

"Do you want a whippin'?"

"All right."

Mom lifted the phone to her ear again. "Kids can be such a pain in the ass. Now where were we? Oh yah...what did she say?"

Sally sighed and headed for the front door. Outside, the sky was darkening and the streetlights winked on.

"Hi, Sally." Her little next-door neighbor friend was standing by the front gate. She wore blue shorts and a white blouse with a ketchup stain on the front. Her face was dirty.

Delighted, Sally asked, "Trisha, how come you're out so late?"

"My dad is asleep on the couch, and my mom's at work. Wanna play some jacks?" She held out her open hand, displaying silver jacks and a red rubber ball.

"Sure." Sally bounded out the gate with renewed happiness. Sitting on the front sidewalk Indian style, she arranged her dress so her panties wouldn't show and pulled up her bobby socks a little.

Trisha sat across from her and tossed the jacks. She was only five and had the jacks scattered out too far.

"I had a bad dream," Sally said, taking the red ball from Trisha. "You want to hear about it?"

"Will I be scared?"

"I was."

"Forget that. Bounce the ball."

"After I tell you, first. There was this snake, you see. This big snake was chasing me. He was in the grass going really fast, and I ran and ran, but I couldn't get away."

Trisha's eyes got big around.

"Then there was this tall fence, and I tried to jump up, but I couldn't reach the top. A loud hiss came from behind me, and when I turned around, the snake's mouth was wide open with fangs coming at my face. I woke up just before it bit me. I was never so scared in my whole life. I screamed as loud as I could, but my mom was on the phone and didn't hear me."

"Bounce the ball," Trisha said, exasperated.

A silver car pulled up to the curb. The door flew open, and a man came toward her. Sally suddenly felt afraid, like he was the snake. Quickly, she resituated her dress, which had hiked up her thighs a little while she was telling Trisha about the dream.

"Have you seen my little puppy?" the man asked in a soft voice. He had curly brown hair and looked worried. "Her name is Candy. I can't find her. She might get run over by a car. Will you help me find her?"

Though the lost dog troubled Sally deeply, she shook her head. "My mom told me never talk to strangers."

The man bent over. His open hand came down close to her knee. "Candy's only about this tall."

Sally scooted back to get away from the snake's hand. He grabbed her leg.

A wave of panic engulfed her, a huge fear like she had in the dream. "Run, Trisha. Tell my mommy. Tell my mommy." Sally kicked and screamed, but another hand suddenly covered her mouth and nose. She couldn't breathe.

He muscled her into the silver car.

***

The car raced away, tires smoking down Route 22, and the light turned foggy.

"You don't have much time to find her," Wach-el said to Justin. *"She has a seventy-four percent chance of being killed within the first three hours."*

"Please find Mikey too," Sadie said and stepped back into the light.

Justin felt a pang in his chest. She wouldn't be able to cross over to everlasting peace and happiness until her soul was put to rest over what had happened to her little brother. As for Darren, he didn't know it yet, but he had a date with the devil.

With a clap of thunder, Justin dematerialized back to earth, back to his grave, and back to his rotting body.

***

Footsteps and hollow voices echoed through the halls of Deckers County Morgue. Tiled floors and whitewashed walls could not erase the aura of death around Captain Holland. His eyelids felt heavy with exhaustion. He could hardly bear to watch the autopsy in progress.

On the stainless steel table in the examination room, a

child's lifeless form lay in a swirling puddle of water tainted with bloody body fluids. Small organs floated in jars of formaldehyde. Little Michael Cross had been found in a dumpster behind Deckers Lumber and Landscape. The coroner, Dr. Yee, worked skillfully and displayed no emotion as he drew diagrams and took notes documenting the boy's bruises and crushed throat.

Holland's healing bullet wound throbbed. He adjusted his left arm in the sling, a constant reminder of how Billy Denton had damn near killed him during the jailbreak.

The smell of formaldehyde in the room intensified. He thought he was going to vomit. Then he felt a familiar pressure on his chest and realized the stench was Justin Graves, though the ghoul had not revealed himself. "Justice? Where are you?"

Yee grumped. "There is no justice for this kind of crime."

Justin's raspy voice reached only Holland's ears. "I'm here to help."

"We've got to find out who did this," Captain Holland said.

Dr. Yee nodded and went about his gruesome task.

"Darren Drake did it," Justin said.

Holland knew that preppy overgrown adolescent with the silver BMW. "How do you know it's him?"

"I talked to Mikey's sister, Sadie."

"But she's dead."

"I talk to dead people, Captain."

"Oh, right." Holland thought he'd never get used to working with a dead detective.

"I've got more bad news. Darren just abducted another child."

Holland looked left and right, up and down. Justin's voice seemed to be coming from every direction. "Boy?

Girl?"

Yee looked up from his work. "You'd better get some rest, Captain. You're talking to yourself."

"Girl," Justin said.

"I'll be back," Holland told Dr. Yee and ran outside to the squad car, his wound burning. He cursed Billy Denton and got in behind the wheel.

Judging from the stench that accompanied Holland into the car, he surmised Justin had followed him. "Where are you?"

"Go, go," Justin's voice said.

Holland started the car, turned on the overheads, and peeled out of the parking lot. His car interior smelled like a hot meat locker. "Where are we going?"

"Last time I saw Darren, he was headed out of town on Route 22."

Holland rolled down his window to get some fresh air. "Maybe we can cut him off at Miller Junction." He flipped on the siren and screamed past cars that were veering for the shoulder. "Where do you suppose he's headed?"

"Deckers Gulch," Justin said. "He's familiar with that territory. His dumping grounds."

Holland glanced at the passenger seat. Justice had materialized. He was hanging onto the armrest and the dash, his face rotten and pale, his molars reflecting the headlights of oncoming cars. His tattered brown coat shed dirt and worms all over the seat. "Better buckle your safety belt," Holland said.

"Do I have to remind you I'm already dead?" The car hit a bump. Justin put a bony hand on top of his cowboy hat. Dust flew. "Can you go any faster?"

"Who did Darren kidnap?" Holland asked as he barreled toward Miller Junction, steering with one hand.

"Six-year-old Sally Williams."

Terry Wright

"Nice family. I know them well."

"Her mother is a drunk."

"I didn't say it was a perfect family."

"She ignored Sally, thought of her as a nuisance, and put her in danger by telling her to go outside and play after dark."

"We can't watch our kids every second, Justice."

"Don't people understand? Molesters and abductors are a fact of life. They are out there. You can't recognize them because they blend into the community. They appear to be upstanding citizens, usually have families of their own, and they hold respectable jobs and live in tidy homes that hide their despicable secrets."

"And most of them are never discovered," Holland added. "We can't stop them all."

"But parents can protect their children by paying attention to them, taking an interest in their activities, especially around the neighborhood, and watching over them when they are outside playing. Too many parents take their children's safety for granted."

"I may be guilty of that from time to time."

"It only takes one time—"

A silver BMW shot through the intersection at Miller Junction.

"There he is." Holland accelerated, and within moments the cruiser was riding the Beamer's rear bumper.

Darren hit the gas. The chase was on.

***

Darren Drake, the dickhead, had enough of this bullshit. The cops were on his tail, and the little bitch in the back seat was screaming like a possessed demon.

"Let me go. Let me go."

"Shut up, you little brat."

She was tied up real good, but he didn't have any duct tape to put over her mouth.

"I want my mommy."

He shot a glance to the rearview mirror, which brightly reflected the cruiser's emergency lights. One cop car behind him was all he saw, but he was sure they'd called for backup. If he was going to get away, he'd have to do something pretty damn quick. Maybe he could get the cop car to back off.

Darren slammed on the brakes and braced for a jolt.

The cop car crashed into the back of his BMW.

Metal crunched and glass shattered. The blinding lights went out behind him. Wrestling the steering wheel, he shot a glance to the rearview and saw the cruiser crash into a guardrail and explode into flames. It rolled a few times and slammed into a signpost.

"Ya dumb bastards." He cackled. "Now you're all mine, sweetheart," he said to the little bitch, now frozen in fear on the back seat. The silence was a welcome relief.

Ten miles down the highway, he found the dirt road that wound its way through a heavily forested valley toward Deckers Gulch. He'd been here many times before. The most recent time he'd dumped Sadie's body. This time he was going to dig a grave. It was going to be a lot of work, but nobody would find this little girl's body.

"I want my mommy."

So much for peace and quiet. "Shut up."

***

Justin gritted his molars and hoped he wouldn't lose them in the crash. Captain Holland hadn't reacted fast enough to the BMW's brake lights. He'd swerved to the right but still caught the Beamer's rear bumper. The swerve turned into a skid, and the guardrail might as well have been a brick wall. Everything started spinning and flipping, crashing and banging. Justin didn't know what was worse, the jarring impacts with the ground or the searing heat of the fire as the fuel tank exploded. He tumbled around the inside the car like laundry in a dryer. Now he wished he'd fastened his seat belt.

Holland let out a guttural scream.

A door flew open, and Justin found himself sliding across the pavement, his left arm bone torn from its socket and flames chewing on his long brown coat. His cowboy hat flew off into the darkness. Whatever meat he had left on his elbow was now grated to the bone. The squad car banged and crashed down the shoulder ahead of him, a ball of whirling fire that hit a signpost and landed upside down, the wheels spinning wildly.

The BMW sped away into the night.

Justin came to rest on his back, the Texas night sky ablaze with stars. He knew his wife was waiting for him somewhere up there. He'd find peace with her, no more misery and death. However, his time on earth wasn't up yet. He still had to free his daughter's soul from the devil. So everything good that awaited him in eternity would just have to wait a little longer.

He got up and stamped his feet. His right ankle was giving him trouble, pointing his toes to the right, and he struggled to get his left arm bone back into its shoulder socket. One good thing about being dead, it didn't hurt.

He staggered toward the burning car with deep concern for Captain Holland's condition.

***

Darren found the place he was looking for and parked the BMW between the trees. The little bitch started screaming her head off again.

"Go ahead, sweetheart. Ain't nobody going to hear you out here."

"Let me go home."

He hit the trunk release button and got out of the car.

The Coleman lantern lit, he grabbed the shovel, a hunting knife, and a blanket so his knees wouldn't get stuck with pine needles. Next, he yanked the little bitch out of the car, and with the hunting knife, cut the ropes binding her feet. He couldn't wait to get under that little dress of hers.

"Now walk that way."

"It's dark."

"Shut up and walk."

"Please, mister. I'm afraid."

Darren grinned. "It'll be over before you know it."

The swaying lantern made the shadows slant this way and that. A slight breeze rustled the pines. There was no path, so the little bitch kept getting tangled up in the underbrush. He had to carry her half the way. About fifty yards into the woods, he came to the small clearing he was looking for. The ground was level here. He laid out the blanket. "Sit."

"Untie my hands. The ropes are hurting me."

"Shut up."

Now for the hard part. Work before play. Slamming the shovel into hard earth, he went about his task feverishly, knowing full well the finality of what he was doing. The hole didn't have to be very big, but it had to be deep. The cops were never going to find this little bitch.

***

Even as fire chewed up the hem of his long coat, Justin limped toward the burning car. It rested on its roof. Flames leaped from the trunk area and quickly invaded the car's interior. Hanging by his seat belt, Captain Holland wasn't moving. Justin reached in and pressed the buckle release. Holland slumped to the ceiling.

"Come on, Captain. You've got to get out of here."

His body was dead weight. With the flames lapping closer, Justin struggled to pull him out through the driver's window, all the while knowing the BMW was getting farther away. Should he abandon the Captain and go after Sally and her captor?

Save the children, the light had said.

But he couldn't let his ex-boss and best friend burn to death. Besides, three hours hadn't lapsed yet. Wach-el could have been stating statistics on the conservative side. There had to be enough time left to save little Sally and Captain Holland.

With great effort, Justin managed to get Holland halfway out the window by the time his pant legs caught fire. He regained consciousness and started screaming. "Help. Help."

"Crawl, Captain." Justin reached around the doorpost and released the fire extinguisher. As Holland scrambled clear of the car, Justin sprayed the Captain's burning pants with white powder, which roared from the extinguisher's nozzle. Then he turned the spray on his own flaming coat.

Smoldering, Justin and Holland sat on the pavement, back to back, the flaming car illuminating the area around them. Holland was breathing hard. Justin stared into the darkness. "I've got to find them."

"Go ahead." Holland gulped air. "But they won't be easy to track down."

Justin rubbed his fleshless chin. "Deckers Gulch is a big place. I figure he'll stay high and take the jeep trails."

"Where's your cowboy hat?"

A wind came up. Justin's hat rolled to him like a tumbleweed.

"How'd you do that?"

He donned his hat. "Wish me luck," and he was gone.

In spirit form, Justin flew over the ground like a stealth fighter. His night vision was like an owl's, his hearing acutely tuned as any bat. Human activity below would not go undetected, but Deckers Gulch was a wilderness area with five thousand square miles of forest and rugged terrain.

Time was running out for Sally Williams.

***

Darren had been digging for an hour. The grave was deep enough.

"I'm cold," Sally whimpered. "And hungry. Take me home."

He clawed his way out of the hole and scrambled over the pile of dirt. "I've had enough of your bellyaching." He tossed the shovel down beside the hole. "What do you think this is, some kind of picnic?" He dropped to his knees on the blanket and unzipped his zipper. In the lantern light, her eyes went wide with terror as he exposed himself. "Ever see one of these?"

She started screaming.

"You can touch it if you want."

She kept screaming.

"This is child's play," Darren shouted. "This is how we love each other, but you'll never live to tell my friends that I'm a dickhead. You won't tell anyone." Now he was really getting excited.

A horrible odor came in on the breeze. *Skunk?*

The little bitch screamed louder.

He tried to ignore the ballooning stench. "Touch it. I'm your father. Do as I tell you. Touch it. Touch it." His stomach started churning. A skunk must've fallen into the hole. Or maybe it was a whole family of skunks. The stench was ruining his good mood.

Then a grating voice came from the grave he'd just dug. "Darren."

Panic shot through him like a rifle blast. *What?* He quickly put himself away. He'd never been caught with his pants down before. Now everyone would know he was a dickhead. It would be humiliating. He couldn't let that happen. Whoever spoke from the grave would have to be buried there...right alongside the little bitch.

Darren grabbed the hunting knife and peered over the pile of dirt. To his amazement, a smelly old cowboy with gray hair glared up at him with red eyes aglow. He was lying in the bottom of the grave like it was a hammock on a Caribbean beach.

Darren showed him the knife. "Who the hell are you?"

"My name is Justin Graves," the cowboy said. "But you can call me Justice."

Darren twisted the knife at him. "Your name is mud, mister."

Justin rose up like Christ on Easter Sunday. "We'll see about that."

This was way beyond anything Darren could handle. His mental condition was on overload anyway. Now his only thought was to save himself, and what better leverage would he have than the little bitch. He turned around, yanked her off the blanket, and held her from behind with the knife blade across her throat. "Back off. I'll kill her, I tell ya."

Justin floated backward. "Don't hurt her."

Sally bit Darren's hand, the one that held the knife. Her teeth broke skin and dug into flesh.

Darren let out a yell and tried to pull his hand from her clamped teeth. He dropped the knife. She stomped on his foot. He tried to push her away, but she wouldn't let go of his hand. In all the confusion, the old cowboy was suddenly on him. A bony fist cracked against his temple. He saw stars spinning dizzily.

The ghoul grabbed the girl.

Confused and disoriented, all Darren could think to do now was run. And run like hell, but he tripped over the goddamned shovel he'd tossed on the ground next to the grave. The hole rushed up to meet him. When his face hit the bottom, his neck bones cracked. Everything went black.

***

The next day, Captain Holland strode up to Sally's doorstep. She ran out with open arms. "Did you bring Justice?"

"He's around here somewhere, I'm sure."

Sally hugged Holland's neck. "Justice needs a bath."

"Hello, Captain." Mrs. Williams stood at the open door, sober as a nun on Christmas morning. "I'll never take Sally for granted again."

Her husband stepped up behind her. "We're grateful to you, Captain."

"She's a lucky girl." Holland set her down.

"I bit the bad man." Sally twirled around in her dress.

Trisha ran up to her. "Want to play some jacks?" She held out a handful of silver jacks and a red rubber ball.

"Sure." They sat facing each other on the sidewalk. "But I get to toss them this time."

Mr. Williams asked, "What have you learned about Darren Drake? How many victims?"

"One victim is too many. Darren was just a small part of a vast network of pedophile, molesters, and abductors in this country. We seized his computer and hacked into his email contacts. Arrests are being made as we speak, from

Los Angeles to Oklahoma City and beyond."

A breeze stirred the air. The smell of decay nearly overpowered Captain Holland.

"It's Justice," Sally squealed. "Pee-whew."

Justin materialized in front of Holland. "How are you feeling, Captain?"

"I've been beaten, shot, and set on fire. How do you think I feel?"

"Glad to be alive, I'm sure."

"Well, you're not looking so good either."

Justin limped to Sally and knelt to her level. "And how's my little hero?"

"I love you, Justice." She bounced the red ball and scooped up jacks.

Mrs. Williams smiled at her. "Children are so innocent. How could anyone prey on them?"

Justin stood, favoring his right foot. "Pedophilia is the soil from which molesters and abductors grow. It's the dirt of the devil. There's nothing you can do to stop the perverse, but you can watch over your children and give pedophiles one less target to go after."

"Good advice, Justice," Mrs. Williams said. "We've learn our lesson."

"Now if you'll excuse me." Justin tipped his cowboy hat. "I have other matters to attend, namely one Billy Denton."

"Revenge is a dead end street, Justice," Holland said. "When are you going to let it go?"

"When I get *my* daughter back."

"What about her funeral? Don't tell me you're going to miss that important event in her life, as well."

"No. I've learned my lesson too."

With a gust of wind, the ghoul was gone.

Roses for the Dead

J ustin Graves alighted on the sun-drenched grounds of Deckers Memorial Gardens, up near a stand of trees that overlooked a green landscape and tombstones planted in perfect rows. He'd attended more than his fair share of funerals. A month ago he was guest of honor at his own interment, and today he'd come to bury his daughter, Christy.

Inhaling the scent of mowed grass, he could see her polished coffin on a bier next to a freshly dug grave, the mound of dirt covered with a blue tarp. His hollow chest panged, not from the gunshot wounds that killed him, but from a terrible guilt eating his insides like maggots on spoiled meat. If he'd been a better father, his daughter would still be alive.

Mourners gathered around the gravesite. Some sat in folding chairs, others stood under a black canopy that shaded an array of flowers and wreaths and burning candles. Bits of hushed conversation reached his rotted ears.

"Poor girl," someone said. "She should've dumped that boyfriend of hers a long time ago."

"She deserved better than Billy Denton."

"Can you imagine being murdered by a man who professed to love you?"

"Her father tried to keep them apart."

"He didn't try hard enough."

"Some kids just can't be helped," someone else added.

Justin swallowed dust. No one could understand how it had been with them, the constant power-struggle between father and daughter. He'd tried, damn it, tried to warn her about Billy, but she wouldn't listen.

"He loves me, Dad."

"What do you know about love?"

"I hate you."

Justin hobbled toward the casket, dragging his broken right foot, a casualty of the car wreck he and Captain Holland had survived while chasing the child abductor.

Survived? Justin huffed. How strange he'd thought of that word. However, being dead afforded him some advantages. His approach to the grave went completely undetected.

Removing his dusty cowboy hat, he reached out a bandaged hand and touched Christy's casket. His rotted fingers felt the polished wood and brass handles, and he could smell the fragrance of a dozen white roses that lay on the coffin lid. But no matter how beautiful the setting, the thought of his daughter lying inside that dark box wrenched his battered soul. He would cry if his dry eye sockets would let him. She was only sixteen years old. How he wished he could savor the warmth of her smile one more time, hear her songbird voice, if only for a moment.

A car door slammed behind him. Captain Harold Holland exited a police cruiser parked at the curb. He paused a moment, donned a gray cowboy hat and surveyed the scene. The pudgy, round-faced Texas Ranger wore a black bow tie, his finest western suit, and polished boots. A circle-star badge glistened from his chest, but the blue and white sling on his left arm looked out of place. Bags under his eyes told Justin his partner hadn't slept well.

As the captain approached, Justin glanced down at his own apparel. The circle-star badge pinned to his dirty brown coat may have shined like brand new, but when he spread the filthy lapels, he stared hauntingly at the scattered array of bullet holes in his chest and the slash wounds that would never heal. Worms wriggled out between exposed rib bones. His muddy cowboy boots needed a good buffing, as well. This was no way to dress for his daughter's funeral, but these were the clothes he was buried in; these were the clothes he was condemned to wear whenever he crawled from his grave.

Subdued voices greeted the captain as mourners gathered around him, some holding umbrellas against a punishing sun.

"How's your shoulder?" someone asked.

"Hurts like hell," he grumped. "Bullets tend to do that."

"Is it true about you and Justin Graves?" a woman chimed in. "Are you helping each other fight crime?"

Holland tipped his hat. "Thanks for coming." He gestured to the casket. "If you'll excuse me, I've got my respects to pay."

"How did you know where to find the girl?" a man asked. He sounded like a heckler at a cheap standup comedy club.

Pressing on to the casket, Holland removed his cowboy hat and stood for a reverent moment before speaking. "God, Christy," he whispered. "I wish your father could be here, but he's still busy chasing bad guys."

Close up like this, Justin could see the bulge from a bandage under the captain's coat. It may have looked like a shoulder wound to some, but he'd been shot in the upper chest, under his clavicle, which caused excruciating pain when he moved his arm. Thus the sling. He was lucky Billy Denton didn't kill him during the breakout at Decker's City Jail.

Holland set his palm on the coffin. "Your father was a damn good man. I'm sorry you two didn't get along, but I

Terry Wright

want you to know he loved you very much." Holland
paused, inhaled slowly and winced. "I blame myself, you
know. If only I'd given him more time off work to spend
with you...but you've got to understand; he was my best
detective. I needed him."

Head bowed, he signed.

"Okay, you needed him, too. Deckers needed him.
Hell, the whole damn state of Texas needed him. I
shouldn't have been so selfish. I'm sorry." The captain's
chin quivered as he fought back tears.

Best friends were hard to find, Justin knew, but the
captain had no call blaming himself for what happened.

"Justin's in a tight jam now, Christy," Holland went
on, his expression dark. "You see...he told me about the
deal he'd made with the devil: one hundred souls in
exchange for yours. It's insane."

Justin didn't think so. Guilt was a powerful motivator,
redemption a worthy goal. Love would conquer all,
including the devil, or so Justin hoped.

"If he'd just let you go," Holland added, "he could
cross over to eternal peace and happiness with Eleanor, but
he won't, so he's stuck in the afterlife, walking the line
between life and death, still chasing bad guys. He thinks
it's his fault you turned to a life of crime. We all know it
was Billy's fault, but your father's so damn stubborn."

Justin felt compelled to materialize so only Captain
Holland could see him. The transformation produced a gust
of wind that swirled around the mourners, tugging at
umbrellas and clothing and causing a moment of alarm. It
only took a split second for him to appear next to Holland.
"It's my fault, Captain. Not yours."

Holland jumped back, his face pinched as he waved
his hat in an effort to ward off the stench. He must've
known better than to say anything, or the others would see

him talking to himself and think he'd gone mad.

"I put my job before my daughter. Now our eternity is at stake. The question is, do Christy and I spend it together in hell with the devil, or together in heaven with Eleanor?"

Turning shoulder-to-shoulder with his dead detective, Holland spoke out the corner of his mouth. "You scared the crap out of me, Justice."

"We were never a family. Her mother died in childbirth. Christy blamed herself. I buried myself in my work. Now I have to pay the price. It's my problem. You stay out of it."

"I want Billy Denton stopped just as bad as you do." Holland's whispered tone sounded firm on that point.

"What chance do you stand against a demon from hell?"

"That punk doesn't scare me." He indicated the sling. "I took one bullet from him already."

"You got lucky. He could've killed you."

"And now I've got to watch my back because a damn ghost is out to kill me. How am I going to explain that to Sandra?"

"Your wife doesn't need to know. I'll protect you."

"Yeah. How did that turn out for Billy Denton?"

Justin looked at his bandaged left arm and hand, recalled how he'd tried to save Billy from falling to his death inside the old mine. It wasn't Justin's fault that his rotted flesh had turned to mush in Billy's desperate grasp. And word got around hell that Billy and the devil had a mutual enemy in Justin Graves, so they'd teamed up against him.

"Billy has the same powers I do, only none of the rules. I'm not allowed to use violence—"

"They set you up to fail, Justice." Holland's voice was still a whisper.

Terry Wright

"Yeah. Hell is full of cheating bastards. I should have expected as much."

"Then give up, Justice. Cross over. Be done with it."

"You know I can't leave Christy behind."

"Can't? You mean you *won't*." Holland turned to face Justin, voice rising. "Look at you, all shot up like someone used you for target practice. Broken foot, bandaged hand, your left arm, hell, half the meat on your face is sliced up or gone. I can see your jawbone and molars, for Christsake."

"I know I'm not a pretty sight."

"That's the only dead body you'll ever have. It's not going to hold up long enough for you to get a hundred souls. You'll lose by default and—"

"Uh-hum."

Holland stopped, slowly turned his gaze to the other mourners. They were staring at him as if he were a crazy man arguing with dead air. "Ah...sorry, folks. "

The preacher stood nearby, Bible resting in the crook of his arm, a concerned slant on his brow. "Captain," he whispered. "Are you all right?"

"Ah..." Holland groaned. "I'm on some pretty heavy pain medication." He indicated his wound. "Makes me babble. Don't let me hold up the service."

"If you're sure."

"Yes, please. Go ahead."

The preacher opened his Bible and faced the attendees. "We are gathered here today to bear witness for Christy Graves..."

"You've got to be more careful around other people," Justin said to Holland.

"You're gonna get me locked up in a psycho ward."

"...a troubled soul set upon bad times..."

Holland held his cowboy hat low. "Let me get

someone to help you...to patch you up."

"I don't want your help."

"Don't be so damn stubborn."

"...we pray the Lord look after her soul..."

Mourners began weeping, every head bowed in prayer.

Thump, thump. Thump, thump.

Justin heard the noise. It was coming from inside Christy's casket. If he'd had a heart, he was sure it would've leaped into his throat. At first he thought she was alive, banging on the lid, trying to get out, but when the bier started creaking like the springs of a cheap motel bed, he thought she was in there jumping on the mattress. The commotion made no sense.

"...accept this lost lamb into heaven..."

As the creaking got louder and faster, his dread began to rise. He looked back at the mourners and realized they were unaware of what was happening. Then the coffin began bouncing violently. Grunting noises came from inside, a man's deep-throated groaning, followed by a scream...a woman's...his daughter's scream. *Christy?* A shot of acidic adrenalin slugged Justin's corpse, made every maggot in his chest writhe.

"...where she can sing with the angels..."

He dropped his cowboy hat and rushed forward, tried to steady the jostling coffin.

"What the hell are you doing?" Holland demanded.

"He's in there." Justin couldn't believe it, banged his bandaged fist on the coffin. "Billy Denton is in there with my daughter."

Holland stepped back, aghast. "You gotta be shittin' me."

"He's raping her dead body."

"...and know your true love..."

Christy screamed again, but it sounded like an echo from the depths of hell. The grunting intensified: louder, faster, deeper. Justin tried to steady the coffin, but his broken foot gave out, and with his arm and hand bandaged, he didn't have the coordination or strength to hold the casket still.

Pounding. Thumping. Grunting.

Panic-stricken, Justin stepped back and prepared to dematerialize and charge the coffin when a wailing moan reverberated from inside, the wail of a demon in the throes of a climax so intense the concussion knocked him to the ground.

"...and let your peace guide her through eternity..."

Justin scrambled to his feet. "I'll kill the bastard."

Holland grabbed Justin's dusty coat sleeve and pulled him back. "Don't forget the rules."

"Screw the rules."

"No violence."

Justin tugged against Holland's firm grasp, went nose-to-nose with him. "Then let the devil have his dues."

Suddenly Holland's cheeks turned pale. His wide-eyed gaze was riveted on the coffin. "Look."

Justin whirled around.

The white roses jumped as Billy's ghostly body rose up from the casket like a slimy mosquito emerging from its larval shell floating on pond scum. Only from hell could Billy project such an image, Justin knew, and Holland could see it, too, no doubt some kind of twisted psychological warfare.

"Howdy, boys," Billy said, dripping slime. Stacked silver rings in his earlobes glistened, and his forked goatee glowed red as hell's own fire. Standing ankle deep in the casket lid, he pulled up his blue jeans, zipped his zipper, and buckled his belt. "Yeah. I needed that."

"...protect her from evil..."

Justin lunged at Billy, but Holland held on. "You can't fight him, Justice."

Billy sat on the roses, crushing the delicate petals, and turned canted eyes to Justin. "The devil has made me just like you."

"You're nothing like me." Justin ground his molars, hoping it would help him hold his temper.

Dropping from the casket to the ground, Billy stood before Justin, chest puffed out and smelling like sweaty socks. "We both love your daughter."

"Rape isn't love." Justin wanted to slug him, but Holland held fast.

"And she's just as good dead as she was alive." Laughing, Billy grabbed his crotch and pumped his hips. "She's still my little whore."

Justin's vision tunneled. He charged the disrespectful punk, but Holland wedged himself between them. "Cool it, Justice. He's not worth it."

Reaching around Holland, Justin tried to grab the punk by his barbed-wire-tattooed neck but got a handful of white roses instead. The coward from hell was gone.

Billy's voice resonated inside Justin's hollow skull. "No violence, Justice." His laughter echoed off.

"Billy's screwing with your head," Holland said. "Cross over. Save yourself."

"I'm going to kill him for that."

"He's already dead."

"Then I'm going to make him wish he was alive."

"Think it over real good," Holland advised. "Your daughter, your wife, your family, don't throw it all away for revenge."

"...in your mercy she will shine, oh Lord..."

Still seething, Justin rearranged the white roses just as

they were, though he knew they'd never moved. The simple task gave him a moment to cool off, let Holland's words sink in. If Justin broke the devil's rules, Christy would burn in hell forever, and he'd never see Eleanor again, but spend eternity in a pool of maggots endlessly feeding on his hell-flesh. The stakes were too high to lose his temper over Billy Denton.

Stepping back from the coffin, Justin faced the captain. "I've got to stay focused. One hundred souls."

Holland set a hand on Justin's shoulder. "Then let me get a doctor to fix you up so you'll stand a fighting chance."

Justin looked down at his broken right foot, the cowboy boot bent at an odd angle, and then at the dirty bandage wrapped around his left arm and hand, the only thing holding the meat on the bone. His chest and neck and head were blasted with bullet holes. Since he'd made this deal with the devil, he'd been beaten, stabbed, speared, shot up, and set on fire. It didn't take a brain surgeon to know his dead body wouldn't last much longer.

"...and dwell in your house forever..."

He retrieved his cowboy hat from the ground. "What doctor's going to work on the likes of me?"

"The coroner," Holland replied.

"At the county morgue?"

"Dead people are Dr. Yee's specialty. How about this afternoon?"

Justin shuddered at the prospect of lying on a cold stainless steel table, but if he was going to stay in one piece long enough to save his daughter's soul, he'd have to accept some help. "I'll be there." He donned his cowboy hat.

"...ashes to ashes, dust to dust..."

With a gust of wind the ghoul was gone.

Justin Graves

***

Captain Holland gripped the cruiser's steering wheel with his right hand and sped away from Deckers Memorial Gardens. Veering around a slow-moving garbage truck, he felt the weight of a monkey on his back. A dead monkey. And there was no shaking Justin Graves.

Rumors abounded. He had an ally in his fight against crime. A ghost. A joke. How could anyone believe such a thing? Desperation over the crime problem in Deckers? Total lack of confidence in law enforcement? Mob mentality? Of course, he'd never admit the truth to anyone: Justin Graves was back from the dead. Holland had to keep it to himself, carry that monkey on his back all alone.

He turned down Deckers Boulevard and headed across town toward home. Sandra was worried sick when he'd left this morning. She kept asking him about the car wreck. How did it happen? Was he all right? He didn't want to talk about it. Darren Drake had kidnapped the girl. Holland was chasing him when the squad car crashed. The bad guy got away. In ten years of marriage, he'd never brought his work home with him, and he wasn't about to start now.

Although the car's air conditioning beat back the midday desert heat, his left arm felt sticky in the sling. He hoped the bullet wound hadn't started bleeding again. At a red light, he removed his cowboy hat and set it on the seat beside the G-Net computer terminal. Good thing the maintenance boys had quickly readied this Crown Victoria for service. His last car ended up in a scrap yard. He couldn't remember the crash, but he owed his life to Justin Graves for pulling him free of the burning, overturned wreck. Suddenly the weight of that dead monkey on his back didn't feel so heavy.

At Dallas Drive, he turned right and pulled up in front

of his house. Sandra's minivan gleamed in the driveway. He noticed the lawn needed mowing, the shutters needed a fresh coat of paint, and the porch rail listed outward. The nails had pulled loose from his kids climbing on it. None of those chores would take much time, just getting to them was the problem.

He donned his cowboy hat, and as he piled out of the car, the Texas heat hit him like a billy club. Beating a path up the walkway toward his front door, he checked his watch. Just enough time to change out of his funeral duds and be on his way to meet Justin at the morgue. Holland had no idea how he was going to dupe Dr. Yee into patching up a corpse. Found it on the side of the road, he could say. Or grave robbers dug it up.

As lies formed in his head, the front door flew open and his kids bounded out. "Daddy. Daddy."

Cory wore his blue and white baseball uniform and cap. Tufts of brown hair stuck out over his ears. He'd tucked the mitt under his arm and propped the ball bat on his shoulder. And Tina's yellow sundress swished around her knobby knees as she ran. The legs of a rag doll flailed as she clutched it to her side. It warmed his heart to see them so happy that he'd come home. Too bad he had to leave right away.

"Hurry, Dad," Cory said as he ran up to him. "We're going to be late."

Late? Late for what? Uh-oh. The ball game this afternoon. He scooped Tina up in his good arm. At six years old, she was light as a daisy. He remembered telling the kids he'd go with them after the funeral. At the time, he didn't know Justin Graves would be there. Plans had changed.

Cory twisted the brim of his ball cap around to the back. "I'm pitching, you know."

Of course he knew, but what could he say that a nine-year-old would understand? He set Tina down.

She hugged the rag doll. "Mom said I could take Julie."

By now he'd made it to the porch steps. Cory beat him to the door where Sandra stood leaning on the doorframe with her arms crossed. Wearing tight blue jeans, a white t-shirt under a denim vest embroidered with flowers, and with her blond hair combed straight down past her shoulders, she was a sight to behold. "Hi, babe."

"How are you feeling?"

"Tired." He kissed her cheek. "My wound hurts."

"You better get ready."

"Look..." He took a hesitant breath, thinking there was no easy way to say this. "I can't go to the game."

A storm brewed in her big brown eyes. "What?"

He hoped it would blow over quickly. "Something's come up. I have to go to the morgue."

"I can't believe you're doing this again."

"Dad," Cory cried. "You promised."

Tears flooded Tina's eyes.

He'd rather face ten armed felons than his disappointed family. "I'm sorry."

"What's so damn important, Harold?"

"Police work." He wasn't about to tell her he was going to meet Justin Graves. "It can't be helped."

"Mom," Cory shouted. "It's not fair."

Tina bawled.

"Go play out back," Sandra said to the kids. "I'll talk to your father."

Cory's shoulders slumped. "Come on, Tina. We don't need him anyway."

That hurt. Holland watched them run off around the house toward the back yard. He wished he could withdraw his offer to help Justin get patched up. Let him rot—

"You've got a lot of nerve." Sandra shook a finger in his face. "Disappoint me all you want, leave me alone to worry myself to tears, slip in and out of bed without so much as a touch, but how dare you disappoint your kids again. It's all they've talked about this morning, spending the afternoon with you."

Choking on the guilt sandwich she'd just shoved down his throat, he removed his cowboy hat. "This isn't easy for them, I know, babe, but they have to learn to be flexible. Plans change in a cop's family." He reached out to touch her cheek but she jerked her face away.

One thing he knew about her. She loved him. She'd get over it, but the scornful look on her face was something he rarely saw. "I'll make it up to them."

"We're sick and tired of being second in your life, Harold."

"I don't have time for this conversation now." He knew the words were like putting a loaded gun to his head. He swept past her into the house, hung his hat on the hook by the door, and moved through the front room, normally well kept, but today, toys and clothes were scattered about. The washing machine churned in the utility room, and he saw the dark TV in the corner, couldn't remember the last time he'd sat down long enough to watch it.

Sandra dogged behind him. "Are you listening to me?"

How could he not? He rushed into the bedroom. What was she thinking, that all their problems could be solved right now? He carefully peeled the sling off his left arm and tossed it on the smooth bed comforter, all the while feeling Sandra's impatient stare from the doorway behind him.

"What's so important that you have to cancel our plans?"

He wanted to tell her about Justin Graves, but he didn't dare. It was his responsibility to protect her from his job. Being a cop's wife was stressful enough without adding ghosts and goblins and the gory details. "You wouldn't believe me if I told you."

"Try me." She folded her arms and leaned against the dresser. "And I want the truth."

Gingerly, he removed his suit coat and set it on the bed. Anything to stall for time. He hoped the phone would ring.

"I'm waiting, Harold. What's going on?"

Maybe he should tell her everything, if for no better reason than to stop this interrogation. "Nothing is going on."

"You think I don't hear people talking?"

Damn. She could've been a Texas beauty queen contender, but she didn't like being the center of attention, especially being gossiped about. He worked his white shirt over his bandaged shoulder. "Don't listen to anyone—"

"I overheard Mrs. Wells this morning. At the market. Her husband's a paramedic. She was telling the checker—"

"Stop it." He turned to face her. "Don't believe anything you hear."

The stern look on her face turned to wide-eyed horror. She was staring at his chest. Startled, he looked down, saw a bruise cutting diagonally across his chest and belly like a jagged-edged swath of ugly blue paint.

"When did you get that?" She stepped forward, touched his chest.

He flinched. "Seat belt. I took a pretty hard jolt."

"You told me you were all right."

"It's nothing compared to this bullet wound." He indicated his left shoulder.

Sandra stepped back, looked past him as if she'd just

Terry Wright

landed on the moon. "Mrs. Wells' husband said you were trapped in the car."

"I don't remember what happened. I was out cold."

"You told the paramedic Justin Graves had pulled you out. The paramedic didn't believe you. Everybody knows Justin is dead. So he asked you where Justin went, and you said he went after the girl."

"I was in shock, delirious, didn't know what I was saying."

"You started the rumor about Justin Graves. Why would you do that if it wasn't true?"

"I didn't—"

"Do you know what our kids will have to put up with in school now, from their friends, the smirks, the ridicule?"

He turned away from her. She was right. What could he say? He'd panicked when the paramedics asked him who'd used the fire extinguisher. He didn't have time to explain, tried to rally his forces to help Justin find the girl, figuring nobody would believe him anyway. They didn't. Said he was in shock, hallucinating. It all turned into fodder for town gossip. Thanks to Mrs. Wells. There was nothing he could do to undo it now.

From the closet, he grabbed a gray western shirt, struggled into it. Silent. Buttoning buttons. Thinking of a way out of this mess, coming up with nothing.

"You're screwing up our lives, Harold, and for what, your fascination with Justin Graves? He's dead. Get over it. Move on."

He sat on the bed. If she knew the truth, maybe she'd understand. He looked up at her leaning against the dresser, arms crossed, frowning, and felt like he was about to confess to murder. "It's not a rumor, Sandra. Justin Graves saved my life."

She stiffened like she'd been stabbed in the back.

Justin Graves

"He's busted up pretty bad. I've got to get someone to patch him up, the coroner, I hope."

She just stood there, mouth agape, an incredulous expression glaring back at him.

"It's the least I can do for him."

Staring with brown, vacant eyes, she pursed her lips, silent, like she was thinking real hard. Not a blink. Not a word.

"So you see, it's important that I meet him at the morgue this afternoon."

Finally, "You're a real piece of work, Harold, coming up with a cock-n-bull story to get out of taking your kids to a ball game."

"It's not like that at all. I want to go with you—"

"But I'm not going to let you do it to them again."

"Look." He fought to stay calm, upbeat. "I'll meet you at the game as soon as I'm done. We'll hit the pizza parlor for dinner. What do you say?"

But she was on a roll. "No wonder you've been acting strange lately."

"How should I act with a ghost for a partner? It's not in any training manual I've ever read."

"Oh, my God." She gasped. "You've gone over the edge. You actually believe your own lie." She started backing toward the door, wide-eyed, like he was from the Twilight Zone. "You're out of your mind."

"See? I told you you wouldn't believe me."

"Nobody's going to believe you, especially your kids." Turning to leave, she stopped. Turned back. "But let's say I do, just for the sake of argument, believe you. Justin is a ghost. Right? He's dead. He'll be dead for a long time. So come with us to the game. Get him patched up on Monday. What's the rush?"

She really had him on the spot with that one. "It's not

~251~

like I can call him on his cell phone. It doesn't work that way."

"Just how *does* it work, Harold?"

He didn't like the stern set of her jaw, couldn't bear to look at her, buried his face in his hands. "I don't know. He just shows up—"

"You're grieving, Harold. I understand. Justin was your best detective, your best friend. You miss him. But he's dead. He's gone. Your kids are still here. They need you."

He looked up. "You think I don't know that?"

"Then stop making up stories—"

"Damn it, Sandra. Give me a break. You asked for the truth. I told you the truth. What's more, he made a deal with the devil but the devil isn't playing fair. Now a demon from hell is out to get him...make him lose his daughter, his eternity. Justin's in no condition to fight a demon. I've got to help him." He stood, tucked in his shirttails and looked up in time to see her wipe a tear from her cheek. God, he hated making her cry. He shouldn't have raised his voice. "I'm sorry I shouted." He moved toward her.

She put out her hand to stop him. "You're the one who needs some serious help, Harold." She stormed out the doorway.

It felt like the air in the bedroom left with her. Swallowing a sense of dread, he already regretted telling her the truth. Now she thought he'd gone mad. He wriggled into the sling.

Car doors slammed. An engine cranked and fired up. By the time he made it to the front door, the minivan had already backed out into the street. The chirp of tires spoke volumes for Sandra's mood. He could only wave goodbye as his family drove off to the ball game.

It wasn't just a game he'd miss, but time with his

family that he could never get back. Tonight's pizza seemed a meager exchange for an afternoon without them. But even as his heart ached, he knew he had to do what he had to do. He grabbed his cowboy hat from the hook and locked the door on his way out.

In the garage, he found the furniture dolly. He couldn't let Justin *walk* into the county morgue. Dr. Yee would never again trust another dead body to be really dead.

Holland wheeled the dolly out to his car, opened the trunk, and stuffed it in sideways, careful not to damage the computer, video recorder, and radio equipment mounted inside. Of course, the lid wouldn't close, so he tied it down with the dolly strap.

A glance back at the house sent memories rushing to the surface. He saw Tina on the porch, jumping rope. The Band-aid on her knee. The boo-boo he'd kissed to make it all better. And Cory kneeling beside his new fire truck, cranking up the ladder, all smiles under his red fire-chief helmet. Sandra sat on the porch swing, watching the sunset, sipping wine. A toast to the future. Christmas lights aglow around the picture window. Sounds of laughter, then crying, then Cory said, *"Come on, Tina. We don't need him anyway."*

Damn. The dead monkey on his back suddenly weighed a ton. He should've kept his mouth shut.

Jumping in behind the wheel, he started the cruiser and tore off toward downtown, wondering how much more trouble he would get into before this was over.

***

The autopsy room in Deckers County Morgue gleamed with polished stainless steel fixtures, the sinks, the counters, and the table, which Dr. Yee commonly referred to as the *Slab*. He prided himself on cleanliness, as did most of his colleagues, his instruments sterilized and the gray-painted floor kept spotless, regardless of the fact that his patients were already dead. And he always wore blue paper booties over his tennis shoes, latex gloves, and a facemask. In this room, on this slab, one of two, he'd investigated thousands of deaths in his thirty-three-year career, but the corpse he now looked down at was the smelliest, most bizarre carcass he'd ever seen. Captain Holland had carted it in on a furniture dolly.

"Justin Graves, you say?"

Holland's wide eyes stared out over the top of his surgical facemask. "Somebody dug him up, damn grave robbers, shot him full of holes, broke his foot, worst case of corpse abuse the Texas Rangers has ever seen."

Corpse abuse? The carcass stunk worse than a rotting beached whale, its stench overpowering the Smelleze odor control pouch suspended above the slab. Yee's eyes watered, Justin stunk so bad, but like it or not, death fascinated Yee, even the messy, smelly part of it most people never experienced.

He strained to examine Justin's long coat, saw it wasn't only perforated with bullet holes and encrusted with mud, but scorched black, as well. "The grave robbers set him on fire, too?"

"Some people's kids." Holland shrugged.

Breathing through his mouth to lessen the reek, Yee slid a head-prop under Justin's skull and brushed aside his shoulder-length gray hair. Round dead eyeballs stared out blankly from dark sockets, the pupils fixed and dilated. His rotting skin had the color and texture of elephant hide. "There's a lot of decay here."

"W-water damage," Holland stammered out. "It seeped into his coffin."

Justin Graves

Justin's jaw plopped open.

"But his clothes are dry," Yee noted.

"Weird, huh."

Yee closed Justin's jaw then let it go. It plopped open again. "Why did you bring him here?"

"Sew him up some, you know, his face, his arm and hand, and while you're at it, can you fix his broken foot?"

Glancing at Justin's cowboy boots, he noticed how the right one lopped over oddly. "What for? It's not like he'll ever use it again."

"We can't bury him looking like this," Holland said. "He was a proud Texas Ranger."

Yee understood the loyalty between Holland and his dead homicide detective. Justin Graves had earned a reputation for himself, so much so that everyone called him Justice, his peers and criminals alike. However, the captain's request to restore a corpse to some form of presentable condition went beyond reason.

Lifting Justin's left hand, Yee peeled back the tattered bandage and inspected a muscle tear that went up into the coat sleeve, exposing bone. "Strange injury," he muttered.

When he dropped the hand, it plunked back down on the table, limber as could be. "Something's not right here," Yee said. "No atrophy of muscles and ligaments." Moving to the flopped boot, he turned the foot toe-up, let it go, and watched it flop over again. "He's so limber, he could've been walking only yesterday."

"It's all that groundwater—kept him loose and juicy."

"That's impossible." Deckers was surrounded by desert. Groundwater would lay far deeper than any six-foot grave at Memorial Gardens.

He spread open Justin's coat lapels, saw worms wriggle out bullet holes in a tattered gray shirt. Bleached rib bones. A tarnished circle-star badge. Slimy white maggots churned inside Justin's chest, feeding on the dead man's heart. The sight didn't sicken Yee as much as it intrigued him. Where there were maggots, there had to have been flies. The corpse couldn't have been buried all this time, unless flies got into the casket somehow. Captain Holland appeared to be pulling a fast one. "How long do you say this corpse has been out of the grave?"

"Since last night."

It had to be a lie. "Then how do you account for all these maggots?" He gestured to Justin's chest.

"How the hell should I know? Just help him out, doc. I don't got all day."

Yee glanced at the refrigerated body bins recessed in the wall, thought of his workload: seven hundred autopsies a year, three waiting, two toxicology tests, five signoffs from City Hospital. Shaking his head, he looked at Holland. "I don't have time for this charade."

"Justin deserves a decent body when we rebury him."

"He was a good man, I know this, but he doesn't need what you ask. He doesn't care."

"I care." Holland grumped. "And you should too. This town, Deckers, and the whole damn state of Texas should care. He gave his life in our service."

Yee felt certain the captain would hound him until he agreed to patch up his dead friend, but how would Yee explain this case in his daily log? *Patch up half-rotted corpse of Texas Ranger.* It would take less time to do it than to argue about it. Then he could get back to his real work. "I'll sew him up quick, okay? You satisfied?"

"Thanks, doc."

"But the least you could do is be straight with me."

"It's complicated."

Stepping to an under-counter drawer, Yee retrieved a curved *ski* needle and several packets of #4 non-absorbable suture. He'd heard the rumors. Captain Holland had a crime-fighting ally, a ghost, they'd said. Justin Graves. How else could Holland have found that abducted girl way back in the woods? He would've needed supernatural help, especially after he'd wrecked his cruiser during a high-speed chase.

And Justin's corpse looked as if it had been in a car wreck. Lacerations, broken bones, burned coat, Yee had seen these kinds of injuries hundreds of times. They could have been sustained in the same wreck Holland had survived. Accident investigators believed someone had pulled the captain from the burning squad car, but he was alone when emergency crews arrived. Word spread that a ghost had saved Holland's life. They'd been working together to find the girl. Yee wondered how rumors like that got started and ran the suture through the needle's eye.

He didn't believe in ghosts...well...not entirely. Strange noises in the morgue would make his skin crawl. And Grandma Yee often talked of ying and yang, life and death, spirit and flesh. The supernatural wasn't totally impossible. However, he was a doctor, a forensic scientist. He believed in facts. Fact number one: this corpse didn't look like any corpse he'd ever seen. And fact number two: Captain Holland's concern for it bordered on the macabre. The facts added up to something fishy going on.

Yee stabbed the needle through the torn flesh on Justin's cheek, pulled the suture tight, and then glanced up at Holland, saw him sweating beside the *Slab*. "Are you going to tell me what's going on or not?"

"You don't want to know," Holland replied.

"I've heard rumors about you and Justin Graves."

"So have I."

Yee skewered the skin beside Justin's upper lip. If Holland had a secret, he was determined to keep it. "People believe what they want, I suppose."

"What can you do about his foot?"

Another stitch, another pull: Justin's rotting flesh stretched over his exposed molars. Yee wondered why the captain was so worried about the dead man's foot...unless the corpse was actually capable of walking around like some kind of ghoul. It wasn't probable, of course, but still, what if the rumors were true? What if Grandma Yee was right? *Spirit and flesh.* Justin's foot would have to be in good working order. Problem was, the morgue wasn't stocked like a hospital. He tied off a stitch, looked up at Captain Holland. "I don't have any titanium pins around here to fix a broken bone."

"A broomstick and a couple radiator hose clamps should do him," Holland said. "It's not like there's risk of infection."

Yee knew Justin would need something stronger than a broom handle to support his weight. Thinking that gave Yee the willies. But still... If he was going to fix the foot, he'd better fix it good.

From the tool tray, he picked up a cranial hammer and held it up to the light. Stainless steel glistened. It felt heavy. Indestructible. It could work. He smiled.

Holland gave him a funny look.

"I'll attach the handle to the leg bone, the hammer head to foot, clamp it down real tight...if I had clamps."

"What kind of clamps?"

"Go to Deckers Auto Parts." Yee pulled down his facemask. "Get a handful of big hose clamps. Meanwhile, I'll finish stitching him up and get that boot off."

Holland removed his facemask and rushed to the door, his blue paper booties scraping on the polished floor. "I'll be right back."

The door closed.

Alone with the corpse, Yee continued sewing up the face. Each stick of the needle released a pungent poof of rot odor. All the while, he felt as if he were being watched. He glanced around, looked behind him.

Nothing.

He looked down at Justin's round eyeballs staring out blankly. "You are one messed up cop, Justice."

The eyeballs moved.

Yee jumped back so fast he nearly stuck himself with the needle. He felt the fire of adrenaline race up the back of his neck and pool in tingles at the base of his skull. His heart pounded as he stared at Justin's eyes, daring them to move again. They didn't.

"Grandma Yee, give me strength." Hands shaking, he went back to work stitching rotted flesh. No way would he look at those eyes again.

Terry Wright

Police Impersonator

A ndrew Loudon coasted his white 1996 LT-1 Caprice cruiser up to the stoplight on Deckers Boulevard. As usual, he quickly glanced at the vehicles stopped around him: an old lady in a Volvo on his right, a young woman driving a minivan on his left, and in the rearview mirror, a Ford pickup appeared beyond the array of phony antennas mounted on the car's trunk lid. Satisfied he had an audience, he took a moment to admire his reflection in the mirror, his official California Highway Patrol sunglasses and his macho butch haircut. Yes, he looked like a cop, and he felt powerful driving this retired police car he'd purchased at auction. Impressed with his persona, he reached for the phony radio mike clipped to the dashboard.

"Officer Loudon... All clear... 10-4." A tingle skittered up the back of his neck. He knew no one had heard his transmission over the radio. It didn't work, but with the mike still pressed to his lips, he glanced again at the young woman in the minivan. He imagined pulling her over, talking to her officially while she cowered in his presence yet wishing he would take her somewhere to be interrogated privately. Just because she was looking straight ahead did nothing to dissuade his fantasy. He knew what the whore wanted.

Behind him, the guy in the pickup lit a cigarette, and the old lady on his right was looking the other way. Nobody was paying any attention to him. This called for extreme measures. After activating the blue and red flashing lights across the top of his windshield, he lurched the Caprice into the intersection, against the red light. Cross traffic honked at him, so he switched on the siren he'd wired under the hood. The sudden wail caused drivers to brake and swerve as the Caprice accelerated in simulated urgency. After clearing the intersection and peeling away, Andrew whooped and hollered. "That got their attention," he shouted, his heart pounding like a crazed drummer. "Man, was I cool, or what."

Two blocks later, he shut off the lights and siren, slowed down, and made a right turn onto Bradley, a tree-lined street between Texas Mall and the Baptist church. There, a Deckers police car idled in the parking lot. With nerves of steel, Andrew pulled up alongside the patrol car and rolled down the window. "Evening, Dale."

The officer looked up. "What are you up to now, Andrew?"

"Making the rounds, you know how it is."

"When are you going to get a real job?"

"I'm just trying to help."

"You shouldn't be wearing that shirt."

"It was my dad's shirt." Andrew knew it wasn't illegal to wear an old police shirt. Besides, the patches had been removed from the sleeves. "What are you doing?"

"The hard part of this job your daddy hated most, paperwork."

"Was there a burglary?" Andrew picked up a hand-held police scanner lying on the seat and displayed it to the officer. "I didn't hear anything on my radio."

"Nothin' that exciting. How's your momma?"

"The same." She hadn't said two words since the shooting.

"You be careful, ya hear?"

Andrew nodded and tore off, the LT-1 Caprice now roaring down Bradley. Tires squealing, he turned into the

Terry Wright

alley behind Texas Mall and slowed the cruiser to a crawl. Though it wasn't yet dark, he turned on the post-mounted spotlight anyway and shot the beam across a row of dumpsters. Heart racing, he knew his father had felt the same excitement while patrolling the streets back then. After he was gunned down, the other officers took young Andrew under their wings, let him go on *ride-alongs* and taught him the lingo. Now, at 22, as he crept down the alley, he was satisfied to be this close to real police work.

At the end of the alley, he spotted a vacant Ford Escort illegally parked in a loading zone. He was about to call the station on his cell phone to report the infraction when he saw the car moving, rocking on its springs, and he had a good idea what was going on. Yes, this was something every cop dreamed of encountering.

Heart rate climbing in anticipation of what he might see, he rolled the Caprice up to the Escort's front bumper, shined the spotlight on its windshield, and emerged, gun in hand. "You in the car," he shouted with authority. "Show me your hands."

Wide-eyed teenagers sat up. The boy's shirt was off; the girl's blouse was unbuttoned. He couldn't see anything good from this vantage point. "Let me see your hands." Man this was exciting. He was scaring the hell out of them.

The kids winced from the bright spotlight and used their hands to shield their eyes. Andrew moved to the driver's window and tapped it with the barrel of his gun. The girl was frantically pulling up her panties. Andrew got a brief glimpse of white thighs. How cool was that?

Finally, the boy rolled down the window. "We aren't doing anything, officer."

The salutation pleased him. "Let's see some IDs."

"Are you a real police officer?" the boy asked as he scrutinized Andrew's apparel.

The girl swatted his arm. "Don't argue with him, Jimmy."

Andrew flashed his father's old badge and bent to the window so he could see the girl better. "How old are you, young lady?"

"Fifteen."

And a nasty whore already. "Jimmy Norton," he read from the boy's driver's license and handed it back to him. "You want to go to jail tonight?"

"We were just making out."

"Give me your phone numbers. I'm calling your parents."

"No. Please, I'll do anything," the girl said.

Andrew wrote down their phone numbers and retreated to his car. When he sat behind the wheel, his heart was beating a hundred miles an hour, but he was cool. Now he had to make them sweat for a few minutes. While waiting, visions of the nasty whore's white thighs kept him company. *I'll do anything.. I'll do anything.* Her pleading words reverberated through his mind. *Anything?* His imagination ran wild until a cold rush of fear came over him. The boy. He would be a witness. Andrew's fantasies came unwound. It would be impossible to get away with sexually assaulting the girl. He threw the Caprice into reverse and sped away.

"What's the matter with you?" he berated himself, pounding the steering wheel with his fists as he careened onto Deckers Boulevard.

"You're a chicken."

"No I'm not." He wanted to arrest that nasty little bitch, put her in the back seat, and take her someplace private for interrogation. He was the law around here. She had to obey him. Those were the rules. In his mind, he'd rehearsed it a hundred times. It was easy. He was so close.

What happened this time?

"Officer Loudon is a chicken, a chicken."

"I'm not a chicken." He floored the accelerator, passing cars with imagined impunity. "Next time. Next time I'll show you I'm no chicken."

***

It was going on closing time at Deckers Bar and Grill when Tracy Farrow tossed back her auburn hair and threw the last dart. "Ten."

"Yes."

All her friends gathered around, patted her back, and shrieked with joy. Martin, her worthy opponent, offered up the prize. "One more beer for Tracy," he shouted to the waitress. "It's on me."

"Last call," she announced.

Tracy really didn't want another beer; she'd had two already, and her kidneys were floating, but it was Friday night, what the heck? She sat at the bar. The pep rally wasn't until noon tomorrow. She could sleep in.

"You're a lucky girl," Martin said and sat next to her. "Pretty and bright, and wicked with the darts."

"And a damn sexy cheerleader," another guy put in.

One of her girlfriends added, "She worked hard to make the squad."

"She's got the moves," another added.

"You guys are the best friends a girl could have." She offered up a toast with her newly delivered beer. "I'm looking forward to the pep rally."

"Deckers University is lucky to have you," a perky blonde said.

"What's your major?" Martin sipped his beer.

"Elementary education."

"Why do you want to be a teacher? There isn't any

money in it."

"Everything isn't about money, Martin. Kids need—"

"Hey," the bartender broke in. "You kids need to go home. I'm closin' up."

"Yah, yah." Martin set down his unfinished glass of beer. "How about giving me a ride, Tracy? I know it's out of your way, but...well...I don't have a car."

"No problem."

It was six miles out of her way, but the drive helped her clear her head of the smoky, noisy bar. She knew she wasn't drunk; she hadn't been drunk since she was sixteen, but nonetheless, with the window down, she felt refreshed by the time she dropped Martin at his apartment. "See you at the pep rally tomorrow." He waved as she drove away.

This time of night in Deckers, the streets were deserted. Thoughts of tomorrow's rally and her acceptance speech occupied her mind. It wasn't long before she turned left onto Bradley and drove past Texas Mall. She lived with her parents about a half-mile from the Baptist church, on a tree-lined suburban road.

Suddenly, a siren wailed behind her. Startled, she glanced at her speedometer, and convinced she wasn't speeding, she shifted her attention to the rearview mirror. Red and blue lights flashed from the windshield of the car behind her, and a blinding spotlight came on. Her throat clutched. It was obvious that a police officer in an unmarked car wanted her to stop, but for what reason she didn't know. Had she accidentally run a red light? Did she make an unsafe left turn? Surely this was a mistake, she assured herself and pulled to the shoulder.

Driver's license in hand, she watched the outside mirror and waited for the policeman to approach. Minutes passed in tense silence. She figured he was running her license plate number through the system. He wouldn't find anything incriminating, but whatever she'd done to warrant this stop, she hoped he wouldn't give her a ticket. Finally, the police car door opened, and silhouetted by the bright spotlight, a dark form approached her window and tapped on the glass. "Step out of the car, ma'am."

"What have I done?"

"Get out of the car." He stepped back, and now in the spotlight's glow she could see his hand hovering over a holstered gun. He was wearing dark glasses, dark pants and a dark shirt with a badge pinned to the pocket, but there were no patches on his sleeves to identify his department or rank.

"Who are you with?" she shouted through the closed window.

"Undercover DUI Enforcement," he replied. "Now get out of the car."

"I'm not drunk."

"Then you have nothing to worry about."

Of course she didn't. She opened the door and got out. "I'll prove it to you. What do you want me to do, walk the line? There isn't one around here. How about I recite the alphabet. A-B-C—"

"That won't be necessary, miss. I can smell beer on your breath from here." He displayed a pair of handcuffs. "Turn around. Put your hands behind your back. You're under arrest."

"This isn't necessary," she said but complied with the officer's order. She was sure everything would be straightened out at the police station.

He administered the handcuffs somewhat clumsily, and being this close to him now, she sensed his inexperience and nervousness. Confused, she watched him rifle through her car and take her purse. He was sweating profusely and talking to himself, saying something under his breath about a chicken. Panic began to set in. "What's your name, officer?"

Mute, he muscled her to his unmarked police car and shoved her into the back seat.

"Who are you?"

"I'm the law around here."

***

In the afterlife, Justin had just gotten comfortable in his favorite hammock. He'd been out late, on the coroner's slab, getting his rotted flesh sewn together and a hammer clamped to his right ankle. Though here he was perfect in every way, back in the land of the living, he was still a fright to see.

The light brightened. *"I have disturbing news for you, Justice,"* a low and hollow voice said.

Justin tipped his hat to shade his eyes. "What else is new, Wach-el?" He didn't welcome the interruption.

"Look." The light parted, revealing an abandoned car on a dark road and a driver's license that had fallen to the pavement. *"It belongs to Tracy Farrow. She dropped it when she was abducted by a police impersonator."*

That got Justin to his feet. Police impersonators revered the job but didn't have the intestinal fortitude to do the work to become a real cop.

"He has just made his first arrest."

A jolt of anger belted Justin in the gut. He knew the dedication and training that went into his profession, and he took it personally when someone pretended to be someone of the same caliber. Some impersonators were just punks trying to be tough guys, but others were criminals who'd chosen this MO to perpetrate their crimes.

"Police impersonators are dangerous in many ways. By counting on their victims' unquestioning cooperation,

Terry Wright

they gain entry to homes, rob motorists on the open highway, abduct children from playgrounds, and rape and murder women who trusted and respected them as bona fide police officers."

"And now an impersonator is prowling the streets of Deckers."

"His desire for the excitement of law enforcement has taken a fatal turn."

"Oh, no."

A mist seeped from the light and swirled around Justin's feet. Moments later, a young woman rose up from the mist, her auburn hair dancing on her shoulders. "Is this the pep rally?" Her eyes were filled with confusion.

"I'm sorry..." Justin removed his hat. "It's not."

"I have to get to the pep rally. All my friends will be there."

Justin stepped forward, offering his hand. "We don't have any pep rallies here, ma'am."

"Who are you?"

"Don't worry. I'm a police officer."

Her eyes shot open wide with fear. Backing away from him she cried out, "You don't look like a police officer. You're a cowboy."

"I'm a Texas Ranger, ma'am."

"You're an impersonator, too."

"I assure you—"

"Get away from me."

The mist rose up and took her away.

"She'll never cross over in that state of mind. You have to help her."

Justin felt sick inside, being shunned by someone he wanted to help. "She doesn't trust the police anymore."

"Do you blame her?"

"I blame the impersonator."

Justin Graves

"There he is." The light revealed an LT-1 Caprice cruiser pulling in behind a car on an isolated stretch of Texas road. *"Go get him, Justice."*

***

"Oh, dear. Dad is going to kill me." Cindy was returning home from a Bible-study group. She'd promised her father she wouldn't get in trouble if he'd let her use his Z28 Camaro. Now, an unmarked car was pulling her over. So okay, she was going ten miles an hour over the speed limit, but she could have been doing a hundred and forty if she wanted. There weren't many cars that could keep up with a Z28.

With red and blue lights flashing behind her, she turned on her signals and looked for a safe place to pull over on the dark shoulder. Suddenly, there was a bump, and a sickening smell exploded inside the car. She thought she'd run over a skunk. The smell stung her eyes to tears, and a salty taste burned the back of her throat. Retching, she was trying to swallow when a grating voice said, "Don't pull over, ma'am."

She couldn't believe her eyes. A disgusting old man was sitting in the passenger seat, his muddy clothes making a mess of her dad's upholstery. Gray hair dangled from under his dirty cowboy hat, and worms wriggled from holes in his filthy long coat. His leathery face was stitched up, Frankenstein style, but she could still see yellowed molars and white bone. The sight and smell of him sent waves of terror roiling in her stomach. "Get out of my car, mister."

A spark of crimson light shined from his eye sockets. "Keep driving, ma'am." His breath reeked of decayed flesh.

"I'm warning you, there's a cop behind me."

"Just punch it."

"Who are you?"

The gas pedal slammed to the floor.

"What the..? Cindy gripped the steering wheel with both hands. "What are you doing?"

"I don't mean to frighten you, ma'am. I'm trying to save your life."

Fighting tears of panic, she couldn't understand why the old cowboy wanted her to run from the police. She'd only seen high-speed chases on YouTube, but in her worse nightmares, she never believed she'd ever be in one.

The Z28 accelerated to 100 miles per hour, and the unmarked police car was still on her tail. "Why are you doing this to me?"

The ghoul tipped his cowboy hat, and dirt rained down around him. "I'm a police officer," he said hoarsely. "Justin Graves, Texas Rangers." He pulled back the lapel of his coat, revealing the gleam of a circle-star badge, rib bones, and rotted flesh. "The man in the car behind you is a police impersonator."

"How was I to know that?"

The Z28 took a right hand curve with ease; the Caprice with siren wailing fishtailed behind them but remained in hot pursuit.

"You have the right to know who is pulling you over," Justin said. "Remember, you don't have to stop for an unmarked car on a dark or isolated road."

"I was just about to pull over for that creep. What should I have done?"

"You could've driven to the nearest lighted area...a shopping center, a gas station, or a convenience store, anyplace where there are people around. Once you've stopped, you shouldn't roll down your window, but ask for identification loud enough to be heard through the glass."

"And if he shows me a badge?"

Justin Graves

"You can't be sure it's legit. Call 911 and ask the dispatcher to verify that a legitimate traffic stop is in progress. You can also request a marked police car be sent to your location."

"But what if he's not an impersonator? He'll think I'm not cooperating."

Justin nodded. "Real police officers wearing plain clothes and driving unmarked cars understand your concerns, and they know your rights."

"Then why am I driving a hundred and twenty miles an hour?"

"The impersonator may think he's a police officer, but he hasn't had the training to handle that Caprice in a high-speed chase."

"But I've never driven this fast before either."

"Leave the driving to me."

She took her hands off the steering wheel. "If this car gets a scratch—"

The ghoul disintegrated right before her eyes.

"Justin. Get back here."

***

"Oh, so the little bitch is going to run, huh?" Andrew activated his siren and accelerated after the Camaro. "Well you don't know who you're dealing with, whore. I'm the law in these parts." His heart was pumping hard as he reached for his phony radio mike. "Attention all cars. I'm in hot pursuit of a red Camaro. Female suspect wanted for intensive interrogation." He was thrilled by his demeanor and impressed with his professionalism.

By now, the LT-1 Caprice's 5.7 liter fuel injected engine was cranking out 205 horsepower and tearing up the highway at 130 miles an hour, but unbelievably, the Camaro was staying two and three car-lengths ahead. "How dare she run from me? It's contempt of cop."

"You're no cop. You're a chicken."

"Shut up, Dad."

"You're a disgrace to my name."

"But you're the one who got killed."

"I was doing my job."

"You were shot by a hooker, for Christ's sake. Now they're all going to pay."

"Every young woman's not a hooker."

Suddenly, a stench ballooned inside the car. He must've run over a bunch of skunks.

"Ah-hum."

Surprised at the sound, Andrew shot a glance to the passenger seat. An old cowboy was sitting there, stinking up the Caprice cruiser. How did he get in here?

"Give up the chase, Andrew," he said in a sandpaper voice.

"Who the hell are you?"

"Name's Justin Graves." He tipped his hat. "But you can call me Justice."

"You smell awful."

"I'm fine, really."

"Shouldn't you be in the morgue?"

"Actually, I was. Got a hammer for a foot now."

Tires screeched through a curve in the highway. The Camaro was getting farther ahead. "You're messing up my concentration, old man. Can't you see I'm right in the middle of a high-speed police pursuit?"

"You don't deserve to wear your father's badge."

"I'm going to finish what he started."

"Your father never murdered anyone."

"This town is full of whores. One killed my father. She destroyed my mother and ruined our lives."

Justice shook his head. "Officers die in this business

all the time; families get torn apart, but what you're doing disgraces us all."

"I'm the law around here," Andrew shouted, but his outburst caused him to lose control of the powerful Caprice cruiser. It shot over the centerline, crossed the oncoming traffic lane, careened onto to the shoulder, and then magically fishtailed back across the road to the lane where it belonged.

"How about pulling over, Andrew, before you wreck this car?"

"Screw you." He drew his gun and shot the ghoul pointblank.

Justin gritted his teeth. "I take that as a no."

Andrew fired again and again until the gun was empty, but the ghoul didn't slump over in the seat. "Die, damnit, die."

"I've already done that," Justin said. "Now it's your turn."

The police scanner lying on the seat came alive. "All units converge." From every direction, patrol cars appeared, overheads flashing, sirens wailing, tires smoking.

"Where did they come from?"

"Now the hunter becomes the hunted," Justin said. "You should've given up when you had the chance." he disappeared in a brilliant flash of light.

Deckers Police cars surrounded the Caprice and worked in unison to box in the impersonator. It was an incredible show of driving skill that gave Andrew the chills, but seeing the Camaro's taillights way down the road filled him with rage. "She's getting away."

He hit the gas and crashed the Caprice into the police car in front of him. The car beside him fishtailed, and the car behind him rammed his rear bumper. Andrew lost control of the phony cruiser. It careened into the guardrail with a horrendous crash. Sparks flew from the fenders, a tire blew, and the Caprice catapulted into the air.

"Justice!"

The Caprice came down sideways, slammed into the pavement and flipped and rolled and crashed end over end. Parts flew everywhere as it exploded in a ball of fire.

***

Sitting on the guardrail, Justin watched the police officers and fire rescue pull the charred body of the impersonator from the wreckage and place him on an unzipped body bag. Dr. Yee would soon have another customer.

Holland ripped the badge from Andrew's scorched shirt. "You're a disgrace to your father." They zipped the bag shut.

Rummaging through the wrecked Caprice for evidence, the investigators found a hand-held police scanner, handcuffs, an empty gun, red and blue flashing lights, and a siren. "Where did he get all this stuff?" an officer grumbled.

"Police equipment is easy to purchase," another replied, "on the internet."

"Perfect for nut-jobs like that guy." He indicated the body bag being loaded into the coroner's van.

Tracy materialized beside Justin. "Will they find my body now? It's so cold in that shallow grave."

"Soon," Justin replied. "First, they have to connect Andrew to your murder."

"I'm glad Cindy made it home all right."

"Without a single scratch on her father's Camaro," Justin noted with pride.

"Thank you, Justice." She touched his rotting arm. "What was that guy thinking?"

"Police impersonators aren't common," Justin assured her. "But there are enough of them around to warrant a few precautions."

Tracy sighed. "I'm going to miss my friends."

Justin smiled. "You'll make new ones on the other side."

An investigator searching the car held up a sooty purse in relatively good condition. "Look what I found."

"Hey, that's mine," Tracy shouted. Of course, no one could hear her.

"That purse will put you in Andrew's car and they'll start looking for your body. Now you can cross over."

She gazed at him with a crook in her brow. "Why haven't you crossed over, Justin?"

"I've got a score to settle with the devil."

He tipped his hat to the cheerleader, and with a gust of wind the ghoul was gone.

The Perfect Crime

P ete whistled. "Come on, boys." King and Cong, two Rottweilers, came running, their muscular frames undulating with each massive stride. Clumps of grass flew up from under their paws. "Time for supper."

Bounding in through the back door, they careened into the kitchen and headed for their gallon-size metal bowls now heaped with chicken parts and beef livers and garnished with green beans. These healthy 110-pound brothers ate twenty pounds of food a day.

Chomping and slurping and gasping huge gulps of air between bites, their meals were quickly devoured.

Pete glowed with pride...until Martha stomped into the kitchen. "Get outta here." She grabbed a broom and started whacking Pete. "How many times do I gotta tell ya to feed them nasty critters outside?"

King and Cong escaped through the closed screen door, tearing it to shreds.

"Someday, Martha, I swear." He showed her a fist.

Hands on her ample hips, Martha went nose-to-nose with Pete. "What are ya gonna do, you skinny wimp? Takes them big-ass dogs to make ya feel like a man. Give ya some delusion of power over the beasts. Well, it ain't workin', ya fool."

"Do you have to be so damned mean?"

"Mean? I'll show you mean." She slapped him upside the head. "Get outside and pull them weeds outta my garden."

Pete rubbed a hotspot growing on his temple. "But I'll

miss my TV shows."

Martha huffed. "All ya ever do all weekend is sit around watching that damn detective crap, true crime, and them FBI fellas huttin' down killers. It's for pussies, I tell ya. A waste of time. What's wrong with watching them ass bustin' football games or a good fishin' show like real men do?"

"You know I don't like that stuff."

"Cuz you ain't man enough, that's why. Now git outta here."

With Martha's broom stinging his bottom side, Pete stumbled out the back door.

"And clean up that dog shit."

Anger burned hot as a blowtorch in his chest. That woman was going to be the death of him. He joined his dogs in the yard and sat Indian style in the grass amidst piles of dog crap scattered all around. Hell. He'd just cleaned it up two days ago. King and Cong had watched him scoop up the poop, their tongues flapping, each oblivious to the stinky messes they'd made.

Fact of life: *big dogs leave big piles.* Seemed like all his dogs did was eat and shit all day.

But they were his buddies. Who else would go with him up to Cedar Ridge, across Pine Bluffs, or even down the back forty of Dead Man's Canyon? Not Martha. She didn't like the great outdoors, but he lived to enjoy the wide-open spaces.

Deckers, Texas, was surround by a vast desert, and he knew most every crag and gully by heart. He'd been hiking the area most of his grown life. With King and Cong trotting along, the bears didn't even bother them, not that he'd seen any bears. Now, if he could just get that lucky with Martha. She was worse than any old bear, and his dogs were smart enough to give her a wide berth.

Terry Wright

Eat and shit all day.

There was no fixing Martha. As she got older and fatter, she got uglier and meaner. He couldn't blame her much, though. Hell, he'd be pissed off at the whole world if he was that ugly, but she was a fair bride back in the days when she liked to ride the wild pony. Now, the only riding she'd been doing lately was riding his ass.

He sighed. Right now, on his favorite TV show, Detective Curland was probably on the trail of some husband who'd killed his wife, buried her body in the backyard, and poured a cement slab over it, or possibly a psycho killer who took some poor street whore out into the bush, bashed in her skull, did her like he loved her, and then dug her a shallow grave. Those killers should've watched the TV shows about how detectives figured out who committed crimes like that. The cops had forensics and cadaver sniffing dogs. And Curland was really good at lying to suspects to trick them into confessing. And most dumb killers left something behind at the crime scene, like DNA evidence, fingerprints, or fibers, and even a speck of blood on the wall they'd missed when cleaning up.

Oh, they'd try to clean up their messes, all right, but they didn't know how Luminal could show the investigators where blood had splattered or pooled even after the killer had wiped it up. Hell, they'd even taken drains apart to find blood in the plumbing, and sometimes they'd pull up floor tiles to reveal where blood had seeped down through the cracks. Oh yeah, cops like Detective Curland were smart.

Pete was smart too. He'd seen all their shows. He knew all their tricks. The secret to not getting caught was twofold: don't make a mess, and leave nothing behind, preferably not even a body.

"Git to work," Martha yelled from the screen door,

what was left of it, anyway.

He scanned the poop piles and thought how much more pleasant they were to be around than Martha. She should be so lucky to be a pile of dog shit...which sounded so true he had to chuckle. He glanced at King and Cong, all happy-tailed. An idea struck him.

King whined. Cong barked.

He patted his dogs. "Don't worry, boys. I got a plan for her. We're going to be free."

Eat and shit all day.

***

Saturday morning, Pete rose early and dressed in some old work clothes he'd not worn for many years. King and Cong were barking in the backyard. They hadn't been fed breakfast yet, on purpose.

Martha sat up in bed. "You better shut up them damn dogs."

"They're hungry."

Martha wiped away a clump of hair stuck to the side of her face. "What are you doin' up so early, dressed like that and all?"

He showed her a short length of rope he'd been holding behind his back. "Remember how you told me them detective shows were a waste of time?"

"So?"

"You're wrong." He lunged at her, whipped the rope around her neck so fast she had no time to resist. Her eyes bulged, more from surprise than pressure, which he was now applying with force, twisting the rope. This way there'd be no blood-splatter evidence.

She kicked some, and croaking noises came from her throat.

But he was careful not to apply too much pressure. He

didn't want to break her larynx, because blood would run out of her mouth and seep down into the mattress. It would take her longer to die this way; she'd suffer more than necessary, which was kind of a bonus. He had her pinned down good, too, so she couldn't scratch him, or otherwise leave any marks of a struggle or his skin under her fingernails.

She went limp, finally, but he didn't release his hold on the rope for four minutes, until he was sure her heart had stopped. Everything was going as planned. Detective Curland would be stumped.

Struggling with her bulky dead weight, he managed to rip off her nightgown, then packed it in her suitcase, along with some of her underwear, a couple of dresses, makeup, and shoes. There'd be no question she'd packed up to leave. Then he dragged her naked body into the bathroom and flopped her into the tub. He'd already covered the walls and floor with plastic and removed the shower curtain, which he'd re-hang later.

Now for the hard part. Working with the axe and hacksaw, a makeshift cutting board, and the carving knife they'd used every Thanksgiving for the last ten years, he started to dismember Martha.

One thing about those detective shows became suddenly evident. They never showed the real horror of murder, the blood and guts, or the smell and the sick feeling it made in a man's stomach. Did he mention the blood? How could any one person have so damn much of the stuff? Fearing it would clot and clump and end up clogging the drain, he turned on the faucets full force.

King and Cong yelped and scrapped in the backyard.

Pete went about his gruesome task. He cut off her arms and legs first, stripped flesh from the bones, and using the dog bowls and mop buckets for catch basins, put

Martha, bit by bit, through the meat grinder clamped to the sink counter. It all looked like hamburger. Then he opened up her belly. Putrid innards spilled out like fat spaghetti.

Yuk!

Occasionally arm-swiping sweat from his forehead, he suffered through the gore and stench until he'd ground up every part of Martha and hacked all her bones to splinters. Late evening arrived by the time he'd cleaned up the bathroom and stuffed all the plastic and his bloody clothes into the suitcase with Martha's belongings.

He carried the heavy metal dog bowls to the kitchen, and opening the back door, he whistled. "Come on, boys. Time for supper."

King and Cong came running, bounded into the kitchen, and slid up to heaping bowls of ground Martha. As always, their meals were devoured posthaste. And that night they had seconds.

Eat and shit all day.

***

It took all week to feed Martha to King and Cong. Dog shit piled up in the back yard.

In the meantime, he replaced the plumbing in the bathroom and tossed the suitcase, meat grinder, carving knife, axe, hacksaw, and empty ChloraSorb bottle in a Dumpster behind Deckers Hardware then waited for the trash truck to haul it away. It would be ten feet deep in the landfill by dusk.

That weekend, he and his dogs went hiking in Dead Man's Canyon. They brought Martha along this time, to the great outdoors, in a garbage bag that barely fit into his backpack. King and Cong had sat with their tongues flopping wetly as Pete collected their dog shit from the backyard then said a little prayer over the big bag of

Terry Wright

excrement: "Ashes to ashes, shit to shit," or something with that flavor.

During their daylong hike across the desert and down into the narrows, he scattered dog shit here and there along the way, in and among the bushes, down crevices, and around rocks until nothing was left of Martha's shitty remains in the backpack.

Detective Curland would never be able to prove foul play; he'd never find any trace of her body should Martha's whereabouts ever come into question. She'd simply packed her suitcase and left him. Wives left husbands all the time.

Pete knew he had committed the perfect crime.

He found a nice shady spot under a crop of evergreens and sat on a rock at the edge of a deep gully. The vista was spectacular up here, the only good thing in his life worth living for, besides King and Cong. His unwitting accomplices sat in front of him, their tails wagging as they tilted their heads and watched him pull ham sandwiches and apples from his belly pack. The bottle of red wine he'd brought along would top off the celebration nicely.

A slight breeze rustled the trees. Then everything became perfectly still.

He extracted the cork from the wine bottle and took a swig. "To Martha," he hailed. "To dog shit."

King and Cong whined.

He tore a sandwich in half and offered each piece to his dogs. "Dessert," he said. "Something to wash Martha down with." He chuckled. "A Martha chaser, you might say."

King and Cong gulped down their booty without even chewing.

Then a fecal stench rose in the air.

"All right. Which one of you is the wise guy?"

They both panted. Nobody fessed up to passing gas.

Justin Graves

The gut-wrenching odor got worse. Pete was beginning to think he'd picked a bad spot for his little picnic. Ruling out Martha's remains, he figured there must've been an open outhouse pit somewhere nearby. He leaned forward and peered into the gully, saw nothing but rocks and sage all the way down to the dry river bed. Nothing around him but sand, rocks, and pines. No outhouse, no sewage treatment facility... The growing stench made the wine in his stomach turn sour.

King and Cong yelped and ran off down the hillside.

"Hey. Get back here." He stood, but suddenly felt dizzy like he'd gotten up too fast. The wine bottle slipped from his grasp and shattered on the ground. Then a pressure on his chest made inhaling difficult. Christ. He was having a heart attack.

"Hello, Pete," a raspy voice said from behind him.

Stilled by surprise, he clutched his chest and slowly turned around. What he saw gave him a fright, a cowboy shedding dirt from his long brown coat. He must've fallen off his horse and got dragged through a pasture full of cattle dung. God, he stunk something awful. And skin on his jaw was missing; his exposed molars looked like they'd never seen a dentist. What the hell was he doing here in the middle of nowhere? "Who are you, mister?"

He tipped his dusty cowboy hat. Deep red eyes set in dark sockets seemed to bore a hole into Pete's soul. "Name's Justin Graves, but you can call me Justice."

Seizing his composure, "I'd offer you some wine," Pete said, "but as you can see..." He pointed to the puddle where the bottle had broken. "I'm fresh out."

Seemingly unconcerned, the nasty cowboy approached, his boots crunching dirt. "Martha is upset with you."

Yeah, right. "How is it you know Martha?"

"I talked to her."

Impossible. The old cowboy not only smelled like shit, he was full of shit. "You want an apple?"

"We watched you feed her body to the dogs, Pete."

His heart lunged in his chest so hard he truly believed he'd fall over dead from cardiac arrest. This couldn't be happening. "You know my name?"

"I know how much she hated those dogs. She told me everything."

Pete wasn't stupid enough to tell Justin that he couldn't have talked to her because he'd killed her. That would be a Detective Curland trick to get a confession out of him. Pete could've written the script for that pitfall. "She left me for another man. No way you talked to her."

Worms wriggled out of a circle-star badge pinned to Justin's filthy brown coat. He parted his coat lapels, revealing rotted flesh and exposed rib bones. "I talk to dead people."

"That's gross." The sight of him was worse than Martha splayed open in the bathtub.

"I'm a homicide detective, deceased, as you can see, and I know you killed your wife."

Pete fought to remain cool, focused. "There's no proof of that."

"You watch TV crime shows. There's always proof."

Pete stepped away from the smelly old ghoul, careful not to get too close to the edge of the ravine. "You don't know what you're talking about."

"That's what they all say about us dumb cops."

"If you're so smart, what evidence you got against me?"

"Did you consider the hardware store security cameras? It's all on tape, you dumping the evidence of your crime in the dumpster."

"Why would anyone look at a security tape of the dumpster? She's not even missing."

Justin grinned, or maybe he yawned, it was hard to tell. "You're right. She's not missing. I know exactly where she is."

"You're lying. Cops don't have to tell the truth."

"She's in the afterlife awaiting justice for her murder. Only then will she be able to cross over to everlasting peace and happiness."

"That's malarkey. There's no proof a murder was committed. No body. No murder weapon."

"Come on, Pete. How do you think I knew where you dumped the evidence? Martha and I watched you. I tipped off the cops. Detectives are combing your house for clues as we speak. How's that for malarkey?"

Pete frowned. He'd been extra thorough. Completely. Not a trace. Clean bed sheets. Clean bathroom. Clean dog bowls.

"And I know your dogs have been eating well lately."

The words felt like a knife going into his chest and twisting, carving out a hollow place that quickly filed with doubt. What could he have left behind? Nothing. Nothing at all. "The cops aren't going to find anything. And you're bluffing about the evidence." He'd seen it hauled away.

"You sure?"

"Of course." Pete gulped. Of course he was sure. Okay, maybe he wasn't absolutely sure.

Justin crossed his arms. Bones creaked. "Nine out of ten killers leave something behind. Some call it divine intervention, a dog hair, a seed pod, a tire impression. What have you forgotten, Pete?"

These trick questions kept popping into the conversation. Detective Curland must've trained this guy on devious police interrogation techniques. "There's nothing to forget."

"Oh, yeah? Then...ah...where's the rope?"

"The rope? What rope?" It was in the suitcase, deep in the landfill by now. He'd put it in the suitcase...or... well, now he couldn't remember what happened to the rope he'd strangled Martha with, but he wasn't going to say anything that would incriminate himself.

"It's under your bed," Justin said, his voice grating.

Pete's chest tightened. "How the hell do you know what's under my bed?"

"When you stripped off Martha's nightgown, the rope fell to the floor and you inadvertently kicked it under the bed. Out of sight. Out of mind."

"You've been snooping around my house?"

Justin tipped his hat. "I made a deal with the devil to save my daughter's soul. I gotta get a hundred bad guys, and let's see...I think you're next on the countdown. The devil is waiting for your soul."

"The devil knows about me?"

"Hey, you made his top one hundred list. That's got to be worth something."

"Oh, shit." Pete could hardly breathe.

Justin sneered. "They're going to find the rope, and you're going down for Murder One."

Pete slumped on the rock. His dogs were gone and his celebration was completely ruined. "She made my life miserable, don't you see?"

"That's not a capital offense, Pete. You should've divorced her instead of killing her. She's really pissed off at you now."

"What else is new?" He exhaled. "I can't believe that old nag didn't go straight to hell."

"Feeding her to the dogs like that, Pete, how could you do such an awful thing?"

Justin Graves

"Ironic." Pete had to laugh. "She hated my dogs."

Justin looked around. "It's nice up here. Enjoy the view while you can. The police will be here soon. I hear the cells on death row are only eight-by-ten."

"I can't go to prison. I need this, the wide-open spaces. And who's going to take care of my dogs?"

"I'll see they get a nice home, but one thing's for sure. They'll be eating regular dog food from now on."

He sighed. "I thought I'd committed the perfect crime."

"There's no such thing."

With a gust of wind the ghoul was gone.

Pete stood, the consequences of his failure far greater than he could bear. There was nothing left for him now. He stepped to the gully's edge, looked down to the craggy dry riverbed below, and took the last step of his life.

Eat and shit all day.

Junk Science

As the sun set over Texas State Prison, in the death chamber, Todd Cunningham lay on his back, arms and legs strapped down to a god-awful gurney, and panic swelled in his stomach like a boiling thunderhead. He feared he'd puke his last meal of pork chops, fries, and chocolate cream pie. Ceiling lights shined down so bright that the man standing over him looked hazy as he went about the task of stabbing a needle into his arm. The bastards were about to kill him for nothing.

"I'm an innocent man," he cried. "You convicted me of a crime I didn't commit."

"Shut up," a guard ordered.

"I've been here for twelve years for something I didn't do."

Nobody would listen. They hadn't believed him, not once over all the years of appeals, all the way to the state supreme court. The evidence spoke for itself, the judges had ruled. One count arson. Two counts murder.

"I didn't set that fire. I didn't kill my kids." A second needle pricked his arm, probed for a vein. Todd clenched his fist. "Bastards."

"Don't make this any harder than it already is."

He knew these guys were only doing their jobs. They didn't really convict him of felony arson and two counts of first-degree murder. A jury did that. They believed the prosecution's expert fire investigator who showed proof of arson, proof an accelerant was used to start the fire, and proof of motive: he was angry at his wife for not coming home from a bar.

Damn right he was angry. The slut got a few beers in her and thought she was the Queen of Sheba. Flirting, flaunting her cleavage, talking trash to the men standing around the pool table. They were very appreciative and attentive, of course. Laughing. Groping. He couldn't take it anymore, stormed out of the bar with divorce on his mind. Once he got home, he'd sent the kids to bed upstairs and fell asleep on the couch. That's what he did. And he awoke to a raging inferno.

Nobody believed him, damn it.

The warden entered the death chamber. He handed an official-looking document, a warrant from the state of Texas, to the executioner, some guy dressed in a white smock, but he wasn't a doctor. The real doctor would come in and pronounce him dead when it was over.

"You're making a big mistake."

As the warden stood by the wall-mounted phone, a curtain opened to reveal a lighted room beyond a glass panel. There she was, sitting in the front row, the Queen of Sheba herself. Come to witness the execution of the man who'd killed her kids.

She just glared back at him. The whore would go to her grave thinking he was a monster.

Next to her sat the state's expert witness, Jeff Wallace, fire investigator and goddamned liar. It didn't happen like he'd told the jury. There was no madman storming through the house, spilling gasoline from a can he'd kept in the garage. He wasn't cursing his wife and condemning his children to die. Just because his arson trained dog had alerted on the presence of an accelerant didn't make his story true. The dog was wrong. Wallace was wrong. The state of Texas had no reason to kill him.

On the other end of the front row sat a lawyer from the Public Defender's office. He'd pleaded Todd's case to the jury; the gas can was empty because it wasn't safe to store flammables in the garage, not because Todd had emptied it throughout the house in a fit of rage. The lawyer even proposed Todd's wife had come home and started the fire while he was asleep on the couch. *That should create reasonable doubt*, he'd said, but the prosecution showed that she'd left the bar with three men to snort cocaine and screw in a cheap motel room. An airtight alibi. Some wife he had there, huh? The whore.

"I didn't do it," he screamed.

The warden patted Todd's shoulder. "May God have mercy on your soul."

A burning sensation oozed up his arm.

"I'm innocent."

Head swimming, he glanced at his wife, saw her fists clenched under her chin, her face wrenched in anger. She might have thought she was getting justice; instead she was witnessing a murder. *My murder.* The defense lawyer hung his head. He knew it. He'd tried to stop it, but he couldn't beat Jeff Wallace, who sat straight-backed in his chair, his chin up, proudly looking on. Todd glared at him, and even as the room began to wobble and blur, he hoped to relay the intense hatred he felt for the man responsible for this outrageous miscarriage of justice.

The bright lights began to fade. He turned his eyes to the ceiling, felt tears well in his eyes. Maybe now, at least, he would be with his kids again.

***

In the light of the afterlife, where souls were purged of hate and despair before crossing over, Justin Graves sat in his chair and played Solitaire with a deck of cards the light had supplied. He didn't need a table on which to deal the cards; they floated in midair before him. King of spades, Queen of hearts, Jack of clubs. Five of diamonds goes on six of spades. Such a mindless game, but it helped divert his thoughts from Christy sitting in hell with the devil, waiting for her father to deliver salvation.

Ace of spades, King of spades, Queen of spades, he might win this game—

"Justice."

There it was again, Wach-el's deep, throaty voice in the light, and always at the most inopportune times. "What is it now?"

King of diamonds, Queen of clubs—

The cards disappeared. "Hey."

"You have a visitor."

Looking up to the light, he saw a figure descend and alight on the misty plane before him.

"This is Todd Cunningham. He was executed in Texas for the arson murder of his children."

"Serves him right." Justin wondered why he wasn't in hell where he belonged. "Or is there more to this story?"

"I didn't do it." Todd held out his right arm so Justin could see the puncture wound left from the lethal injection needle. "Nobody believes me."

"What makes you think I should?" In all his years as a homicide investigator, Justin knew better than to take the word of a suspect, much less a convicted child murderer.

"This will interest you, Justin." The light produced a Decker's Herald newspaper article with a headline that read: *Arson Investigator Top in Profession.*

"Good for him."

"Jeff Wallace has uncovered more arson fires than anyone else in his field: ninety-nine percent, to date. An unusually high percentage, don't you think?"

"I don't know anything about arson investigation," Justin said, though it seemed unlikely that so many fires were intentional.

"His conclusions are based on unproven theories, outdated assumptions, and junk science. He makes it appear as though a crime has been committed when, in fact, there is none."

"See..." Todd said. "Believe me now?"

Justin frowned. "If you didn't start the fire, what did?"

The light surged and parted, revealing a scene from the land of the living. Streetlamps flashed off a red pickup careening down a tree-lined residential road. The truck skidded to a stop in front of a bi-level house with a well-manicured lawn, and out of the driver seat bailed Todd Cunningham, spitting mad.

"It was just after midnight," Todd explained. "I wasn't in a very good mood."

Justin watched Todd storm to the house.

Inside, two kids, dressed in pajamas, watched an old console TV.

"Where's Mom?" the oldest boy asked.

"David was nine," Todd said as he watched these past events play-out through teary eyes.

"Time for bed."

"But dad—"

"You heard me." He collapsed on the couch.

The smaller child, a girl, scurried up to him, clutching a puppy. "Night, daddy." She kissed his cheek.

"Sally was only six," Todd sobbed out.

Time fast-forwarded to a quiet living room. Dim streetlight seeped in through a chink in the curtains and revealed the puppy as it bounded down the stairs, scampered past Todd sleeping on the couch, and scooted behind the television set. There the puppy chewed on an already well-chewed cord.

"In Todd's deep sleep, there's no way he could've

heard the sparking of the short-circuited cord or the puppy yelp."

A glow began to illuminate Todd's face, growing brighter by the second. Black smoke crept across the ceiling above him. The television became an inferno, igniting the wall, the carpet, the curtains, and the furniture. By the time Todd awakened, fire was already climbing the stairs.

"I'd never been so scared in my life," Todd said. "There was no way I could get to my kids. The thick smoke, the heat, I couldn't get through it. Singed my hair, scorched my clothes. I don't even know what happened to the little dog."

Justin wondered about that too, until he watched Todd bolt out the front door. Through a cloud of billowing smoke, the puppy darted out and scampered into the night.

The image dissolved.

Wach-el explained the science. *"As the carpet burned, the synthetic fabric, glue, and dyes melted into hydrocarbon and caprolactam, which flow in much the same way any flammable liquid flows, and when it too burns, it leaves the same burn-patterns as gasoline on the floorboards under the scorched carpet. Fire investigators used to think that was evidence of arson. They know better now."*

Justin understood how an investigator might make the wrong assertions, but a trained arson dog? "How could his dog have been mistaken about the presence of an accelerant?"

"A dog can locate the residual odor of hydrocarbon, but it's up to the investigator to collect samples, run further tests, and make the call."

Justin thought about that. "It would be in the investigator's best interest to find evidence of arson. No arson, no need for an investigation, no money. Plenty of motivation for fabricating evidence."

"Or Wallace flat-out lied about what he found," Todd said. "He's a weasel, I tell ya. He needs to pay for what he did to me." Todd rubbed the needle wound on his arm.

"Your children are waiting for you on the other side," Justin told him. "Revenge is no reason to make them wait any longer."

"I hear your wife is waiting for you there too, Justice. What's keeping you here?"

"Redemption," Justin said and left it at that. Christy's horrible predicament was none of Todd's concern.

The light pulsed. *"Todd can't cross over until this is settled."*

"All right, Todd." Justin stood. "But I'll need your help."

"Anything."

"When this is over you may regret you said that."

***

Inside the redbrick firehouse of Deckers Station 23 sat two gleaming red fire trucks and one white Ford Expedition with fire chief emblems on the doors. The aroma of paste wax permeated the air, as spiff equipment was always the order of the day. Ceiling lights reflected off polished cement floors sectioned off in red and yellow stripes. Jeff Wallace gave his black lab, Chops, full reign on his short leash. Nose to the floor, he led the way to the chief's office. The Cunningham execution had nailed the lid shut on yet another successful arson case. As he slipped through the open door, Jeff expected praise for another job well done.

"Congratulations, Inspector Wallace." Chief Robert Daniels rose from his high-backed chair behind a massive walnut desk. Baseball trophies adorned the abundant shelving around the room, and the black glassy eyes of a bull elk head stared down from the wall.

With Chops sitting at his heel, Wallace shook the chief's hand. "Thanks."

"Deckers seems to be crawling with arsonists lately. I don't know what we'd do without you, Jeff."

"Just doing my job, sir."

It felt good knowing he earned his keep in the department. He didn't have the balls to fight fires himself, but when it came to arson investigation, he was the pro. No one ever doubted him; nobody ever would. He patted Chops' side. "Good boy."

"That's quite a dog you got there, inspector."

"Best arson dog in the business." Who would ever know what Chops really smelled in all that burned debris? Soot mostly. Smoke, for sure. The national average for sniffing out accelerants was somewhere around forty-one percent. Chops had a ninety percent success rate. Came from training and reading the dog the way it was necessary to keep their services in demand.

"You must be proud—"

Beep. Beep. Beep.

The fire alarm stopped the chief.

Dispatch came over the intercom. *"One eighty one, Engine two, Engine four, Battalion twenty-three, one eighty one, house fire, two twenty Texas Drive, visible flame and smoke."*

Daniels snatched his fire chief helmet from a hook on the wall. "Let's roll."

***

Already on scene, Captain Holland sat in his squad car and watched the abandoned house burn. Even from his position a half block away, the acrid smell of wood smoke seeped into the car and stung his nostrils. Justin Graves sat in the passenger seat, his elbow propped out the open window in a casual manner, like he wasn't the least bit worried that his cockamamie plan wouldn't work.

"If Wallace declares the fire an arson, what does it prove? It is arson. You set the fire."

"By shorting out the electrical," Justin replied.

As flames tore through the front windows, and smoke churned into the sky, Holland remembered how Justin had stuck a wrench into the main fuse box with his bare hands. Sparks flew like welding flack. The stench of burnt flesh turned the air nauseous, until finally the wallboards ignited. Justin tossed the damaged wrench on the floor, brushed his smoking hand on his coat, and then led the way out of the house to wait for the fire to grow.

"Any legitimate inspector would see the obvious cause of this fire," Justin said. "But my bet is Jeff Wallace will claim an accelerant was used."

"So what? An old abandoned house is burned down. Nobody's going to care."

"Things are not always what they appear." Justin pointed to the burning house.

Holland couldn't believe his eyes. A man stood in the front yard, arms flailing. Soot soiled his t-shirt and slacks, and smoke swirled from his ratty hair. He must've come from inside the burning house.

"My kids are in there," the man cried. "I couldn't get them out."

Cold terror raked Holland's spine. He could've sworn that house was abandoned.

A child's scream cut through the air like hurled razor blades. Holland's throat seized. And then he heard another scream. Two kids? How could he have missed them when he inspected the house? He'd made a horrible mistake.

"They're gonna burn to death." Holland acted without thinking, elbowed the car door open.

Justin grabbed him by the arm. "Let it play out my way," he said in a gravelly stern voice.

Holland yanked against Justin's grasp. "I'm not going to sit here while children die."

Effortlessly, Justin pulled him back into the car. The door slammed shut as if by an invisible hand. "It isn't easy to get justice. Sacrifices must be made, whether real or perceived. It's a painful process, horrifying at best, but if the stakes aren't high enough, Wallace's investigation may drag on for months. I've got to make it personal for him, make him act recklessly. Trust me, captain. It has to be this way."

More screams shrieked through the air. Holland wanted to get out, do something, at least find out for himself if those screams were real or not, but a supernatural force rooted him in his seat.

The man on the lawn fell to his knees, pressed his palms over his ears. "I couldn't get them out."

Doing nothing went against everything Captain Holland stood for, against every instinct he possessed. "This better work, Justice."

No answer.

"Justice?" He looked to the passenger seat and saw that it was empty. Holland groaned. "I'm gonna have nightmares for the rest of my life."

***

A horrific scene greeted Jeff Wallace and his driver, Fire Chief Robert Daniels, as they pulled up in the chief's Ford Expedition, overheads flashing and siren wailing. Two fire trucks roared up behind them and stopped near a fire hydrant. With urgency, firemen scrambled to work, hauling hoses and breaking out ladders. Some donned protective fire gear, helmets and oxygen tanks. This would be an all-out assault on the fire.

Chief Daniels sprang from the vehicle. Wallace watched him run past a man kneeling on the front lawn.

"My kids are in there," he cried.

Their screams tore through the air.

"My God." Wallace jumped out and ran toward the hysterical man. His hair was singed and his clothes were scorched. "What happened?"

"My kids are in there." His face was buried in his hands.

"How many?"

The sobbing man didn't answer.

Wallace shook the man's shoulder. "How many, damn it?"

"I couldn't get them out."

He looked toward the burning house. Streams of water arced into the inferno, striking hot timbers that sizzled and hissed in protest. White clouds of steam melded with black curling smoke and belched outward to swirl around the firemen who held their positions.

The children kept screaming.

Panic rising, Wallace rushed up to Chief Daniels. "Aren't you going to send someone in?"

Daniels shook his head. "It's too dangerous. The whole damn structure is involved."

"Where are the screams coming from?"

"What screams?"

"My kids are in there," the man shouted, still holding his face in his hands.

It was as if he couldn't say anything else. Wallace turned to the father who'd left his children inside to die. "How did the fire start?"

The man looked up, a blank stare in his eyes. Wallace's heartbeat stuttered at the sight of him. "You?" Todd Cunningham in the flesh. "You're dead. Executed. I was there. I saw you die."

"My kids are in there," he wailed.

The screams died down as each young life ended.

"I couldn't get them out."

By now, the firemen had knocked the blaze back far enough that a few of them could make entry. They had to check for any possible victims; make sure no homeless people had taken shelter inside the abandoned house. Wallace knew it was standard operating procedure for the Deckers Fire Department. He hoped they'd find the children alive.

Within moments, a fireman appeared with a small body and laid it at Wallace's feet, a body charred beyond recognition; it could've been a monkey for all he knew. Then another child was brought out, its stiff little arms outstretched, fingers burned off the hands, small mouth agape. Its eyeballs had exploded in their sockets. And the smell was something awful.

Firemen covered the small bodies with a yellow tarp, but that didn't erase the horrific images from Wallace's mind. It was the most terrible thing he'd ever seen. All his investigations, all his conclusions, all the scenarios he'd presented to all those juries hadn't prepared him for the true terror of witnessing the death of children by fire. The impulse to exact justice overwhelmed him. Todd Cunningham was going to pay for letting these kids die.

"I couldn't get them out."

Wallace glanced at Daniels who was directing his men. They were getting the fire under control. He looked at the Expedition where Chops watched the goings on through the side window. As soon as the fire was out, he'd have

Terry Wright

Chops make a sweep through the house. The fresher the crime scene, the more solid the evidence, but this time it would be just a formality. He knew the man on the lawn, Todd Cunningham, was responsible for this. His singed hair and scorched clothes proved it was arson. The accelerant he used obviously back-flashed on him when he lit it. No doubt in Wallace's mind, Cunningham would get the death penalty.

"You're under arrest." Wallace wrenched the man's hands behind him and slapped on the cuffs.

"What are you doing?" Chief Daniels shouted.

"It's him again," Wallace said. Sweat trickled down his face. "Todd Cunningham."

Daniels gave the man a good hard look. "No it isn't."

"Of course it is." Was the chief blind?

"Do you realize what you're saying, Jeff? You're IDing a dead man. Do you know how crazy that sounds?"

It sounded perfectly logical to Wallace. "He killed those kids. I know it. And I'll prove it." It was that simple. "In the meantime, he's not going anywhere."

"Where did you get handcuffs?"

"Chief," came over Daniels' handheld. "We need you on the north side right away."

He cast Wallace a sharp glare. "Don't do anything until I get back." He hurried off.

An approaching police siren grabbed Wallace's attention as a Texas Rangers unit pulled up. He recognized the captain who got out. Captain Holland. They'd worked on past cases together.

"What do you have here?" Holland asked him.

"Hold this man for investigation of arson," Wallace said with authority.

Holland examined the distraught man. "Who is he?"

"Todd Cunningham."

Justin Graves

"Is that right?" the captain asked the man. "Are you Todd Cunningham?"

"My kids are in there."

"Jesus. He's in shock." Holland removed the handcuffs and returned them to Wallace. "I'll take it from here."

He watched the captain place Cunningham in the squad car and peel off.

Just then, a smell worse than burnt flesh wafted through the air. It was as if the small corpses had already begun to rot. He pinched his nose and looked around, saw an old cowboy standing next to him. With all the noise, it was no wonder he hadn't heard him approach, but why did the smelly bastard have to stand so close?

The cowboy removed his dusty hat and looked down at the covered bodies. Shoulder-length gray hair shielded his face from view, but it appeared the cowboy knew the young victims of this fire. Wallace decided to lend him some assurances. "I'll get a conviction against bastard who did this, don't you worry."

The cowboy donned his hat and turned to face him, a sight he wasn't prepared to see. The man's face was stitched up like a softball. By God, it was an ugly job. And from the brown and crooked condition of his teeth, Wallace figured the cowboy should see a dentist. But when he looked into those round eye sockets that seemed to glow red, a chill skittered up the back of his neck. "Who the hell are you?"

"Name's Justin Graves, but you can call me Justice."

"I should call you an ambulance." Wallace batted at the man's foul breath.

"Won't do me any good. I'm dead."

That wasn't hard to believe, but still, Wallace believed the guy to be a street bum looking to gawk at dead children.

"Move along before I have you arrested, mister."

"Todd didn't kill his kids."

"You know Todd Cunningham?" Had to be more than coincidence, Wallace assumed.

"Texas put an innocent man to death, thanks to you."

"A jury believed he did it."

"You gave them misinformation based on junk science."

"Now you're going to stand here and tell me how to do my job?"

"Look," Justin rasped. "I'll make this as painless as possible. Tell the DA you'd made a mistake in the Todd Cunningham case. You want to withdraw your testimony."

"Over my dead body."

"And you'll never investigate another fire again."

"Screw you, Justice."

"Listen real good, Jeff. You get one chance to redeem yourself. An electrical short in the main fuse box caused this fire. Check it out for yourself, but whatever you do, don't blame this one on Todd."

"You're out of your mind, old man. I've got two dead kids here and the murderer in custody."

"Come clean on this case right here and now or pay the consequences."

"That's it. You're under arrest for obstruction." He twisted Justin's arms behind him, slapped on the handcuffs. "Chief. I need another squad car over here."

In one smooth motion, Justin handed the handcuffs back to Wallace. "Last chance."

"Hey." He stared at his unlocked cuffs in disbelief. "How did you do that?" When he looked up, the cowboy was gone. "Son of a bitch."

Chief Daniels approached. "What is it now, Wallace?"

"Did you see that cowboy?"

"What cowboy?"

Oh brother. If he tried to explain it, Chief Daniels wouldn't believe him anyway. "Never mind." He stepped to the Expedition and let Chops jump out. "We're going in."

***

The chief watched Wallace and his black lab go inside, even though the firemen hadn't finished mopping up. "Be careful in there, inspector. The ceiling isn't stable."

A Texas Rangers car pulled in, and Captain Holland emerged. "Did he find anything yet?"

"He just went in," Daniels replied, concerned about the structural integrity of the house. Normally, Wallace would've waited for a safety check before entering with his dog, but this time he seemed in an unusual hurry to begin his investigation.

"There's something we have to discuss about this case," Holland said, gesturing to the house. "It's a sting operation."

"What are you talking about?"

"Inspector Wallace is under investigation for evidence tampering."

"Nonsense. He's the best—"

"Look at how many arson cases he's handled, over twice the national average."

"Deckers has had a string of arsonists, true."

"God only knows how many innocent people have been convicted because of him."

"He's been an efficient investigator." Daniels couldn't think of any reason to doubt Wallace's conclusions.

"We started this fire," Holland said. "But we didn't use an accelerant; we shorted out the main fuse box."

"Why wasn't I informed of this operation?"

"The fewer people who knew, the better, less chance of a leak. We don't know if anyone else is involved."

"God, I hope not." Daniels feared a conspiracy within his department could ruin his career.

"I've found it," Wallace shouted from the blackened doorway. "It's arson, all right. Chops picked up on an accelerant right away. I'm going to nail that damn Cunningham, this time for good."

"What the hell's he talking about?" Holland asked. "Cunningham was put to death three days ago."

Daniels knew full well what this was about. His insides knotted at the thought of his best investigator deliberately reporting the facts wrong. He looked at Holland. "The main fuse box, you say?"

Holland nodded.

"I'm going to find out once and for all." Daniels sprinted to the door, shoved Wallace aside, and rushed inside the blackened house. The air reeked of smoke and soot. Creaking sounds came from the weakened ceiling, and judging from the water seeping down through the drywall, he figured the attic was plumb full. Thoughts of retreating outside were overruled by his need to know the truth, so he pressed on.

Drawing his flashlight, he made his way around the burned out interior, careful not to trip on all the floating debris. He found the fuse box in the kitchen back wall. Right away, in the light beam, he saw residual flack from heavy electrical arcing. It had gotten so hot the metal had turned blue. And a quick sweep of the light revealed the heavy burn damage surrounding this area. It had actually exposed two-by-four wall joists that looked like standing columns of charcoal. No, it didn't take an expert to determine the origin of this fire. Yet his top investigator blamed it on the use of an accelerant. Why? Did he do it for money? The city paid him well for his services. Or did he do it for fame, to be the best in his field at all costs? One thing for sure, Wallace was one sick bastard.

Fuming mad, Daniels made his way back through the front room, quickly picking up his steps as he passed under a sagging, creaky ceiling that wouldn't hold up much longer under the weight of the water in the attic.

Once outside, he ordered his men to cordon off the area. "Nobody goes in. The ceiling is about to collapse." And looking at Holland, "You're right."

"Here comes our man," Holland said, indicating Jeff Wallace's approach from the Expedition.

"My report." Wallace handed it to the chief.

"What's the rush?" Daniels eyed the report. *Arson,* it read. *Traces of an accelerant found.* The dumb bastard had already put it in writing.

"We've got the suspect in custody," Wallace announced. "Todd Cunningham."

Daniels had no choice. The guy just kept digging his hole deeper. "Captain Holland, arrest him." He indicated Wallace.

The investigator stepped back. "Now wait a minute."

Holland got out the cuffs. "Put your hands behind your back."

"What the hell is this?"

"Evidence tampering for starters," Daniels said. "And the murder of Todd Cunningham if I have my way."

Wallace bolted. Holland grabbed him by the jacket, spun him around, but he broke free and dashed inside the house.

"Get out of there," Chief Daniels shouted. "The ceiling is going to collapse."

"Then you don't dare come in after me."

"We'll work it out, Jeff." That's all Daniels needed, a

standoff. One hour, two, eight, he doubted they had that many minutes.

"You never doubted me before, chief. It's that cowboy, I tell you. He set me up."

"What cowboy?"

"I'm the expert—"

The house shuddered. Wood cracked. The ceiling came down with a horrendous crash and blast of soot followed by a deluge of water.

Chops took off running, tail tucked between his legs.

With no regard for their own safety, firemen stormed through the door and started clawing through the rubble, lifting timbers, tossing aside soaked insulation and breaking up slabs of drywall. One of their own had fallen. Whether he was a good guy or a bad guy, Daniels knew it didn't matter to his men.

***

Justin Graves floated inside the house. It didn't matter that the space remaining between the ceiling and floor only amounted to three inches at best. His ghostly form contorted as needed for him to gain access to the crushed fire investigator, whose body was convulsing under the extreme pressure. Blood oozed from his mouth, nose, and eyeballs. In moments, he'd be dead, but he didn't need to be conscious to hear Justin's voice.

"You should've taken my advice, Inspector Wallace."

"I can't breathe."

"Now all your cases will be reexamined."

"I'm dying."

"Innocent prisoners will be released."

"Help me."

"Deckers will have to pay out millions in settlements. Your fraudulent legacy ends right here...in disgrace."

"I'm the best..."

"Todd Cunningham can now rest in peace."

"I don't want to die."

"And where you're going, fire reigns supreme."

"No."

The man's soul released from the body. Justin felt it float a moment, and then it disappeared on its spiraling journey down to hell.

Todd's ghostly form appeared beside Justin. "He'll never bear false witness again." Little David and Sally were with him. "I can cross over now."

"Was it worth it?" Justin asked, knowing the horror they'd relived to reenact the disaster.

"There's nothing I wouldn't do for my kids." Todd hugged them close. "Including relive the worst night of my life."

"I know you'd have climbed those burning steps if you could have."

"Yeah, but compared to your problems, Justice, this charade was a cakewalk. I've got my kids back while your daughter still languishes in hell."

"But I'm one soul closer to setting her free."

"Good luck, Justice."

With a gust of wind the ghoul was gone.

Terry Wright

Dog Fighter

In the dark confines of the small space, Benny felt the tire jack jabbing him in the back. Ropes burned his wrists, and every bump reminded him of how bad he had to pee. He breathed through his nose on account of the duct tape over his mouth. Being trussed up like a holiday ham wasn't what he'd expected. It was all a big misunderstanding. Now he doubted he'd get out of this trunk alive.

Maybe Cisco's homeboys would drive the car into a lake, watch it sink. Or perhaps park it in some remote backwoods and use it for target practice. They had an arsenal of stolen semi-automatic pistols, M-16s, and even an Uzi. Or maybe they'd park the car somewhere and set it on fire. Oh man, please don't set it on fire. Jesus Christ, he didn't want to burn to death.

The car jerked to a stop. Both doors opened and slammed shut. Benny gritted his teeth. The trunk lid popped, letting in a rush of air. Beefy hands grabbed him, yanked him out. He tried to tell the bastards to take it easy, but his words came out muffled. *"Tkkk mmms ssee."*

As they propped him up against the rear fender, he got a good look around. Industrial part of town. Long rows of warehouses on each side of an alley. A spackling of security lights illuminated dumpsters down the way. The homeboys were going to shoot him and throw his body in the trash. Sure as hell. *I didn't do anything wrong.*

A four-door Caddy pulled up, white, with windows tinted black, and chrome spinners. The sight of Cisco's car made Benny's bladder burn.

The driver door opened, high-top Nikes slapped pavement, and a banger in Decker's South Side gang got out, all five-foot-two of him, skinny as a nail, though his oversized Steelers jacket made him look bigger. He wore baggy pants so low that his Fruit-of-the-Looms was showing. Benny could break the punk in half, given the chance.

"All right, Benny," Cisco said. "Time to settle up."

Mmmm ppppddd uuunnn.

Cisco stalked up while slugging his left palm with his right fist. "Where is my bones?"

Cringing, Benny wished this wasn't a meeting about the money. When would he learn that gambling ain't his bag? He couldn't speak, so he just shook his head.

Cisco motioned to one of his homeboys. The bastard yanked the tape off Benny's mouth. Felt like it took lip skin with it, but he wasted no time trying to lighten the mood. "Cisco, bet you never thought you'd see the likes of me again."

"The money, wise guy."

"I'll get it. You know me, man." The words came out gritty as sand. Fear had sucked the spit out of his tongue. "I'd never weasel out on a bet. Butch killed Chaser, won fair and square. I just need to make another score, man. I'll get you the money. Give me a chance."

"I already gave you a chance."

"That wasn't my fault. The North Side brothers jumped me and took your blow."

"You are a liar." Cisco backhanded Benny across the face. "You sold it and kept the cash."

Benny saw stars. "I didn't. I swear."

This time Cisco slugged him in the stomach, buckled him over, winding him bad.

"On my mother's grave." Benny wheezed, fearing a

Terry Wright

beat-down wouldn't be the worst of it. Homeboys held his arms, kept him from keeling over.

Cisco smiled wickedly, pinched Benny's cheek. "How about...I make you a wager."

Betting had gotten Benny into this jam in the first place, on dogfights. Cisco had the meanest dog of all, Butch, a sixty-five pound pit bull that killed Chaser like he was just a squirrel. Less than two minutes in the pit. A real blood frenzy. Sure, Chaser was a long shot, but long shots paid off bigger. Damn dog cost him a grand he didn't have.

"I'll pass on your wager," Benny managed through clenched teeth.

Cisco grabbed Benny's hair, yanked his head back. "I make the rules. You cannot pass." He shoved Benny's head down, stepped away. "Cut him loose, dawgs."

"Huh?" Had Benny heard the gangbanger right? *Cut me loose?*

The homeboys drew their knives.

Or cut me good? Benny wondered how much that was going to hurt, but sure enough, they cut his arms free. Rubbing his wrists, he saw Cisco retreating to his car. "Thanks, man. You won't regret this." He started to walk off.

A homey stepped in front of him, big as a brick wall.

"But..." Benny showed him his freed hands.

Homeboy turned him around to face the Cadillac. Benny saw Cisco standing next to the rear door, now joined by his son, Pauley, eight years old. The boy held a small dog in his arms, a beagle like Snoopy. What the hell was he doing here?

Cisco knelt to the boy. "Watch what happens when a scumbag reneges on a bet."

"You gonna kill him, papa?"

He tousled the boy's hair. "No. Not me, son."

A sharp pain stabbed Benny's bladder. If Cisco wasn't going to kill him then who was going to do the deed? He cast a frightful look at the homeboys. Nah. They'd have killed him already. Obviously Cisco planned for his son to watch something especially horrid. This wasn't Sesame Street, for God's sake. "Come on, Cisco, give me a break, will ya?"

Cisco stood. "How fast can you run, Benny?" He pointed down the alley. "You make it to the other end alive, you win, all bets are off. You get your juice back."

Benny's momma didn't raise no fool. "You'll cap me in the back. Nobody can outrun no bullet."

"But if you do not make it..." Cisco opened the rear car door, revealing a big cage with a barred door and a chrome latch. "You die."

With a vicious growl, a dog charged the cage door, banged its muzzle into the bars like it felt no pain.

Butch!

Benny peed in his pants. "That ain't funny, Cisco."

The pit bull's black eyes bored into Benny like he was a slab of fresh meat.

Cisco reached for the door latch.

Butch growled.

Stepping back, Benny's heart started banging against his ribs. "You gotta be shittin' me, man?"

"I will give you a head start," he offered. "Count to five. Ready? One..."

Adrenaline hit Benny's bloodstream like a runaway train.

"Two..."

He took off down the alley, panicked feet nearly tripping him up.

"Five..."

"Five?" Benny heard the latch spring, the cage door

swing open. Butch's bulk hit the pavement with a scrambling thud.

"Sorry," Cisco shouted. "My math, it is not so good."

The cheating bastard, Benny cursed as he flew past dumpsters, hoping to find one with an open lid. Nothing. Blood pumped through him so hard he could hear it in his ears. Dog claws scraped pavement behind him...at breakneck speed, gaining, in spite of his all-out sprint, lungs burning, mind maddened with fear.

Butch hit him like a cement truck, knocked him to the ground, teeth gnashing, throat growling. Benny heard a scream like no scream he'd ever heard. His scream.

Bear trap jaws clamped down on his left forearm, fangs tore meat and snapped bone. Horrendous pain rifled through his body. He could smell the dog's foul breath.

"Down, boy," he shouted.

Butch shook him like a dead rabbit.

"Call him off. Call him off." Benny fought back. Kicking dog balls. Pounding his right fist into a muscular ribcage. The more Benny fought, the more he bled and the more blood-frenzied Butch got. Crazy. Benny's arm couldn't hold off the dog any longer. It gave way to the tremendous pressure of canine teeth and jaws. As the muscles tore and the forearm separated from his elbow, Benny's scream echoed down the alley that proved longer than his lifespan.

Butch shook the stub like a chew toy then lunged for Benny's throat, crushed his windpipe and cut off his air. Gagging, he felt hot blood gush out his nostrils. Strength leaked from him, the will to fight gone. Poor Chaser must've felt the same way when he was fiercely overpowered in the fight pit. Terrified. Helpless.

This was no way for dog or man to die.

***

Strolling a golf course in the afterlife was actually walking on clouds. Cirrus blanketed the fairways, cumulonimbus towered in the rough, and traps were black holes in the universe. They were like that on earth, too, Justin recalled as he lined up for his tee shot on the ninth hole. No need to use a golf tee, though; the ball simply hovered above the cotton-soft ground. Whacking a ball around helped take out his frustration over Christy's predicament in hell, which he couldn't do anything about until the next bad guy came around, his next case, and it seemed Billy Denton was lying low, for now. Justin was just about ready to swing when a disturbance in the light interrupted his concentration. The cloudy golf course began to churn and boil like a brewing storm.

"Justice." The light spoke in Wach-el's deep voice.

"Can't you see I'm in the middle of my game?"

Everything around him erupted into smoke and flame. An ethereal wind tore at his long brown coat. He had to hang on to the brim of his cowboy hat to keep it from flying away. The afterlife was a strange place, where tormented souls found solace before crossing over to everlasting peace, but never had he experienced its serenity so violently disturbed.

"You have a visitor, Justice...a visitor from hell."

"I work for the other side," Justin shouted into the tempest.

"Make your friends wherever you can find them, Justice."

A figure appeared in the fiery storm, limping forward, a man wearing shredded clothes that whipped in the wind.

"This is Benny Nevaro, petty crook, smalltime hustler. Con man. He has a rap sheet ten feet long."

Justin leaned on his golf club. "What's he want with me?"

Terry Wright

"He lost a bet on a dog fight, got himself killed."

"You expect me to have sympathy for him?"

"Hear him out, Justice." The voice in the light faded away, taking the golf club with it.

"Hey. I was two under par." But the game was over. He couldn't remember finishing a round up here anyway, sighed and turned to his approaching visitor.

As Benny drew closer, the true horror of his condition became evident: wide open eyes ringed in white, severe facial lacerations leaking blood, and air hissing from a splayed-open throat, the jugular still spewing. Torn meat hung from his left elbow where his forearm used to be attached.

"What happened to you?" Justin asked.

"Dog bite," Benny replied in a sputtery voice.

He probably deserved what he got, but still, Justin wondered why the light had allowed a man condemned to hell to disturb the serenity of the afterlife. "What are you doing here?"

"I didn't come for myself, man." The blood spilling out of him dissolved as it fell. "I'm a criminal, always been, took people for whatever they got, including Cisco. Yeah, I boosted his blow. Stole his bones...his cash. So what? He's got everything already. Cadillac. Fancy duds—"

"What's that got to do with me?"

Yellow flames reflected a fiery vision from the land of the living. Justin and Benny turned to see a tall fence materialize in the darkness of night. Beyond it, a warehouse appeared, flat roof and corrugated steel walls stippled with perimeter lights. The sounds of riotous revelry reached Justin.

A smoky scene came into focus, inside the warehouse, a string of hanging light bulbs around a low-walled dirt pit and a gathering of excited people. Justin first noticed the diversity of their apparel: men dressed in expensive business suits or blue jeans, women in flowing gowns or short-shorts and bikini tops, like a cross-section of America all in one place. They clutched wads of cash in their fists and shouted out bets to a short skinny guy flanked by a couple thugs.

"That's Cisco," Benny rasped, spitting blood. "A banger with a winning fight dog's got juice, commands respect in the gang. If it weren't for Butch, Cisco would be lying in a ditch somewhere. He's nothin' but a twerp on a head trip."

Rap music hammered the air, annoying Justin.

"His dog Butch, like most fight dogs, ain't raised with no tender loving care. He got beatings, sleep deprived, constant exercise. Butch never ate dog food from a bowl either. Cisco fed him live rabbits, cats, and other dogs. He learnt to kill to eat and grew up a druggy for fresh blood. In the pit, it's called a blood frenzy, and once the bloodletting is started, it's got to be satisfied. Butch won't quit till he's got his fill."

Justin knew fight dogs had it rough, but animal abuse and dog fighting, though illegal, weren't capital crimes.

As the betting reached a fever pitch, the vision panned the area, past the ring of dangling light bulbs to a dimmer part of the warehouse. Rows of caged dogs came into view, barking, growling, and yapping. Two men, trainers, Justin assumed, stood at a treadmill where a dog ran to exhaustion, tongue flopping. From the rafters, a dog hung by the neck, swinging back and forth on the rope, still as death.

Bleeding profusely, Benny explained, "If a dog loses a fight, the owner loses his juice. So he kills the dog in the cruelest way he can think of, hanging, drowning, even skinning it alive."

Terry Wright

"And you want me stop the dog fights?"

"No man, I want you to save Cisco's son, Pauley."

"Why would you care what happens to a kid?"

"One minute in hell can shed a whole new light on the consequences of livin' a life of crime."

Justin wouldn't argue with that.

"Cisco killed me, used the dog to do his dirt, made Pauley watch me die. So I want to bust his hold on the kid, the way he's schoolin' him to be mean. Won't get me any juice in hell, but what the hell."

"I won't come between a father and his son," Justin said. Family was too important.

"Then watch this." Benny pointed to the fiery light. "See if you don't change your mind."

The vision panned back to the unruly mob pressing in on the lighted pit. Within its three-foot-high boarded walls, Butch stalked side to side, sniffing the dirt, growling. Justin didn't want to see a dog fight. He was about to protest when he saw a boy standing at the wall, clutching a small beagle.

"That's Pauley," Benny said.

He looked like a nice kid, real Norman Rockwell the way he held the dog, all droopy.

Cisco approached the boy, pointed to the fight pit. Pauley shook his head, wouldn't look at his father. Tears began streaming down his cheeks as he hugged his little dog. Cisco tugged on the beagle's scruff, but the boy wouldn't let go. His cries could be heard over the cheering crowd.

Justin now understood what the father demanded of his son.

Cisco shook the boy's arm. Butch charged the wall, darted away sharply, growled, turned in frantic circles, barking like crazy.

~316~

"Do it." Cisco slapped the boy upside the head.

Slowly, Pauley lifted the small beagle up and held it over the wall.

"No shit," Justin muttered, wishing the vision was only a nightmare.

Pauley looked once more to his father. There was no reprieve in his eyes. With a trembling hand, the boy dropped his dog into the pit. Growling, Butch charged. The image dissolved into a stormy cloud of fiery light splattered with red spots.

Justin felt sick. He'd seen a lot of blood and gore during his years as a Texas Ranger, but this hit him hard, not only for the beagle's fate, but for how Cisco's cruelty would affect the boy.

Benny stood stone-faced. "What better way to toughen up a kid than to give him a dog, let him feed it, love it, and then make him send it to its death."

Justin sat in a chair the light had provided. The thought of killing Cisco came to mind, but thoughts like that could get him in trouble with the devil.

"It's all about the juice, man."

"I don't get it. The devil wants Cisco's soul." Justin glared at his dog-mauled visitor from hell. "He wants my soul, too, damn it. Hell, he wants every soul, yet he releases yours long enough to ask me to save a boy from his own father. It doesn't make any sense. Why would he do that?"

Blood spurting from his neck, Benny moved closer to Justin. "It wasn't the devil's idea, no, some chick talked Satan into sending me to see you."

That caused Justin's ethereal soul to jump from the chair. "A chick?"

"A good lookin' squeeze, too. Ah..." Benny paused in thought while eternal rivulets of blood trickled down his face. "Sittin' on a throne of fire, man. She's got some juice with the devil. Christy...that's it...that's her name."

"My daughter." Justin fell back into his chair. All around him the afterlife churned in hellish red and yellow flames. He felt numb.

"She used to babysit little Pauley back when she was still kickin'."

That was entirely possible. Christy ran with Billy Denton's East Street Gang for so long, she could've met other bangers, could've watched Pauley from time to time.

"Christy wants you to save him. The devil wants you to do it for her."

No way. The devil cheated at Solitaire. This request had more to do with their deal than a banger boy's future. "You think that's it?" Justin shot to his feet. "You dumbass," he shouted at Benny. "The devil used you to set me up. He doesn't care what Christy wants, but he thinks I'll kill Cisco if she's okay with it."

"You'll have to kill his homeboys first."

"It's a trap, all right."

Benny stepped back, a look of confusion on his bleeding face. "I-I don't know about no trap, man."

"But we're not going to let him get away with it."

"We? What...?"

Justin raised his arms to the hellish fire, and a massive explosion sent a black cloud of smoke swirling through the afterlife. Now masked in darkness, he worked Benny's transfiguration. As the smoke cleared, he batted the air with his cowboy hat until white light gleamed all around him.

Benny coughed. The dead banger's new form slowly became visible; he was the spitting image of Justin himself, same sewn up face, same molars, same cowboy hat drizzling dust, same grimy long coat and shiny circle-star badge. Behind him, radiating light beams gave the clone an aura of authority. "What have you done to me, man?"

"You're the decoy."

He eyed the badge pinned to his coat. "I'm a cop now?"

"Don't let it go to your head." Justin tossed him the Winchester.

"What's this for?"

"You're going in first."

***

The warehouse lights dimmed, and the rap music fell silent. Caged and fed, the fighting dogs settled in for the night. Except for an occasional yap or growl, little else reminded Cisco of the evening's festivities.

He sat at a table illuminated by a single bulb. Butch, the killer of beagle puppies, lay at his feet. Two homeboys, armed with M-16s, stood guard on either side of them. The pile of money on the table needed counting, but Cisco's attention was on his son, Pauley. The boy had curled up in a fetal position on the nearby ratty couch, and he was crying like a girl. So what if Butch had killed his little beagle? No reason to cry about it.

When is he gonna man up?

Dogman, one of the trainers, along with his partner, Snoops, strode up from the back where the dogs were kept. The homeys were heavily armed.

"Looks like a kickin' haul tonight." Snoops took a seat in front of the money. "And we only lost two dogs."

Dogman handed out cigars and passed around a lighter. "Congratulations, Cisco."

He inhaled smoke, still staring at his boy. "I should whoop his ass, give him a good reason to cry."

"He'll get over it." Dogman puffed life into his cigar.

Gritting his teeth, Cisco scowled at Dogman. "At this rate he will never have no juice."

Terry Wright

Dogman sat at the table. "Just go easy on him."

"The poodle is makin' me look bad." Cisco leaned forward. "Ya know what I do when that happens." He looked down at Butch lying at his feet then kicked him in the ribs.

The dog yelped and scrambled to his feet, growling at Cisco.

"Down, boy," he commanded.

Butch cowered and lay down.

"I got juice with that dog, man, not because I loved and pampered him, but because I made him scared to death of me."

"Ain't right to treat your dog like that," Dogman said. "He's not a pet. He's a fighting dog, and Pauley's just a boy."

Snoops blew cigar smoke. "Boy's gotta learn. Same as a dog."

"Butch knows I am the boss." Cisco examined his cigar. "A good woopin' will straighten Pauley out too."

"Leave me alone, papa," Pauley shouted, his face buried in the couch cushion. "I hate you."

Cisco shot to his feet so fast the chair fell over. "Do not diss me, boy."

Cigar clamped in his teeth, Dogman leaned forward and grabbed two handfuls of money. "Let's count the cash and go home."

Suddenly, the stench of dog shit swirled in the air. Cisco covered his face with his hand, glared down at Butch. "Ah, damn, why you go and fart like that?"

Butch licked his chops.

Snoops and Dogman looked pallid, like they were going to puke. The smell kept getting worse and worse but not from the dog...maybe from somewhere deep in the warehouse. "What the hell is going on back there?"

Justin Graves

The homeboy guards started hacking.

Pauley kept crying.

"Somebody open a window," Cisco shouted. "Jesus."
That's when he saw a cowboy step from the shadows. He just stood there like Wyatt Earp at the OK Corral, cowboy hat cocked on his head, long brown coat, and Winchester rifle at his side. *Rifle?* "He's packin'." Cisco ducked under the table and crouched behind Butch's sixty-five pound body to use it as a shield. "Cap him, bros."

The homeboys opened fire with their M-16s set on automatic. Snoops pulled his Uzi and started banging away. Dogman threw his body over Pauley on the couch. Butch stood, eyes fixed on the cowboy and growling. To keep the dog from charging into a spray of flying lead, Cisco held him back by the collar.

Shell casings tinkled across the floor, and the acidic reek of gunpowder quickly overpowered the stink of dog shit. Cisco watched between the dog's legs as bullets tore into the cowboy, each impact spewing a poof of dust. *They got him.* His body jolted spastically from the pummeling barrage, but he wouldn't go down. Instead, he raised his Winchester and started pumping out rounds.

Snoops got capped first, flew out of his chair and slammed to the floor, not three feet from Cisco, legs splayed and blood spurting from his forehead. His gun landed beside him.

Cisco nearly retched, scooted sideways toward the gun, his heart beating wildly. He glanced back at his homeboys firing away, wishing they'd hurry up and put the dude down. But one after the other, the homeboys hit the floor, bleeding.

Butch started yapping. The smell of all that gore had stirred him into a blood-frenzy, but Cisco held him by the collar, not wanting to lose his shield.

Terry Wright

When the gunfire stopped, he peered around his dog. The cowboy was still standing. Butch yapped and tugged; he wanted to get at him bad.

"Dogman..." the cowboy shouted, "take the boy and get out of here."

Cisco seethed. Who was that cowboy to give orders around here? He had no juice, but Dogman and Pauley fled anyway. How dare them take orders from a stranger? Now it was just Cisco, Butch, and the cowboy left in the warehouse. And yapping Butch wanted blood, but Cisco had to hold him until he could get the dropped gun.

"Cisco..." the cowboy said. "Bet you never thought you'd see the likes of me again."

That voice...it damn near stopped Cisco's heart. The cowboy sounded like Benny, Benny Nevaro, the thieving prick who stole Cisco's blow and his bones. No wonder Butch was frantic to get at him. The dog recognized his scent, even in that cowboy get up, under which he probably wore body armor, but still, Butch had already killed him once. He wanted his blood again.

How the hell was Benny alive now?

The cowboy-Benny stepped forward, rifle raised at Cisco. "Get up, you coward."

This was it. He was going to die.

Suddenly, the floor bubbled up around the cowboy's feet, causing him to stop and look down at a caustic pool of roiling sewage.

The acrid smell made Butch yelp and pull back.

Cisco keeled over and held his nose. *What the hell is that shit?*

From out of the steaming sewage rose slimy white tubular grubs, swaying and writhing, a dozen or more: three feet, five feet, eight feet high. The giant maggots made slurping sounds as they surrounded the cowboy. Whirling, he fired his rifle, but the bullets had no effect on the maggots' squishy bodies.

A round mouth ringed with wiggling feelers and jagged teeth popped out of a maggot and swallowed the cowboy's rifle, arm and all. Another maggot clamped onto his left leg, crunching bone. Yet another chomped on his remaining arm. Benny screamed.

Then a ghostly image appeared, the head of a man suspended in midair, a familiar face with a forked red goatee and silver rings in his eyebrows. Billy Denton from the East Street Gang. He was dead too, Cisco knew, and pressed his hands to his face, wishing the nightmare would end.

"Justice," Billy said to the cowboy. "You have broken the rules. Now the devil has come for his dues." Cackling laughter echoed within the warehouse walls.

"No," the cowboy shouted. "You're makin' a mistake, man."

Billy's image faded along with his laughter.

Mouth open and teeth gnashing, an eight-foot maggot swooped down on the screaming cowboy. It slurped in his head, hat and all, slowly sucking him in up to his eye sockets then his nose hole and his bony jaw until his screams became just a murmur. And when he was gone, the bubbling pool of sewage and monster maggots sank into the floor and disappeared.

Butch licked his chops.

Shaking, Cisco got to his feet, glanced around and suddenly realized he'd cheated death. Relief and joy spilled out in uncontrollable laughter. He'd faced the demons of hell and lived to tell about it. That meant only one thing. He had more juice than God himself.

Butch growled.

Cisco stopped laughing, felt a pang of dread as he

looked at his dog. Butch had alerted on something in the shadows. *Now what?*

Heavy footsteps. Raspy breathing. Someone was there, all right. Cisco bent to pick up Snoops' gun. By the time he straightened, that damn cowboy had stepped from the shadows. This time he had no rifle.

"You again?" Cisco pointed the gun at him. "Have you not had enough for one night, Benny?"

The cowboy tipped his hat. "My name is Justin Graves," he said in a gravelly voice. "But you can call me Justice." The stench of rot wafted on his breath.

That wasn't Benny's voice. And up close like this, he could see stitches in the cowboy's face, sewed up like Frankenstein's monster. Gray hair cascaded from his hat to his shoulders, and he stunk as bad as that cesspool from hell. Butch growled at the cowboy, but Cisco held the collar. In his other hand, the gun wavered. "What do you want?"

"I'm here to save your son from a life of crime."

"He don't need savin'." Cisco spat. "But you do."

Cisco pulled the trigger, shot the cowboy dead center in the chest. He just stood there like Benny did. Was this the night of the living dead twins? Cisco fired again and again until the gun clicked empty. *Damn it.* He threw down the gun. "I'm warning you, man. I'll sic my dog on you."

Butch growled like mad.

"I know a nice couple in Dallas," Justin said and stepped forward. "They'll take Pauley in—"

"Nobody's takin' my kid nowhere."

"They'll give him a good home, good education."

"He's schooled just fine where he is."

"You're preening him to be a criminal," Justin said.

"That's none of your Kool-Aid, man."

"You're not fit to be a father."

"He's gotta have juice to survive in the hood."

"Gangbanging. Dog fighting. Dope dealing. There's a much better life waiting for him in the real world."

"Go to hell, Justice."

"Been there, done that. Now it's your turn."

"Then bring it on, bro." Cisco released Butch's collar. "Get him, boy."

Growling, Butch charged Justin, knocked him over. His cowboy hat flew off, and he hit the ground in a cloud of dust. Holding up his left arm to ward off the dog was a useless attempt at self-defense. Butch tore into the cowboy's coat sleeve, ripping it open, and sunk his teeth into rotting flesh.

"Kill him, Butch." Cisco wanted to jump up and down, he felt that elated.

The cowboy was pinned on his back. He used his feet to pivot in a circle so his body tripped up the dog, but Butch held on, tearing rot from bone. Cisco expected to see blood spewing everywhere, and when he didn't, he felt his stomach cramp. Butch was after the blood, but he wasn't getting any. That had never happened before.

Growling, Butch let go of the cowboy's ragged arm bone and bit into his left thigh. The dog had worked himself into a blood frenzy, biting and tearing at Justin's leg. Cisco had never seen him act so wild and out of control, a masterpiece of brutality in motion.

"You're a dead man, Justice."

Inexplicably, Butch stopped the attack, sniffed Justin's bloodless leg wounds, and then leered at Cisco.

"Blood frenzy," Justin said. "It needs to be satisfied...'til he gets his fill. That's the way you trained him, right?"

"Benny tell you that?"

Head low and growling at Cisco, Butch licked his

chops. Drool stretched to the floor.

Cisco stepped back, felt the weight of Butch's deadly stare. "Benny's just a thief and a snitch."

"Thanks to him, I was able to get you alone." Justin stood. "I wasn't allowed to use violence against your bodyguards. He didn't know that."

Butch took a crouched step toward Cisco, teeth bared.

"Easy, boy." Cisco had seen that blood lust glare before...but never directed at him. He felt dizzy with fright.

"And Benny had plenty of reason to kill you and your homeys. I knew he'd start shooting. And like I figured, Billy Denton thought Benny was me and sucked him back to hell where he came from."

Snarling, Butch charged Cisco.

"When you see Benny down there, be sure to tell him he's got juice with me."

Scrambling backward, Cisco wished he hadn't wasted all those bullets. "Down, boy."

The dog kept coming.

"Stop."

All Cisco saw was teeth and jaws.

"Justice—"

Chomp.

With a gust of wind the ghoul was gone.

Hate Crime

I n the darkened room of a rundown house on the forgotten side of Deckers, 41-year-old Jenny Vandenburg lay curled up on a tattered mattress, her body wracked with chronic pain from an old bullet wound. Her wheelchair was parked an arm's reach away, and in her right hand, she clutched a bottle of pain pills. It had been an agonizing five years since she'd been shot, and tonight, for the first time, she knew peace would come to her.

She shed no tears; she'd already cried enough: for herself, for her growing sons, and for the stranger whose life she'd tried to save that fateful night. Back then she was a heroine, a Good Samaritan they'd called her. The mayor honored her, showered her with praise and financial assistance, and as she convalesced, her optimism and fighting spirit were an inspiration to everyone in town. However, after countless surgeries, the doctors finally told her they couldn't fix her spinal wound. The bullet had done too much damage. So they prescribed for her an array of pills that did little or nothing to relieve her suffering. The public's attention soon waned, and she found herself left with the crushing reality of getting through each painful day. Through it all, her sons had grown out of childhood, and now she lay in bed, hardly able to sit up.

Today's news had dealt her the final blow. She'd thrown the newspaper on the floor when she saw the headlines: *Burnham Freed.* Now despair over her agonizing paralysis and the outcome of the trial made her contemplate the only remedy she had left. She just wanted to get it over with.

Her 15-year-old son poked his head in the bedroom door. "Mom, can I have a Hot Pocket?"

"Yes, dear," she said weakly.

"Are you all right?"

"I don't want to live anymore."

"You always say that, Mom."

"Where's your brother?"

"Watching TV in his room."

"Go to bed soon, both of you."

"Goodnight, Mom." He closed the door.

"Goodbye," she whispered to herself. Mostly she feared what would become of her boys. After all, she'd endured all this misery to raise them properly. Now, they were nearly young adults. They'd been forced to mature much too quickly due to the circumstances that arose from that horrible night she was shot. If she had it to do all over again, she wondered if she would've turned the other way when those skinheads accosted the black stranger at the bus stop. Right now, she didn't know. Right now, she didn't care. The pill bottle came up to her lips, and with a mighty gulp, she took the last medication she'd ever need.

***

In the afterlife, the light flickered and glowed, an indication to Justin that there was something he needed to know. He sat in his recliner and set his cowboy hat on his knee.

"A hate crime was committed five years ago," the angel Wach-el said from the light. *"Its final victim has just died, and she will come to you, Justice. While you are waiting, I want to show you what happened."*

The light parted, revealing a scene from the past. A bus stop appeared on a downtown street corner.

Justin Graves

"It was after two o'clock in the morning."
Only a dim streetlamp lit the area. A slight-framed black man wearing a baseball cap sat on the bench.
"His name is Edmond Day."
Justin noticed how unassuming the man appeared, even frail.
"He has just finished his shift at the hotel where he works as a bellhop. He sends most of his wages to his village in Africa where his wife and three children live. They had dreams of coming to America."
Justin nodded in admiration of the immigrant and then noticed a woman approaching the bench.
"Her name is Jenny Vandenburg. She's a single mother of two fine boys and works as a nurses' aide at the hospital nearby. It's a paycheck-to-paycheck existence for her, but she's determined to make life better for her sons."
"Hello," Jenny said to the black man, Edmond Day. He tipped the bill of his ball cap, and she sat next to him.
A commotion down the street quickly drew their attention to two men walking toward the bus stop. Justin's throat clutched at the sight of them. They wore chain-laced leather vests, camouflaged pants tucked into combat boots, and black gloves with the fingers cut off. Their heads were shaved, and more alarming, they displayed tattoos of swastikas, exploding atom bombs, hooded KKK figures, and burning crosses.
"These skinheads have just left their jobs at a gas station and are headed for the Fourth Reich Bar, a Mecca of white supremacists and the Neo-Nazi movement."
Swapping obscenities and laughing, they bantered back and forth as they approached, but when they spotted the small black man sitting on the bus stop bench, their demeanor suddenly changed.
"Whatta we have here?" the larger of the two

Terry Wright

skinheads said and elbowed his buddy.

Justin felt the air become charged with tension.

"The big guy's name is Gary Burnham."

The shorter skinhead stepped in front of the black man and loomed over him. "Black people don't belong here," he growled. "This is white territory."

"Leave him alone," Jenny said to the skinheads.

"Stay out of this, bitch," Burnham spat.

Jenny glared at them both.

"I am a peaceful man from Africa," Edmond Day said in his own defense. "It is good that I see you, yes?"

"Shut up," Burnham growled. "Nobody said you could talk to us." He grabbed little Edmond Day, punched him, choked him, and then frisked his pockets. In the struggle, the ball cap fell off his head, and Jenny retrieved it from the ground.

"Stop it," she shouted. She was trying to give the hat back to Edmond, a clear attempt to distract the skinheads, when the shorter skinhead pulled out a gun and shot the black man four times.

"Come on," Burnham said, holding up a few dollars and a cheap watch that he'd pilfered from the dead man.

The killer cast Jenny a menacing glare. "She's a witness."

"Then shoot the bitch," Burnham said.

To Justin's horror, the skinhead shot her. Then they took off running in opposite directions. Justin felt a suffocating chill. "Did they get away with it?"

"The shooter was convicted and sentenced to life in prison, but this crime is not about him. It's about Gary Burnham. He too was convicted of murder and sentenced to life plus forty-eight years."

"So all's well that ends well," Justin stated matter-of-factly.

Justin Graves

"Problem is, his lawyers won a retrial based on a technicality. And instead of going to trial again, Burnham copped a plea and got a 12-year sentence. With time served, he's getting out of prison today."

"I don't understand..." Justin scowled. "The law specifically states that if a murder occurs during the commission of a felony, all participants are considered equally guilty of the murder."

"But in this case, the District Attorney did not want to put Jenny through another trial. She was willing to testify again, mind you, but because of her previous outbursts in court during the first trial, the DA elected to accept the plea bargain, rather than risk a sympathetic jury."

"What happened?"

"Jenny was a flamboyant and outspoken woman who sometimes made her point with profanity. In the original trial, when Burnham's defense lawyer attacked her credibility as a witness, she swore at him. He claimed her outburst prevented Burnham from getting a fair trial."

"Is that why he got a new trial?"

"No. The appeals judge did not consider that argument because the technicality issue was enough to warrant a new trial."

"What was the technicality?"

"The trial judge wrongfully accepted into evidence a video confession made by the shooter to a television station, rather than bring him into court. In the video, he bragged about killing a black man, and though he didn't implicate Burnham, the defense claimed it could have prejudiced the jury to the notion that Burnham was guilty by association with the confessed killer."

"But he *was* guilty by association."

"The judge should've made the shooter testify in person. Burnham had the right to face his accuser."

Justin began to get the picture.

"It was a tremendous blow to Jenny's crusade to see that justice was served for Edmond Day."

"But the shooter was put away for life. That had to have been some consolation."

"Even so, the instigator of the violence was a free man. That injustice and the constant pain of her wounds were more than Jenny could handle. She committed suicide." The light dimmed. *"Here she is now."*

"I can walk," Jenny said as she stepped from the light and stood before Justin. Amazement shined from her smiling face. She wore a long white robe and held her palms out, upturned. "There's no more pain. I'm light as a feather."

"There are no wheelchairs here, ma'am."

Her rosy cheeks glowed for a moment, and then as if she came to a sudden realization, her smile vanished. "I cannot cross over until Gary Burnham pays for his crime. He beat that poor man, robbed him..." She began to weep. "And now he is coming back to town."

***

A Greyhound bus squealed to a stop in a downtown terminal, and as the doors opened with a hiss of compressed air, passengers began to disembark. Gary Burnham muscled his way down the aisle, pushed a couple college kids out of the way, and knocked an old lady back down into her seat.

"Young man?"

"Stuff it, ya old bag." As his combat boots hit blacktop, cool autumn air brushed over his clammy shaved head. Earlier, on the bus, he'd changed into his leather vest and camouflaged pants and tossed his go-to-court clothes out the window. Now he was headed for the Fourth Reich

Bar. He'd convinced the parole board that he'd abandoned his white supremacist beliefs; all men were created equal, and he was sorry about what happened to Edmond Day. It was all bullshit, of course, but it got him released from prison early.

Truth was, for the last four years, he'd relished the thought of shooting another black man. And he'd let everyone in the cell block know how much he hated blacks. Oh, his white supremacist ravings pissed off the black inmates, but they couldn't get close to him because he'd kept a circle of compatriots around him. His white peers looked up to him, thought he was a hero for the Aryan cause. They'd kept him safe from black retribution, but working in the prison laundry, he was forced to wash the blacks' stinking socks and underwear. It was humiliating, and though he couldn't do anything about it then, now he was free, and he would get his revenge; he was going to take back the city for the white people.

The Fourth Reich Bar was busy as usual. Heavy-metal music assaulted the air; bourbon and schnapps flowed freely. A giant swastika hung on the wall behind the bar, along with black-and-white photos of Nazi SS troopers and the dead bodies of Jews stacked like cordwood. *Ah, the good old days.* Burnham grinned.

Pool balls cracked together, and boisterous cheers rose. He saw familiar faces: Spike and Dutch, and the Dayton brothers; Haskins and his clan were there too. In the war for white supremacy, they'd all committed so-called *hate crimes* and never got caught. Then, to Burnham's delight, he saw new faces, which meant that the movement had grown in his absence. Everyone's heads were shaved, and they all displayed their racist tattoos proudly. He felt right at home exchanging knuckle-bump greetings with fellow compatriots, and he was quickly

Terry Wright

invited to the bar where a boilermaker awaited him.

"Welcome back." The bartender's name was Mitch, and he was the baddest sonuvabitch in the place. Mitch slid an army issue Colt across the bar. "I been savin' your piece for ya."

Burnham shoved it under his vest, gave Mitch a *Heil Hitler* salute, and downed the drink.

Pats on the back and high-fives went all around. Two more drinks awaited him, and another three after that. Before long, the whole damn room was spinning. He laid his head on his arms on the bar, closed his eyes, and welcomed the lofty sensation of freedom among his people.

About that time, the music suddenly changed to rap, and a sharp pang of anger stabbed his guts. When he looked up, he froze. There was a black bartender standing in front of him. Burnham jumped up, staring in total disbelief, his heart beating hard. The bartender looked like Edmond Day. At first, Burnham figured it was the booze wreaking havoc with his mind, but when the black man said, "It is good that I see you, yes?" Burnham knew that something terrible had gone wrong.

"Hey, boys," he shouted over the rap music. "We got us a black boy in here." Cackling, he looked to his left and couldn't believe his eyes. He looked to his right, and panic swelled inside him. There wasn't a single white man in sight, just stern black faces with white-ringed eyeballs looking at him as if *he* were the oddity.

He whipped around only to find more black brothers gathering behind him. With venomous glares, they were inspecting the tattoos on his arms: the swastikas, the burning cross, and the hooded KKK. The rap music was getting louder, and he began to sweat. "Mitch," he called out.

But when Mitch didn't answer, Burnham's anger

~334~

flared. His compatriots had betrayed him. Obviously, they'd slipped out of the bar while his head was down, and the blacks came in to...to what? To get revenge?

Suddenly, a nauseating smell assailed him, the air reeking of dirty socks and piss-stained underwear, but a million times worse than anything he'd encountered in the prison laundry. He cupped a hand over his mouth and swallowed down a wave of bile. That's when he spotted the only other white guy in the place, at least he might have been white at one time, an old cowboy approaching from a dark corner. He wore a bullet-riddled long coat that drizzled dirt, and his face appeared to be more bone than flesh, all road-mapped with stitches. Tangled gray hair reached down to his shoulders. As he neared, the stench grenaded, but for some unknown reason, the blacks paid him no mind. "Who are you?" Burnham demanded.

The ghoul came within spittin' range. "My name is Justin Graves," he said in a voice like grated stone. "But you can call me Justice."

"What are you doing hangin' out with all these black folks? Got you no white pride?"

"I talked to Jenny Vandenburg and Edmond Day."

"That's not possible. They're dead."

"I talk to dead people...because I'm dead, too."

"You're just a crazy old cowboy."

"You think I look like this because it's fashionable?" The words hissed through Justin's exposed molars.

Grimacing, Burnham looked the ghoul up and down. "You should see an undertaker."

"I saw what happened that night at the bus stop. I know you were the instigator, an accessory to murder, and a thief."

"So what? My lawyer got me out early." He glanced at the crowd of black men around him. "Where did all these darkies come from?"

"They're friends of mine," Justin said. "And they're not very happy with you right now."

"Screw 'em."

"I'll make you a deal. Denounce your Aryan allegiance, and I'll assure you safe-passage out of this bar."

"I can take care of myself." Burnham slipped his hand under his vest where he'd stashed the Colt.

"Better yet..." Justin upped the ante. "I'll help you start a new life, line you up with a good job where you'll meet a beautiful woman who'll love you and give you children."

"You can't do that."

"I have the power to do anything. I'll even rid you of those hateful tattoos."

"You ain't touchin' my tattoos, mister. What are you, some kind of Black-Lives-Matter lover?"

Justin simply nodded.

"Then you'll die with the rest of them." Burnham pulled the gun and shot Justin point-blank. He staggered backward in surprise and clutched his chest. Satisfied, Burnham whipped around and shot the black bartender right between the eyes.

A feeling of power came over Burnham, and he twisted left, now aiming at a wide-eyed black man sitting on the next barstool. The gun banged again and again and again. Black bodies fell like Dominoes, and Burnham let out a holler of total elation. However, the next time he pulled the trigger, the gun only clicked. Black men rushed toward him.

Alarmed, he looked up and saw Justin at the front door, waving goodbye.

"Justice!"

The black men jumped him and beat him to a pulp.

Justin Graves

***

Two days passed. Yellow police tape remained strung across the entrance to the Fourth Reich Bar. On the corner, the bus stop bench still stood, a stoic reminder of the place where so many lives were ruined. Justin sat on the bench between the misty forms of Jenny Vandenburg and Edmond Day. He realized there were actually two people murdered that night; only Jenny's life hadn't ended as quickly as Edmond's. Hers had dragged on for five torturous years.

"Hate is like a virus," Jenny said to Justin. "It spreads with no compassion for its victims. I'm just glad Burnham is back in prison where he belongs."

Edmond put his arm around Jenny and asked Justin, "Why did this man kill so many of his friends in that bar?"

Justin shrugged. "The police are baffled."

"He killed a lot of innocent people."

"Don't fret about them, Mr. Day." Justin shook his head. "They were all guilty of doing something illegal."

Jenny sighed. "At least Burnham won't get off on a technicality again."

"And he won't last long in prison," Justin assured her. "The white supremacists who protected him from the black prisoners won't associate with him this time, not after killing their compatriots in the bar. He'll get shanked in the shower. The devil will have him soon."

"I only wanted him to pay for what he did to me and Edmond," she replied. "Even though Burnham didn't pull the trigger that night, he was just as guilty as his buddy."

Justin tipped his hat to her. He knew she'd done the most courageous thing anyone could ever do. She'd put herself in harm's way for a stranger and paid dearly for doing the right thing. "Jenny, you'll always be a hero to me."

"Thanks, Justin."

"Cross over. Find your eternal peace and happiness. You deserve it."

"I wish you were going with me."

"Yeah, well...I haven't yet paid my dues to the devil."

With a gust of wind the ghoul was gone.

Behind the Badge

Officer Stone sat in his patrol car behind Krueger's Gym, drumming his fingers on the steering wheel. The muggy Texas night made his neck sweat. He was itching for a good fight.

"Carmichael and Thorp are slower than dirt," he said to his partner, Gil Baker, riding shotgun.

"Quit your bitchin'. They'll be here."

Stone allowed Baker to shoot off his mouth like that. He'd once said that Deckers PD was the last hole-in-the-wall department that would hire him. After a brutal arrest caught on video in Los Angeles last year, Baker was lucky to get this job. "Goddamned bureaucrats," he'd said. "I should've plugged 'em all with hollow points."

Stone had been impressed enough with Baker's badass-cop attitude that he'd requested him to be his partner.

A squad car came down the alley with its lights off.

Adrenaline jolted Stone's heartbeat up a notch. "About time they got here."

Tires crunched gravel, and the car stopped. Doors opened. Two cops got out. Carmichael, a brut of an officer with arms the size of railroad ties, lumbered up to Stone's open window. "We ready?"

"Fuller's inside keepin' watch," Stone said. "Last we heard, Carson was working out on the heavy bag."

Thorp, a neckless weightlifter, ambled up beside his partner. "Carson is undefeated, Stone. The boxing champ around these parts."

"He's a punk." Stone pushed open the door and pulled

his six-foot-six frame out of the car. Standing a head above the others, he balled a fist. "Don't let this baby-face fool you." He pointed to his soft smile then frowned. "I can take him with one hand tied behind my back."

Thorp grimaced. "I'd rather bench press 400 pounds."

Baker jumped in with his two cents for Stone. "I know you've busted a lot of heads in your time, but Carson, he'll be tough to beat, not like that snot-nosed kid at Camp Pendleton you killed."

"It was an accident," Stone said.

Carmichael grinned. "You can't bullshit us."

These guys were the best partners in crime a police officer could ever ask for. "Okay, boys. Let's roll."

Stalking toward the back door of Krueger's Gym, Stone remembered when he was a Marine drill sergeant and how he'd broken a recruit's neck. It wasn't an accident. Top Brass had ordered their drill sergeants to go easy on the new troops in basic training; the poor babies missed their mommies. One kid bucked his authority. A bad apple in the barracks wasn't acceptable. During hand-to-hand combat class, Stone broke the kid's neck, kind of like pulling a weed from the garden, got rid of the problem, but the Marines labeled Stone an undesirable, gave him a hardship discharge, and swept the murder under the carpet.

Five years later, after being fired from two other departments for using excessive force and the unjustified discharge of a firearm, he found himself in the company of these good ol' boys in Deckers PD. Thorp had five shootings on his record, two deaths. Carmichael liked to play both sides of the street, took bribes and kickbacks, and broke a few legs along the way. And Fuller, who was watching Carson inside Krueger's Gym, had racked up three civil lawsuits against Pasadena for police brutality. Fuller always carried a *drop*, a gun or a knife that he could plant at the scene, just in case someone made a bad call.

Yeah, the good ol' boys, the misfits and undesirables of law enforcement, they'd found a common bond here in Deckers. It wasn't all about police work, though. They'd spend three nights a week at the police gym, three at the shooting range, and one at Molly's Hideaway getting laid.

Stone followed the good ol' boys into Krueger's Gym. Tonight, he'd come here to kick Carson's ass, put him in his place after some snitch heard him talking trash against the police department's good-old-boy policies. Stone wasn't afraid of muscles and knuckles. He wasn't afraid of anything.

Floorboards creaked under his boots as he made his way down a dingy hallway lit by one naked ceiling bulb that winked on and off. Cigar smoke hung in the air like swamp gas. Passing by the men's room, he smelled the stink of urine and vomit and crappy toilets.

Fuller met them in the hall. "There he is." He pointed. "Carson."

The champ must've been 290 pounds of hard-packed flesh and bone, his black skin shining with sweat, his wide ivory-ringed eyes glaring at the good ol' boys as they entered the gym. A boxing ring with sagging ropes took up most of the center floor. Barbells and weight machines lined the far wall, and the heavy bag hung from the ceiling on a stout chain. The gym smelled like moldy cheese.

Some of the toughest men in Deckers gathered around the newcomers. Most were heavily tattooed; some were missing teeth. They all looked pissed off at the intrusion of law enforcement.

Clutching the bag as if it were his lover, Carson gave Stone a fat-lipped grin. "You boys come to play?"

Stone handed his gun belt to Baker. "Just me."

The good ol' boys stood tall, hands on their hips, their

Terry Wright

eyes daring anyone to start a rumble.

Carson's eyes narrowed and his smile showed perfect white teeth. He let go of the bag, flexed his biceps, and puffed out his chest. With muscles rippling, he stepped forward, fists balled. "So I see. You came for a boxing lesson."

"Not quite." Rolling up his shirtsleeves, Stone flexed his biceps and put up his fists. "I'm here to give you a lesson in keeping your mouth shut." Talking tough often weakened an opponent's resolve, broke down a man's self-confidence, and made tough-guys wonder if they were tough enough.

Carson huffed. "You'd risk getting that pretty-boy face of yours messed up?"

"You don't scare me."

"I will." Carson came at him full force.

Stone let loose a barrage of quick punches, each one well placed sledgehammer blows that could have knocked out a horse.

Knuckles cracked on jawbone. A couple of Carson's white teeth clattered on the floor. Blood spewed from his mouth. His smile wrenched into a fearsome snarl as he growled like a crazed beast and lunged forward.

Sidestepping, Stone nailed him with a fist to the back of his neck, something he'd learned in the Marines, a quick way to disable an attacker.

Carson went down like a sack of shit. Moaning sounds came from his throat.

Stone felt invincible. "Anybody else?" He showed his fists to the throng of thugs standing around.

There were no takers.

***

In front of Deckers High School, Nate stood toe-to-toe

with his girlfriend, Jasmine, wishing she wasn't so pissed off at him.

She crossed her arms and glared, her pretty black face scrunched up like a dried prune. "No, I tell yah, yah hear?"

He squinted against the last rays of the setting sun. "You're jiving me, girl."

"You know I ain't. No man of mine is gonna leave me hangin' out around this dump. A girl's got to keep her priorities straight."

"But I gotta do my duty for my country."

"You know Buddy Chester, now he ain't figurin' on doin' no duty. He can take care of me just fine whilst you're gone away to that army place."

"Graduation's in a week, girl. You know what my recruiter said. They need volunteers to help fight the terrorists. Why you gotta go on like this?"

"Ever since you turned seventeen you think you're some kind of big man. But you ain't nothin' but a skinny little black boy with stupid dreams."

Nate wanted to scream and kick and throw a fit, but he held his temper, something he'd always had trouble doing in the past, and doing it now wasn't easy. Why couldn't she understand? "I thought we was in love."

She turned her back on him. "It's over, you and me. I got Buddy now."

"But—"

A black Ford Taurus screeched up to the curb. Doors popped open. Buddy Chester got out, along with a few of his black brothers from Deckers High. Standing taller than six foot, he put on his Foster Grants. "Got a problem, fool?"

"Shit," Nate said under his breath.

Jasmine batted her eyelashes. "Oh, Buddy. This creep's been hastlin' me."

Creep? Nate couldn't believe it. Up until a few minutes ago, he was her boyfriend, but right now he didn't have time to worry about *her* attitude. The brothers had gathered around him, looking all bad from the hood. Gulping, he held up a *black power* fist. "Be cool now, homeboys."

Buddy pulled a switchblade that made an ominous clicking sound as it snapped open. "I'm gonna cut yah, nigga."

Panic raced through Nate like a storm of fire. Anger fueled the flames. First his girl dumped him, called him a creep, and then this steroid-infested African Amazon called him the N word. If Nate took off running now, Jasmine would know he was a coward. He wasn't about to give her that pleasure. Besides, one thing he'd learned from his dad: show no fear. He took a step back, slipped a hand into his baggy jeans, and pulled out a pocketknife.

The brothers started laughing.

"What you gonna do with that little thing?" Buddy asked.

"Back off, bros." Nate waved the knife. Right about now he wished he'd sharpened the damn thing. "Leave me alone."

One of the brothers grabbed him from behind. Another snatched the knife from his hand. They threw him on the ground. Buddy kicked him in the ribs.

Gasping air, Nate heard Jasmine laughing as they piled into the Taurus and sped away.

"Bastards." Nate felt like breaking something. He'd lost his girlfriend, his pride, and his knife. Clutching sore ribs, he got up off the ground and headed for home.

***

Mrs. Washington, five years widowed, sat in her

antique wooden rocker and worked knitting needles on a Penn State sweater she was making for her only son, Nate. The chair creaked on the hardwood floor of a modestly furnished living room. Times like this she couldn't help but brag about her son, soon to graduate from Deckers High School. "Nate is going to look so fine in this sweater when he's at Penn State."

Next-door-neighbor Millie Prescott sat on the sofa, sewing a needlepoint picture of potted flowers. "Gets mighty cold up there in winter. Anna, you must be awful proud."

"It's been a tough road for Nate. Oh dear Lord, when his daddy was killed, he was mad at the whole world."

Millie sighed. "The boy got his self kicked out of school first year. Caused such a ruckus, he did."

"That temper, Jesus, I thought it would be the death of him."

"He got on better than my Bruce, though," Millie said. "First juvenile hall and now county jail. I fear he'll be doing hard time in a Texas prison some day."

"That's what gang bangers get, sorry to say."

"I'd be calling the police near every time he'd come home, all tanked up and bustin' down my door. Didn't want him around when he was like that. Out of control kids deserve to be locked up."

"I've been blessed." Anna tied off a row of yarn.

The front door banged open. Nate stormed into the living room. "I hate her." he shouted. "She's a whore."

Anna set the knitting in her lap. "Now calm down, son. Tell me what happened."

"Jasmine and Buddy Chester, I hope they have white babies."

"Is that any way to talk?" Anna could only hope to keep her son's anger in check. She'd seen him like this

Terry Wright

before, and it made her skin turn to gooseflesh.

He paced the living room, his Reeboks squeaking on the floor. "She dumped me for the town bully just 'cause I told her about me joining up with the army."

"Don't be talking like that, Nate honey. You're going to Penn State."

Nate rushed up to the rocker, got down on one knee. "I'm going to drive a tank like my daddy did."

"And he got his self killed doin' it."

"It was a war, Momma."

"You think I'm gonna stand for you makin' the same mistake as your daddy? Well, you got another think comin', young man. You're goin' to Penn State. I've been savin' up all my life."

Nate grabbed the sweater from her lap and threw it on the floor. "You can't make me."

Millie got up from the sofa. "Do as your momma tells you, boy."

Nate leaped to his feet. "Get outta here, yah nosey old bag."

"Well I never…"

He kicked over the coffee table.

"Nate. Stop it."

Millie Prescott ran out, screaming into the night.

***

The good ol' boys gathered outside Krueger's Gym. High-fives all around. "You showed that punk," Baker said.

Stone rubbed his knuckles. "Guess he was wrong about me being afraid of him."

Fuller put in, "You're not afraid of anyone, Stone."

A call came over the radio. *"Domestic disturbance, 549 Pine Lane. Code three."*

Stone opened the car door. "Let's go."

Baker rode shotgun. Fuller sat in the back seat. They peeled out of the alley and careened down Main Street. Carmichael and Thorp followed behind them, driving like mad.

Stone got on the radio to dispatch. "What's going on over there?"

"Neighbor called it in. Kid next door is out of control."

"Fuckin' punk," Baker said.

"We're on it," Stone reported and signed off.

Baker hit the siren switch.

Stone shut it off. "We'll go in real quiet."

Moments later, they rolled to a stop in front of 549 Pine Lane.

As Stone got out of the car, he heard shouting inside the house, a woman's voice. "You're going to Penn State."

"I'm going in the army, Momma."

Sounded like a disrespectful punk to Stone, probably despised authority like that snot-nosed recruit.

Car doors slammed behind him. Carmichael and Thorpe had arrived on scene but not as quietly.

"Now look..." the woman shouted. "The cops are outside."

"Tell them to go away."

"Millie must've called them."

Stone rallied the good ol' boys. "Thorp, take a position at the front window. Carmichael, cover me on my left, Baker, my right. Fuller, back me up."

They ducked low and stalked to the front door.

A plump black woman appeared behind the screen. "It's all right, officers," she said. "My boy don't mean no harm."

"We got a complaint, lady."

"Don't pay him no mind. He's just upset—"

"Step aside." Stone pushed his way inside the house, hand hovering over his gun.

"You can't come in here lest I say it's okay."

Fuller shoved the black woman out of the way. She fell backward into her wooden rocker, which cracked and splintered, sending her to the floor with a thud. Her knitting scattered, and she let out a yelp.

A skinny black boy rushed to her side. "Momma."

"Hands up," Stone ordered and pulled his gun.

The boy didn't obey, just hovered over his mother sprawled on the floor. "Momma."

She moaned. "I think my back is broke."

Stone shouted at the kid, "Show me your hands." His adrenaline level was on overload from the fight at Krueger's Gym and the fast drive to this scene of domestic disobedience. He had no patience for this punk kid and his wailing mother. "Get down on the floor, boy."

Baker and Thorp flanked Stone, their hands on their weapons.

"Leave us alone," the boy cried out.

Stone stepped forward. "Do it now."

The punk grabbed a knitting needle off the floor and pointed it at him. "Get out of our house."

"Drop the weapon." Stone aimed his gun at the boy's heart.

The black woman on the floor shrieked. "He don't mean no harm."

"Drop your weapon." Baker ordered, his gun drawn too.

"Leave us alone."

Fuller drew his gun. "Drop it, kid."

Nate held the knitting needle point to his own throat. "Get back or I'll kill myself."

Stone had taken enough crap from this punk. He

pulled the trigger, twice, a double tap, just like he'd been trained to fire a gun at a perp. More gunfire rang out around him: two, four, six shots banging, muzzles flashing. The aroma of gunpowder ballooned in the air.

The kid's body fell limp over his mother, as if he was still trying to protect her.

Blood pooled on the floor.

The black woman screamed and fainted.

**

Surrounded by the warm glow of the afterlife, Justin kicked off his boots and settled back in his favorite recliner, which the light had supplied. Though he wanted to close his eyes and rest, visions of his daughter, Christy, her soul being violated by the devil somewhere down in the chasms of hell, tormented his mind. And with her killer on the loose, his soul now an advocate for evil, Billy Denton could derail Justin's deal with the devil at any time. One hundred souls for Christy's pardon from hell, but one slipup from Justin and they'd both spend eternity there together.

The devil would win.

A droning sound filled the afterlife, and the light pulsed like a nightclub strobe. *"Justin."* Wach-el's deep voice reverberated from the firmament. *"A young man has fallen victim to police brutality."*

"What did he do?"

"This boy's name was Nate Washington, a promising young man who wanted to serve his country, like his father had, in the army. His only crime was trying to protect his mother after she was brutally assaulted by overzealous police officers. Take a look."

The light parted, revealing a scene from the land of the living. A modest front room in a modest home somewhere in Deckers, Texas.

Terry Wright

"549 Pine Lane," Wach-el said.

A large black woman lay sprawled on the floor amidst the splinters of a broken rocking chair. She appeared unconscious, but the boy lying across her abdomen had been shot full of bullet holes that leaked blood and pooled on the floor beside them.

"Nate and his mother, Anna."

Deckers police officers stepped into the scene, guns drawn. One bent down, yanked a knitting needle from the boy's clutched fist, and tossed it aside.

"Officer Stone," Wach-el narrated. *"And his partners. They call themselves the good ol' boys."*

Justin swallowed a lump in his throat.

Sirens wailed through the afterlife.

"Back up," Stone said.

Carmichael asked, "What are we going to do?"

Fuller handed Stone a knife. "Drop this."

Stone holstered his gun, examined the knife, a six-inch stiletto, and smiled.

Baker handed him a handkerchief. "Wipe it."

Stone wiped the knife clean of prints and dropped it next to the pool of blood. "Good work, boys. Carmichael, call for medical. Fuller, get out the crime scene tape, and don't any of you forget to put on your sad faces when internal affairs starts asking questions."

They high-fived each other. This wasn't their first rodeo.

"Those cops had no reason to shoot that young man," Wach-el said. *"You can't let them get away with it."*

Justin stood. "You're right." The recliner dissolved into the light. His cowboy hat appeared in his hand, a Stetson, and he set it on his head.

"What are you going to do?"

As if by slight-of-hand, Justin produced a stiletto

exactly like the one Stone had dropped. "I've got an idea."

***

Police Commissioner McDougal called the hearing to order. Captain Holland and several ranking officers from the Texas Rangers sat to the right of him at a long conference table. They'd been called in to serve as the outside investigative agency on the Deckers PD shooting case. On his left sat members of Internal Affairs and the shoot team. Citizens, including Anna Washington, the deceased boy's mother, sat in chairs behind a polished wood railing.

Matter at hand: the shooting of Nate Washington.

First to testify: Officer Stone. "Yes." He sat stoically in a chair facing the investigators. This wasn't the first time he was accused of using excessive deadly force. "We were called to 549 Pine Lane on a domestic disturbance."

"And what did you encounter when you arrived?" McDougal asked, his tone as flat as if he were reading from a dictionary.

"The suspect was highly agitated."

"Nate Washington?"

"Yes."

"What did you notice when you made entry?"

"A coffee table was overturned, and a rocking chair was broken."

"Who was in the room?" McDougal asked.

"Nate and his mother."

"Where was she when you first saw her?"

Stone sat straight-faced on the witness stand. "She was sprawled on the floor."

"That's a lie," Anna Washington shouted from her spectator's seat. "I met the officers at the door—"

McDougal slammed down his gavel. "Please, Mrs.

Washington, let him speak or I'll have you removed."

"But he's lying. They pushed me—"

The Commissioner showed her the palm of his hand. "Hold your tongue and let me get to the truth. Now, as you were saying, Officer Stone."

"She was on the floor."

"Did you push her?"

"Of course not."

"Liar," Mrs. Washington shouted.

"I'm warning you," McDougal said, pointing his gavel at her.

"I'm sorry, but—"

"One more outburst and you're out of here. Do you understand?"

"Yes, sir."

McDougal went back to Officer Stone. "Nate's mother was on the floor. Was she injured?"

"Yes," Stone said, stone-faced. "She said her back was broken."

"And you assumed Nate had caused this injury?"

"He was the only other person in the room."

"And where was he?"

"The suspect stood over his mother. He had a knife in his hand."

This time Anna Washington shot out of her chair. "That's not true. My Nate, he didn't have no knife."

McDougal hammered the gavel. "Deputies, remove her from the room."

"They killed my boy," she yelled as two brute deputies dragged her out. "In cold blood." Doors closed but Stone heard her screaming from down the corridor. "Nate didn't have no knife."

"Carry on, officer," McDougal said.

"He wouldn't drop the knife. We warned him several

times. When he lunged at us, we had no choice but to open fire in self-defense."

"Is this the knife?" McDougal held up a six-inch stiletto sealed in a plastic bag.

"Yes."

"Were you in fear for your life?"

Stone scrunched up his face. "I was terrified."

Looking at the other officers, Carmichael, Thorp, Fuller, and Baker, "Gentlemen," McDougal asked. "Is your consensus the same?"

The good ol' boys nodded.

Leaning back in his chair, McDougal cleared his throat. "I'd have been in fear of my life too, with one of these things coming at me." He dropped the knife on the bench. "I rule the shooting was justified."

The Texas Rangers conferred with each other. Captain Holland stood. "The knife is convincing evidence enough for us to agree, sir."

McDougal hammered his gavel. "The officers are free to go."

***

In the dark police station parking lot, the good ol' boys rallied between a row of Deckers' squad cars, huddled around Stone as he passed out cigars. "That's the end of that." He lit a cigar and passed the silver Zippo around to his comrades.

Thorp pulled fire into his cigar. "Thanks to Fuller's drop."

"Never leave home without it." Fuller blew smoke.

Stone grinned. "One less punk in the world."

He'd no sooner said the words than a gust of wind stirred the night, bringing with it an odor that reminded him of the men's room in Krueger's Gym. Or was it the stench of Deckers' stockyards and slaughterhouses? He noticed the good ol' boys' faces turn sour, Thorp clutching his stomach, Carmichael gagging, and Baker coughing. Fuller's face turned white, his nostrils flaring. Stone thought he was going to be sick. "What the hell is that stink?"

A voice like sandpaper rasped from the darkness. "Excuse me, boys."

Stone whipped around, saw an old man standing in front of a squad car. Deep dark eye sockets glowed red out from under a dusty cowboy hat. His face looked battered and sewn like an old sock. The long coat he wore shed dirt that vanished before it hit the ground. For an instant, Stone felt a sharp stab of fear in his chest, a novel response to an impending conflict. "Who the hell are you?"

"Name's Justin Graves." The cowboy tipped his hat. "But you can call me Justice."

"You better move along, mister, before we run you in for vagrancy."

Baker covered his nose. "The mission on 12th Street has a free shower. I suggest you us it."

Justin rubbed his jaw. Flesh peeled away, exposing more bone. "Cops like you give us all a bad name."

Carmichael stepped forward. "Watch your mouth, old man."

"You don't know nothing about cops," Thorp put in, poking his cigar at Justin.

"I'm a Texas Ranger." He spread open his coat, revealing a ragged gray shirt. Decaying rib bones showed through the tatters, and old bullet holes in decaying flesh had been closed up with sutures. New wounds bled maggots and worms. The stench made the night air taste rank as fresh manure. When he closed the coat, a circle-star badge suddenly gleamed from the left lapel.

Justin Graves

Stone began to see a problem. Some time back, he'd heard of a Texas Ranger who was killed in a gun battle at a warehouse in Deckers. Either this was a perfectly executed hoax, or the good ol' boys were in big trouble. Rumor had it that the dead homicide detective came back from the grave to help Captain Holland get justice for victims of crime. "Justin Graves, you say?"

"I have something for you." Justin held out his bony hand and displayed a six-inch stiletto.

Stone about flipped. "Where did you get that?"

"Jesus," Fuller said. "It's my drop."

Baker gasped. "How'd he get it?"

"Come on, boys," Justin said. "You can figure it out."

"He switched 'em," Thorp said.

"Wrong." Justin shook his head. "It's identical to the one in the evidence room. Same make. Same model, but this one has your fingerprints on it, Fuller, and yours too, Stone, when he handed it to you to make the drop."

"I wiped it clean," Stone said. "You've got nothing."

"I'm Justin Graves. I can put Thorpe's fingerprints on Carmichael's ass if I wanted to."

"He set us up," Baker hissed.

"When McDougal figures it out, he's going to slap you boys with evidence tampering on top of murder one. You bullies are finished hiding behind the badge."

Carmichael spit. "Son of a bitch."

"We'll get the death penalty," Thorpe said.

"However," Justin added. "I'll give you a way out of this mess. Go back in there and tell the truth, cop a plea, make a deal for jail time, you'll live, maybe even long enough to see daylight again."

Baker jumped in, "Cops in prison don't last long."

"We could get shanked in the yard," Thorpe added.

"Take your chances," Justin said, "or face the devil

~355~

for your deeds. I'll guarantee you one thing. In hell, your guns are not allowed."

"Screw you, Justice. We're not admitting we did anything wrong." Stone drew his gun. "Give me the knife."

"And there's also the question of your fingerprints on a certain knitting needle." Justin produced it from his coat pocket. "Remember touching this?"

"How do you know I touched it?"

"I saw you take it out of the dead boy's hand—"

"You weren't there."

"I'm everywhere. Do we have a deal?"

Stone had heard enough of the old man's bullshit. He fired two rounds into the ghoul, double-tapped him good. Dust flew. The bullets tore clear through Justin's rotting corpse and shattered the squad car windows behind him.

Fuller and Baker started firing, too. Bullets pinged off hoods and peppered fenders. Carmichael and Thorpe got into the act, each squeezing off rounds that penetrated decaying flesh and exploded radiators and overhead lights.

Gunshots echoed through the night, but the smelly cowboy just stood there. A smile formed on Justin's leathery lips. "I take that as no deal."

With hot adrenaline spilling into his veins, Stone emptied his gun into the ghoul but only managed to tear up more police cars, sending glass and shards of metal flying.

Justin laughed. "You guys are making a mess."

"We're gonna kill you," Stone shouted.

"You're too late. I'm already dead."

The good ol' boys reloaded and gave it their best shot, shooting up every cop car in the parking lot as Justin disappeared and reappeared in various places.

Captain Holland rushed out of the police station. Several Texas Rangers followed him, guns drawn. "What the hell do you boys think you're doing?"

Justin Graves

The gunfire stopped, plunging the parking lot into silence. Stone looked at Baker, and then Thorp. Carmichael shrugged. Fuller frowned. "A prowler, sir."

"Jesus H Christ. Are you all crazy?"

Stone pointed at Justin. "He's standing right there."

"They can't see me," Justin said. "But they'll hear this." He held out the stiletto and dropped it. In slow motion, the knife tumbled down and struck the pavement with a clanking sound that echoed off into the night.

"What was that?" Holland asked.

Stone's throat went dry. "Not-nothing."

A spine of light glinted off the blade, attracting Holland's attention. "That looks like the same knife Nate Washington threatened you boys with." He picked it up with pinched fingers. "Even in this light I can see fingerprints on it."

"It wasn't my idea," Fuller said. "The kid had a knitting needle. That's all. It was Stone who planted the knife. I had nothing to do with it."

"Liar," Stone shouted. "It was your drop."

"Captain," Thorpe said. "I want to change my testimony. I'll tell you the truth."

"Arrest these men," Holland ordered his rangers.

Stone couldn't believe he'd just been ratted out by the good ol' boys. His career was finished. He'd go to prison, maybe even get a needle in his arm. "Why you lousy..." He turned his gun on Fuller and blew a hole in his head.

Holland's rangers fired point-blank at Stone. A dozen muzzle blasts flashed in the night. Stone's heart stopped beating before his body hit the ground.

"Drop your weapons," Holland ordered the other good ol' boys. They surrendered without further bloodletting.

With a gust of wind the ghoul was gone.

The Evil in this World

D eep in the Cavern of Terrors, the pool of red goo and nightmares belched, expelling Leon onto the rocks. He could've been tarred and feathered if Billy had any feathers. "Where have you been?"

"Time out." He flung goo from his hands and stomped his feet. Every bit of his demon body was covered in the fetid slime. He wasn't laughing anymore.

"Time out?" Billy frowned from his uncomfortable precipice. "Like with a dunce cap in the corner and all?"

Bony bats flittered around them like the hecklers of hell. Leon grabbed one from midair, broke its neck, and tossed the bones into the goo. "Maggots, biggest ones you ever seen. I must've got ate and shit out a thousand times. That's the devil's idea of *time out*. What are you doin' down here?"

"Watching the bats."

"Ain't you supposed to be gettin' killed by Justin Graves?"

"I'm working on it."

"Then why you watching bats?"

"I want to fly like them."

Leon wiped a glob of slime from his demon face then assumed his usual squatty posture on the rock next to Billy. "Fly like those little shits...what for?"

"Not little. Big. I mean really big. Scary big. The bones nightmares are made of big."

"Yeah." Leon squinted. "That could be scary...but if this big-ass bat had your face, now that would be piss-in-the-pants scary."

Anyone else would have taken that comment as an insult, but not Billy. "And Justin would know it's me for sure."

Leon bobbed up and down. "He'll try to kill you, guaranteed."

"I gotta make damn sure, so—"

"You're gonna kill Captain Holland, right?"

Billy smiled. "After I kill his wife and kids, of course."

"That'll piss him off...oh yeah...Justin will have to kill you for that."

"Can you make me bat-shit scary?"

Leon stood, held his hands out to the red pool. "Icknay."

The surface boiled and rose up until the broken-necked bat emerged from the goo, no longer a handful of bones but a whole truckload fully assembled. Its scream shook the chamber walls as its bony wings flapped with long whooshing strokes that pulled it free of the goo to land on the rocks below Billy.

"Now that's what I'm talking about."

Leon turned his upheld hand to Billy. "Icknay."

Like a fast elevator ride, Billy's soul merged with the bony beast. Its snouted skull formed wicked teeth, and Leon recognized Billy's red chin beard and the silver rings that pierced the bones around the bat's ear-holes. With demon and bat-bones now one, Billy was truly the stuff of nightmares. The screams of a thousand demons couldn't have drowned out the ultrasonic echo-location screeches from the giant Billy-bat as it took flight.

Leon turned his hands to the bats roosting on the rocky ceiling. "Icknay."

They all took flight, swirling and swooping, their ultrasonic chirps a cacophony of echoes throughout the chamber. Like fighter jets to the mother ship, they circled the flying monster Leon had made. He stood on the rock and swept his hand to the tunnel. "Fly. Fly. Fly."

Billy bat banked toward the black maw and led his swarm of little killer bats down the tunnel toward hell's fiery exit.

***

It was past midnight when Captain Holland parked the police cruiser in front of his house. The windows were dark, his family asleep inside. A broken family...cop father on the job 'til all hours, kids left to the events of their lives without him, mother and wife at her wits end. She thought he needed some serious mental help. "I'm not crazy," he mumbled to himself.

He got out and locked the car. A streetlamp and a bit of moonlight illuminated the walkway to his front door. He entered quietly, hung his hat on the hook. Shadows slanted across the walls. Down the hall, he checked on Cory. His room looked like a bomb went off in there. Tina's room was nice and neat. They were both sound asleep. In the master bedroom, he left the ceiling light off, removed his jacket and holstered gun. The gun went in the gun-safe in the closet. The jacket went on the floor.

"Harold?"

"Go back to sleep."

She turned on the nightstand light. "What time is it?"

"Late. As usual." He used the boot-jack to get his boots off.

"You said you were coming home right after the hearing."

"Something came up."

"Don't tell me it's Justin Graves' fault you're late."

He peeled off his shirt. Could have been Justin had a

hand in the parking lot melee at Deckers PD. He might have put the stiletto on the pavement. The crime lab's nightshift found Stone and Fuller's fingerprints on the *drop*. Justin probably caused the good ol' boys to shoot up nearly every squad car in the lot. He shucked out of his trousers. "I haven't seen him."

"Our life's not been the same since he was killed."

Holland crawled into bed. "Two Deckers officers died tonight. In the parking lot. I had to wait for the coroner to take the bodies to the morgue. Dr. Yee was not happy about working tonight."

"Your life's a nightmare, Harold. I don't want to hear about it. I'll never get any sleep."

The light went out.

***

Justin made it back to his grave in Deckers Memorial Gardens. As usual, he had to dig his way back into his coffin, but this time the digging wasn't easy. The good ol' boys had shot him up pretty bad. Bullets had torn meat from bone. Rotted muscle wasn't strong to begin with, but now his arms and hands were nearly useless. His left knee was blown out, right hip broken, countless ribs turned to splinters. A couple of molars had exploded.

Still, he'd managed to get into his eternal resting place and braced for the swirling trip back to the afterlife.

He waited. Nothing happened.

"Wach-el?" he groaned out. "What's the hold up?"

Light blasted from the lid in front of his face, so bright that his eye sockets would have fried if it hadn't dimmed to a swirling mist. *"Justice, beware."*

The mist revealed the depths of hell, the fire and smoke and screeching of demons. Bones flew through the firmament, scattered helter-skelter, spinning and swirling and tumbling. Justin cringed against the onslaught and the growing chitter. "What's all that noise?"

"That is the sound of echo location. Blind as a bat is not blind at all. They are flying from hell by the hundreds but lead by only one demon."

The bones flying through the misty light began to take form: backbone, neck bone, leg bone, tail bone...and wing bones, more finger bones than arm bones. Bat bones for sure, and this flying skeleton was no little bat, but a giant bat with a red chin beard and silver rings around ear hole bones.

"Billy Denton."

The terrible screeching grated on Justin's nerves.

"He's not coming for you, Justice. He's coming for Captain Holland and his family."

"Not if I can stop him."

"To stop him you'll have to kill him, and if you kill him, you'll lose, and the devil will have your soul...and Christy's too, forever."

"How can I beat a dead giant bat?"

"Bats have few natural enemies and no real defenses other than maneuverability in flight. They're quicker than a bird because their wings are light and their bones are flexible. On the ground they are clumsy and slow."

"So the trick is to keep Billy on the ground."

"His soul is in the bat's skull. Shoot for the wing bones and not for the brains."

"Billy doesn't have any brains."

The vision in the mist revealed one final horror, the armada of small bony bats trailing the giant Billy-bat.

Justin's rotted heart lurched. "I'm going to need more firepower."

The light supplied him with two big pistols. *"They never need reloading."*

Justin Graves

"I'm in no shape to fight a demon bat."

"Dr. Yee is working late tonight."

"I can't just waltz into the morgue looking like this."

"Then Harold Holland and his entire family will die."

"Why do you always have to be right?"

"Better hurry."

Justin dug his way back out of the grave and transported himself to Deckers County Morgue.

***

Afterhours as it was, the hallways and offices were dark, but for a shank of light from the small window that looked into the medical examiners' lab. Justin squinted from the glare as he peered in to see both 'slabs' occupied. On the left, Officer Stone lay naked with a white towel across his crotch. Water from the running faucet hose swirled red with blood as it funneled down the drain. His torso was a pincushion of bullet holes. On the right, Fuller lay there with a hole in his head, courtesy of Stone's execution bullet. Dr. Yee, dressed in a white lab coat, was cutting off Fuller's police uniform with a big pair of scissors. This was no time to be interrupting the doc's work, but then, when was there ever a good time for Justin to introduce himself?

The lab was so brightly lit, there were no shadows to hide in, no way to let his presence be gradually known, so he made his body invisible and opened the door.

Dr. Yee must've sensed motion or heard something. He stopped cutting the dead man's shirt and looked up.

The door swung closed.

He brandished the scissors. "Who's there?"

Justin projected his voice to come from every corner. "My name is Justin Graves."

Yee stepped back until the counter stopped him,

scissors at the ready. "Justin is dead. I saw him with my own eyes. What kind of sorry-assed prank is this?"

"You had your doubts, doc, especially after you saw my eyes move."

A terrible realization darkened Yee's eyes. He angled the scissor-point downward. "What do you want?"

"Captain Holland is in grave danger, and his family, too. I need your help to save them."

"Holland?" Yee turned a full circle. "So it's true...the rumors about you two?"

"We have an unofficial partnership. I'd have kept it between the two of us if not for what's coming."

"Coming? What's coming?"

"Death. Straight out of hell, and I'm running out of time to stop it."

Yee shuddered. "If this is for real...show yourself."

"Don't be alarmed by the sight and smell of me."

A blast of wind blew through the lab, swooping up papers and dislodging Stone's towel. From out of thin air, Justin appeared in all his rank ghoulishness.

Yee dropped the scissors and slapped a hand over his nose and mouth. "What the hell happened to you?"

Justin limped to the counter, set down his Winchester and pulled two pistols from under his mud-encrusted coat. "I had a run-in with the good ol' boys." He set the pistols next to the rifle and, with a broken index finger, indicated the two dead cops. "I need you to patch me up again."

***

Lately, there'd been very few moments when Holland felt as if his life might have returned to normal, like now, sitting at the breakfast table with his wife and kids. That sense of family seeped into his battered mind, and he seriously considered breaking all ties with Justin Graves.

The dead homicide detective had become a liability instead of an asset. He was destroying their marriage.

"You're awfully quiet this morning," Sandra said to him, her oatmeal barely touched.

"I was just thinking how much I love you all."

"We love you too," Cory said. He wore his baseball cap backwards.

Sandra set down her spoon. "Then why do you torture yourself with this job? The Texas Rangers...you live and breathe murder and mayhem every day, every night. The stress is destroying your sense of reality, Harold. Get another job, a nine to five. Spend more time with us."

"Yeah, Dad," Tina chimed in. She looked so cute, so innocent, sitting there in pigtails with rag-doll Julie in her lap. "You're never home anymore."

Sandra smiled. "Deckers Hardware is looking for counter help."

She'd never believe Justin Graves was back from the dead. He sipped coffee and eyed her over the rim of the cup. Maybe it was time for him to give up law enforcement, get a safe job—

Crunching metal and shattering glass stopped his train of thought, sure as any wrecking ball. It sounded like a traffic collision had occurred outside, right in front of his house. Cory and Tina looked at each other like 'oh boy.' Sandra glared at Harold in terror. He was already on his feet, heading to the front picture window, when the crashing sounds came again, and again. He peeled back the curtains to a vision he could never have imagined in his worst nightmares.

Sandra's minivan lay on its roof in the middle of the street, burning. "What the hell?" And a giant skeletal bat of some kind, skin and bones less the skin, was attacking his squad car. On bony wings that couldn't possibly create flight, the monster hovered over the wreck, grabbed it with its claws by the bumper, lifted it and dropped it again. It hit the pavement with another horrendous crash. The son of a bitch was turning his car to scrap metal.

Once he swallowed the initial shock of that sight, he noticed hundreds of smaller bats swirling in the sky, the morning sunshine glinting off their white bones. Neighbors were fleeing down the street, some dressed for work, others in their nightclothes. Bats swooped in on the easy pickings. Hell had come to Deckers, Texas.

Sandra rushed up behind him and screamed.

The giant hovering bat flitted around, faced the window, and shrieked. Holland noticed the red chin beard and silver rings. Then an angry face materialized in the bat's skull. Holland recognized that face right away. The realization chilled him to the bone.

"Billy Denton."

Sandra grabbed Holland's arm. "You know that guy?"

"He killed Justin Graves." He turned to her and his kids standing behind him. "Quickly. Our bedroom." Holland had to get to his gun in the safe.

"What's he doing here?"

"It's a long story. Now go. Everyone."

Tina clutched Julie and ran without question. Cory stopped long enough to grab his baseball bat by the kitchen door. Holland held back behind Sandra long enough to see the front window implode, the curtains tear from the rods, and the bony mass force its way into the living room. The bat-beast spread its wing bones, but there wasn't enough room for it to fly, only thrash about, destroying the television, upending the lamps, and overturning the couch. Grounded, it lumbered forward on its folded wing elbows and dragged its body of bones. Its echo-location screeched with each wretched step.

Holland thought his heart would fail him. He raced down the hall to the bedroom with the giant bat in hot pursuit. Billy was able to rearrange the bat's bones to accommodate the narrow hall, and Holland knew no doorway would stop him.

He darted into the bedroom and shut the door that could not protect them. "Kids. In the closet. Sandra, help me with this." He pushed on one end of the dresser, and they slid it in front of the door. "Hurry." He ushered her into the closet where he knelt to the gun safe. His trembling hand failed to dial the combination correctly, once, twice, then the door opened with a click. He grabbed the gun just as the bedroom door exploded in a hail of splinters. Billy bulled past the dresser as if it wasn't there. The bed slammed into the wall; the nightstands fell in a heap.

"Harold," Sandra cried. "Shoot him."

Gritting his teeth, Holland fired the revolver into the bat's skull, each report loud and smoky in the closet, but Billy-bat kept pulling itself forward by its bony wings and screeching like the devil himself. No more bullets, no escape. It suddenly became evident why Billy had destroyed the cars first. Holland threw the worthless gun at Billy's bony head.

Billy responded by jamming his toothy snout into the closet and snapping at Tina. The beast pulled back with Julie in its crushing jaws.

"No," Tina screamed.

Like a pit bull, the bat shook Julie. Stuffing flew through the air and floated down to the floor.

Cory charged out of the closet, swinging the baseball bat. "Let go of Julie." He struck Billy in the kneecap bone, re-cocked the bat and belted him on the snout. Julie's cloth carcass flew into the wall. A claw shot out and grabbed the bat, broke it, easy as a toothpick.

Terry Wright

"Cory, get back in here," Holland yelled.

Huddled with his family in the closet, Holland feared the end of their lives was close at hand. "Sorry," he whispered to Sandra. "I didn't know that helping Justin Graves would come to this."

Billy dragged himself to the closet and looked over his victims as if they were fruit to be picked from a bowl.

The stench of decomposition suddenly ballooned in the room. Cadavarine and putrescine gases permeated the air and clung to every surface. The kids gagged and choked. Sandra turned white. "What's that smell?"

"It's time you meet Justin Graves."

From out of the bedroom debris stepped the ghoul, Winchester strapped to his back, a pistol in each hand, and cowboy hat firmly planted on his skull. The circle-star badge on his coat gave off a blinding gleam, and his eye sockets glowed a deep red.

Billy-bat reeled up and screeched at the intruder.

"Hello, Billy," Justin said in a gravelly voice. "You're going back to hell." Both pistols spit fire and lead, shattering wing bones, leg bones, rib bones; each blast dropping the giant bat down a notch, a bit at a time until Billy's demonic vessel could no longer provide him with earthly transport. He was forced to abandon the bat bones and materialize before Justin.

"Shoot me, Justice. Put an end to this madness. You cannot win."

Justin twirled the pistols gunfighter-style and stuffed them under his belt. "Go back to your boss. Tell him I'm going to win and make him look like a fool."

"You want me to tell him something that stupid? He'll kill the messenger."

"What do you care? You're already dead."

"There're things worse than death down in hell. I've

seen the suffering. Smelled it."

"And thanks to you, my daughter is in the thick of it."

"As long as the devil favors her, she'll be spared the eternal torture and pain of hell's fiery pits. So don't screw things up."

"I don't trust the devil as far as I can spit."

"She's where she belongs, Justice. Don't believe me? Just shoot me. You can spend eternity with both of them."

"Don't do it." Holland stepped from the closet. "Cross over, Justin. Spend eternity with Eleanor. Leave the living to fight the evil in this world. It's not your job anymore."

Billy laughed. "When are you guys going to learn? You can't fix evil. You can only hope to coexist with it."

Sandra joined her husband to stand before Justin and Billy Denton. "I've changed my mind, Harold. Your job as a Texas Ranger is your life, a life of fighting evil. I'm sorry I ever doubted you." She nodded to Justin. "Officer Graves. Good to see you again."

He tipped his hat. "You too, ma'am."

Tina emerged from the closet and rushed directly to Billy Denton. "You killed Julie." She pounded on his chest. "Why do you have to be so mean?"

Cory picked up the broken pieces of his baseball bat and said nothing.

"Yeah, well, sorry about that, kids. I don't know what got into me." Billy waved his hand. The ball bat parts joined together, and Julie's innards floated back into her cloth body. The rag-doll healed, he handed Julie back to Tina. "Here you go."

Julie hugged her doll and cried with joy.

Cory test-swung the ball bat. "Hey. It's good as new."

Justin removed his dusty cowboy hat and held it over his heart...well...where his heart used to be. "Billy. That was kind of you."

"It's the last thing you expected me to do, I'm sure." He offered his hand to Justin. "You're a good man, Justice. You don't deserve to lose your soul. I won't be back."

Justin shook the hand of his killer. "I can't say I'm going to miss you."

"Fair enough." Billy Denton dissolved in thin air, as did the bat bones scattered about.

Sandra ushered the kids to the destroyed bedroom door. "I'm sure your dad and Justin have things to discuss."

"Bye, Justin," Tina and Cory said as they left.

Holland frantically dusted himself off. "Justice. There's a horde of demon bat-bones attacking the citizens of Deckers. I hope you've got a lot more bullets."

"Wach-el took care of the bats."

"Who's Wach-el?"

"An archangel who's earning his fiery sword by helping me. He sent a swarm of locusts to Deckers. Those bats were starving and went after the locusts. As Billy departed, so did the bats and bugs. Deckers is again a safe place to live."

"That's a relief, Justin. Now what about you?"

"Billy's right. I can't beat the devil, and maybe Christy *is* where she belongs."

Holland threw up his hands. "Finally you see the light."

"But I won't quit chasing bad guys. There's too much work to do. Besides, I kinda like being your silent partner."

"You mean this isn't over yet?"

He slapped a grody hand on Holland's shoulder. "Not as long as there's evil in this world."

"But Justice—"

With a gust of wind the ghoul was gone.

About the Author

There's nothing mundane in the writing world of **Terry Wright**. Tension, conflict and suspense propel his readers through the pages as if they were on fire. His mastery of the action thriller has also won him International acclaim as an accomplished screenplay writer. A longtime member of the Rocky Mountain Fiction Writers, he coordinated their annual Colorado Gold Writing Contest for six years, received their highest award for service, The Jasmine Award in 2012, and was nominated for the 2014 Writer of the Year.

A Vietnam Veteran, USAF, retired auto repair shop owner, certified private pilot, and an avid Harley Davidson enthusiast, he now spends his time editing and publishing authors for TWB Press and Amore Moon Publishing (www.twbpress.com).

He lives in Centennial, Colorado, with his wife, Bobette, and their Yorkie, Taz.

Visit Terry's website at TerryWrightBooks.com.

More novels and short stories from Terry Wright

 **The 13th Power Quest, Book 1**
The search for the secret of the universe
Science Fiction novel, series, technology, action, adventure
www.twbpress.com/the13thpowerquest.html

 **The 13th Power Journey, Book 2**
Mankind's first journey across the galaxy
www.twbpress.com/the13thpowerjourney.html

 **The 13th Power War, Book 3**
And then came man, and war, and death
www.twbpress.com/the13thpowerwar.html

 **The Duplication Factor**
Behold the first human clone
Science Fiction novel, thriller, action, adventure
www.twbpress.com/theduplicationfactor.html

 **Black Jack**

A Denver detective searches for his wife's killer

Crime drama novel, thriller, action, mystery

www.twbpress.com/blackjack.html

 **The Pearl of Death**

Historical thriller, novel based on the world's largest pearl

www.twbpress.com/thepearlofdeath.html

 **The Grief Syndrome**

An immortal man fights to save the world

Science Fiction, novel, futuristic, action, thriller

www.twbpress.com/thegriefsyndrome.html

 **Undead in Paris (a screenplay)**

Vampire wars: the old ways vs the new ways

www.twbpress.com/undeadinparis.html

 **Z-motors - The Job from Hell**
An unemployed master mechanic finally gets a job
Zombie short story, thriller, satire
www.twbpress.com/zmotors.html

 **Street Beat**
A woman reporter matches wits with a serial killer
Crime drama short story, action-thriller, romance
www.twbpress.com/streetbeat.html

 **Return Me to Mistwillow**
A dusty ghost town gets a visitor from the past
Ghost short story, Colorado history, action, thriller
www.twbpress.com/returnmetomistwillow.html

 **Wilderness Rampage**
A motorhome vacation trip turns deadly
Action adventure short story, bad guys and a bear
www.twbpress.com/wildernessrampage.html

www.twbpress.com

www.ingramcontent.com/pod-product-compliance
Lightning Source LLC
Chambersburg PA
CBHW051127030726
47504CB00004B/748